Matthew Arnold

Schools and Universities on the Continent

Matthew Arnold

Schools and Universities on the Continent

ISBN/EAN: 9783337396503

Printed in Europe, USA, Canada, Australia, Japan

Cover: Foto ©Andreas Hilbeck / pixelio.de

More available books at **www.hansebooks.com**

SCHOOLS AND UNIVERSITIES

ON THE CONTINENT

BY

MATTHEW ARNOLD, M.A.

FOREIGN ASSISTANT COMMISSIONER TO THE SCHOOLS ENQUIRY COMMISSION; ONE OF HER
MAJESTY'S INSPECTORS OF SCHOOLS; FORMERLY FOREIGN ASSISTANT COMMISSIONER
TO THE COMMISSION FOR ENQUIRING INTO THE STATE OF POPULAR EDUCATION
IN ENGLAND, AND PROFESSOR OF POETRY IN THE UNIVERSITY OF OXFORD

London

MACMILLAN AND CO.

1868

PREFACE.

I WAS in 1865 charged by the Schools Enquiry Commissioners with the task of investigating the system of
education _for the_ middle and upper classes which prevails in
France, Italy, Germany, and Switzerland. In the discharge
of this task I was on the Continent nearly seven months, and
during that time I visited the four countries named, and
made as careful a study as I could of the matters to which
the Commissioners had directed my attention. The present
volume contains the report which I made to them. I have
here adapted it to the general reader's use, and divested it of
some details which for his use were unnecessary.

It is the education of the poor, not the education of the
middle and upper classes, which principally occupies public attention in this country at present. In Switzerland, more than
in any other country with which I am acquainted, all classes
use the same primary school; and in Switzerland, therefore,
I had occasion to touch upon the primary school,—the school
of the poor,—because there this school forms a link in the
chain of schools in which the middle and upper classes are
educated. Accordingly, the English reader will in the following pages find a full account of the primary school system
in Canton Zurich,—a region free like England, industrial
like England, Protestant like England. School attendance
is obligatory there, and the schools are very good; both in
their goodness and in all the important points of their system
resembling the schools of Germany, of which, therefore, and of
their system, the reader, after acquainting himself with the
Zurich schools, will be able to form a clear notion.

I hope the growing interest in the subject of popular education will induce my countrymen to inform themselves accurately what on the Continent the primary school, at any rate, is, and what a different sense words bear according as they are applied to popular education here, or on the Continent. At present, when in canvassing the subject of English popular education the example of the Continent is adduced, the example is in general perfectly fallacious, because the terms which we employ are perfectly ambiguous, or our application of them perfectly inaccurate. It is constantly said,—no less a personage than the secretary to the National Society, Mr. Wilson, said it at the Society's last general meeting,—that 'it appears that in 1858 the proportion of scholars to population was, in England and Wales, 1 to 7·7; in Holland, 1 to 8·11; in France, 1 to 9; and in Prussia, 1 to 6·27.' It is at once argued from thence, as Mr. Wilson argued, that 'our own country, therefore, is in advance of Holland and France, and not far behind Prussia.' Mr. Pease, at the annual meeting of the British and Foreign School Society in May last, said: 'Prussia supplied an education superior to that of any country in the world, and he was glad that ours fell but little short of it.' To the same effect Mr. Joseph Spencer, at the recent Congregationalist Meeting in Manchester, met the weighty and impressive speeches of Mr. Baines and Mr. Morley on our educational condition, by saying that ' he believed we did not stand behind any country except Prussia.' Still more recently, Lord John Manners has declared that ' our primary education is ahead of all the countries in the world except Prussia;' and this, he added, ' is shown by figures which no one doubts and everybody admits.' No wonder, therefore, that anti-alarmists should, like Mr. Wilson, pronounce it ' highly satisfactory to find that, notwithstanding many confident assertions to the contrary, the state of education in England and Wales will bear favourable comparison with the state of education in the most

advanced of continental countries, even in Prussia, where
attendance at school is compulsory.'   No wonder that a san-
guine man should even go a little beyond this, and, like Mr.
Joseph Spencer, pronounce that ' the system of education in
Prussia being surrounded with so many things which are
objected to in England, he believed we might be considered
on an equality with Prussia.'

But when these gentlemen congratulate themselves because
it appears that the proportion of scholars to population is in
England and Wales 1 to 7, while in Holland it is only 1 to 8,
in France only 1 to 9, and even in Prussia not more than
1 to 6, there is a fallacy in their use both of the word
appears and of the word *scholars*, which requires notice.   In
the first place, that in England and Wales the proportion of
scholars to population is 1 to 7, *appears* in a very different
way, and on very different evidence, from the way and the
evidence by which the proportion of scholars to population in
France or Prussia is established.   For France or Prussia
such statistics are got from a series of administrative
authorities, with machinery and power to collect them.
For England, the statistics come from the Education Commissioners of 1859.   These Commissioners have themselves
told us how they procured their information.   They had no
series of administrative authorities through whom to collect
it; such a series does not exist in England; it could not, as
we are often told, be tolerated by a high-spirited and intelligent people like ourselves.   The Commissioners sent en-
quirers, with no power to enforce an answer to their questions,
through about one-eighth of England; and from the information thus obtained for about one-eighth of the country,
they made a generalisation as to the remainder.   The only
information they could get of the same quality and trust-
worthiness as the information on which the continental
returns are based, was for that minority of our schools which
is in connection with the Committee of Council.   It was

not, of course, the Commissioners' fault that the returns, by which it appeared to them that the proportion of scholars to population was, for England and Wales, 1 to 7, were of this incomplete kind; they had no means of getting complete returns. But it is obvious how different a sort of appearing is this by which the English rate of scholars appears to be 1 in 7, from that by which the foreign rates appear to be 1 in 9 or 1 in 6. The English Commissioners *guess* their proportion; the foreign authorities *know* theirs. Therefore we ought not to say: 'It *appears* that in England 1 in 7 of the population is in school, in France 1 in 9, in Prussia 1 in 6;' but we should say: 'It is *thought likely* that in England 1 in 7 of the population is in school; it is *ascertained* that in France 1 in 9 is in school, in Prussia 1 in 6.' Perhaps this ought not wholly to extinguish the high satisfaction with which, as Mr. Spencer and Mr. Wilson say, the comparison of English education with that of continental countries is calcu'ated to fill us; but at all events it must tend to somewhat abate it.

In the same way, a fallacy lurks under our use of the word *scholars*. England, says the secretary to the National Society, is in advance of Holland and France, and not far behind Prussia, because our proportion of scholars to population is not far behind Prussia's, and is in advance of that of Holland and France. I feel that I ought to apologise, in passing, to that admirably educated people, the Dutch, for even quoting what they must think such an impertinence as the assertion that England is in popular education ahead of Holland; but the impertinence comes, in truth, from those who utter it being the victims of an ambiguous use of words. They do not know what the continental nations mean by the word *scholar*. They do not know that the continental nations and we mean something wholly different by it. Prussia means by a scholar a child who has been subjected from his sixth year to his fifteenth to obligatory instruction, either in public schools under certificated teachers who have had a three years' train-ing in a normal school, or in private schools under teachers who produce the same, or higher, guarantees of competency. France means by a scholar a child who is either in a public school under a certificated teacher, or in a private school under a certificated teacher. Both public and private schools must, in France, be under certificated teachers, and both are liable to State-inspection; the public schools alone, however, to complete inspection, the private schools to partial inspection only. But then, of the children,—some four millions and a half in number,—who are counted as scholars of the primary schools in France, nearly three millions and a half are in public, completely inspected schools; there are no more than 922,000 in private, partially inspected schools. In England, on the other hand, out of some two millions and a quarter of chil-dren whom our Education Commissioners count as scholars, there are only 920,000 in schools with certificated teachers, or under any public inspection, complete or incomplete, whatever; all the rest are in schools which give no tangible guarantees of any kind, which do not, therefore, in a foreigner's eyes, possess any real claim to style themselves schools, and their pupils scholars, at all. It is probable that some of these schools are schools coming up to the foreign standard of what a school is, and with scholars coming up to the foreign standard of what a scholar is. It is known that very many of them fall immeasurably below this standard. But how many come up to it, and how many fall below it, we have no certain means of knowing; no certain means, therefore, of ascertaining our proportion of scholars, in the continental sense of the word, to population. All that is certain is, that the proportion of 1 to 7 is not the true one, because it counts very many children as scholars who, on the Continent, would not be counted as such. It is true that Mr. John Flint, the registrar to the English Commissioners of 1859, says in a re-markable letter to the *Times*, that in reckoning scholars he regards quantity not quality, and that he has nothing to do with quality; and for English purposes this view of a scholar may perhaps serve very well; but it is obviously illusive when we are comparing school-returns with the foreigners, who do not regard quantity of scholars merely, but who regard quality also.

So far are the foreigners from accepting our estimate of what constitutes a scholar, or thinking, with the secretary of our National Society, that the state of education in England and Wales will bear favourable comparison with the state of education in the most advanced of continental countries,— so far, I say, are they from this, that a foreign Report on education, which I have now before me, goes on, after re-marking that the number of our school children over ten years of age diminishes every year, to sum up our condition as follows :—*L'Angleterre proprement dite est le pays d'Europe où l'instruction est le moins répandue.'* The reporter does not consider that 1 in 7 of our population is a scholar, in the sense in which 1 in 9 of the population of Holland is a scholar, or he would not speak in this manner. Not finding any complete returns of our school population, and not being disposed, even if they found them, to accept Mr. John Flint's law of disregarding quality, foreigners seek elsewhere for data enabling them to compare our primary instruction with their own. They produce statistics showing that, in the Prussian army, the proportion of illiterate recruits is 2 per cent. ; in the French army 27 per cent. ; in the English army 57 per cent. Even allowing these statistics to be trustworthy, it must be admitted that, recruited as our army is, the comparative instruction of our recruits is not a fair test by which to try our popular education as pitted against that of France or Germany. It is a sounder test, perhaps, than the generalisation of the Education Commissioners of 1859, applied in conformity with Mr. John Flint's law ; but it is not an accurate test. Probably, with the sort of civil administration we possess, and are proud of possessing, we cannot obtain the means of accurately comparing our popular education with that of the Continent. But then Mr. Wilson and Mr. Spencer and others ought to beware of building too much upon an inaccurate comparison of it.

In short, it is expedient for the satisfactory resolution of these educational questions, which are at length beginning seriously to occupy us, both that we should attend to the experience of the Continent, and that we should know precisely what it is which this experience says. Having long held that nothing was to be learned by us from the foreigners, we are at last beginning to see, that on a matter like the institution of schools, for instance, much light is thrown by a comparative study of their institution among other civilised states and nations. To treat this comparative study with proper respect, not to wrest it to the requirements of our inclinations or prejudices, but to try simply and seriously to find what it teaches us, is perhaps the lesson which we have most need to inculcate upon ourselves at present. No ability or experience in the judge who pronounces on these matters can make up for his not knowing the facts. Mr. Fraser and Canon Norris both of them assert, that our inspected schools at present are at least equal to the best primary schools of any other country, if not superior to them. Many others amongst us say the same thing. Mr. Lowe, the author of the Revised Code, thinks 'our system, though partial, may compare favourably with any system in the world;' and evidently, by what he says of America, he believes that our English schools must necessarily be superior to those of less favoured countries, where, as he says, 'examination as practised under the Revised Code in England is totally unknown.' Mr. Fraser, again, lays it down as certain, that our inspectors and inspection are better than those of any other country. I have every interest in accrediting all possible good report of our inspectors and our inspection; but, having seen those of the Continent, I am not of Mr. Fraser's opinion. Neither am I of his, and Canon Norris's, and Mr. Lowe's opinion as to the equality, if not more than equality, of our inspected schools with the best primary schools of the Continent. I have that high respect for the abilities and judgment of these three gentlemen, that if I understood them to have seen with their own eyes the best primary schools of Holland, Switzerland, and North Germany, as well as our own schools, and then to have arrived at this favourable judgment of the English schools, I should at once defer to their opinion, and conclude that my own judgment, which is not so favourable to the English schools, was mistaken. But now I do not understand them to have seen the Dutch, and German, and Swiss schools and inspectors with their own eyes; but they speak from report, or from the pleasant impressions they have received from English inspectors with whom they have come in contact, or from their warm admiration of the Revised Code. This admiration goes so far with some people, that Lord Hartington boldly says of Mr. Lowe, who produced the Revised Code, that English education owes more to him than to any other man living. And no doubt Lord Hartington knows; but he does not tell us the grounds on which he has built up his knowledge.

I have seen Dutch, German, and Swiss schools, I have seen their inspection; and I think both them and their inspection, in general, better than our schools and inspection at present. I think, as a matter of fact, they are better; and I think, as a matter of likelihood, it seems likely they should be better. The working-class in Zurich or Saxony is, in general, less raw and illiterate than ours; and every one knows that children brought up with raw and illiterate parents are more stubborn material as scholars, than children brought up in more civilised homes. Then these Swiss and German children are obliged to be under teaching from their sixth to their fifteenth year. Mr. Fraser thinks it vain even to talk of

keeping in school the mass of our children after their tenth
year. Then again, in Prussia, the regular school-course for
primary schools consists of the following matters: religious
instruction, reading, writing, the mother-tongue, object
lessons, geography, history, physics, natural history, arithmetic, drawing, needlework, gymnastics, singing. Prussian
inspection extends to all these matters, and the German
nature abhors making instruction mechanical. In England,
since the Revised Code, the school-course is more and more
confined to the three paying matters, reading, writing, and
arithmetic ; the inspection tends to concentrate itself on these
matters ; these matters are the very part of school-teaching
which is most mechanical, and a natural danger of the
English mind is to make instruction mechanical. Finally,
the Swiss or German schoolmaster has in general had a three
years' training in a normal school, is a public servant, enjoys
much consideration as discharging an important function,
and through bodies such as the School-Synod described in a
later part of this volume, makes his voice heard in the school
legislation and school regulation of his country. With us
he has an inferior training, has no sort of representation by
which to make his ideas and experience reach the Education
Department; while, as to his status, there was no part of
Mr. Lowe's reforms on which he valued himself more, and
which more recommended itself to many people, than that by
which he made the schoolmaster know his place, and got rid
of the danger and impropriety of seeming to give him rank
as a public official. For my own part, I have always looked
with some apprehension upon this check administered to the
schoolmaster ; because it seems to me of the first importance,
in dealing with any organism, not to do anything *to depress
its powers of life* ; and the powers of life in our public education were undoubtedly the schoolmasters, animated by the
hopes, advantages, and belief in their mission, which Sir
James Shuttleworth had given to them. To have administered

a check to a body of which some members were pragmatical, and to have escaped the danger, so grave in the eyes of the country gentlemen, of having in our schoolmasters a band of public servants, appear to me a doubtful compensation for having discouraged the whole body of schoolmasters, and thereby lowered for the present, and till some action other than ours comes in to repair what we have done, the powers of life of our whole public education. This way of thinking, however, seems contrary to that of many able people in this country, and, being so, is probably erroneous; only, as their way of thinking assumes that our schools under the Revised Code may compare favourably with any schools in the world, I should be glad if my countrymen would try to acquaint themselves with the best continental schools, and satisfy themselves by actual observation whether this is so. It is not so very rare for English people to find themselves at Basle, or Berlin, or Leipzig, and the primary schools on the Continent are in general thrown open readily enough to visitors. If Mr. Fraser, after bringing to bear on the best foreign schools the same keen eyes and shrewd judgment which he has brought to bear on English and American schools,* were then to assure us that he thought our schools and inspection better, I should be much staggered in the contrary opinion, and even inclined to surrender it to the authority of so much more capable a judge. But at present he and other good judges seem to lie under a sort of disadvantage in giving their judgment for the one of two things, without having seen the other.

Even where we have made up our minds as to the course which in this or that school matter we wish to adopt, it can do us no harm to see what is the course followed by the continental schools in this particular, and why they follow it. Take the matter of schoolmasters' certificates, for

---

* As to the significance of the American schools, which Mr. Fraser, from personal observation, can compare with those of England, see the note at p. 244 of this work.

instance. Certain influential people amongst us have schools with uncertificated teachers; they object to being forced to employ certificated teachers; and yet they demand to be allowed to try and earn the examination grants offered by the Revised Code. They say that it is hard to oblige a small rural place to maintain a teacher of the same class as a town. This sounds plausible; yet it is interesting to know that, in Prussia, it is just in the small rural places that the elementary school is made of the most complete and effective kind, because in these places the burgher or middle school of towns,—a second stage of school, higher than any elementary school we have,—cannot be provided. But then people say, that the Revised Code pays for results, and that when they offer results, they ought to be paid for them without any more questions being asked. Certainly they seem to have a case as against the eminent author of the Revised Code, who declared the other day at Edinburgh in plain words: ' It is the business of the State to ascertain results, and to pay in proportion to them.' Many persons, accordingly, think their demand ought to be granted, and granted, perhaps, it will be. But at least it is curious and interesting to know that on the Continent, these influential employers of uncertificated schoolmasters, instead of being allowed to earn public grants, would have their schools closed by public authority. No doubt this is one of ' the many things,' as Mr. Spencer says, ' surrounding foreign education which are objected to in England;' but there is always some profit in having these things in black and white. The foreigners defend their arbitrary proceeding by saying, that the public has an interest and a right to take securities of the schools which educate its children; and that, ' to ascertain results,'—that is, to examine all school-children once a year for a few minutes in reading, writing, and arithmetic,—is an unsound security, while the employment of a teacher who has passed three years under the best training for him the country can give, is a sound security. It will be objected not only that this foreign doctrine is at variance with Mr. Lowe's high authority, but also that it is un-English to regard the mass of the public, the parents of school-children, instead of regarding influential managers, because in England we have reversed Sieyès's famous rule, and say: ' Nothing *for* the people, everything *by* the people.' And against such an objection I do not presume to contend; only I urge that we may as well know, in all its nakedness, the foreign practice and the foreign theory in this matter.

As to compulsory education, again, denominational education, secular education, the continental precedents are, I maintain, to be studied for the sake of seeing what they really mean, and not merely for the sake of furnishing ourselves with help from them for some thesis which we uphold. Most English liberals seem persuaded that our elementary schools should be undenominational, and their teaching secular; and that with a public elementary school it cannot well be otherwise. Let them clearly understand, however, that on the Continent generally, everywhere except in Holland, the public elementary school is denominational,* and its teaching religious as well as secular. Then as to compulsory education. It may be broadly said, that in all the civilised states of Continental Europe education is compulsory except in France and Holland. The opponents of compulsory education quote Mr. Pattison, to show that in North Germany ' compulsory attendance is a matter which produces comparatively little practical result.' They quote a report of mine, to show that in French Switzerland ' the making popular education compulsory by law has not added one iota to its prosperity.' But yet the example of the Continent proves, and nothing which Mr. Pattison or I have said disproves, that in general, where popular education is most prosperous, there it is also compulsory. The compulsoriness is, in general, found to go along with the prosperity, though it

* Of course with what we should call a conscience clause.

cannot be said to cause it; but the same high value among a people for education which leads to its prospering among them, leads also in general to its being made compulsory. Where the value for it is not ardent enough to make it, as it is in Prussia and Zurich, compulsory, it is not, for the most part, ardent enough to give it the prosperity it has in Prussia and Zurich. After seeing the schools of North Germany and of German Switzerland, I am strongly of this opinion. It is the same thing as in religion. The vitality of a man's religion does not lie in his imposing on himself certain absolute rules as to conduct; but, in general, if his religion is vital, it will make him lay on himself absolute rules as to conduct. Above all, it will make a newly awakened sinner do this; and England, in spite of what the secretary to the National Society says, I must take leave to regard, in educational matters, as a newly awakened sinner.

Therefore I do not think the example of Prussia and Switzerland will serve to show that compulsoriness of education is an insignificant thing; and I believe that if ever our zeal for the cause mounts high enough in England to make our popular education 'bear favourable comparison,' except in the imagination of popular speakers, with the popular education of Prussia and Switzerland, this same zeal will also make it compulsory.

But the English friends of compulsory education, in their turn, will do well to inform themselves how far on the Continent compulsory education extends, and the conditions under which alone the working classes, if they respect themselves, can submit to its application. In the view of the English friends of compulsory education, the educated and intelligent middle and upper classes amongst us are to confer the boon of compulsory education upon the ignorant lower class, which needs it while they do not. But, on the Continent, instruction is obligatory for lower, middle, and upper class alike. I doubt whether our educated and intelligent classes are at all pre-

pared for this. I have an acquaintance in easy circumstances, of distinguished connections, living in a fashionable
part of London, who, like many other people, deals rather
easily with his son's schooling.   Sometimes the boy is at
school, then for months together he is away from school, and
taught, so far as he is taught, by his father and mother at
home. He is not the least an invalid, but it pleases his
father and mother to bring him up in this manner. Now I
imagine no English friends of compulsory education dream
of dealing with such a defaulter as this, and certainly his
father, who perhaps is himself a friend of compulsory education
for the working classes, would be astounded to find his education of his own son interfered with. But if my worthy
acquaintance lived in Switzerland or Germany, he would be
dealt with as follows. I speak with the school-law of Canton
Neufchâtel immediately under my eyes, but the regulations
on this matter are substantially the same in all the states
of Germany and of German Switzerland. The Municipal
Education Committee of the district where my acquaintance lived would address a summons to him, informing him
that a comparison of the school-rolls of their district with
the municipal list of children of school-age showed his son
not to be at school; and requiring him, in consequence, to
appear before the Municipal Committee at a place and time
named, and there to satisfy them either that his son did
attend some public school, or that, if privately taught, he
was taught by duly trained and certificated teachers. On
the back of the summons my acquaintance would find printed
the penal articles of the school-law, sentencing him to a fine
if he failed to satisfy the Municipal Committee; and, if he
failed to pay the fine, or was found a second time offending,
to imprisonment. In some continental states he would be
liable, in case of repeated infraction of the school-law, to be
deprived of his parental rights, and to have the care of his
son transferred to guardians named by the State. It is

indeed terrible to think of the consternation and wrath of our educated and intelligent classes under a discipline like this; and I should not like to be the man to try and impose it on them. But I assure them most emphatically,— and if they study the experience of the Continent they will convince themselves of the truth of what I say,—that only on these conditions of its equal and universal application is any law of compulsory education possible.

Of the education of the middle and upper classes, however, I have no need to speak at length here, for almost the whole of the following pages is devoted to that subject. It is not, like popular education, a subject which very keenly interests at present our educated and intelligent classes. It concerns their own education, and with their own education they are, it seems, tolerably well satisfied. Yet I hope that here again these classes,—above all I hope that the great middle class which has much the widest and the gravest interests concerned in the matter,—will not refuse their attention to the experience afforded by the Continent. Before concluding that they can have nothing to learn from it, let them at any rate know and weigh it.

To three points particularly let me invite their consideration. In the first place, let them consider in its length and breadth the facts, established in the following pages, that on the Continent the middle class in general may be said to be brought up *on the first plane,* while in England it is brought up *on the second plane.* In the public higher schools of Prussia or France 65,000 of the youth of the middle and upper classes are brought up; in the public higher schools of England,—even when we reckon as such many institutions which would not be entitled to such a rank on the Continent,—only some 15,000. Has this state of things no bad effect upon us? If the training of our working class, as compared with the working classes elsewhere, inspires apprehension, has the training of their employers, as compared with employers elsewhere, no matter of apprehension for us?   There are people who say that the labour questions which embarrass us owe their gravity and danger at least as much to the inadequacy of our middle class for dealing with such questions, as to the inadequacy of our working class.   'English employers of labour,' these people say, 'are just now full of complaints of the ignorance and unreasonableness of the class they employ, and of suggestions, among other things, for its better instruction.   It never occurs to them that their own bad instruction has much to do with the matter.   Brought up in schools of inferior standing, they have no governing qualities, no aptitude, like that of the aristocratic class, for the ruling of men ; brought up with hollow and unsound teaching, they have no science, no aptitude for finding their way out of a difficulty by thought and reason, and creating new relations between themselves and the working class when the old relations fail.'   I do not say that this is certainly so, but I say that the bearings of our education on the matter,—our education both in itself and in comparison with that of the Continent,—are at least worth studying.

The second point is this.   The study of continental education will show our educated and intelligent classes that many things which they wish for cannot be done as isolated operations, but must, if they are to be done at all, come in as parts of a regularly designed whole.   Mr. Grant Duff, who directed his attention to educational matters long before they were in everybody's talk as at present, has pointed this out with great truth and clearness.   Our educated and intelligent classes, in their solicitude for our backward working class, and their alarm for our industrial preëminence, are beginning to cry out for technical schools for our artisans. Well-informed and distinguished people seem to think it is only necessary to have special schools of arts and trades, as they have abroad, and then we may take a clever boy from our elementary schools, perfected by the Revised Code, and put him at once into a special school. A study of the best continental experience will show them that the special school is the crown of a long co-ordered series, designed and graduated by the best heads in the country. A clever boy in a Prussian elementary school passes first into a *Mittelschule*, or higher elementary school, then into a modern, or *real*, school of the second class, then into a *real* school of the first class, and finally, after all these, into the special school. A boy who has had this preparation is able to profit by a special school; to send him there straight from the elementary school, is like sending a boy from the shell at one of our public schools to hear Professor Ritschl lecture on Latin inscriptions.

I come, lastly, to the third point for our remark in Continental education. These foreign Governments, which we think so offensively arbitrary, do at least take, when they administer education, the best educational opinion of the country into their counsels, and we do not. This comes partly from our disbelief in government, partly from our belief in machinery. Our disbelief in government makes us slow to organise government perfectly for any matter; our belief in machinery makes us think that when we have organised a department, however imperfectly, it must prove efficacious and self-acting. The result is that while, on the Continent, through Boards and Councils, the best educational opinion of the country,—by which I mean the opinion of men like Sir James Shuttleworth, Mr. Mill, Dr. Temple, men who have established their right to be at least heard on these topics,— necessarily reaches the Government and influences its action, in this country there are no organised means for its ever reaching our Government at all. The most important questions of educational policy may be settled without such men being even heard. A number of grave matters enumerated in the following pages,*—our system of competitive examinations, our regulation of studies, our whole school legislation, —are at the present moment settled one hardly knows how, certainly without any care for the best counsel attainable being first taken on them. On the Continent it is not so; and the more our Government is likely, in England, to have to intervene in educational matters, the more does the continental practice, in this particular, invite and require our attention.

In conclusion. There are two chief obstacles, as it seems to me, which oppose themselves to our consulting foreign experience with profit. One is, our notion of the State as an alien intrusive power in the community, not summing up and representing the action of individuals, but thwarting it. This notion is not so strong as it once was, but still it is strong enough to make it opportune to quote some words from a foreign Report before me, which set this much obscured point in its true light :—

‘ *Le Gouvernement ne représente pas un intérêt particulier, distinct, puisqu’il est au contraire la plus haute et la plus sincère expression de tous les intérêts généraux du pays.*’

This is undoubtedly what a government ought to be, and if it is not this, it is the duty of its citizens to try and make it this, not to try and get rid of so powerful and essential an agency as much as possible.

The other obstacle is our high opinion of our own energy and wealth. This opinion is just, but it is possible to rely on it too long, and to strain our energy and our wealth too hard. At any rate, our energy and our wealth will be more fruitful and safer, the more we add intelligence to them; and here, if anywhere, is an occasion for applying the words of the wise man :—‘ If the iron be blunt, and a man do not whet the edge, then must be put forth the more strength; but wisdom is profitable to direct.’

* See pages 282–3 of the following work.

CONTENTS.

CHAPTER I.

DEVELOPMENT OF SECONDARY INSTRUCTION IN EUROPE.

CHAPTER II.

THE FRENCH SECONDARY SCHOOLS FROM THE CONSULATE TO THE PRESENT TIME.

CHAPTER III.

GOVERNMENT, ADMINISTRATION, AND TEACHING STAFF OF THE FRENCH SECONDARY SCHOOLS AT PRESENT.

CHAPTER IV.

MATTERS TAUGHT IN THE FRENCH SECONDARY SCHOOLS.

CHAPTER V.

THE *LYCÉES.*

CHAPTER VI.

PRIVATE OR FREE SCHOOLS AND COMMUNAL COLLEGES.

CHAPTER VII.

CHARACTER OF DISCIPLINE AND INSTRUCTION IN THE FRENCH SECONDARY SCHOOLS.

CHAPTER VIII.

SUPERIOR OR UNIVERSITY INSTRUCTION IN FRANCE.

CHAPTER IX.

DEVELOPMENT AND HISTORY OF THE ITALIAN SECONDARY SCHOOLS.

CHAPTER XXI.

THE SCHOOLS OF SWITZERLAND.

CHAPTER XXII.

GENERAL CONCLUSION. SCHOOL STUDIES.

CHAPTER XXIII.

GENERAL CONCLUSION CONTINUED. SCHOOL ESTABLISHMENT.

I.

FRANCE.

CHAPTER I.

DEVELOPMENT OF SECONDARY INSTRUCTION IN EUROPE.

ORIGIN OF OUR PRESENT SECONDARY SCHOOLS—THEIR DEVELOPMENT BEST TRACED IN FRANCE—ROMAN PERIOD—MEDIÆVAL PERIOD—UNIVERSITY OF PARIS—CREATION OF COLLEGES—THE INSTRUCTION IN THE MEDIÆVAL SCHOOLS—THE UNIVERSITY OF PARIS AND THE RENAISSANCE—SCHOOLS OF THE JESUITS—THE OLD SCHOOLS ABOLISHED AT THE REVOLUTION—NEW PLANS—FOURCROY'S LAW (1802).

POPULAR EDUCATION has sprung out of the ideas and necessities of modern times, and the elementary school for the poor is an institution which has no remote history. With the secondary school it is otherwise. The secondary school has a long history; through a series of changes it goes back, in every European country, to the beginnings of civilised society in that country; from the time when this society had any sort of organisation, a certain sort of schools and schooling existed, and between that schooling and the schooling which the children of the richer class of society at this day receive there is an unbroken connection. In no country is this continuity of secondary instruction more visible than in France, notwithstanding her revolutions; and in some respects France, in that which concerns the historical development of secondary instruction, is a typical country. All the countries of western Europe had their early contact with Greek and Roman civilisation, a contact from which their actual books and schools and science begin; France had this more than any of them, except Italy. All the countries of western Europe had in the feudal and catholic Middle Age their universities, under whose wings were hatched the colleges and teachers that formed the germ of our actual secondary instruction; and the great Middle Age university was the University of Paris. Hither repaired the students of other countries and other universities, as to the main centre of mediæval science, and the most authoritative school of mediæval teaching. It received names expressing the most enthusiastic devotion: the *fountain of knowledge*, the *tree of life*, the *candlestick of the house of the Lord*. 'The most famous University of Paris, the place at this time and long before whither the English, and mostly the Oxonians, resorted,' says Wood. *Tandem fiat hic velut Parisiis . . . ad instar Parisiensis studii . . . quemadmodum in Parisiensi studio . . .* say the rules of the University of Vienna, founded in 1365. Here came Roger Bacon, Saint Thomas Aquinas, and Dante; here studied the founder of the first university of the Empire, Charles the Fourth, Emperor of Germany and King of Bohemia, founder of the University of Prague;* here Henry the Second in the 12th century proposed to refer his dispute with Becket; here, in the 14th, the schism in the papacy and the claims of the rival popes were brought for judgment. In Europe and Asia, in foreign cities and on battle fields, among statesmen, princes, priests, crusaders, scholars, passed in the middle ages this word of recognition, *Nos fuimus simul in Galandia,*—the Rue de Galande, one of the streets of the old university quarter, the *quartier latin* of Paris.

The countries of western Europe, leavened, all of them, by the one spirit of the feudal and catholic Middle Age, formed in some sense one community, and were more associated than they have been since the feudal and catholic unity of the Middle Age has disappeared and given place to the divided and various life of modern Europe. In the mediæval community France held the first place. It is now well known that to place in the 15th century the revival of intellectual life and the re-establishment of civilisation, and to treat the period between the 5th century, when ancient civilisation was ruined by the barbarians, and the 15th, when the life and intellect of this civilisation reappeared and transformed the world, as one chaos, is a mistake. The chaos ends about the 10th century; in the 11th there truly comes the first re-

---

* Founded 1348.

establishment of civilisation, the first revival of intellectual life ; the principal centre of this revival is France, its chief monuments of literature are in the French language, its chief monuments of art are the French cathedrals. This revival fills the 12th and 13th centuries with its activity and with its works ; all this time France has the lead ; in the 14th century the lead passes to Italy ; but now comes the commencement of a wholly new period, the period of the Renaissance properly so called, the beginning of modern European life, the ceasing of the life of the feudal and catholic Middle Age. The anterior and less glorious Renaissance, the Renaissance within the limits of the Middle Age itself, a revival which came to a stop and could not successfully develope itself, but which has yet left profound traces in our spirit and our literature,—this revival belongs chiefly to France. France, then, may well serve as a typical country wherein to trace the mediæval growth of intellect and learning ; above all she may so stand for us, whose connection with her in the Middle Age, owing to our Norman kings and the currency of her language among our cultivated class, was so peculiarly close ; so close that the literary and intellectual development of the two countries at that time intermingles, and no important event can happen in that of the one without straightway affecting and interesting that of the other. As late as the year 1328 we find French an alternative language, at Oxford, with Latin ; the students are to use *colloquio Latino vel saltem Gallico*. With the hostility of the long French Wars of Edward the Third comes the estrangement, never afterwards diminishing but always increasing. To this day it is impossible to read the French literature of the true Middle Age without feeling that here is the moment when the life of the French nation comes really closest to our own ; thought and expression have both of them much which we recognise as akin to us, which we have in a great degree retained, while the French have gone away from it to a thought and expression more effective no doubt for many purposes, but more unlike ours. To show how this is the case with thought and style would need more space than I have here at command ; one example out of a thousand,—the word *rescouer*, for

instance, 'to rescue,' which the French had in the Middle
Age, which we have still, but which the French have no
longer,—will show how it is the case with language.

Roman civilisation in Gaul, as in other parts of the empire,
organised a system of schools. Before the ruin of that civilisation in the fourth century, there were great schools in
important towns, Vienne, Lyons, Bordeaux, Arles, Agen,
Clermont, Perigueux; and at these schools, Christian children
began to appear. Then came the invasions of the barbarians,
and the break-up of the old order of things. For some time
schooling ceased to be a concern of lay society; it went on in
the shelter of the church and for the benefit of the ecclesiastical body. The great schools from the 4th century to the
12th are the monastery schools, such as the school of Saint
Victor at Marseilles, of Lérins in the isles of Hyères, of Saint
Claude in Franche Comté, of Saint Médard at Soissons.
There were 400 monks studying at the school of Saint
Médard in the sixth century. A famous monastery school for
women also, that of Chelles near Paris, existed as early as
the time of the Merovingian kings. But as a new state of
society gradually formed itself and became solid, signs appeared of the lay class too coming to school. A decree of
Pope Eugene II., in 826, ordered that *in universis episcopiis
subjectisque plebibus et aliis locis in quibus necessitas occurrerit,
omnino cura et diligentia adhibeatur ut magistri et doctores
constituantur, qui studia literarum, liberaliumque artium
dogmata, assidue doceant.* The Council of Aix-la-Chapelle,
in 816, had divided the school into interior and exterior;
the first for novices in training for the Church, the second
for lay boys. In 855 this arrangement was carried into
effect at Fleury sur Loire, one of the schools which Theodulf,
Bishop of Orleans, employed by Charlemagne in his plans of
social reconstruction, had founded. At Fleury sur Loire was
formed a school expressly for the sons of laymen, the youth
of the upper class; it was called *Hospitale Nobilium.* The
Palace School of Charlemagne is well known. Charlemagne's
astonishing efforts at reconstruction were, however, premature; after his death followed another period of confusion
and slow formation. But about the 11th century we see

feudal society, with institutions naturally developed and destined to endure for a long while, in possession of France, England, and Germany. From about the 11th century, date the beginnings of an instruction which has, with many changes of names, impulses, and objects, been going on uninterruptedly ever since.

Our Stephen Harding, the third abbot of Citeaux, and the true founder of the great order of the Cistercians, was studying at the School of Paris in 1070. The name of Abelard recalls the European celebrity and immense intellectual ferment of this school in the 12th century. But it was in the first year of the following century, the 13th, that it received a charter from Philip Augustus, and thenceforth the name of University of Paris takes the place of that of School of Paris. Forty-nine years later was founded University College, Oxford, the oldest college of the oldest English University. Four nations composed the University of Paris,—the nation of France, the nation of Picardy, the nation of Normandy, and (signal mark of the close intercourse which then existed between France and us!) the nation of England.* The four nations united formed the faculty of arts. The faculty of theology was created in 1257, that of law in 1271, that of medicine in 1274. Theology, law, and medicine had each their Dean; arts had four Procurators, one for each of the four nations composing this faculty. Arts elected the rector of the University, and had possession of the University chest and archives.

The pre-eminence of the Faculty of Arts indicates, as indeed does the very development of the University, an idea, gradually strengthening itself, of a lay instruction to be no longer absorbed in theology, but separable from it. The growth of a lay and modern spirit in society, the preponderance of the crown over the papacy, of the civil over the ecclesiastical power, is the great feature of French history

* Another mark of this close intercourse is the choice of a patron by the nation of France; this patron was Saint Thomas of Canterbury. That of the nation of England was Saint Edmund, the Saxon martyr-king. In the 15th century, when the Hundred Years' War had separated France and England, the nation of Germany took the place of ours, and Saint Charlemagne took that of Saint Edmund. In 1661 Charlemagne was made by statute the common patron of the University.

in the 14th century, and to this century belongs the highest development of the University. But the ecclesiastical power never abandoned its claims to a control of education; it had numerous means of action on the University, and it waged a constant war for mastery, often with success. The Chancellor of the Cathedral of Notre Dame was the ecclesiastical chief, as the rector was the academical chief, of the University; the seal of the University, for the first twenty years of its existence, is the seal of its ecclesiastical chief, the Chancellor of Notre Dame. When, between 1221 and 1225, the University struck, for the first time, a seal of its own, the Chapter of Notre Dame complained to the papal legate at Paris of the usurpation, and the legate ordered the seal to be broken. The scholars rose in insurrection, assailed the legate's house, and compelled him to fly. The dispute was referred to the Pope, and at last Innocent IV., in 1244, granted to the University a seal of its own.

But the licence to teach, the crown of the University course, was conferred by the ecclesiastical power, the Chancellor of the Cathedral. Not till he was provided with this licence could the candidate appear before the masters of his faculty, and receive from them the bonnet of doctor in law, medicine, or theology, of master in arts. So far the University had to admit the intervention of the authority of the metropolitan church. Nor was it successful in freeing itself from the intrusion of the mendicant orders, who saw in the right of teaching a powerful means of influence. The Dominicans, on an occasion when the University had shut its schools, in 1229, offered themselves as teachers of theology; the University refused to them and the Franciscans the degree of master and the privilege of teaching; but on an appeal to the Pope the University had to give way, and in 1257 Saint Thomas Aquinas and Saint Bonaventura were made doctors in theology by the Chancellor, and admitted to teach in Paris. The admission of the other orders followed.

But the importance of the University in the 13th and 14th centuries was extraordinary. Men's minds were possessed with a wonderful zeal for knowledge, or what was then thought knowledge, and the University of Paris was the great fount from which this knowledge issued. The University and those depending on it made at this time, it is said, actually a third of the population of Paris; when the University went on a solemn occasion in procession to Saint Denis, the head of the procession, it is said, had reached Saint Denis before the end of it had left its starting place in Paris. It had immunities from taxation, it had jurisdiction of its own, and its members claimed to be exempt from that of the provost of Paris; the kings of France strongly favoured the University, and leaned to its side when the municipal and academical authorities were in conflict; if at any time the University thought itself seriously aggrieved, it had recourse to a measure which threw Paris into dismay,— it shut up its schools and suspended its lectures.

In a body of this kind the discipline could not be strict, and the colleges were created to supply centres of discipline which the University in itself,—an apparatus merely of teachers and lecture-rooms,—did not provide. The 14th century is the time when, one after another, with wonderful rapidity, the French colleges appeared. Navarre, Montaigu, Harcourt, names so familiar in the school annals of France, date from the first quarter of the 14th century. The College of Navarre was founded by the queen of Philip the Fair, in 1304; the College of Montaigu, where Erasmus, Rabelais, and Ignatius Loyola were in their time students, was founded in 1314 by two members of the family of Montaigu, one of them Archbishop of Rouen. The majority of these colleges were founded by magnates of the church, and designed to maintain a certain number of bursars, or scholars, during their university course. Frequently the bursarships were for the benefit of the founder's native place, and poverty, of which among the students of that age there was no lack, was specified as a title of admission.

Along with the University of Paris there existed in France, in the 14th century, the Universities of Orleans, Angers, Toulouse, and Montpellier. Orleans was the great French school for the study of the civil law; Reuchlin and Theodore Beza studied it there. The civil law was studiously kept away from the University of Paris, for fear it should drive out other studies, and especially the study of theology; so late as the year 1679 there was no chair of Roman or even of French law in the University of Paris. The strength of this University was concentrated on theology and arts, and its celebrity arose from the multitude of students which in these branches of instruction it attracted.

One asks oneself with interest what was the mental food to which this vast turbulent multitude pressed with such inconceivable hunger. Theology was the great matter; and there is no doubt that this study was by no means always that barren verbal trifling which an ill-informed modern contempt is fond of representing it. When the Bishop of Paris publicly condemned, as current in the University, such propositions as these: *Quod sermones theologi sunt fundati in fabulis ; Quod nihil plus scitur propter scire theologiam ; Quod fabulæ et falsa sunt in lege christiana sicut et in aliis ; Quod lex christiana impedit addiscere ; Quod sapientes mundi sunt philosophi tantum*, it is evident that around the study of theology in the mediæval University of Paris there worked a real ferment of thought, and very free thought. But the University of Paris culminated as the exclusive devotion to theological study declined, and culminated by virtue of that declension. A teaching body with a lay character could not have been created by the simple impulse to theological study. The glory of the University of Paris was its Faculty of Arts, its *artiens*, as they were called ; it was among the students in this faculty that the great ardour showed itself, the great increase in numbers. The study of this faculty was the seven arts * of the *trivium* and *quadrivium*; the three arts of the *trivium* were grammar, rhetoric, and dialectic ; the four of the *quadrivium*, arithmetic, geometry, astronomy, music. This was the liberal education of the middle age, and it came direct from the schools of ancient Rome. In the work, still extant, of Martianus Capella, an African grammarian established at Rome in the fifth century, the arts of the *trivium* and *quadrivium* are set forth in order, in a mixture of prose

---

* Enumerated in this line of middle-age Latin verse :
Lingua, tropus, ratio, numerus, tonus, angulus, astra.

and verse; and this book was one of the chief text-books of
the Middle Age, and its great guide to a liberal education.
Such an education was apparently possible with the programme offered by the seven arts. Rhetoric included poetry,
history, composition,—the humanities in general; dialectic
took in the whole of philosophy. The mediæval teacher of
grammar had for his text-books the grammars of Donatus
and Priscian, grammars coming from fully competent authorities, and quite sufficient, if properly used, for the teacher's purpose. The great monastery schools of Cluny, Saint Victor,
and the Bernardines, assigned three years to grammatical
studies, and the University professed to admit to its teaching
no student who was not already grounded in them; *qui nescit
partes, in vanum tendit ad artes.* But a measure of the good
sense of the grammatical studies of the time is supplied by
Donatus moralizatus, the grammar of Donatus *moralised,* as
was then the fashion with all books used for instruction.
' What is the *pronomen* ? ' the learner is made to ask. ' Man
is thy *nomen,*' the teacher answers, ' sinner is thy *pronomen.*
Therefore, when thou makest thy prayer to God, use thy *pronomen* only, and say, " O heavenly Father, I call not upon
thee as man, but I implore thee as sinner." ' Again : ' Why,'
the learner asks, ' is the preposition the consideration of the
joy of the elect ? ' The answer is : ' *Quia illi præponuntur
damnandis.*'

The scholastic philosophy remains a monument of what
the Middle Age achieved in the favourite art, the art which
starved all its six sisters,—Dialectic; but what was really the
instruction given and the proficiency acquired in the humanities and mathematics it is not so easy to determine.
The word mathematics was at that time synonymous with
magic, as is shown by a hexameter line in a poem for the
use of the schools,—a line equally unpromising for their
mathematics and for their scholarship : *Datque mathematicos
comburi theologia.* The arithmetic most in esteem was that
of the computers, which dealt with epacts, the golden number, the dominical letter, and all the calculations necessary
for framing the ecclesiastical calendar. But a catalogue of
the Sorbonne library, in 1290, shows that among the books

was a treatise on geometry in French, *Practica Geometriæ in Gallico*, of which the first words are quoted in the catalogue. The catalogue of the same institution, in 1338, has several copies of a Latin version of Euclid's Geometry. There is no mention of any work on algebra or mechanics. In the Sorbonne catalogue of 1290 appears Ovid; in the catalogue of 1338 he is joined by Terence, Virgil, Horace, Lucan, Juvenal, Statius. Ovid was the favourite poet, and a special, though a curious, object of moralisation. Numerous translations of the Latin classics were made for John of France and Charles V., showing that much attention and interest was already drawn to these works; but the frequent mistakes show also how imperfect was the mastery of them by that age.

The Council of Vienne, in 1311, decreed that at the Court of Rome, and in the four Universities of Paris, Oxford, Bologna, and Salamanca, there should be classes of Hebrew, Arabic, and Chaldee. Pope Clement V. is said to have at the same time enjoined the study and teaching of Greek. It is certain that in the monasteries of the Dominicans, who for their missions in the East needed the Oriental languages, individuals acquired a knowledge of them; the Dominicans of Dijon in 1439 give themselves, in a document which has been preserved, the name of *Massorii*, as the inheritors of the tradition of the Jewish doctors. The same order, renowned for its devotion to learning, sent members of its body to learn Greek in Greece itself, and as early as the 13th century produced translations of Aristotle, Plato, and Proclus. But it is evident that the study of Greek and the Oriental languages was confined to a few individuals, and did not pass into the general school instruction of the time; for the project of founding the study of these languages, as something still lacking to the schools, appears again and again in the 15th century. In 1455, and again twenty-five years later, the schools of Paris propose the establishment of a chair of Hebrew, as still a desideratum; and an envoy of the Greek Emperor, Manuel Palæologus, found at Lyons, in 1395, no one who could understand his language.

The eminence of the University of Paris was in the scholastic philosophy; its culminating moment was the 14th century, its greatness was mediæval. It did not follow the growth of the time, assimilate the new studies of the Renaissance and the 16th century, make itself their organ, and animate with them the French schools of which it was the head. Ramus, the chief representative among French teachers of the new studies and their spirit, who took as the subject of his thesis for the degree of master of arts: *Quæcumque ab Aristotele dicta essent, commentitia esse*—marking thereby the gulf which had begun to separate men's spirit from the old learning—Ramus, though he began his career as a servitor at the College of Navarre, passed his life in bitter conflict with the University, by which he was twice condemned, once for his anti-Aristotelian heresies, once for his Calvinism. The languor of the retrograde spirit took possession of the University, and, with the University, of the colleges and schools of France, which depended on it. The one learned institution which imbibed the spirit of the Renaissance, which seriously established, for the first time in France, instruction in Greek and Hebrew, which kept meeting by the creation of successive chairs, chairs for mathematics, philosophy, medicine and surgery, anatomy and botany, the wants of the modern spirit, and which was spared by the Revolution when all the other public establishments for education were swept away,—the College of France,—this institution was a royal foundation of Francis the First's, and unconnected with the University. A few names like that of Rollin stand out in the annals of the University teaching of France, between the Renaissance and the Revolution, and command respect; but in general this teaching was without life and progress.

The Jesuits invaded the province long ruled by the University alone. By that adroit management of men for which they have always been eminent, and by the more liberal spirit of their methods, they outdid in popularity their superannuated rival. Their first school at Paris was established in 1565, and in 1762, two years before their dissolution, they had eighty-six colleges in France. They were followed by the Port Royalists, the Benedictines, the Oratorians. The

Port Royal schools, from which perhaps a powerful influence upon education might have been looked for, restricted this influence by limiting very closely the number of their pupils. Meanwhile the main funds and endowments for public education in France were in the University's hands, and its administration of these was as ineffective as its teaching. The only college whose pecuniary state was solid was the College of Navarre, and Navarre was administered not by the University, but by the *Cour des Comptes.* The University had originally, as sources of revenue, the Post Office and the *Messageries,* or Office of Public Conveyance; it had long since been obliged to abandon the Post Office to Government, when in 1719 it gave up to the same authority the privilege of the *Messageries,* receiving in return from the State a yearly revenue of 150,000 livres. For this payment, moreover, it undertook the obligation of making the instruction in all its principal colleges gratuitous. Paid or gratuitous, however, its instruction was quite inadequate to the wants of the time, and when the Jesuits were expelled from France in 1764, their establishments closed, and their services as teachers lost, the void that was left was strikingly apparent, and public attention began to be drawn to it. It is well known how Rousseau among writers, and Turgot among statesmen, busied themselves with schemes of education; but the interest in the subject must have reached the whole body of the community, for the instructions of all three orders of the States General in 1789 are unanimous in demanding the reform of education, and its establishment on a proper footing.

Then came the Revolution, and the work of reform soon went swimmingly enough, so far as the abolition of the old schools was concerned. In 1791 the colleges were all placed under the control of the administrative authorities; in 1792 the jurisdiction of the University was abolished; in 1793 the property of the colleges was ordered to be sold, the proceeds to be taken by the State; in September of the same year the suppression of all the great public schools and of all the University faculties was pronounced. For the work of reconstruction Condorcet's memorable plan had in 1792 been

submitted to the Committee of Public Instruction appointed
by the Legislative Assembly. This plan proposed a secondary
school for every 4,000 inhabitants ; for each department, a
departmental institute, or higher school ; nine *lycées*, schools
carrying their studies yet higher than the departmental
institute, for the whole of France ; and to crown the edifice,
a National Society of Sciences and Arts, corresponding in
the main with the present Institute of France. The whole
expense of national instruction was to be borne by the State,
and this expense was estimated at 29,000,000 of francs.

But 1792 and 1793 were years of furious agitation, when it
was easier to destroy than to build. Condorcet perished with
the Girondists, and the reconstruction of public education
did not begin till after the fall of Robespierre. The decrees
of the Convention for establishing the Normal School, the
Polytechnic, the School of Mines, and the *écoles centrales*,
and then Daunou's law in 1795, bore, however, many traces
of Condorcet's design. Daunou's law established primary
schools, central schools, special schools, and at the head of
all the Institute of France, this last a memorable and enduring creation, with which the old French Academy became
incorporated. By Daunou's law, also, freedom was given to
private persons to open schools. The new legislation had
many defects. There was no provision for the reception of
boarders in the central schools. There was no hierarchy of
teachers ; all the professors were of equal rank and independent one of another. The country, too, was not yet settled
enough for its education to organise itself successfully. The
Normal School speedily broke down ; the central schools were
established slowly and with difficulty ; in the course of the
four years of the Directory there were nominally instituted
ninety-one of these schools, but they never really worked.
More was accomplished by private schools, to which full
freedom was given by the new legislation, at the same time
that an ample and open field lay before them.

They could not, however, suffice for the work, and education
was one of the matters for which Napoleon, when he became
Consul, had to provide. Fourcroy's law, in 1802, took as
the basis of its school-system secondary schools, whether

established by the communes or by private individuals; the Government undertook to aid these schools by grants for buildings, for scholarships, and for gratuities to the masters; it prescribed Latin, French, geography, history, and mathematics as the instruction to be given in them. They were placed under the superintendence of the prefects. To continue and complete the secondary schools were instituted the lyceums; here the instruction was to be Greek and Latin, rhetoric, logic, literature, moral philosophy, and the elements of the mathematical and physical sciences. The pupils were to be of four kinds: *boursiers nationaux*, scholars nominated to scholarships by the State; pupils from the secondary schools, admitted as free scholars by competition; paying boarders, and paying day-scholars. Three Inspectors-General were appointed for these schools, who were to be assisted by three Commissioners taken from the Institute.

CHAPTER II.

THE FRENCH SECONDARY SCHOOLS FROM THE CONSULATE TO THE PRESENT TIME.

UNIVERSITY OF FRANCE. THE PRESENT ORGANISATION OF THE FRENCH SECONDARY SCHOOLS IS FOUNDED UNDER THE FIRST EMPIRE — THE FRENCH SECONDARY SCHOOLS UNDER THE RESTORATION AND THE GOVERNMENT OF JULY 1830 — REVOLUTION OF FEBRUARY, 1848—CHANGE IN POSITION OF THE UNIVERSITY OF FRANCE—ORGANIC SCHOOL LAW OF MARCH 15, 1850 — THE FRENCH SECONDARY SCHOOLS FROM 1850 TO THE PRESENT TIME.

THE work now really began, and the present secondary instruction of France dates directly from the Consulate. The four greatest of the old schools of Paris were adopted, re-named,* and set to work. In the course of a year and a half 30 *lycées* and 250 secondary schools were started and in operation. More than 350 private schools received aid, while inspectors-general and members of the Institute traversed France to ascertain the educational condition of the country, and what were its more pressing requirements. The Normal School, the unique and best part of French secondary instruction, was launched at last ; ' a boarding establishment for 300 pupils, for the purpose of training them in the art of teaching the letters and sciences.' In 1810 it was fairly at work. Meanwhile, from 1806 to 1808, Napoleon had established the centre in which all these schools, and all the schools of France, were to meet, the new University, the University of France. The freedom of teaching conceded by the Revolution was now withdrawn, for the control of the whole public instruction of France belonged henceforth to the University, no school being allowed to exist without the authorisation of its Grand-Master, no schoolmaster to

---

* The *Lycée Impérial*, the *Lycée Napoléon*, the *Lycée Charlemagne*, and the *Lycée Bonaparte*.

give instruction unless he was a member of the University and graduated in one of its faculties. These faculties were five,—theology, law, medicine, letters, mathematical and physical sciences. The grades were three,—the baccalaureate, the licence, the doctorate. The licence answers to our degree of master of arts. Twenty-seven *academies*, or University centres, each with its rector, council, and staff of inspectors, were formed in the principal towns of France, and they carried on, under the authority of the grand-master at Paris, the administration of the University.

The University was not a mere department of that State, it was an endowed corporation. It had a revenue of about 2,500,000 of francs. Of this the fixed part proceeded from a permanent charge, granted to the University, of 400,000 francs a year upon the public funds, and from the property, real and personal, of the old universities and colleges, so far as this property was still unappropriated and at the State's disposal. This latter source proved so inconsiderable that the average income accruing to the University from the whole of its landed estates did not exceed 16,000 francs a year. The variable portion of the University revenues was far the most important. This consisted of dues paid for examinations and degrees, and of a contribution, one-twentieth of the fee paid for their schooling, from all the scholars in the secondary schools of France. With these revenues the University paid the expenses of its administration, the expenses of its faculties, and the charge of the Normal School. The public scholarships founded in the lyceums and the insignificant contribution made at that time by the State towards the expenses of primary instruction were paid in the form of a subvention from the Minister of the Interior.

The legislation of the Empire accomplished little for the primary instruction of France, but the secondary instruction it established on a firm footing, and with the organisation which in the main it still remains. In 1809 a statute restored to Greek and Latin their old preponderance in this instruction, effacing a mark which the Revolution, by the prominence given to scientific and mathematical studies, had left upon it. It thus resumed the mainly classical character common to it in the corresponding institutions all through Europe. In 1813 the Empire had thirty-six *lycées*, with 14,492 pupils, of whom 3,500 held public scholarships; in the private schools,—if private they can be called, when their teachers had to be members of the University, their studies and discipline to admit University inspection, and their students to pay the University tax,—there were 30,000 pupils. The Restoration changed the title of the public schools from *lycée* to that of *collége royal*, and made an important division of the subvention paid by the State to secondary instruction, assuring part of it to the maintenance of the public scholarships, part of it to the payment of the teaching staff. The whole of the subvention had hitherto gone to pay the scholarships endowed by the State, and the teaching staff had been paid out of the school-fees of the pupils. In the disasters of France the number of pupils in the schools fell off greatly, and their payments became irregular. The Government of the Restoration wished to secure the position of the teaching staff, which had thus become very precarious. In order to effect this, it increased its subvention, but paid fewer scholarships than formerly, in order that it might pay teachers instead. The municipalities, as well as the State, had by the legislation of the Empire been bound to provide a certain number of scholarships in the *lycées* with which they were locally connected. But the municipalities, and even that of Paris, had already, in the general pressure, resisted the obligation of providing their own share of scholarships; and when the State, reducing its own number of scholarships, left that of the municipalities unaltered, and besides ordered the prefects to see that they were regularly paid, the resistance grew stronger still. The government had to yield to it, and the number of scholarships at the charge of the municipalities was reduced by nearly one-half, while the reduction in the number of State scholarships was still maintained. The amount of free schooling in the French *lycées* was therefore seriously diminished. This diminution, however, was not ill-suited to the circumstances of the time, and soon began to be viewed with favour. With the reviving prosperity of

France families of the middle class became more and more capable of themselves meeting the moderate charge of their children's education; the higher class, about whose ability to pay there could be no question, but who had hesitated to avail themselves of the new public schools, began more and more to use them; and a class whom the prodigal supply of State scholarships had attracted to the State schools, a class without the means of purchasing from their own resources a liberal education, were, it was said, not proper recipients of such an education, were rendered useless and discontented citizens by it, and would be the better for being excluded from it. So strong was the feeling in favour of this exclusion, that at the very outset of the new and liberal Government of 1830, the report of a Commission recommended it to the Chamber of Deputies in urgent and even harsh terms. At the same time the better payment and the continued extension of the teaching staff in the public schools were desired on all sides. Under this impulsion the State grant for scholarships steadily declined, that for the teaching staff steadily increased. Between 1815 and 1830 that for the former sank from 988,000 francs to 822,300; that for the latter rose from 812,000 francs to 927,500. The Government of Louis Philippe, having undertaken the serious task of dealing with primary education, was unable at first to give much attention to secondary; when, however, M. Guizot's memorable law of 1833 had founded primary instruction, a succession of ministers set themselves to improve and develop the secondary schools. The number of *lycées* had risen, under the Restoration, from 34 to 40; under the Government of July it rose to 54. The contribution of the State to their support greatly increased. But the increase was entirely for the fixed expenses, as they are called, of the public schools, expenses in which the payment of the teaching staff forms the grand item. These, from 920,000 francs, which was their amount in 1830, had risen, when the Revolution of February overthrew the Government of July, to 1,500,000 francs. The subvention for scholarships had fallen in the same period from 822,300 francs to 710,950 francs.

The University had been made by Napoleon an endowed

corporation, and not a ministerial department, in order to give it more stability and greater independence. The grand-master was, however, to all intents and purposes, the Minister of Public Instruction, and when in 1824 the head of the University, M. de Frayssinous, took this title of Minister, the change was one of name and not of substance. But the spirit of uniformity and method which the French bring to their system of public accounts is very strict, and gradually it began to be said that the University was in fact a public department with a special budget of its own, collecting and spending its revenues without supervision or responsibility, and that this was bad public economy. It was urged that the University ought to bring its estimates before the Chamber of Deputies, submit its accounts to the regular auditors of the national expenditure, and collect its revenues through the agency of the public collectors. The *Cour des Comptes* obtained an order to have the University accounts laid before it, and it found them irregular and unsatisfactory. In 1834, after a long discussion, the special budget of the University was suppressed, and the collection of its revenues and the control of its accounts assimilated to that of the other public departments. It was left in the possession of its endowment and property, an honour more nominal than real, since it no longer had the management of them; but it was thought that by retaining, as the possessor of an endowment and of property, the character of a *personne civile*, it might attract bequests and fresh endowments,* of which a department of State had no chance.

* So many questions arise, in England, about endowed schools, that I will take this opportunity of saying what is the state of the law, in France, about endowments for education.

These endowments are of far less importance in France than in England. In the first place the Revolution made a clean sweep of all old endowments; what exist date from a time since the Revolution. In the second place the French law sets limits to a man's power of disposing of his property, which in England do not exist. In France by the *Code Napoléon* (Art. 913, and the articles following) if a man leaves one legitimate child, he may dispose of one-half of his property, and no more, away from him; if he leaves two, he may dispose of one-third, and no more; if he leaves more than two, of one-fourth, and no more. If he has no children, a certain proportion of his property is similarly secured to his nearest representatives within certain limits. The amount of property free to be disposed of in benefactions is thus smaller in France than in England.

Its schools meanwhile continued to prosper, and had never
been in so flourishing a condition as they were when the

In England a man names an individual to be trustee, or a number of individuals
to be trustees, to carry into effect a charitable bequest, on conditions assigned by
him at pleasure. In France this cannot be done. A founder must entrust his
bequest for charitable purposes to a *personne civile*, defined as an *être fictif, auquel
la loi reconnaît une partie des droits qui appartiennent aux personnes ordinaires, et
qui peuvent recevoir des libéralités*. Such a *personne civile* must be either a public
establishment (for instance, a public hospital, a parish church, a commune) or an
establishment of public utility.

An establishment, not being a public establishment, can only be made an
establishment of public utility, and capable therefore of receiving an endowment,
by a decree of the Council of State, a body which prepares Government bills, and
is, besides, the highest administrative body in France, to which the most important
matters of administration,—conflicts between the different departments of State,
questions of jurisdiction between the administrative and the judicial authority,
&c.,—are brought for final settlement.

The recipient, therefore, of an endowment must be a *personne civile*; but to
enable even a *personne civile* to accept an endowment an express authorisation of
the administrative authority is in each case required, and the natural heirs are
heard on the other side. They are not heard on any point of law; if any such
arises it goes to the ordinary legal tribunals; they are heard on the question
whether the bequest was a proper one for a man in the testator's condition of
family and fortune to make. In some cases it is the prefect who gives this
authorisation, with the advice of the *conseil de préfecture*; in general, and always
when there is opposition on the heirs' part, it is the Council of State.

Illegal, immoral, or impossible conditions attached to a benefaction or bequest,
are by the law of France null and void. The Council of State calls upon the
living donor to rectify such conditions before his benefaction can take effect; in
the case of a bequest, authorisation is given with reserve as to illegal conditions,
which are set aside.

A bequest to an establishment for purposes not within the legal attributions of
that establishment is thus set aside. For instance, if a bequest is left to a church
for a school, it cannot take effect, because the law does not recognise school-
keeping as an attribution of a church; so the Council of State authorises the
commune, which is by law a school-keeping establishment, to accept jointly with
the church, and the commune manages the bequest.

Again, a bequest to an elementary communal school, saddled with the condition
that the school shall be taught by the religious for ever, is set aside, because the
school law of France gives to the communal and departmental authority the right
of deciding for themselves whether a communal school shall be under lay teaching
or the teaching of the religious. A condition giving to an authority other than
that named by the school law of France the nomination of a communal teacher, or
the selection of the free scholars in a communal school, would be equally invalid.
So would a condition forbidding a private school to be under Government inspection, or enabling it to be under an uncertificated teacher; because by the
French law all schools, private as well as public, must admit inspection, and must
have a certificated teacher. Private schools are at present not inspected as to
their teaching; there is now before the Council of State a law for putting under
inspection the teaching as well as the buildings, healthiness, morals, &c., of
private schools which enjoy their endowment by virtue of an authorisation.

. It is to be remembered that public establishments and recognised establish-

Revolution of February broke out. Their pupils, 9,000 in 1809, 15,000 in 1830, numbered 20,000 in 1848. Their grant from Government at that time reached, as I have already mentioned, the sum of 1,500,000 francs; the sums received from scholars' fees for board and instruction exceeded 6,200,000 francs. The staff of professors and other school functionaries had never been so fully organised or so well paid. But the University had enemies whose attacks grew with time stronger and stronger; of these enemies the most persevering, passionate, and formidable were the clergy. Its lay character made it particular obnoxious to them; they constantly assailed it with the charge that it instructed and did not educate; they attacked its constitution, its studies, the orthodoxy of its teachers, and even their morality. It is difficult perhaps to find a perfectly precise sense for the charge that an institution instructs and does not educate, but it is well known with what great and damaging effect this charge can be used. The monopoly of the University made the charge the more dangerous, at the same time that this monopoly recruited the ranks of the University's chief assailants, the priests, with auxiliaries from quarters the most opposite, whose interests or whose principles it wounded. With the fall of the Orleans dynasty fell the privilege of the University. In 1848 the government of General Cavaignac struck the first blow at its academical organisation, which had remained unchanged since the Emperor Napoleon's decree first founded it in 1808. The 27 academies, which had carried on the administration of the University for forty years, were reduced to 20. Then came the law of March

ments of public utility, have their rules of management for institutions depending upon them, which cannot be set aside by the directions of a testator. A commune is a public establishment, and the school of a commune follows a certain order of management fixed for such institutions. The congregation of the Christian Brothers is a recognised establishment of public utility, and the order of management of the Christian Brothers' schools is fixed by the statutes of the congregation, statutes which have had to obtain the Government's sanction.

In general, therefore, the action of founders is greatly limited in France, as compared with England.

A proper *personne civile* having been properly authorised to enjoy an endowment, the administrative authority does not further interfere. A man's heirs, however, may, if the legal conditions of his endowment are not complied with, bring an action before the ordinary legal tribunals for a restitution of the property to them.

15, 1850, the organic law which now governs public instruction in France, and which transformed the regulation of this
instruction completely. By this law persons not members
of the University became free to open schools, and the exclusive privilege of the University ceased. The shadow of a
corporate and endowed existence which had been left to it
ceased also; its endowment no longer appeared as an item of
the public debt, its estates were made part of the public
domain. Eighty-six academies, one for each department of
France, at first replaced the old academical organisation of
1808; but very soon * these 86 academies were reduced to
16, each academy including in its district several departments; and this is the organisation in force at the present
moment.

Before I come to the schools as they now exist a few words
must be given to the immediate effect produced upon them
by the legislation of 1850. The unsettled state of the times,
the derangement of many private fortunes, and the opening
of a number of private schools, at first affected the *lycées* very
unfavourably. The sums received from the pupils in them
for board and lodging fell from 6,204,693 francs in 1848 to
5,191,666 francs in 1851. This diminution in the receipts,
. as the State refused to make it good, necessitated a reduction in the payments to teachers and functionaries. With
all the economy that could be exercised the embarrassment
was great and increasing, when the government, in 1853, hit
on the simple expedient of raising the fees for board and
schooling, which had remained nearly stationary since they
were first fixed in 1802. The fee for board in a Paris *lycée*
had been 600, 700, 800, or 900 francs, according to the pupil's
place in the school. It was now fixed at 950, 1,050, 1,150,
and 1,500 francs. The fee for schooling, which had at first
been a uniform fee of 60 francs, and then had been raised to
100 francs, was made, according to the subjects taught, 120,
150, 200, or 250 francs. Proportionate additions were made
to the school charges in the departments, where these
charges are always lower than in Paris.

Far from emptying the public schools, this rise in their

* In 1854.

charges answered perfectly. The old charges had been very low, the new charges were not in themselves high, and were accompanied by an improved and developed programme of studies. The return of tranquillity and the growing wealth and prosperity of the country enabled families to support them the more easily. The *lycées* filled again, and the new scale of charges produced an addition of 800,000 francs in the yearly amount received from their scholars. In 1855 the number of *lycées*, which had been 54 before the February Revolution, had risen to 63; the number of pupils in them, which had fallen to 19,000 in 1851, had in 1855 increased to 21,219. The communal colleges at the charge of the towns where they are situated had been less successful. The law of 1850 required every town which wished to preserve its communal college to bind itself to pay for five years its teachers' salaries; several municipalities refused to saddle themselves with this obligation. Their colleges passed out of their hands into those of a private proprietor, generally an ecclesiastic; and thus out of the spoils of the communal colleges, though not out of those of the *lycées*, the new private schools which the law of 1850 admitted into existence did, to a certain extent, enrich themselves. In 1857 the communal colleges were only 244 in number, having been 306 in 1849; eight of the chief of them, however, had in the meanwhile been converted into *lycées*. The pupils in the communal colleges had numbered 31,706 in 1849; in 1855 they numbered only 28,219.

So the public secondary schools of France had, in 1855, in round numbers, 49,500 scholars. The total expenditure for these schools was (again in round numbers) 19,500,000 francs, or 780,000*l*. The expenditure for the *lycées* was 480,000*l*.; that for the communal colleges 300,000*l*. For the *lycées* the State contributed about 76,000*l*.;* for the communal colleges, which are municipal institutions, barely 4,000*l*. The State subvention for 1855 to French secondary instruction may be put, therefore, at about 80,000*l*.; the municipal subvention to the communal colleges amounted to

---

* 1,301,908 fr. for the *dépenses fixes*, and 635,237 fr. for scholarships.

nearly the same sum. There remained 620,000*l*. (216,000*l*. for the communal colleges, 404,000*l*. for the *lycées*) to be raised by the schools themselves. The State subvention, exclusive of the grant for scholarships, gave, in 1847,* an average of 28,900 francs for each of the 54 *lycées* then existing; in 1855, when the *lycées* numbered 63, the State subvention of the year gave an average of but 20,665 fr. for each *lycée*. The aid was insufficient even with the increased fees charged, and the total expenditure for 1855 on the *lycées* outran the total receipts by 354,052 francs, about 14,160*l*.

At the present moment France has 74 *lycées*, 20 more than she had in 1847, and 11 more than she had in 1855. She has 247 communal colleges, 59 less than she had in 1849, but three more than she had in 1857. In these schools she has 65,832 scholars; 32,794 in the *lycées*, 33,038 in the communal colleges. Thus the 74 *lycées* have very nearly as many pupils as all the 247 communal colleges together. And while the number of pupils in the *lycées* tends to increase, and is about 1,000 more this year than last, in the communal colleges it tends slightly to diminish, and is about 100 less. The state schools have altogether 15,000 more scholars than in 1855, a sign of the advance of the country in prosperity. The amount of state aid received by them is much higher than in 1855, a time of reduction and distress; it reaches, including the grant for state scholarships, 3,000,000 of francs in round numbers, a third more than in 1855, 120,000*l*. now to 80,000*l*. then. Of this sum the *lycées* receive 1,900,000 fr. for their fixed expenses, and 868,000 for bursarships;† the communal colleges receive 223,000 fr., having received less than 100,000 fr. in 1855. The mean rate of grant to each *lycée* is still, however, slightly below what it was in 1847, though nearly one-third greater than the rate of 1855. It is intended to place a *lycée* in every department of France, and five new ones are at the present time in progress.

---

* In this year the subvention was 1,560,750 fr.

† The actual number of bursarships in the French *lycées* is now 1,057, divided among 1,588 holders. It is worthy of note that the ten colleges of Paris alone, before the Revolution, had 1,046 bursars, almost the number of the bursarships for the whole of France at present.

CHAPTER III.

*GOVERNMENT, ADMINISTRATION, AND TEACHING STAFF OF THE
FRENCH SECONDARY SCHOOLS AT PRESENT.*

GOVERNMENT, ADMINISTRATION, AND ORGANISATION OF THE FRENCH SECONDARY
SCHOOLS—MINISTRY OF PUBLIC INSTRUCTION—IMPERIAL COUNCIL OF PUBLIC IN-
STRUCTION—ACADEMIC COUNCILS—DEPARTMENTAL COUNCILS—INSPECTORS-GENE-
RAL—ADMINISTRATION OF THE FRENCH LYCÉES—REGULATIONS AS TO THEIR
FUNCTIONARIES AND PROFESSORS—AGGREGATION—THE NORMAL SCHOOL—POSITION
AND PAYMENT OF TEACHERS IN THE FRENCH LYCÉES.

HE who has seen one *lycée* or communal college in France,
I will not say has seen all, but at any rate may consider
that he can form for himself a pretty accurate notion of all.
In all, the course of studies is very nearly the same, following programmes drawn up by authority. In all, the books·
used are very nearly the same, specified in a list drawn up
by authority. In all, the professors and principal functionaries of every kind are appointed by the Minister of Public
Instruction, and can be dismissed by him. In all, the
arrangement and training of classes, the arrangements for
boarding, the hours of work and recreation, the means of
recreation, the mode of government, and the whole system
of discipline, are the same.

The Minister of Public Instruction is the head of this vast
organisation. His office, in Paris, has six divisions, under
himself and his secretary-general. Each of these six divisions
has its chief, and is divided into two bureaux, each, again,
with its head. First come the three divisions for superior
instruction, secondary instruction, primary instruction. The
first bureau of each of these is for the *personnel* of the branch
of public instruction administered by the division,—treats,
that is, all matters relating to persons, appointments, and
studies; the second bureau is for the *matériel* and *compta-
bilité,*—whatever relates to buildings, finance, or accounts.

The three remaining divisions have charge, one, of the department's business with the Institute and with the public libraries; another, of its business with the scientific and literary establishments (such as the Museum of Natural History, the French school at Athens, the observatories of Paris and Marseilles, &c.) in connection with it; the third, of the expense of the central office, and of the general revision of the whole finance and accounts of the department. Under the Minister's presidency is the Imperial Council of Public Instruction, which in concert with him fixes the programmes of study in the state schools and the books to be used in them. It is also consulted as to the formation of new state schools, and as to the whole legislation and regulation of French public instruction. The important measures which have lately been introduced and passed for the furtherance of professional instruction, as it is called,—measures of which I shall have to speak presently,—were all of them thus brought by M. Duruy, the present minister, before the Council, and there discussed. Certain members of the Council formerly proceeded from election; in 1852, under the pressure which then caused, in France, the strengthening of the hand of government everywhere, proposal by the Minister of Public Instruction and nomination by the President of the Republic was substituted for election in these cases. The Emperor still nominates on the Minister's proposal; but M. Duruy's disposition has certainly been rather to enlarge the part of action for others than to keep all action for himself; thus he has lately given to the functionaries of public instruction, whom the law of 1852 gave him the power to dismiss off-hand, the security of a committee of five, chosen out of the Council of Public Instruction, by whom the case of the functionary whose conduct may be in question is to be examined, his defence heard, and the merits of the case reported on.

But the names of the actual members of the Council guarantee its fitness for its functions, whether it comes from election or from nomination. The Minister is the President, and M. de Royer, the Chief President of the *Cour des Comptes*, is Vice-President. The great bodies of State are represented,

so is the Church, so are the Protestants, so are the Jews, so
is the law, so is the Institute, so are the schools, public and
private. There are thirty-two members, with a secretary ;
and among the thirty-two, not to speak of the great official
personages, are M. Franck, M. Silvestre de Sacy, M. Guigniaut,
M. Milne-Edwards, M. Michel Chevalier, M. Ravaisson, M.
Dumas the chemist, M. Le Verrier, and M. Nisard. It will
not be disputed that these are men whose opinion on matters of instruction may with propriety and advantage be
asked.

After the Imperial Council come the Academic Councils.
By the law of 1854, as I have said, the number of the
academies, or University centres, was fixed at 16. They are
now, by the addition of academies for Savoy and Algiers, 18.
This Minister of Public Instruction is the titular Rector of
the Academy of Paris, and the ordinary functions of the
rectorate are in this academy discharged by the Vice-Rector.
In the other academies they are discharged by the Rector,
who must have the degree of doctor in one of the faculties,
and who is the head of the superior and secondary instruction of the departments which form the district of his academy, and the president of the academic council. The main
control of primary instruction, including the right of nominating the schoolmasters, was in 1854, by a change made
from political reasons, but which nearly all friends of education condemn, taken away from the rectors and given to the
prefects. The rectors are assisted by academy inspectors, of
whom there must be one at least (at Paris by a special rule
there are eight) for each department comprised in the academy. As there are only 17 academies for France, most of
them, of course, have a district of several departments; the
academic centre, the residence of the rector and the seat of
the faculties, is in general placed in the most important chief
town of their departments. In the other departments of the
district the academy inspectors exercise in fact the functions
of rector, having their offices in the several chief towns,
entering the names of candidates for degrees in the different
faculties, and inspecting the public schools. All their reports on these schools converge, however, to the centre of the

academy, to the rector's office; and from these reports, from the reports of the immediate authorities of the schools, and from his own inspections, the rector makes up the monthly report which he is bound to transmit to the Minister in Paris. With the rector is placed, to form his council, not only the academy inspectors of his district, but also the deans of faculties, and seven other members chosen every three years by the Minister. These seven are an archbishop or bishop from the district, two ministers of the Catholic, Protestant, or Jewish worship, two members of the magistrature, and two public functionaries or other notables of the district. The well-known M. Coquerel is thus a member of the academic council of Paris, and M. Devienne, the First President of the *Cour Impériale*, is another. This council consists of some 30 members in the academy of Paris, where the academy inspectors are very numerous; in the other academies it consists of from 15 to 20 members. It holds two sessions a year, lasting about a fortnight each, when it receives reports from the academy inspectors and deans of faculties on the whole instruction of the district, and deals with all questions which come before it respecting the administration, finance, discipline, or teaching of the public schools.

There is also, for each department of France, a Departmental Council, of which the prefect is president, and the academy inspector, a primary inspector, the bishop and an ecclesiastic named by him, a representative of the Protestant and of the Jewish communions, the chief law-officer of government in the department, a judge, and three or four members of the Council General,* are members. The primary inspector, the Protestant and Jewish representatives, the judge, and the members of the Council General, are named by the Minister of Public Instruction. This departmental council has to do with primary rather than secondary instruction; with the public secondary schools it does not meddle, but certain matters affecting the private secondary schools come before it from the academic authority, with appeal to

---

* The Council General is an elective body consisting of the notables of the department.

the Imperial Council of Public Instruction in Paris. Of these matters I shall speak by-and-by. The departmental council meets twice a month.

Besides the Minister, the Imperial Council, and the academic authorities, six inspectors-general have special superintendence of secondary instruction. Three of these inspectors are for letters, three for sciences; every year they are sent by the Minister on tours of inspection, and they visit the *lycées*, the more important communal colleges, and a certain number of private secondary schools.

Now I come to the *lycées* themselves. Their administration, properly so called, is in the hands of a provisor, a censor, and a steward, who themselves take no part in the teaching, but who admit the scholars, correspond with the parents, keep the accounts, manage all the household economy, superintend the discharge of his duties by each member of the establishment, and maintain the discipline. There are also two or more chaplains, and the great *lycées* of Paris, which receive a very large number of boarders, have also a certain number of officers, with the title of General Superintendents, attached to the governing body. To all French *lycées* is attached a Council of Administration, revising the conduct of their business affairs, and each academy has a Commission of Health, charged with the care of the sanitary interests of the establishments of public instruction in the academic district. A Central Commission of Health exists for the special benefit of the Paris *lycées*. But, in the first instance, the governing and administering body in a French *lycée* consists of these three functionaries,—the *proviseur*, who is the chief of all, the *censeur*, and the *économe* or steward. Then come the teachers, professors of different degrees of rank. Then the *maîtres répétiteurs*, on whom falls the task of that constant supervision of the boys out of class hours, for which French schools have with us in England such a notoriety. The professors give their lessons and are then free to depart. They have nothing whatever to do with the boys out of school hours. The *maîtres répétiteurs*, or *maîtres d'étude*, as they are more generally called,—the ushers, as we should call them,—are with the boys when they are preparing their lessons, and at their meals, and at their recreation, and in their dormitories. The highest class of these ushers assists the boys in the preparation of their lessons; a lower and far larger class is inadequate for this task of tutor, and is simply charged with the duty of superintending and reporting.

All these functionaries, from the *proviseur* to the *maître d'étude*, are nominated by the minister. The *proviseur* and the rector, indeed, present for the minister's acceptance candidates for the post of *maître d'étude* and of teacher of the lower classes in the communal colleges; and the rector has to keep a record of service and seniority among the professors in the *lycées* of his academy, which record, no doubt, guides the minister in making his nomination. Still the mass of patronage vested in the minister must appear to our eyes extraordinary. But it is right to say that the law in France has imposed conditions on the minister's exercise of his patronage which inevitably keep it within strict bounds. As the rector must be a doctor in some faculty, and the academy-inspector must be a licentiate (intermediate between a bachelor and a doctor, and answering to our master), so each functionary of the *lycée*, from the *proviseur* to the *maître d'étude* must present some guarantee of intellectual capacity. The *proviseur* must be a licentiate. The *maître d'étude* must be a bachelor of letters or sciences. But it is for the professor's office that the most stringent security is required. To be a full professor (*professeur titulaire*) the title of *agrégé de lycée* is necessary. We have nothing corresponding to this in England. It is not a university grade but a special certificate or diploma. The examination for it requires the possession of a university grade, and covers the whole ground of the intended professor's teaching. The title exists for superior instruction also; there are *agrégés de faculté* as well as *agrégés de lycée*; to be full professor in a faculty, indeed, guarantees beyond the *agrégation* (for example, the rank of doctor or of member of the Institute) are demanded; but even to be acting professor (*professeur suppléant*) in a faculty, the title of *agrégé* in that faculty must be obtained; and to obtain it the candidate has to pass a strict examination in the matters which he will have to teach.

The *agrégés de lycée* are of seven orders, corresponding to the kinds of instruction given in the *lycées*. There are *agrégés* for the classes of mathematics, of natural sciences, of philosophy, of higher classics, of lower classics, of history and geography, of modern languages. To be an *agrégé* for any one of them the candidate must be twenty-five years old, and must have had five years' practice of teaching in a public or private school. A certain maturity and experience are thus ensured at the outset. Then the intending *agrégé* for the classes of mathematics must possess the degree of licentiate of mathematics, and that of licentiate either of physics or of natural sciences ; for the classes of natural sciences the same ; for the classes of philosophy, the degree of licentiate of letters (master of arts), and that of bachelor of sciences ; for the higher classical division, the degree of licentiate of letters ; for the lower, the same ; for the classes of geography and history, the same ; for those of modern languages, a certificate of fitness (obtained only after examination) to teach them.

These preliminary securities being taken, the candidates undergo a written examination. If they fail in the written examination they are rejected. If they pass in it, they proceed to a *viva voce* one. In every case the examination is based on the programme of the classes for which the candidate wishes to become *agrégé*, and the oral examination includes one or more lessons delivered as if to a class. The programmes of the different classes are, as I have already said, fixed by authority. I will just mention in passing what the candidate for the *classes supérieures de lettres* (higher classical division) has to do. His paper-work consists of a piece of Latin verse, a piece of translation from French into Greek and Latin, a piece of translation from Greek into French, a Latin essay and a French essay, one on a philosophical the other on a literary subject, and a piece of translation into French from a modern language, English or German. In his *viva voce* he has to correct aloud two exercises of boys in the higher classical division of a *lycée*, to translate with full comments and explanations a passage from a Latin and Greek author read in the *lycées*, and to

comment on a passage from one of the French classics read
there. He has also to translate a passage from an English
or German book. Finally, he has to give, as if to a class,
a lesson on either grammar, classical literature, philosophy,
history, or modern languages, at his own choice.

Having proved his fitness by his examination, the candidate is then nominated professor in a class of the order for
which he has obtained the title of *agrégé*. But he cannot be
employed in a class of another order without obtaining by
examination the title of *agrégé* for that class; thus an *agrégé*
for the higher classical division cannot be employed in a
mathematical class or a class for natural sciences, nor can an
agrégé for the lower classical division be employed in the
higher. The spectacle so often seen in English schools of a
classical master teaching, without any real acquaintance with
his subject, mathematics, or modern languages, or history,
is not to be seen in France.

The pupils of the Normal School (*École Normale Supérieure*) can hold the place of professor without being *agrégés*;
but they cannot hold the more important and better paid
post of *professeur titulaire* without this test, they can only be
divisional,* acting, or assistant professors (*professeurs divi-
sionnaires, suppléants, or adjoints*). And the examinations of
the Normal School are in themselves a test, and a very strict
one, of the fitness of its pupils for their business. I have
already mentioned this admirable institution; it enjoys a
deserved celebrity out of France as well as at home, and
nowhere else does there exist anything quite like it. Decreed
by the revolutionary Government, and set to work by that of
the first Napoleon, it had two periods of difficulty,—one
under the Restoration, when it attracted hostility as a nest
of liberalism, and it was proposed to abate its importance by
substituting for one central Normal School several local
ones; another after the revolution of February, when the
grant to it was greatly reduced, and the number of its pupils
fell off. But it has now recovered its grants and its numbers,

* The full professor (*professeur titulaire*) has the *class*; the class, if large, is
divided, and the divisional professor has charge of a division, as contradistin-
guished from a class.

and few institutions in France are so rooted in the public esteem.   Its main function is to form teachers for the public schools. It has two divisions; one literary, the other scientific. Its pupils at present number 110; they are all bursars, holding a scholarship of 40*l.* a year, which entirely provides for the cost of their maintenance. The course is a three years' one; but a certain number of the best pupils are retained for a fourth and fifth year; these, however, are lost to the secondary schools, being prepared for the doctorate and for the posts of superior instruction, such as the professorships in the faculties.

Every Englishman who has been at Oxford or Cambridge must in France remark with surprise that institutions like these universities of ours, taking a young man at the age of eighteen or nineteen, and continuing his education, with the shelter of a considerable, though modified, control and discipline till the age of twenty-three or twenty-four, seem to be there, for laymen, quite wanting. It is true that in France, as in Germany, there is a superior instruction, a faculty instruction, much more complete than ours, and that our Oxford and Cambridge are, in fact, as Signor Matteucci, who had studied them well, said to me at Turin, not establishments of superior instruction at all, but simply *hauts lycées.* This is true, and it is to be regretted that we have not a better organised superior instruction; still Oxford and Cambridge, in prolonging a young man's term of tuition and prolonging it under discipline, instead of his being thrown at large on the life of a great city, Paris or London, where he follows lectures, are invaluable, and it is in this direction that foreigners may find most to envy in English education. But it must be remarked that there are great government schools in France which in some measure perform the part of Oxford and Cambridge, and supply yearly a body of laymen whose intellectual training has been prolonged, under stringent discipline, for several years beyond boyhood; a body sufficient, even in itself, to keep society fed in the several departments of practice and knowledge with a number of intellectually trained men of a high order, and to preserve the intellectual level from sinking. The Polytechnic

School, which trains civil as well as military engineers for the State, the *École Forestière* (School of Woodcraft), the *École Impériale des Chartes*, the *Ecole Française d'Athènes*, are all of them establishments discharging this function. But the chief of the establishments which discharge it is the *École Normale Supérieure.* This school is in the Rue d'Ulm, in the old school quarter of Paris on the left bank of the Seine, where the Sorbonne, and by far the greater part of the *lycées* and centres of instruction, secondary and superior, are still to be found. The building is large and handsome, something like one of the more modern colleges at Oxford or Cambridge; it has chapel, library, and garden; the tri-colour flag waves over the entrance to it. Everything is beautifully neat and well kept; the life in common which economy compels these great public establishments, in France, severely to practise, has,—when its details are pre-cisely and perfectly attended to, and when, as at the *École Normale,* the resources allow a certain finish and comfort much beyond the strict necessary of the barrack or hospital, —a more imposing effect for the eye than the arrangements of college rooms, though I am far from saying the life in college rooms is not preferable. The pupils, even here, sleep in large dormitories, but the beds are screened from one another by partitions stopping short of the ceiling, in the fashion adopted in some of the more recent Normal Schools for our primary teachers here in England; each student has thus a small chamber to himself.

Last year 344 candidates presented themselves for 35 vacancies, and these candidates were all picked men. To compete, a youth must in the first place be over 18 years of age and under 24, must produce a medical certificate that he has no bodily infirmity unfitting him for the ·function of teacher, and a good-conduct certificate from his school. He must enter into an engagement to devote himself, if admitted, for 10 years to the service of public instruction, and he must hold the degree of bachelor of arts if he is a candidate in the literary section of the school, of bachelor of sciences if in the scientific. He then undergoes a preliminary examination,

which is held at the same time at the centre of each academy
throughout France. This examination weeds the candidates;
those who pass through it come up to Paris for a final examination at the *École Normale,* and those who do best in this
final examination are admitted to the vacant scholarships.
A bare list of subjects of examination is never very instructive; the reader will better understand what the final
examination is, if I say that the candidates are the very
élite of the *lycées,* who in the highest classes of these *lycées*
have gone through the course of instruction, literary or
scientific, there prescribed. In the scientific section of the
Normal School, the first year's course comprehends the
differential and integral calculus, and it will at once be
seen what advanced progress in the pupil such a course
implies. By a favour which has been very rarely accorded
even to authorised inquirers, and for which I am very grateful, I was permitted to be present at several of the lessons
of the school, and I can answer for the preparation and
attention of the pupils, and for the excellence of the teaching.
Better lessons than those which I heard on Lucretius's
account of the plague at Athens, on some chapters of Thucydides, and on the *Femmes Savantes* of Molière, better, whether
as respects the lecturer's performance or the students', I
really cannot imagine. I also heard a mathematical lesson;
on the merits of such a lesson I am unfortunately,—and it is
a misfortune I had continually to regret while discharging
my errand,—most incompetent to give an opinion; but here
too I could see and admire the evident easy mastery of the
lecturer over his subject, the rapidity with which he went, his
constant and dexterous use of the black board; while his
hearers seemed all to be held in hand, and to follow with a
quickness and adroitness answering to his own. In the
third year there is a division in the scientific section, some
pupils giving their chief study to pure mathematics and
astronomy, others to physics and natural sciences.

I found, as I have said, 110 pupils in the Normal School,
all bursars; commoners, to use our expression, are not
received. For these 110 students there are, besides the

director-general and a director of scientific studies and
another of literary studies, 23 professors, or *maîtres des conférences*, as in this institution they are called. The professors
are pretty equally divided between letters and sciences. One
of the most distinguished professors of the scientific section
told me that in this section they were a little under-officered,
and that it would be better if certain of the scientific lectures,
which the students now have to go to the Sorbonne to hear,
where the wants of the audience are not the same as theirs,
could be given at the school itself, and by professors of the
school. This really was the only drawback I could hear of
to the complete efficiency of the school, and this, of course,
was due to the common cause of such drawbacks, want of
funds. The cost of the school last year was 307,610 fr.; in
round numbers, 12,300*l*. The library, laboratory, and collections seemed to me excellent.

The pupils have half-yearly examinations, and they are
practised to some extent, and, under the present Minister,
M. Duruy, more than ever before, in the *lycées* of Paris.
The teaching of the professors keeps always in view the
scholastic destination of their hearers. At the end of the
third year's course the student who has passed through it
with distinction is authorised to present himself at once for
aggregation. Five years' school practice, it will be remembered, is required of other candidates. The less distinguished
student is at once nominated to a *lycée*, but to the post of
assistant professor only, not of full professor; after one year's
service in the capacity of assistant professor he may present
himself for aggregation.

I have been somewhat minute in describing how the body
of professors in the French public schools is formed, because
the best feature of these schools seems to me to be their
thoroughly trained and tested staff of professors. They are
far better paid than the corresponding body of teachers in
Italy; they have a far more recognised and satisfactory
position than the corresponding body of teachers in England.
The latter are, no doubt, better paid; but, with the exception
of the head masters of the great schools, who hold a position

apart, who need eminent aptitudes for other things besides teaching, and who are very few in number, they form no hierarchy, have no position, are saddled, to balance their being better paid, with boarding-house cares, have little or no time for study, and no career before them. A French professor has his three, four, or five hours' work a day in lessons and conferences, and then he is free; he has nothing to do with the discipline or religious teaching of the *lycée*, he has not to live in its precincts; he finishes his teaching and then he leaves the *lycée* and its cares behind him altogether. The provisor, the censor, the chaplains, the superintendents, have the business of government and direction, and they are chosen on the ground of their aptitude for it. A young man wishing to follow a profession which keeps him in contact with intellectual studies and enables him to continue them, but who has no call and no talent for the trying post of teacher, governor, pastor, and man of business all in one, will hesitate before he becomes a master in an English public school, but he may very well become a professor in a French one. Accordingly the service of public instruction in France attracts a far greater proportion of the intellectual force of the country than in England. At the head of the Normal School which I have just been describing is M. Nisard, a member of the French Academy, and the author of a well-known history of French literature; the director of the scientific studies is M. Pasteur, a member of the Institute, and one of the first chemists in Europe. Among the *maîtres des conférences* is M. Gaston Boissier, whose name English readers of the *Revue des Deux Mondes* will recall as the author of some excellent articles on Roman history which lately appeared there; M. Boissier is also one of the professors at the *Lycée Charlemagne*. In the scientific section is M. Hermite, whose name every mathematician knows; M. Hermite is a member of the Institute. But besides names thus widely known, the professorate of the Normal School and *lycées* abounds in names honourably known in their own country as those of men of mark and honourable performance or honourable promise in their several departments of sciences or literature; such are the names (I quote almost at random) of MM. Briot, Berger, Bénard, Jules Girard, Étienne. Two of the most eminent of modern Frenchmen, M. Cousin and M. Villemain, were originally professors in the French public schools; they were both, also, Ministers of Public Instruction. M. Duruy, the present Minister, was a professor, an author of a very good school-book, and an inspector. M. Taine and M. Prévost-Paradol, personages so important in the French literature of the present day, were both of them distinguished pupils of the Normal School. It is clear that this abundance of eminent names gives dignity and consideration to the profession of public teaching in France; it tends to keep it fully supplied, and with men who carry weight with the pupils they teach, and command their intellectual respect. And this is a very important advantage.

The salary of a professor is composed of two parts, the fixed part and the eventual part, as they are called. The fixed salary of a full professor is, at Paris, 4,500, 4,000, and 3,500 fr., according to the division in which the professor is placed; in the departments, 2,400, 2,200, and 2,000 fr.* The fixed salary of a divisional professor is in Paris 1,800 fr. or 1,200 fr.; in the departments it is 1,200 fr. The eventual salary used to be formed by taking nine hundredths of the fee for board and schooling paid by each boarder, and five-tenths of the fee paid for schooling by each day boy. The sum obtained by taking these fractions was in every *lycée* divided between the censor and the professors, and the share received by each was the eventual part of his salary.† But since 1862 the *traitement éventuel* has been fixed at a uniform sum of 3,000 fr. for professors in Paris; for those in the departments it is more than one half less. A professor also receives certain fees for examinations and conferences, and often he gives a certain number of private lectures. I was

---

* There may be in Paris 30 professors at the first-named rate at a time, 35 at the second, any number at the third. In the departments, 133 at the first rate, the same number at the second, any number at the third.

† Formerly the divisional professors had no share in the *traitement éventuel*, but they are now admitted to a share in it.

informed that from all these sources the income of an able Paris professor of the first rank in his calling reached very nearly 10,000 fr. (400*l.*) a year. For my own part I would sooner have this, with the freedom and leisure a French professor has with it, than 800*l.* a year as one of the under masters of a public school in England.

The divisional professors are poorly paid, especially those in the departments, but it is to be said that their condition is, or ought to be, one of passage only; they are on their road to the aggregation and the post of full professor. Meanwhile they, too, may turn their spare hours to account for the benefit of their income.

The position of the great body of the *maîtres d'étude* or *maîtres répétiteurs* is more discouraging. They are extremely numerous; the system of supervision practised in the French schools makes it necessary that they should be so, and their number of course renders it impossible that they should be well paid, or that many of them should rise to the higher posts of the profession. Some of them rise; and distinguished men have begun their career in the post of usher. While superintending the *études,* or workrooms in which the boys prepare their lessons, the usher may be carrying on his own studies for the aggregation, for which a five years' practice in teaching is one of the preliminary conditions, and service as an usher, even of the humblest grade, counts. To rise in this way through the aggregation to the professorate is of course in theory the true career of the usher; the majority of them, however, fail to achieve it, and their regular line of promotion is to become *régents* in a communal college. There are three classes of them,—aspirants, second-class ushers, first-class ushers. An aspirant must be 18 years old, and must have the degree of bachelor of arts or sciences ; a second-class usher must have served for a year as aspirant; a first-class one must have served a year in the second class, and that, if he has the degree of master of arts or sciences, is sufficient; if he has not this degree, he must have served in the second class five years, three of them in the same *lycée.* The higher order of ushers may hold the post of master in the lowest or elementary division of the school, or may be employed to supply the place of an absent professor; they also may act the part of tutor by explaining to the boys in their *étude* any difficulty in their lessons, and by helping them forward with them. Of course in the higher part of the school an ordinary *maître d'étude* has not the attainments necessary for such a task as this. An usher acting as master receives in Paris about 60*l.* a year, in the departments from 40*l.* to 50*l.*; the three grades of ushers not in charge of forms receive from 30*l.* to 50*l.* in Paris, from 25*l.* to 40*l.* in the departments. It is to be remembered that they have in the *lycée* their board and lodging free, and those of them who, being masters of the lower forms, are not required to live in the *lycée*, have an allowance of about 20*l.* a year towards their board and lodging.

The Paris *lycées* no doubt get the best of the *maîtres répétiteurs*, and employ those of the highest grade; I was struck with the generally decent address and appearance of those whom I saw there, and everywhere I was inclined to wonder that for such a post at such a stipend the schools could supply themselves as well as they did. Of course it is not easy to induce the authorities to own that the *maître d'étude*, who is such an indispensable ingredient in that system of constant supervision which they think necessary, is and must be a weak part in it, and a stranger has few means of penetrating in such a matter below the surface; but I am inclined to think, chiefly, I own, from what I have heard from English boys brought up in French schools, that among these many *maîtres d'étude* there is a large stagnating mass in which there is much corruption and much mischief, and that from this mass a great deal that is noxious distils among the boys they are set to overlook, though perhaps the contempt with which the boys are apt to regard the usher makes his influence for harm somewhat less than it might otherwise be. The boys who spoke with disgust and contempt of the body of *maîtres d'étude* spoke, I must add, with great respect of that of professors.

To conclude this account of the governing and teaching

staff in a French public school, I must add that their nomenclature in a communal college is somewhat different from
that in a *lycée*.   The director of a communal college is called
the *principal*, not the *provisor*; the masters are called *regents*,
not *professors*.   The principal must have the degree of
bachelor, and so must the regents; in those colleges which
give the full course of secondary instruction, the regents
charged with the higher parts of this course must be
licentiates.

CHAPTER IV.

MATTERS TAUGHT IN THE FRENCH SECONDARY SCHOOLS.

DIVISIONS AND CLASSES IN A FRENCH LYCÉE—MATTERS TAUGHT IN EACH CLASS.

AFTER the teachers I come to the matters taught. The programme of the French public schools is, as I have said, fixed by authority; the arrangement of classes and studies is the same in all. A *lycée* has three divisions,—an elementary division, a grammar division, and a superior division called often *division for humanities*. The classes, unlike those in our great public schools, have for their highest class not a *sixth* but a *first*. The lowest class is the *classe de huitième;* boys are admitted to it very young, as young as seven years of age, if they can read and write; but even before this class the *lycées* are authorised to place a preparatory class, not numbered, in which the instruction given is mainly that of primary schools,* and does not include Latin. Here children of six years of age are admitted. The very good exercise of learning by heart from the classics of the mother tongue begins even in this preparatory class, and is continued to the top of the school. Latin begins in the *classe de huitième,* and is carried further in *septième*. After *septième* begins another division, that of grammar. It is obvious that when boys are admitted at six or seven years old a serious examination at entrance is out of place; but after the elementary division a boy's access to each division is guarded by an examination, which turns, of course, on the matters taught him in the division he is leaving. The lowest class in the division of grammar is *sixième*, the sixth form in the school, according to the French way of reckoning. Here begins

---

* Primary instruction may be given by a primary schoolmaster, but he must hold, unless he has the degree of bachelor, the full certificate of a primary teacher.

Greek, and also the study of the modern languages. These may be English, German, Spanish, or Italian, according to the wants of the localities and the wishes of the parents, France having a frontier either in contact or in close proximity with all these languages. It may wound an Englishman's vanity to find that the pre-eminence given in the schools of his own country to French is not given in France to English; in the *lycées* of Paris, German and English pretty nearly divide the pupils, the advantage resting, however, with German; partly because this is the native language of important provinces of France; partly because it is of more use to military students, which many boys in the *lycées* are going to be; and partly, no doubt, because in the scientific and intellectual movement of Europe at present England counts for so little and Germany for so much, In Germany, where French is obligatory, as with us, in the schools, and where English is optional, one cannot hear without a little mortification the two languages classified as, the one, the *Handel-Sprache*, the other, the *Cultur-Sprache*; English is the *Handel-Sprache*, learnt for mere material and business purposes; the *Cultur-Sprache*, learnt for the purposes of the mind and spirit, is French.

Drawing and singing are likewise obligatory matters of instruction in the French *lycées*, and are not paid for as extras. Two hours a week are, on an average, given to each. Drawing is taught as a matter of science, not of amusement, and the pupil is carried through a strict course from outline up to ornament and model drawing.

The fifth class (*classe de cinquième*) reads our old friend Cornelius Nepos, but it reads also authors not much, I think, in use in our schools,—Justin, Ælian, and Lucian. The division of lessons is the same here and in the sixth class; ten *classes*, as they are called, a week, and two hours of singing, one of drawing, and two of gymnastics.* A class lasts two hours; so this gives (not counting gymnastics) 24 hours of lessons in the week. The classes are thus divided:

---

* Gymnastics form part of the regular course in the *lycées*, and are not charged for as extras.

seven classes and a half (15 hours) for classics; one class
(two hours) for history and geography; two half classes (two
hours) for modern languages; one half class (one hour) for
arithmetic. The weekly number of classes remains the same
all through the school; but the proportion of time given to
classics and to other subjects varies, and so does the amount
of additional lessons.

In *quatrième*, the head form of the grammar division,
Latin prosody in the classical instruction, geometry in the
scientific, appear as new subjects. An hour less is in this
form given to classics, an hour more to mathematics. An
hour more than in the two forms below is here given to
drawing.

Another divisional examination, and the boy passes into
humanities. Of the *division supérieure* (humanities), the lowest class is *troisième*. Here Latin verse begins, and here, for
the first time in the school, Homer appears. Among the
books read in extracts by this form, and not commonly read,
so far as I know, in our schools, I noticed Terence, Isocrates,
Plutarch's *Morals*, and the Greek Fathers. Mathematics now
get four hours a week; history, which we have just seen
dividing its class with geography, gets the whole two hours;
geography and modern languages become additional lessons,
the first with one hour a week, the second with two. Music
is reduced to one hour. The number of lesson-hours in the
week (still not counting gymnastics) has thus risen from 24
to 26.

In *seconde*, the same proportion between sciences and letters;
but in sciences the programme is now algebra, geometry, and
natural history, instead of arithmetic and geometry. The
distribution of additional lessons remains the same. The
Agricola of Tacitus, the easier dialogues of Plato, the easier
orations of Demosthenes, appear among the books read.

Then the boy rises into our sixth form, called with the
French from old time not first class, but *Classe de rhétorique*.
The classics read are much what would be read in our sixth
form; but in the mother-tongue the pupil studies the *Pensées*
of Pascal, the *Oraisons funèbres* of Bossuet, La Bruyère, Fénelon's *Lettre à l'Académie Française*, Buffon's *Discours sur le*

Style, Voltaire's *Siècle de Louis XIV.*, Boileau's *Art Poétique*, and La Fontaine's *Fables.* Even the selection of a body of English classics like this, excellent in themselves and excellently adapted for the purposes to which they are destined, is a progress which English public instruction has yet to make. Letters have eight out of the ten classes in *rhétorique*, which is the great classical form of the school. Sciences have only one class, divided between geometry and cosmography; but with an object which I shall notice presently, an additional lesson of an hour in the week has been established for the benefit of those pupils who desire to refresh their knowledge of the scientific instruction given in *seconde* and *troisième.* Otherwise the lessons occupy the same number of hours as in those two classes.

But now, after the great classical form of *rhétorique*, comes a crowning of the edifice which we have not, and which in some degree, perhaps, represents that part of education which with us the student gets later, at the University. This is the class of *logique*, or, as it is now officially called, of *philosophie*. The design of this class is thus summed up by the present minister, M. Duruy: General revision of the classical and scientific studies of the three previous forms; instruction in physics; and, above all, as the two characterising studies of this class, philosophy,—making the pupil busy himself with the substance of ideas as in rhetoric he busied himself with their form, and developing his reflection as rhetoric developed his imagination and taste,—and contemporary history. The programme of the course of philosophy divides the subject thus: Introduction, psychology, logic, moral philosophy, theology, history of philosophy. That of the course of contemporary history goes from 1815 to the present time; the professor has to introduce it with a 'rapid summary of the general facts which have modified, from the 15th century onwards, the ideas, interests, and constitution of European society.' He concludes it with 'France's share in the general work of civilisation.' The programme is a skilfully constructed framework, capable of being by a good teacher so filled up as to make the course very interesting and useful. In *philosophie*, the design of this class being such as I have stated, Greek and Latin of course lose their preponderant share in the lessons. In the ten lessons they have now, indeed, only so much share as the language of four out of the nine authors read,—Xenophon (*Memorabilia*), Plato (*Gorgias*), Cicero (*De Republica, Tusculans* and *Offices*), and Seneca (select letters),—gives them; the remaining five authors read are French, and the books are : the Port Royal Logic ; the *Discours de la Méthode* of Descartes ; Pascal's *De l'Autorité en matière de Philosophie*, his *Réflexions sur la Géométrie en général*, and his *De l'Art de Persuader* ; Bossuet's *Traité de la Connaissance de Dieu et de Soi-même* ; and Fénelon's *Traité de l'Existence de Dieu*. But two hours of additional lessons in the week are given to going over the pupil's former classical work, and to Latin composition. The essay, Latin and French, appears for the first time in this form. Sciences now get the large share of five classes a week (ten hours). To algebra, geometry, and cosmography, are added physics and chemistry.

To pass through a form takes a year; the programme of studies for each form covers a year, and the pupil has to go through it. A boy therefore who came at eight years old and began in *huitième*, is seventeen years old when he has finished *philosophie*. Sixteen years is the age at which a candidate is allowed to present himself for the degree of bachelor in arts or science. The degree of bachelor of arts is the natural termination of the literary studies of the *lycée*, and the examination for this degree now turns, by express regulation,* upon the matters taught in the classes of *rhetoric* and *philosophy* in the *lycées*. A youth who has gone through these classes with success has no difficulty in obtaining the degree, and one sees on the benches of the *lycées* pupils who, having completed the age of sixteen, have gone in for their degree, and already got it. Examinations are held twice a year in each of the 16 seats of faculties of letters in France, and in 13 other towns whither the faculties of their respective academies send examiners. The examining jury is composed of three members of the faculty of letters and one of that of sciences. The examina-

---

* *Décret impérial u 27 novembre, 1864, relatif au Baccalauréat ès Lettres.*

tions are public, partly on paper and partly oral, and they last two days. Candidates who fail in the paper-work examination are not admitted to the oral one. The paper-work consists of Latin and French composition, and of translation from Latin into French ; the *viva voce* work, of construing a passage from a Greek or Latin author and explaining a passage from a French one, and of answering questions in philosophy, history and geography, and mathematical and natural sciences. The paper-work counts for three marks, the construing and explaining for two, philosophy for one, history and geography for one, the sciences for two. Failure in any one of these five sections causes the candidate's rejection. If he loses three out of the nine marks distributed between the sections he is equally rejected. The part given to mathematics and natural sciences in an examination for the degree of bachelor of letters, is what will most strike us in going through this programme. A candidate who holds already the degree of bachelor of sciences is of course exempted from the scientific part of the examination. A candidate who has got, in the class of rhetoric or philosophy, one of the chief prizes for classics in the grand annual competition of the *lycées*, is exempted from the literary part of the examination, but the scientific part he must still go through. The dues for the degree of bachelor amount to 100 fr. (4*l*.)

But many of the best pupils of the *lycées* have in view not the arts degree, but a degree in sciences and admission to the *écoles spéciales*, as they are called,—schools like the Polytechnic, St. Cyr, the *École Navale*, the *École Forestière*, the *École Centrale des Arts et Manufactures*. Admission to these schools is a favourite object of ambition in France ; it at once places a young man in a career ; but it is guarded by a strict and competitive examination in mathematics and natural sciences. It is said that a clever boy who has gone through the *lycée* to the end of *philosophie*, and who has followed with diligence the scientific as well as the literary instruction of the different classes through which he has passed, is, at the same time that he has secured a thorough literary education, strong enough in sciences to obtain, with a little previous aid from private tuition, the degree of bachelor of sciences, and to present himself with this indispensable credential at one of the special schools. To encourage boys destined for these schools to complete their course of literary training first, the additional lesson in sciences of which I spoke when I was describing the rhetoric class has been added to the programme of that class. The boy is thus enabled to keep his mathematics fresh at the same time that he goes on with his classics. However, it is admitted that in general a much stricter scientific training than this is necessary for a boy who wants to get into the special schools. Two scientific classes are therefore placed as appendages to the *lycée* system,—the class of elementary mathematics and the class of special mathematics. The class of elementary mathematics puts Greek altogether aside, and of its ten weekly classes gives only one to Latin and French; one is given to history; of the remaining eight, three are given to natural sciences, five to mathematics. Modern languages, geography, and philosophy are provided for by additional lessons of one hour in the week each. In special mathematics, the mathematical and natural sciences have the same share of classes, eight out of ten; but natural sciences get only two of them, mathematics the other six. Latin and history disappear, French literature has one of the two classes left, a modern language the other. An additional lesson of an hour in the week is assigned to work in the laboratory.

After a year in elementary mathematics the pupil is ready for the examination of the degree of bachelor of sciences or that of the Military School of St. Cyr. The class of special mathematics conducts to the more difficult examination of the Polytechnic School, or to that of the scientific section of the Normal School. It sometimes happens that the same student passes for both the Polytechnic and the scientific section of the Normal School; M. Duruy in a recent report notices with pleasure that several students who had thus won the double nomination elected for the Normal School. Nothing could better show the credit with which this excellent institution has succeeded in investing the somewhat unattractive profession of schoolmaster.

But the Polytechnic and St. Cyr have fixed twenty as the highest limit of age for their candidates; the competition, at the Polytechnic especially, is very severe (some people say, too severe), and it is not easy to succeed the first time; a candidate wishes to have time for more trials than one. But a youth who goes through his literary course to the end of *philosophie*, and then takes his two years of mathematics, elementary and special, to fit him for the Polytechnic examination, finds himself with no margin of age to spare, and must succeed the first time or give up his object. Add to this that a boy with a strong aptitude for scientific studies often feels very little disposed for a nine years' conversation with Latin and Greek. Add again, that the parents of a promising boy often feel very little disposed for an eleven years' expense for his schooling, when he might be off their hands in eight or nine. To meet cases of this kind the well-known *bifurcation* had been established. On issuing from the division of grammar, and passing the examination which guards the issue from that division, a boy, instead of entering humanities, was allowed to choose whether his training should be henceforth literary or scientific. The *lycée* offered him his choice between a scientific section, supposed to prepare him for business, for the special schools, for degrees in science and medicine; or a literary section, conducting to degrees in letters and law, and, in general, giving what the world has agreed to call the education of a gentleman. A boy may be admitted at once to the grammar division; three years of classics, therefore, there, and then the *bifurcation*. But even after the *bifurcation* letters kept a strong hold on the follower of sciences; one-half of the school-time was in the scientific section given to literature, modern languages, and history, while in the literary section only one-fifth of the school-time was given to sciences. But neither the friends of letters nor those of sciences were satisfied with the *bifurcation*. It was said that it took the boys too young, before their vocation was sufficiently clear; that it damaged both scientific and literary studies, producing good students in neither. The present minister, M. Duruy, abolished it. The abolition, however, turns out, when one looks closely at it, to be more apparent than real. It is true that a scientific section of the *lycée* no longer exists in name, and that a boy who after he has done with the grammar division remains on at school, must enter *troisième*, the lowest class of the division of humanities, and pass his year there. It is desired, no doubt, by the framers of the new regulations that he should have the benefit of *seconde* and *rhétorique*, if not of *philosophie*, as well; but in these cases, where there is a current of interests which conflicts with the regulations, it is not what is desired, but what is enforced, that is important. The pupil is not obliged to proceed, after *troisième*, to *seconde*, or else leave the *lycée*; a lower division of the class of *mathématiques élémentaires*, under the title of *cours préparatoire*, receives the pupil whose parents wish the direction of his studies to be henceforth scientific rather than literary. He has first to pass an examination in what he has been taught in *troisième*; but once admitted to the *cours préparatoire* his literary classes are reduced to five, and his scientific classes are as numerous as those of *troisième*, *seconde*, and *rhétorique* altogether, and throw into one year the scientific instruction which those classes spread over three. From the *cours préparatoire* he issues into the regular class of *mathématiques élémentaires*, at the end of which follows naturally the examination for the degree of bachelor of sciences, this examination turning on the matters, scientific and literary, taught in the class of *mathématiques élémentaires* in the *lycées*. Afterwards, if, for the Polytechnic or the Normal School, or for any other object, he needs higher mathematical instruction, he goes on into *mathématiques spéciales*.

The changes introduced by M. Duruy have, therefore, made one year of humanities obligatory on the school-boy proceeding to the scientific classes. To this extent they are in favour of classics. M. Duruy urges also, though he does not enforce, a still longer course of humanities before the pupil gives himself to sciences. On the other hand, in his new programme he has strengthened the scientific instruction by introducing more of it into the higher classical forms than was formerly taught there. He has also, in general, simplified, compressed, and reduced the old programme of instruction in the *lycées*. Still more has he done this with that of the bachelor's degrees, both in arts and science. This programme, which was before a very wide one, he has now made identical, as I have said, with that of the *lycée's* two highest classes in humanities, and with that of its class of elementary mathematics. This simplification, the degree in question being for youths of seventeen or eighteen, seems clearly judicious.

CHAPTER V.

THE LYCÉES.

WITH the provision I have described for the supply of professors, they are a body, all through France, of one stamp and training; the pick of them no doubt comes, in the long run, to the Paris *lycées*, but the ablest of young professors may expect to find himself, at some moment in the beginning of his career, at a school in the provinces. The field for him in Paris, however, is large. Paris has seven great classical schools *de plein exercice*, as it is called; that is, in which the full course of instruction which I have detailed above is given. All *lycées* are *de plein exercice*, while of the 247 communal colleges only 152 are so. The rest have only the elementary division and the division of grammar; they do not add to grammar the division of humanities. The seven great classical schools of Paris are the *lycées* Louis le Grand, Napoléon, Saint Louis, Charlemagne, Bonaparte, Bourbon, and the Colleges Stanislas and Rollin. Of these the *lycées* Louis le Grand, Napoléon, and Saint Louis, and the two colleges, take boarders; Charlemagne and Bonaparte take day-scholars only. Most of them retain the site, at least, of an old pre-revolutionary school; Saint Louis is the *Collége d'Harcourt*, founded in that great school-movement of the 14th century which I have already mentioned, by two brothers, members of Philip the Fair's Council, Raoul d'Harcourt, canon of Paris, and Robert d'Harcourt, bishop of Coutances. Napoléon was the old *Collége Henri IV*, and as, from the neighbourhood of the Panthéon, one sees its long pile, flanked by the Church of St. Étienne du Mont, where Pascal lies buried, one must own that a venerable look of old France it still retains. Bonaparte was the *Collége Bourbon*. Louis le Grand was the famous Jesuit school of Clermont, which Louis the Fourteenth one day visited, and the performance of the scholars being admired by one of his suite: 'What would you expect?' said the king, '*c'est mon collége*.' That night the Jesuits erased the name of *Clermont*, fixed in large letters on the front of their building, and the next morning saw *Louis le Grand* in its stead. Louis le Grand is the only one of these Paris *lycées* which managed to live on through the Revolution, notwithstanding the decree suppressing the ancient colleges. The Jesuits had long been expelled, but it had an adroit director at its head; and though straitened by the trials of the time, it was never actually closed.

These seven establishments have a total of 5,968 scholars. Louis le Grand, the largest, has 1,330; Bonaparte has 1,220; Charlemagne 930; Saint Louis 800; Napoléon 688; Stanislas 620; Rollin 380. The *lycée* of Vanves, a mile or two out of Paris, formed to relieve Louis le Grand of its little boys and to give them country air, has 700 scholars; but without counting Vanves, the seven great schools of Paris contain very nearly 6,000 scholars. The nine English public schools which were the object of a Royal Commission's inquiry, have 3,027 scholars. Only six of the nine have really, in public estimation, the rank of great public schools, the rank which the seven great Paris schools hold; still, let them all be counted in, and yet the public classical schools of Paris alone have nearly twice as many scholars as the public classical schools of all England. Nay, of all Scotland and Ireland besides; for these two countries have no public classical schools of the rank of the great English schools or of the Paris *lycées*, and Scotch or Irish parents who desire, and can afford, schools of this rank for their children, must send them to the English schools.

I visited all the *lycées* of Paris, and I believe there is no part of a *lycée*'s organism, from the elementary division up to *mathématiques spéciales*, which I have not seen at work, and no part of the instruction which I have not heard given. The internal management and the working aspect of all these institutions are similar, though the exterior of the buildings is often strikingly different. The modern, handsome, and wealthy appearance of the *lycée Bonaparte* suits its position in the newer and more luxurious quarter of Paris,—the quarter most frequented by visitors,—with the Rue de la Paix, the Grand Hôtel, the Opéra, and the Madeleine for neighbours. On the other side of the Seine, in the old quarter of the schools and the religious, in the neighbourhood of the Sorbonne and Sainte Geneviève, the somewhat dilapidated front of Louis le Grand or Napoléon suits the antiquity and associations of the region. Many of the public school buildings in France, the old school sites and fabrics having been, as I have already said, restored after the Revolution, as far as possible, to their former destination, are in fact very old, and the rebuilding and repairing of the *lycées* and those sanitary works in connection with them which earlier ages neglected, but which are now thought, and rightly, to be of such great importance, are a cause of constant and heavy expense to the government. In this way the whole front of Saint Louis, which stands on the new continuation, upon the left bank of the Seine, of the Boulevard Sébastopol, has just been re-built, and a very handsome building this *lycée* now is. You ring at the decorated entrance in the boulevard, and the porter admits you to the open and spacious vestibule, looking on the school's first great court, surrounded by high white walls with uniform tiers of windows, and communicating directly with the *parloir*, where at all the French public schools a boarder's parents, or those authorised by them, can come and see him between twelve and one, or between half-past four and five. Ascending a staircase, one reaches the *cabinet* of the censor and that of the provisor. The room of the provisor communicates with the apartment where he is lodged (for the provisor lives at the *lycée*), and the provisor's lodging at Saint Louis is most enviable. Its occupant when I was there was M. Legrand, but he has since left it to become provisor at Bonaparte, a much easier post, because at Bonaparte there are no boarders. Every one who has had opportunities of observing must have been struck to see how much work

Frenchmen seem able to do, and to do with spirit and energy; the provisor of a great *lycée* certainly needs to have ability of this sort, with the business and responsibility of a boarding house of some 500 boys pressing upon him. M. Legrand had it to perfection; constantly appealed to, with a rain of letters, messages, meetings, applicants, visitors, perpetually beating upon him, he seemed to suffice to all claims, and to suffice not only industriously but smoothly; but he began his work, he told me, at four in the morning. On several occasions he took me through the different departments of the *lycée*; the internal economy of such an institution could not be better seen than at Saint Louis and with such a cicerone as M. Legrand. The series of large courts for a school of 800 boys, courts generally quiet, but at the breaking up of a lesson or in the short time allotted to recreation noisy enough; spacious and airy, sometimes shaded with trees, but looking, to an ex-schoolboy from any of the great English schools, hopelessly prison-like; on the ground floor round the courts the school-rooms, *salles de classe*, with their professor, and their 30 or 40 boys seated at desks rising one behind the other; or the work-rooms, *salles d'étude*, rooms of much the same aspect and dimensions as the *salles de classe*, but with a *maître répétiteur* presiding in them instead of a professor, and with the boys learning their lessons instead of saying them; above, the refectories with their show of table napkins and silver cups, and the large dormitories scrupulously neat and clean, at one end the curtained bed of the usher in charge, in the door at the other end a window by which to overlook the room from without, and, near it, ingenious mechanical devices by which the visits of the functionary whose business it is to see, so often in the night, that all is well in each bedroom, are recorded, and the controller is himself controlled; then the dispensary and infirmaries, the service done by sisters of charity, with rooms for all stages of illness and the eternal usher overlooking those invalids who are up and together; the linen stores and clothes-rooms, everything beautifully kept, each boy's things ticketed and numbered with the greatest exactness; the bath-rooms, offices, kitchens, the supplies of bread and wine, the soup, meat, vegetables, pastry, all in preparation on a grand scale and all of them which I tasted excellent,—this is what may be seen in every great *lycée* in France; but at Saint Louis, from the newness and freshness of the buildings, and the perfection of finish and order which is reached, it may be seen to special advantage. Finish and order are, however, in the great majority of cases, rules of French administration; and as I have already remarked, the march of a great public service, such as is the service of one of these establishments, has inevitably something imposing in it if regularly and well conducted, which the arrangements of private establishments, in which the individual has, very likely, his tastes more consulted and a life more to his mind, cannot well equal. But when we come to consulting the individual's taste and giving him a life to his mind, we generally come at the same time to expense; a cheap private establishment, without the regularity and economy of a great machine, and without the costly luxury of independent comfort, is a slipshod thing, full of meanness and misery. It is to be remembered that in one of the Paris *lycées* a boy is to have board, instruction, books, writing materials, clothes, washing, medical attendance, and medicine, for 50*l.* a year. The question is, how these may be given best for that money.

The medical service is excellent; the general rate of sickness in the *lycées* is certainly surprisingly low, and probably to the excellence of the medical service,—for ability, completeness, and attention, far exceeding, like that of a great hospital, anything the inmates of the establishment could command at home,—this is in great measure owing. The meals are four in number; breakfast, dinner at noon, the *goûter*, as it is called, at half-past four, and supper in the evening. The breakfast is a slight, and the *goûter* a very slight affair; this latter is in fact a roll of bread and nothing more; the dinner and supper are the substantial meals. The dinner is in general soup, then two dishes and a vegetable, then dessert; there is an allowance of wine. It will be seen how different is the system of meals from ours, or at least from what ours was; but it is in great measure climate and differences of physical organisation which determine the varieties in these things. I have heard some complaints of the way the boys are fed in the *lycées*; not as to the quality of the food, but the quantity, I have heard several people complain, is apt to be insufficient. I give these complaints, on a matter which, with boys, very easily gives rise to them, and where it is not very easy to test their exact justice, for what they are worth.

The boys in a *lycée* have, it must be said, to our notions a long and exhausting day; they rise earlier than our boys, later than boys in Italy (this again is an affair mainly of climate); the boarders in a French *lycée* rise between five and six, and their allowance of school hours is more than ours, their allowance of air and exercise less. The hours of. class are but four a day, from eight to ten in the morning, and from two to four in the afternoon; but this is only a small part of the work-day of the French schoolboy, his hours passed at *conférences*, at examinations, and above all at pre-paring his lessons in the *salle d'étude*, under the eye of the *maître répétiteur*, have to be added to it. It seems to me that the French schoolboy is at lessons, on an average, ten or eleven hours a day, and that his time for meals and recreation is not, on an average, more than two hours. Thursday is a half-holiday, and the only one. Certainly, the boys, at their quarter-hours or half-hours of recreation, seem to enjoy themselves with great spirit, and their gymnastics are pro-bably a better physical training for the short time they have to give to exercise than our boys' amusements would be; but they did not, in general, to my thinking, look so fresh, happy, and healthy as our public-school boys. The master of a well-known *pension*, who had English boys as well as French, assured me that the French boys were not to be judged by their complexions, that they had more endurance and a tougher fibre than our boys, and that when he took them out together on long excursions his English boys, vigorous at first, knocked up sooner than his French boys. This is the old reproach of the Latin races against the northern barba-rian, that he is lusty, and melts and gives way in the sun; there may be some truth in it, and the spirit and gaiety of an English boy do not go with him into his exercise,—he flags in it,—if he does not feel he is at play and free in it; thus it has been observed that gymnastics do not flourish in our schools, they are too much of a drill or a lesson; and for the same reason the volunteer company has not so many or such ardent recruits as cricket or boating. And no doubt the physical energy of the young English *pensionnaire* would show to more advantage if he was matched in cricket or boating with his French comrades, than in gymnastics or a walking excursion, where he is a little damped by the sense of constraint and rule. Still it is hard to believe, and I do not believe, that the confinement, the scanty recreation, and the long school-hours of a French schoolboy are without some·unfavourable effect on his health and development; the long school-hours, however, are an almost inevitable result of placing large boarding schools in the heart of large cities, where space for exercise and freedom of range must be limited, and the boys therefore must be kept more at work to save them from the mischief of being penned up together in idleness with few or no resources of amusement. The placing large boarding schools in large cities is itself, again, an almost inevitable result of having large day-schools attached to the boarding schools; for the supply to large day-schools can only be found, of course, in large cities, and indeed the need for them only exists there. It must be added, besides, that a body of professors such as the *lycées* of Paris are proud, and justly proud, of possessing, is hardly to be obtained out of a large city. Many of these professors have pursuits, independent of their work at the *lycées*, which tie them to Paris; and the *lycées*, if they were planted in the country, amidst better conditions of physical development for their boys. might have some loss in professors to set against the gain in other respects.

The French *lycées*, however, are guiltless of one preposterous violation of the laws of life and health committed by our own great schools, which have of late years thrown open to competitive examination all the places on their foundations. The French have plenty of examinations; but they put them almost entirely at the right age for examinations, between the years of fifteen and twenty-five, when the candidate is neither too old nor too young to be examined with advantage. To put upon little boys of nine or ten the pressure of a competitive examination for an object of the greatest value to their parents, is to offer a premium for the violation of nature's elementary laws, and to sacrifice, as in the poor geese fatted for Strasburg pies, the due development of all the organs of life to the premature hypertrophy of one. It is well known that the cramming of the little human victims for their ordeal of competition tends more and more to become an industry with a certain class of small schoolmasters, who know the secrets of the process, and who are led by self-interest to select in the first instance their own children for it. The foundations are no gainers, and nervous exhaustion at fifteenis the price which many a clever boy pays for over-stimulation at ten ; and the nervous exhaustion of a number of our clever boys tends to create a broad reign of intellectual deadness in the mass of youths from fifteen to twenty, whom the clever boys, had they been rightly developed and not unnaturally forced, ought to have leavened. You can hardly put too great a pressure on a healthy youth to make him work between fifteen and twenty-five ; healthy or unhealthy, you can hardly put too on him light a pressure of this kind before twelve.

The bursarships in the *lycées* are, therefore, not given away by competitive examination among children from eight to twelve; they are given on the ground of poverty, either to the children of persons having some public claim, or to the most promising subjects from the primary schools. This seems to me quite right, and I wish the English reader to remark how here, as elsewhere, we suffer from our dread of effective administration and from the feudal and incoherent organisation of our society. In the hands of individuals and small local bodies patronage like that of our foundation schools becomes outrageously jobbed ; at last the public attention gets directed to this, and the patronage has to be otherwise dealt with ; but there is no body of trained and competent persons with authority to decide deliberately how it may be best dealt with ; so it ends by the local people through whose laches the difficulty has arisen throwing a

sop to Cerberus, and gratifying an ignorant public's love of
claptrap by throwing everything open to competitive examination. On the Continent, there is an Education Minister/
and a Council of Public Instruction to weigh matters of this
kind; so far from jobbing being promoted by this, the
examination test is much more strictly applied in France
than with us, but there is a competent authority to decide
when it is rational to apply it and when absurd. Neither
are there any complaints of the way the *lycée* bursarships,—it
being judged best not to give these by competitive examination,—are distributed ; because here again all that is done is
done with the safeguards of joint action between several
competent agencies, of publicity, and of responsibility. It
is a mistake to suppose that a government bureau, in an
administrative organisation like that of France, has no
checks; it has far more checks than a government bureau
here, which has been extemporised to meet some urgent
want, and is not part of a well-devised whole. The secretary
of our Education Department is almost invited to settle of
his own authority education-questions which M. Duruy,
though a minister, would not settle without referring them
to a Council composed as we have seen. Nay, and even sup-
posing our secretary refers them to his chiefs and they refer
them to the Committee of Council,—how is this Committee
of Council composed ? Of three or four Cabinet Ministers,
with no special acquaintance with educational matters.

The want of more air and exercise for their schoolboys is
a matter which is occupying the attention of the authorities
of public secondary instruction in France ; they are beginning with the greatest sufferers by the old system, the little
boys, and the *lycée du Prince Impérial*, at Vanves, is a fruit
of their awakened solicitude for these children. Vanves is
charming. It lies a mile or two out of Paris on the Vaugirard road. It was a summer villa of the Prince of Condé ;
when the then holder of this title emigrated at the Revolution, Vanves was sold as emigrant's property, and was bought
very cheap by the *lycée* Louis le Grand, which managed, as
I have said, to subsist through the storms of the revolution.
It is now, like every other *lycée*, the property of the State,

and after having for some time served as a juvenile department for Louis le Grand only, it is now an independent establishment for little boys, beginning with primary instruction and carrying them no further than *cinquième*, when they
are passed on, not necessarily to Louis le Grand only,—though
the old connection of Vanves with this *lycée* is felt as a strong
tie,—but to whatever school the pupil chooses. Seven hundred
little boarders (for Vanves takes no day-scholars) of from five
to ten or eleven may be seen here, and a pretty sight they are.
The park and garden are quite delightful, and the ground
beautifully thrown about; the high hill on which stand the
school buildings commands a magnificent view of Paris on
the one side, and of the country towards La Celle St. Cloud
and St. Germain on the other. The buildings have been
of late greatly enlarged, and every improvement in school
construction and arrangements, according to the French
notions, introduced; and whoever wishes to see French
school construction and arrangements at their very best
should go and see Vanves. The school is popular, and no
wonder; at the lodge at the foot of the hill one sees carriages
waiting, and in the glades of the park the mammas whom
they have brought may be descried walking with their little
boys. Being so young the pupils pay the lower rate (40*l.* to
45*l.* a year) fixed by authority for the younger divisions in
the Paris *lycées;* but it is on little boys, they say, not yet
come to the terrible appetite of fifteen, that the great profits
are made ; and while many *lycées* can hardly make both ends
meet, Vanves is in the highest prosperity. It is self-support-
ing, and after paying all its expenses has a profit of 4,000*l.*
a year. Its progenitor, Louis Le Grand, clears a profit of
more than 3,000*l.* Profits of this kind go to the State, the
proprietor of the *lycées*, and are available for the general
expenses of secondary instruction. In this way a prosperous
lycée helps to pull a struggling *lycée* through; but a *lycée*
which brings in plenty of money will always be liberally
treated for its own improvements and extensions.

Vanves has no day-scholars ; its boarders are all housed
on the premises, and all pay about 40*l.* a year. In the
ordinary *lycées* it is not so. These, with scarcely an excep-

tion,* take day-scholars, and do not themselves lodge all their pupils who are boarders. They all charge a rate fixed by authority,† ranging, for their boarders, from 40*l.* to 60*l.* a year; for their day-scholars, from 6*l.* to 10*l.* For the boarder this includes everything; his *tutor,* as we should say, —that is, the professor who gives him the benefit, out of class hours, of certain *conférences* and examinations, and the *répétiteur,* who helps him with his lesson,—as well as his class instruction and his board; for the day scholar, it only includes his class instruction, and he pays from 3*l.* to 5*l.* a year extra, according to his place in the school, for *tutor.* This makes a day scholar's expense come to from 9*l.* to 15*l.* a year. Some boys are half-boarders, passing the twelve hours from 8 a.m. to 8 p.m. at the *lycée,* getting their dinner and their *goûter* there, but not breakfasting, supping, or sleeping; these have the full instruction, and they pay from 22*l.* to 34*l.* a year. The *externe surveillé* is a day-scholar who learns his lessons in the *salle d'étude* under the usher's eye, and is thus off his parents' hands the whole day except an hour in the middle of it, but has no meals at the school; he pays, as an ordinary day-scholar with the full instruction, from 9*l.* to 15*l.* a year, and 80 francs (about 3 guineas) a year besides for superintendence.

But all the boarding-scholars of a *lycée* which takes boarders are not boarders of the *lycée* itself; and many of the day-scholars of a *lycée* which takes no boarders are boarders, though not in the *lycée.* At Louis le Grand, for instance, the greatest of the *lycées,* there are 800 boarders (*internes*) and 500 day-scholars (*externes*); but all these *externes* do not live at home. Charlemagne and Bonaparte have no *internat,* they are day-schools; but the population of Bonaparte is thus divided: day-scholars who live at home (of these, 151 are *externes surveillés*), 707; day-scholars who are at a boarding-house, 493; total, 1,200. And that of Charlemagne thus: day-scholars

---

* At the *Collége Rollin* they are all boarders.

† *Décret du 5 août* 1862. In the elementary division boarders pay 40*l.*, in the grammar division 44*l.*, in the superior division 48*l.*, in special mathematics (where they have, perhaps, the best scientific and mathematical teaching to be got anywhere) 60*l.* Day-scholars pay, in the elementary division 6*l.*, in grammar 8*l.*, in humanities and special mathematics 10*l.*

who live at home, 200 (70 of them *externes surveillés*) ; day scholars who are at a boarding-house, 790; total, 990. A boarding-house of this kind is called in France *pension, institution*; its director is called *chef de pension, chef d'institution.*

These establishments are private, or, as the French prefer to call them, free (*école libre, institution libre*).

CHAPTER VI.

PRIVATE OR FREE SCHOOLS, AND COMMUNAL COLLEGES.

PENSIONS OR INSTITUTIONS LIBRES—THE COMMUNAL COLLEGES—PRIVATE SCHOOLS—
THE SEMINARIES.

PRIVATE or free schools in France are not free in the sense that any man may keep one who likes. To keep one a man must be twenty-five years old, must have had five years' practice in a school, and must hold either the degree of bachelor, or a certificate which is given after an examination of the same nature as the examination he would have to pass for the degree of bachelor. Thus he cannot, as in England, be perfectly ignorant and inexperienced in his business; neither can he, as in England, be a ticket-of-leave-man, for the French law declares every man who has undergone a criminal condemnation incapable of keeping a school. Neither can he have his school-room in ruins or under conditions dangerous to his pupils' health or morality; for if it is a new school he is establishing, he has to signify his intention beforehand to the academic authority of his department, and if this authority makes objection, the Council of Public Instruction in Paris, in the last resort, decides. If within a month the academic authority makes no objection, he is then free to open his school; but it is at all times liable to inspection by the academic authority or the inspectors-general of secondary instruction, to ascertain that nothing contrary to health, morality, or the law, is suffered to go on there. The inspector of a school of this kind does not meddle with its instruction.

Much the most famous of these institutions is Sainte Barbe, near the Pantheon; it is in the neighbourhood of Louis le Grand, and boards a great number of boys who follow the classes of that *lycée*. Sainte-Barbe answers more than anything else I saw in France to a public school with us; I do not mean at all in the mode of management and teaching, which is that of all French schools; but it is not a State establishment, and yet has antiquity, important buildings, a great connection, a *genius loci*, and general consideration. Its head, M. Labrouste, is a member of the Imperial Council of Public Instruction. Many families which frequent the great classical *lycée*, Louis le Grand, have used Sainte Barbe as their boarding-house for generations; the *Collége Rollin* was once held here; and the prosperity of the establishment is now so great that it has recently founded a Vanves of its own for its little boys at Fontenay aux Roses, near Paris; and Fontenay, like Vanves, is well worth seeing. But just because it has this exceptional character, Sainte Barbe, of course, is not a good sample of the French *pensions*; neither is it a good example of the French private schools, because its chief function, though it has classes of its own, is to serve as a great hereditary boarding-house to the frequenters of Louis-le-Grand. So I will go elsewhere for specimens of the *pension*, which now occupies us.

These institutions abound in Paris, and the files of uniform-wearing schoolboys whom one meets in the streets are generally *pensionnaires* going under the care of the master of the *pension* or one of his ushers to or from the *lycée* whose classes they follow. The Commissioners will ask, as I did, why, if a boy is not to live at home, but to be a boarder somewhere, he does not go and board at the *lycée* whose classes he follows. The answer in the case of Sainte Barbe to the question why the *institution* has the preference over the *lycée* is, as I have said, old hereditary connection. But generally the answer is this: parents seek a somewhat less vast assemblage of boys, a somewhat more domestic management, and a somewhat more attentive supervision of studies out of class hours than they find, or think they find, at the *lycée*. At the same time they like the name of the *lycée*, its guarantees, and its professors. So they send their boy to a *pension* where he is with fifty, a hundred, two hundred boys, not with four or five hundred; where the master's wife imports the feminine element into the direction of household affairs, and where their boy gets more looked after in learning his lessons, and better tutored; and then he is to add to this the benefit of the *lycée* professors and the *status* of a public schoolboy.

Two of these *pensions* I visited, besides Sainte Barbe; M. Cousin's in the Rue du Rocher, and the *Institution Massin* in the Marais. A German would hardly think of visiting M. Cousin's *pension*, but it has an interest for an Englishman in being one of the very few boarding-houses which approach in expensiveness our Eton and Harrow. It is in connection with the *lycée Bonaparte,* and is fed, like that *lycée,* from the wealthy and luxurious quarter of Paris. A certain number of great personages send their sons to the classes of Bonaparte, and have a tutor for him at home. This, however, gives the paternal house the benefit of the boy's residence, which, unless the paternal house is very large, is not always convenient; besides, a tutor at all equal to the tutors of a good *pension* is a costly luxury if one has him all to oneself. So many of the great people of the rich quarter send their boys to M. Cousin. His expensiveness has been exaggerated; about 120*l.* a year is the cost for an elder boy there, and the cost for a younger boy is less. M. Cousin's house is a good one, and he has a garden, which, for Paris, is delightful; the meals are said to be very good; the older boys have excellent rooms to themselves; the younger ones are not more than two or three in a room; the time given to recreation is something more than in the *internats* of the *lycées,* and the whole establishment has a more domestic character than they have, and not their rigid, formal, and military air. As to lessons and sports, however, the difference between M. Cousin's and the *lycée* is, to an Englishman's notions, slight; the system is in the main much the same, and necessarily so; but there is no doubt that the preparation of the boys for their classes, and the individual help given them out of *lycée* hours, is much more considerable at M. Cousin's; indeed, one may say roundly that he employs professors where the *internat* only employs ushers. The *conférences* and *répétitions* of the *lycée* are, indeed, by professors, and are designed to meet the want of tutoring; but the amount of these which falls to the *interne's* share is not to be compared with the amount he gets of *salle d'étude* work under an usher, who is as different from a professor as chalk from cheese; and it is the object of establishments like M. Cousin's to make the *maître répétiteur*, as tutor, disappear, and come in only as watchman, and, as tutor, to put the professor in his place. This M. Cousin does, and it is the best ground for his high charges.

I must add that M. Cousin himself is an ex-functionary of public instruction, and that the success he enjoys seemed to me thoroughly well earned.

As M. Cousin feeds Bonaparte, so the *Institution Massin* feeds Charlemagne. As Bonaparte is a somewhat fashionable *lycée*, so Charlemagne is a somewhat democratic *lycée;* selected, in general by poor but clever school-boys from the provinces whose parents wish to give them the advantage of one of the great *lycées* of Paris. It is on the right bank of the Seine, but beyond the wealthy quarter. Charlemagne has no *internat*, yet four-fifths of its pupils are boarders. They board in *pensions* not like that of M. Cousin; and the *Institution Massin* in the Marais close by,—a quarter which has long ceased to be aristocratic and fashionable,—is a good sample of them. It was founded in 1810, at the revival of secondary instruction in France, by M. Massin, from whom it takes its name; its present head is M. Lesage, who has the grade of licentiate, the title of *agrégé*, and was for twelve years a professor at Charlemagne. He too, then, is no adventurer, and may be supposed to know his business. An Englishman can at once see the difference between the domestic arrangements at M. Cousin's and those of a *lycée*, though the general course of study and play will seem to him to be pretty much alike at the two places. At the *Institution Massin* the march of the domestic arrangements and the aspect of the premises seem to me not to differ much from those of the *lycée*. The expense at M. Lesage's differs very little from that at a *lycée;* in France it is a very small body of parents which will exceed this rate, and the *pensions*, therefore,—the immense majority of them,—keep their charges very near the rate of the public schools. At M. Lesage's the charges for boys in special mathematics are slightly lower than those in the *internat* of a *lycée*; for other boys they are from five to ten pounds a year higher. That is to say, a boy in humanities at Charlemagne who boards with M. Lesage, pays M. Lesage for his board and tuition 1,200 fr. a year, and pays the class-fees of Charlemagne, 250 fr., besides; in all, 58*l.* a year. As an *interne* in humanities at Saint-Louis, his board, tuition, and class-fees would all be covered by 1,200 fr. (48*l.*). The same in the lower divisions; M. Lesage's boarders pay the same as the *internes* of a *lycée*, with the class-fees of the *lycée* in addition. The pupils in special mathematics spring at once, if *internes* of a Paris *lycée*, from 1,200 fr. to 1,500 fr., a great leap; the class-fees, however, are the same in humanities as in special mathematics. The increase of 300 fr., then, is for board and private tuition alone; and this increase M. Lesage does not think it needful to make, but charges a boy in special mathematics, like a boy in humanities, 1,200 fr. a year for his board, and 250 fr. a year for his *lycée* class-fees.

A certain number of M. Lesage's pupils are boys who are too backward for the *lycées*, or who, from their age, have not time to follow the *lycée* course; these have their whole instruction at the *pension*, an instruction in the main identical with that of the *lycée*. These pay the same as the other boarders, minus the *lycée* class-fees. Their education, therefore, costs them from 5*l.* to 10*l.* a year less; but it says much in favour of the *lycée* classes that the boys fit for them almost invariably pay the fees and follow them.

The aspect of things at M. Lesage's, the internal arrangements, the large dormitories, the *salles d'étude*, the courts, the chapel, are all to an English eye hardly distinguishable from those of a *lycée*. The meals are the same; a sister is to be seen in the infirmary; there are the two *aumôniers* to give religious instruction to the Catholics, and the Protestant ministers to pick out their sheep and conduct them to the *temple*. There is the same preparation for the degree of bachelor as at the *lycées*, even the same special preparation for the great Government schools as at Saint Louis.* Only

---

* At Saint-Louis the special and elementary mathematics of the ordinary *lycées* are organised with peculiar and minute reference to the examinations of the several Government schools, and take the title of ' École Préparatoire aux Écoles Spéciales du Gouvernement.' There is a two-year course of special mathematics.

there is, or is believed to be, a more effective and sustained tutoring; there is Madame Lesage to give an eye to the younger boys or to invalids; the movement of the whole establishment does not seem so entirely mechanical, and the numbers, though large, are not, as in the *internats* of the great *lycées* of Paris, so vast that a boy feels lost in them. Charlemagne having no *internat*, it is obvious that a boy who does not live in Paris, and wants to go to Charlemagne, must board elsewhere than at Charlemagne. But the notion that a *pension* is more homelike and less barrack-like than the *internat* of a *lycée*, that there is more individual care, and that the tutoring is better done, tells in some degree, no doubt, in favour of an establishment like M. Lesage's, as well as in favour of one like M. Cousin's, though in the case of M. Lesage's, as I have said, the difference from a *lycée* is not very perceptible.

There are *pensions* formed on some special principle of grouping, such as nationality or religion; for instance, for Polish boys frequenting the *lycées*, for Protestant boys frequenting the *lycées*; of course, with this further tie between the inmates, the principle of association becomes still less mechanical. The march of the institution, however, its scale of expense, and the reasons for preferring it, will be found, I think, in nearly all cases pretty much what I have described them.

But the Commissioners will desire to hear of humbler public schools than the great *lycées* of Paris. Let us then take the *Collége Communal* at Boulogne, close at our own door, which almost any of us may have an opportunity of seeing. Again a large, imposing building; it stands in one of the principal streets of the town, and it gives its name, *Rue du Collége*, to one of the side streets. Again the University of France, with its guarantees and inspection; *Collége Communal de Boulogne-sur-Mer; Instruction Publique; Académie de Douai*, is the full style of the institution. 'The public establishments for secondary instruction,' says the organic law,* 'are the lyceums and the communal colleges.

---

* *Loi du 15 mars 1850 sur l'Enseignement*, art. 71, 72, 74, 75.

Boarding-houses may form part of them. The lyceums are founded and maintained by the State, with the co-operation * of the departments and towns. The communal colleges are founded and maintained by the communes. In order to establish a communal college, every town must fulfil the following conditions: it must furnish premises suitable for the purpose, and undertake to keep them up; in these premises it must place and keep up the necessary fittings for the classes, and for the boarding-house too, if the school is to take boarders; it must guarantee, for five years at least, the fixed salary of the principal and the professors, which shall be held to be an obligatory charge upon the commune in case the resources of the college itself, the school-fees paid by day scholars and the proceeds of the boarding-house, are insufficient. The object and extent of the instruction in each communal college shall be determined, regard being had to the wants of the locality, by the Minister of Public Instruction, in Council,† on hearing the proposition of the Municipal Council and the opinion of the Academic Council thereon.'

The Communal College of Boulogne exists in conformity with these provisions of the law. Its inspectors are the rector of the Academy of Douai, the academy-inspector for the department of the Pas de Calais, and any one of the eight inspectors-general for secondary instruction whose tour of inspection brings him that way. It is a communal college *de plein' exercice*; that is, it has not only the elementary division and the division of grammar, but that of humanities also. And it is the college of the municipality, kept in its own hands, and entrusted *en régie* only (as it is called) to the principal as their functionary. Sometimes the communal college is made entirely over to the principal, with a subvention from the municipality, and the condition annexed that he shall take a certain number of scholars on certain terms. Beyond this, he may make what he can out of the school, and he conducts it at his own risk. The principal of the Boulogne College, M. Blaringhem, told me that he had held a municipal college in this manner, but that he preferred

---

* This co-operation consists in the foundation of scholarships (*bourses*).
† This is the Imperial Council of Public Instruction.

to hold it as at present, *en régie*, with a fixed salary.   I asked
him if it was not more lucrative to be able to charge for
one's boarders what one liked, instead of having the tariff
settled by authority; he said, no, because the public school
tariff fixed, with the most rare exceptions, the tariff for all
the schools in the country.   And this is what I have again
and again been told.

So the Boulogne College has its council of administration,
like a *lycée*, to overlook its business affairs, and to go through
its accounts in concert with the principal, as the council of a
lycée goes through them in concert with the provisor.   Only
as the college is a municipal institution, while the *lycée* is a
State institution, and it is the French rule that the administration of a public establishment shall mainly belong to that
public authority,—whether the State, the department, or the
commune,—with which it is in immediate connection, the
council of administration of the Boulogne college is a municipal body.   It consists of the mayor, the ex-mayor, a judge
of the civil tribunal at Boulogne, the president of the Boulogne tribunal of commerce, and two lawyers, one of them a
member of the Boulogne municipal council, the other the
mayor's adjoint.   The scale of school-charges is fixed by this
body in concert with the principal, and with the sanction of
the rector of the Academy of Douai, to which Boulogne belongs.   The charges are much lower for French boys than at
Paris.   A boarder under 12 pays but 23*l.* a year; over 12
but under 15 he pays 25*l.*; above 15, 28*l.*   The day scholar's
fee is the old Paris school fee before 1853, 100 fr. (4*l.*)   For
English boys (of whom there are several) the rate is higher,
because they have to be taught the French language; but
for them the rate is not in itself high; for boarders under 12
years of age, 39*l.* a year, from 12 to 15, 42*l.*, above 15, 48*l.*
English day scholars pay 4*l.*, 5*l.*, or 8*l.*

The school arrangements, hours, and lessons are just the
same as in a *lycée*; there is primary instruction for the little
boys, then an elementary and a grammar division with their
regular classes; then humanities conducting to the degree
of bachelor of letters, and a scientific training conducting to a
degree in sciences, and to the great Government Schools.   The
college staff consists,—besides the chaplain, the teachers of

modern languages and drawing, and a primary schoolmaster,—
of the principal, and twelve regents, one for philosophy, one for
history, three for science and mathematics, seven for classics.
The principal must hold at least the degree of bachelor; eight
of the twelve regents (all above the division of grammar) must
hold the degree of licentiate, the other four must hold that
of bachelor. The degrees of licentiate and bachelor are obtained, as I have said, only by examination. The degree of
licentiate means more than an Oxford or Cambridge degree
of master of arts, for which there is no examination. But I
should like to see in any one of our considerable towns over
against Boulogne,—Dover, Ramsgate, Canterbury,—a public
school with a staff of 13 functionaries holding degrees, literary or scientific, from the universities of Oxford, Cambridge,
or London. And the four other principal towns of the *Pas
de Calais* have each, as well as Boulogne, their public school;
Saint Omer * has a *lycée*, Arras, Béthune, and Saint Pol have
communal colleges.

It is obvious that when the public schools of a country
educate 66,000 of its boys of the upper and middle classes,
the work left for private schools to do cannot be nearly so
considerable as with us. I have remarked already that the
population of the nine schools on which a Royal Commission
reported barely exceeds the half of that of the great classical
schools of Paris alone. But the *Public Schools Calendar* gives
a list, after the nine schools, of all the chief endowed grammar
schools of this country, and of the chief schools of modern
foundation, such as Cheltenham and Marlborough. Certainly
a good many of the endowed schools in the list do not at
present rank as high as even a communal college; but giving
all of them, and all of the schools of modern foundation enumerated in the calendar, the rank of public schools, and
adding their population to that of the nine schools, I find
that our public school boys in England number (in round
figures) 16,000, to match the 66,000 public school boys of
France. I think the English reader will be startled, as I was,
by this comparison. If a public school education is an ad-

---

* Arras is the chief town of the Pas de Calais, but the *lycée* is not always in the
chief town.

vantage, then this advantage is enjoyed by 50,000 more boys in France than with us.

Therefore private education is by its volume a much less important affair in France than with us. I cannot pretend to give any accurate statistics of it. There are said to be 1,395 institutions of secondary instruction in France conducted by laymen or by the secular clergy; the clerical seminaries, therefore,—223 in number,—are included in this body of schools. The 1,395 schools have a total of 112,628 scholars. There are, besides, 33 institutions of secondary instruction belonging to religious corporations; these 33 have a total of 5,285 scholars. This gives, in round numbers, 52,000 boys in private secondary schools, clerical and lay, against 66,000 in the secondary schools of the State. The French Government are intending to bring out a great statistical work on secondary instruction, and this will contain interesting information on the number and population of the private schools; but this work is still only in prospect. I find that Paris contains 131 private secondary schools (*établissements libres d'instruction publique*), but in this number are included establishments like M. Cousin's and the *Institution Massin*, acting mainly as feeders to the public schools; and a very large number of the 131 are places of this kind. If we take the departments, where the private secondary schools are almost universally independent of the *lycées*, we shall be struck with their insignificant number compared with what we are used to in England. Let us take the Academy of Paris. The district of this Academy includes nine departments: Seine, Cher, Eure et Loir, Loir et Cher, Loiret, Marne, Oise, Seine et Marne, Seine et Oise. Setting aside the metropolitan department, the number of the private secondary schools is as follows: in Cher, four; in Eure et Loir, four; in Loir et Cher, four; in Loiret, four; in Marne, six; in Oise, five; in Seine et Marne, eleven; and in Seine et Oise (a department *quasi* metropolitan, of which Versailles is the capital), nineteen; 57 in all. These same eight departments contain four *lycées* * and twenty-one communal colleges.

* The easy access to the great *lycées* of the metropolitan department explains the fewness of the *lycées* in the other departments of this academy district.

Two private establishments which I visited I will mention, because they both enjoy a high reputation. One is the school of Sainte Geneviève in the Rue des Postes, the other is the Jesuits' school at Vaugirard. Like the school at Vaugirard, the school in the Rue des Postes is in the hands of the religious. Both are considerably more expensive than the public schools, keep up a brisk competition with them, and make them very jealous. This is particularly the case with the school in the Rue des Postes, which is a special preparatory school for the Polytechnic, Saint Cyr, the Naval School, and other Government establishments of the kind; the charge is 1,800 fr. a year (72*l.*), and certain matters are extras which are not extras in the *lycées*; a boy here does not cost less than 80*l.* But the course is for not more than two or three years; a boy comes here at the age when he would be entering *mathématiques élémentaires* at the *lycée*; here, too, he gets a thorough mathematical training, but this school aims at uniting this training with a truly religious education (*unir de fortes études mathématiques à une éducation vraiement religieuse* *). I found 300 boys here, with 35 masters, half for superintendence and half for teaching. It is, of course, to its superintendence that an establishment of this kind aims at giving a character entirely different to that of the superintendence in the establishments of the State. For the special scientific training of their pupils these religious are free to use, and do use, along with duly qualified teachers of their own order, the best lay instructors of the capital, the same as the *lycées* themselves employ. Their charges are high, and they can afford to provide thoroughly good teaching. Private tuition is an extra, and their pupils are the sons of wealthy people and can afford this extra. They admit their pupils with careful tests as to character and capacity, and they keep them for the first three months on probation; the seclusion is greater than in the *lycées*; the boys have 'leave out' but once a month instead of once a fortnight; visits in the *parloir* are permitted only twice a week instead of every day. No wonder, then, that this abundance of care, concentration, and appliances bears fruit, and that the candidates from the Rue

---

* The words of the prospectus of the school.

des Postes are remarkably successful in the examinations for
the Government schools.

I was particularly struck with the good appearance of the
boys here. In the *lycées* I had been struck with their good
manners, and the natural politeness they showed, down quite
to the little boys, when tried by the unusual incident of the
entrance of a stranger and a foreigner into their school-room;
I am sure in England there would have been much less
rising and bowing, and much more staring and giggling;
but here, besides having good manners, the boys certainly
looked, I thought, fresher and better than in the *lycées*. They
are a great many of them the sons of the old noble families
of France, amongst which, as is well known, Catholic senti-
ment is strong. They have probably had more advantages
for their health and growth and good looks than the mass of
the *lycée* boys, and the grounds and recreation of the school
itself, though not without a general resemblance to those of
a *lycée*, had something much more attractive in them. The
great religious house, with its large cool galleries looking on
the convents and gardens of that old quarter of Paris, and
the figures of the religious moving about, had certainly a
repose and refreshment for the spirits which in the great
barrack-like machine of a *lycée* is wanting.

The same may be said of the Jesuits' school at Vaugirard.
This school is even more interesting than that of the Rue
des Postes, being a complete school, while that is only a set
of scientific classes. At Vaugirard they go through the
whole course, as in the *lycées*, from primary instruction to
philosophie and *mathématiques spéciales*. Here, too, as in the
Rue des Postes, they are very successful in the examinations
for the great Government Schools; and for the same reasons.
The boys are all boarders; the fees are high (about the same
rate as in the Rue des Postes); no expense need be spared,
and the tutoring as well as the class-lesson is very careful
and good. The instruction is given by the religious, and as
they work for love and for the good of their order, of course
one great cause of expense in lay schools,—the payment of
teachers,—is cut off. I heard the teaching in *philosophie*,
rhétorique, quatrième, and the elementary division. The
Jesuits seemed to me quite to merit their reputation as

teachers. The superior is in every respect a remarkable man. He was a distinguished pupil of the *École Normale;* then he became a Jesuit, and, of course, quitted the service of the State; but his experience in the *École Normale* is no bad thing for his school. The good appearance of the boys struck me here as in the Rue des Postes, and the number of well-known names one heard among the boys was curious, and showed from what class this school is fed. Among the little ones I found a Maronite, and a young American from Mobile who could hardly speak French yet, and was glad, poor child, to be addressed in his own language. The cosmopolitan character of France is well shown by the number of boys from different parts of the world whom one finds getting their education in her schools. At Saint Louis I noticed a boy whose face was evidently that of an Oriental, and found on inquiry that he was the son of a Persian of rank, and had been sent there all the way from Persia.

The instruction at Vaugirard, having the degree of bachelor or the Government Schools in view, cannot but follow, in general, the same line as that of the *lycées*; the tutoring is the great difference. The house, class-room, and recreation arrangements have also a general similarity with those of the public schools, but the sense of a more agreeable, happier, and milder life than that of the *lycée* is felt at Vaugirard, and more at Vaugirard than in the Rue des Postes; for Vaugirard, though still Paris, is the very outskirts of Paris, and of the convent quarter of Paris,—a region full of trees and gardens. The Jesuit school is at the extremity of Vaugirard and gets the air of the country. In the Rue des Postes, too, the boys are older, and it is for the little boys that the cast-iron movement of the *lycée* appears most dismal, and the guidance of the ecclesiastical hand in bringing them up seems most protecting and natural. Something of this ecclesiastical shelter we are used to in the great schools and universities in England; and perhaps it is on this account that in spite of all which is to be said against the Jesuits and their training, I could not help feeling that the Vaugirard school was of all the schools I saw in France the one in which I would soonest have been a schoolboy.

Sorèze, Lacordaire's school, which I have elsewhere * described, was a first-class private school under the Dominicans, as Vaugirard under the Jesuits. The law forbids the title of *lycée* or *collége* to be taken by any private establishments, but the Minister of Public Instruction can authorise certain old established schools of this kind to keep the name of *collége* if they have been used to bear it. It is in this way that two out of the seven great classical schools of Paris, *Rollin* and *Stanislas*, get the title of *collége*. They, however, though not state establishments, not only follow the same course of teaching as the *lycées*, but employ professors of the same stamp. Private establishments are bound, as I have already said, to have for their head the holder of the degree of bachelor at least, or else of a certificate of capacity; but for their assistant teachers they may employ whom they will. But they are bound to keep a register with the full name, age, and birthplace of each assistant whom they employ, and to produce it whenever the inspector requires. And the authorities of public instruction have the power,† in a case of misconduct or immorality, to reprimand, suspend, or altogether interdict from teaching, either the head of a private school or any of his assistants, with the right of appeal, when the penalty goes so far as suspension or interdiction, to the Imperial Council in Paris. A teacher interdicted cannot be employed thenceforth in any school public or private. These powers seem extensive; but I am bound to say that all the private teachers whom I asked informed me that they were exercised in a way to cause no complaint; and that neither as to authorising the establishment of a private secondary school in the first place, nor as to inspecting or interfering with it afterwards, was the action of Government in the least degree unfair or vexatious.

The *séminaires*, where the clergy are educated, are under ecclesiastical management. They are nominally subject to state superintendence; ‡ but so far as I could learn this superintendence comes to nothing, and no inspector ever enters them.

---

* See *A French Eton, or Middle-Class Education and the State.* (Macmillan.)

† *Loi du* 15 *mars* 1850 *sur l'Enseignement,* art. 67, 68.

‡ *Loi du* 15 *mars* 1850, art. 70.

CHAPTER VII.

CHARACTER OF DISCIPLINE AND INSTRUCTION IN THE FRENCH SECONDARY SCHOOLS.

DISCIPLINE IN THE FRENCH SCHOOLS—INSTRUCTION—GREEK—LATIN—VERSIONS DICTÉES—SCHOOL-BOOKS—THE MOTHER-TONGUE—MODERN LANGUAGES—GEOGRAPHY—HISTORY—MATHEMATICS AND THE NATURAL SCIENCES—FOREIGN JUDGMENT OF ENGLISH MATHEMATICAL TEACHING—RELIGIOUS INSTRUCTION—REALSCHULE INSTRUCTION—RECENT ATTEMPTS TO DEVELOPE IT IN FRANCE—M. DURUY'S ENSEIGNEMENT SECONDAIRE SPÉCIAL.

THE long school-hours and the constant supervision in the French schools are favourable to discipline, and the Frenchman is born with a turn for military precision and exactitude which makes the teacher fall easily into the habit of command, and the pupil into that of obedience. French teachers who have seen our schools are struck with the greater looseness of order and discipline in them, even during class hours; and I have seen large classes in France worked and moved with a perfection of drill that one sometimes finds in the best elementary schools in England, but rarely, I think, in our classical schools. Our government through prepositors or prefects, and our fagging, are unknown in the French schools; for the former, the continual presence and supervision of the *maître d'étude* leaves no place; the latter is abhorrent to French ideas. The set of modern opinion is undoubtedly against fagging, and perhaps also against government through the sixth form; one may doubt, however, whether the force of old and cherished custom, the removal of excess and abuses in the exercise of these two powers, and certain undeniable benefits attending that of, at any rate, the latter of the two, may not yet long preserve them in the great English schools. The same can hardly be said of flogging, which, without entering into long discussions about it, one may say the modern spirit has irrevocably condemned as a school punishment, so that it will more and more come to appear half disgusting, half ridiculous, and a teacher will find it more and more difficult to inflict it without a loss of self-respect. The feeling on the Continent is very strong on this point. The punishments in the French schools are impositions and confinement; at Vanves I saw a kind of *punishment-parade,* the culprits being marched round and round a court. The employment of punishments, however, is certainly less than with us, and here, too, the great number of school hours saves the French schoolmaster from a difficulty. It is a part of the censor's business to collect, and to give at the end of every week to the provisor, a report from the usher on the behaviour, and from the professor on the progress, of each boy in the school; at the end of every quarter the provisor forwards the summary of these reports to the parents.

Comparing the instruction with that of our own great classical schools, one is at once struck by the fact that the French schools carry Greek by no means so far as we do. Their Greek composition is next to nothing; there is no Greek verse, and even the Greek exercise has lately been abolished in *troisième* and *seconde,* on the ground that it was the merest grammatical exercise, not carried far enough to give the pupil the least power of really writing Greek, and that an exercise of this sort was out of place after *troisième* began. Different *lycées* have a special reputation for different branches of instruction; thus Saint Louis is famous for mathematics, Louis-le-Grand for the humanities generally, Charlemagne for Greek. But even at Charlemagne the upper boys, whom I heard at lesson under a distinguished professor, M. Boissier, had certainly nothing like the mastery of Greek of the upper boys in our best public schools; one might almost say that in the iambics of Sophocles they could get along pretty well, but that any chorus was decidedly too much for them. The Greek lessons are much fewer in number than with us. The grounding seemed to me good enough. The little boys in *sixième* whom I heard at *Bonaparte* saying their Greek grammar left nothing to be desired.

In Latin the French schools seem to me quite equal with

ours ; perhaps it is from the affinity of the language with their own, but they seem, if there is a difference between our best schools and theirs, to be more at home with Latin, and to take to it more kindly than we do.   They do not, however, get through nearly so much of the Latin authors, but their Latin composition, prose and verse, is very good.   From the specimens I saw I should say they had a Ciceronian and Virgilian tradition just like some of our famous schools, and produced work very much the same as the best of them.   In this respect both we and they, I think, beat Germany, though a German boy has a fuller command of a Latin of a certain kind than either our boys or the French.

Both in Latin and Greek the quantity of writing work done by the French boys strikes an Englishman with astonishment ; the professors seem to be extraordinarily fond of *versions dictées*, as they are called ; a passage from a classic is dictated, the boy takes it away with him, translates it out of class hours, and a good deal of time in a subsequent class hour is given to the revision of this translation of his.   A day boy sometimes makes strange work of the passage dictated, and then, as he has not the *étude* to do his translation in, gets no opportunity of setting himself straight, and is altogether bewildered.   I cannot but think that the French might with advantage write a good deal less, and adopt our plan of making the boys learn and say their lesson out of a book a good deal more.   In our elementary schools I have often regretted that the master teaches the lessons so much, instead of making the boys, as in our classical schools, learn it beforehand ; the French professors proceed more like our elementary teachers in this respect, and then, when the master *teaches* the lesson, of course there has to be a great deal of going over it again afterwards, in the *étude* or the *conférence*.   The lycées have much more of this than our schools, and I am inclined to prefer, at least for teaching classics, our plan, which makes the boy depend more on himself, and, above all, takes him through a great deal more of an author.

The French use books of selections a great deal, and I believe Rugby was rather an exception to the common rule of the English public schools in using them in the higher forms

so very little. I suppose no one who has been used to the
Rugby practice can much like the other. About their school
books in general the French are conservative, and amusing
stories are told of German scholars at Paris pointing out
errors in the received school books, and getting a fine, instead
of thanks, for their pains. It is a just instinct, however,
which makes the French university cling to fixity in its
elementary school books, and their boys learn grammar
better than ours in consequence. A boy does not enter into
the *rationale* of grammar; what he wants is a system of clear
categories to refer the cases in his reading to. What is that
infinitive?—It comes under the *hinc spargere voces* category.—
Why is it *patientiá* after *abutére*?—By the rule that *utor* and
its compounds take an ablative. This is a good mental
exercise for a boy, and he is capable of it; but that he may
practise it with advantage, his categories should be as plain
and few as possible, and should be firmly fixed in his own
mind and in his questioner's. When he is capable of com-
prehending the *rationale* of grammar (quite another affair),
he is of an age to *consult* a grammar, not learn it, and his
grammar can then hardly be too philosophical and full. Half
a dozen grammars of this kind are sufficient for the needs of
a whole school. But we, and the Germans too, keep trying
to put the *rationale* of grammar into the first grammar, the
grammar that is learnt, not consulted; the boy's mental
digestion rejects the *rationale*, and meanwhile the fixity
needed for categories to which he is promptly and precisely
to refer all his cases,—an effort of which his mind is perfectly
capable,—is sacrificed. Thus, with all the faults of the old
Latin grammar, twenty years ago boys of twelve and thirteen
did their grammar work a thousand times better than they
do it now, because the substance of fixity of categories had
not then been abandoned for the shadow of *rationale*. Up to
a certain point, therefore, I think the French authorities wise
in their zeal for fixity of text-book.

From the bottom of the French schools to the top one
finds recitation, reading, and exercises, in the mother tongue.
Writing French is as considerable a part of a boy's work as
writing Latin. So far is this pushed that there are to be

found in France hostile critics of the *lycées* who say that to
judge by their teaching you would suppose every boy in them
was meant to be afterwards by profession a man of letters.
It is probable too much stress may be laid on teaching matters
of literary workmanship and style, graces which, after all,
nascuntur non fiunt; but the reading and reciting from the
classics of the mother tongue and the getting some knowledge of its literary history, is clear gain ; and if the French
attempt to teach too much, and of what cannot be taught, in
style and the art of writing, we do not, or at least did not
when I knew our schools, attempt to teach enough, and of
what can.

M. Duruy is very anxious to promote the teaching of modern
languages in the schools, and that the boys should learn to
speak them, not to read them only. From the beginning of
the grammar division to the top of the school modern languages form a regular and seriously taught part of the school
work, and I have heard the little boys in *sixième* patiently
practised at speaking sentences in English or German. This
attempt, of course, necessitates the employment of foreign
teachers, and then comes the well-known difficulty as to discipline, which the French experience just as we do. Perhaps,
from the many other fields open to Englishmen, the supply
of good English teachers abroad is particularly limited; that
of Germans seemed to be considerably better. I mean, it is
much more common, I think, to find an educated, competent
German, a man in whom his employers have a good bargain,
teaching in a French school, than to find an Englishman of
like stamp there. With these drawbacks much is not at
present effected; but more, I think (still speaking from my
own remembrance of our great schools), than is done with
us ; partly because the conditions of the problem are better
understood, partly because its solution is more seriously
attempted.

Geography forms the object of distinct lessons of which
the graduated course is traced in the ministerial programme.
Neither the German classical schools nor ours teach it, in
general, in this manner; and after the elementary classes it
is surely best taught in connection with other lessons, which

afford plenty of occasions for teaching it, and give a better chance, by attaching it to interesting events, of making it likely to be remembered and more than a dry and soon lost nomenclature. The professor in France uses the black board and traces outline maps with an adroitness and accuracy which may often be seen in our elementary schools, but not often, I think, in our classical.

History, too, is taught according to a graduated programme, which begins in the lowest class of the grammar division with the East,—Egypt and Asia,—and proceeds through Greece and Rome to the history of the modern nations, finishing, as I have already said, in the philosophy class with contemporary history. The programme system, —the programme being drawn, as it is, by a competent hand and with great care,—seems to me of service here. It gives the teacher himself a valuable clue, serves to guide his reading, and leads him to group his ideas and methodise his teaching. I do not think any educated man could read the programme of Middle-Age and modern history for the French *lycées* without profit,—without being reminded of gaps in his knowledge, and stimulated to fill them. The history lessons I heard given to the higher classes were evidence in favour of the system, for they were well-arranged and very interesting.

Modern languages, geography, and history have an *agrégation* of their own; that for modern languages having been introduced by the present minister. They have thus, of course, special professors, and are not taught, as I remember them taught in our schools, by each classical master to his own form.

As often as I approach mathematics and natural sciences, I am confronted by my own ignorance of them, and warned not to say much. Something, however, of what I heard and saw I must report as well as I can. The French have a reputation for their teaching of these matters; their language is excellent for it, and their text-books are clear and good. But what strikes one most, is the prominence of oral teaching here; and oral teaching seems here in its right place. The text-book is merely the basis of the professor's instruction, and by itself can give no idea of what the French mathematical teaching is. In these studies, again, the programmes seem to be of advantage, and the system of revision and repetition of lessons, which in classics I thought pushed too far, is so serviceable in mathematics and natural sciences that it may well have got its currency from its usefulness in these branches. I never shall forget the impression made upon me by teacher and pupils in the class of *mathématiques spéciales* at Saint-Louis, under a young and distinguished professor, M. Vacquant. Teaching so vivid, and a class of fifty so borne along, I should hardly have thought possible. No pupil is allowed to enter the class of *mathématiques spéciales* without being first examined to test his ability to profit by it. But down to the arithmetic of the lower classes the teaching, in this branch, seemed to me always searching and good. A distinguished Swiss, well known to many persons in this country, M. William de la Rive, told me he could trace in the educated class of Frenchmen a precision of mind distinctly due to the sound and close mathematical training of their schools. I heard, too, several lessons in the natural sciences; M. Duruy has sought to strengthen the whole of the scientific teaching at the same time that he did away with the *bifurcation*. The mathematical lessons, however, seemed to me better than the lessons in physics; partly, no doubt, because the latter need an apparatus for illustration and experiment which the former do not, and which a school cannot always procure in due abundance and efficiency. But the French lay the greatest stress on the importance of teaching the natural sciences, and regard mathematics as subsidiary to this object; they severely criticise our Cambridge teaching for devoting itself so exclusively to pure mathematics, and making the instrument into an end. The barrenness in great men and great results which has since Newton's time attended the Cambridge mathematical teaching is mainly due, they say, to this false tendency. Comte's judgment on the study of sidereal astronomy is well known, and the leaning of practice and opinion among French mathematical teachers at present tends in the same direction as that judgment.

In general, the respect professed in France for the mathematical and scientific teaching of our secondary schools is as low as that professed for our classical teaching is high. A French schoolmaster who had seen a number of our schools said to me: 'Your boys do not learn arithmetic, the science of numbers; they learn to reckon (*le calcul*).' And every one who has watched a French teacher employing with his pupils the simple process called *réduction à l'unité*, and has also watched an English boy's bewildered dealing with a rule of three sum, and heard his questions about its 'statement,' which to him is a mere trick, learnt mechanically, not understood, and easily misapplied, has a good notion of the difference between the arithmetic of French and of English schools. I must not forget to add that our geometry teaching was in foreign eyes sufficiently condemned when it was said that we still used *Euclid*. One of the great sins of Cambridge was her retention of *Euclid*. I am bound to say that the Germans and the Swiss entirely agree with the French on this point. *Euclid*, they all said, was quite out of date, and was a thoroughly unfit text-book to teach geometry from. I was, of course, astounded; and when I asked why *Euclid* was an unfit text-book to teach geometry from, I was told that Euclid's propositions were drawn out with a view to meet all possible cavils, and not with a view of developing geometrical ideas in the most lucid and natural manner. This to me, in my ignorance, sounded plausible; but at any rate the foreign *consensus* against the use of *Euclid* is something striking, and I cannot but call the English reader's attention to it.

I have several times mentioned the *aumôniers*, or chaplains, attached to the French public schools. None of these schools, secondary or primary, are secular schools; in all of them religious instruction is given. It is given, too, in the vast majority of private schools. An hour's lesson in the week, certain exercises and prizes in connection with this lesson, and service on Sundays, are what this instruction amounts to in the secondary schools. The provisor and the chaplain regulate it between them; that of Catholic boys is under the inspection of the bishop of the diocese or his delegate, in concert with the provisor. Protestant and Jewish boys receive the religious instruction of their own communion, regulated, *mutatis mutandis*, precisely like that of Catholic boys. The great *lycées* of Paris have Protestant and Jewish chaplains attached to them, just as they have Catholic chaplains. Where Protestants or Jews are not numerous enough for the school to have a special chaplain for them, boys of those persuasions still receive their religious instruction from ministers of their own creed appointed to visit them, and are entirely exempted from the religious instruction of the Catholics. I cannot myself see that the religious lessons (I do not, of course, speak of the services and ordinances of religion) come to very much in secondary instruction, though I must think, differing in this respect from many liberals, that they have an important and indispensable part in primary. But it is indisputable that they give rise neither in France nor Germany to any religious difficulty, as we say, whatever; they are regulated with absolute fairness, and there are no complaints at all of improper interference and proselytism. This, I say, is indisputable; and Protestants and Jews would testify to it as much as Catholics.

Hitherto all the schools spoken of have been classical schools, with Latin and Greek for the staple of instruction, and a greater or less admixture of mathematics and natural sciences with these. But in France, as elsewhere, an important sign of the times is the dissatisfaction with the predominance and omnipresence of Latin and Greek in secondary instruction. The greatest lover of the classics must admit that the modern spirit shows a certain hostility to them; and it is remarkable that in the secondary schools* of that great manifestation of the modern spirit, the French Revolution, only two professors out of fourteen were assigned to classics and *belles-lettres*. Napoleon, as I have already mentioned, did away with the central schools, and restored Latin and Greek to their old supremacy, but the *bifurcation*, which began as early as 1821, showed the tendency to elude, when

---

* The central schools instituted by the Convention in 1793.

it was impossible to gainsay, that supremacy. The upper primary schools, which were instituted by M. Guizot's school legislation in 1833, were another attempt to get rid of difficulties caused by that supremacy. The two great municipal schools of Paris, the *Collége Chaptal* and the *École Turgot,* were another. The *Collége Chaptal* has 1,000 scholars, 600 of them boarders paying 40*l.* a year. The *École Turgot* takes day scholars only, paying from 6*l.* to 7*l.* a year. The director of this latter school, which I visited, is M. Marguerin, a gentleman who was sent by the Prefect of the Seine to see our secondary schools in London, and whose report on what he saw there is well worth reading. In both these establishments Latin and Greek are wholly excluded from the school course, which is filled by French, modern languages, mathematics, natural sciences, and the other parts of what is called a modern education. The Christian Brothers have a successful school of the same kind at Passy. The friends of this new instruction were strong enough to insert in the organic school law of 1850 a paragraph binding the minister to appoint special juries to give certificates to the imparters of the *enseignement professionnel,* as it was then called.* Commissions were set to organise it, but while they proceeded slowly with their task, it so far organised itself that 64 *lycées* out of 74, and nearly all the communal colleges, made some provision for giving it; and last year, of the 66,000 boys in the schools of the State, 20,000 were receiving this modern instruction, while in private schools of one sort and another 40,000 boys were receiving it.

M. Duruy is entitled to speak for his own 20,000 boys at any rate, and he declares that, in their case, with hardly any exceptions, this instruction proved a failure.† The commissions appointed to study the subject reported that this instruction was a failure, too, in the majority of private schools. Its teachers were proceeding at random, without any distinct and well-digested plans; they were ill-paid, and

---

* 'Le ministre, sur l'avis du Conseil supérieur de l'instruction publique, instituera des jurys spéciaux pour l'enseignement professionnel.'—*Loi du* 14 *mars* 1850 *sur l'Enseignement,* art. 62.

† *Circulaire du* 2 *octobre* 1863 *relative à l'enseignement professionnel.*

their position was uncertain; they were, in general, without
the requisite collections and apparatus. A *grande inutilité*,
M. Duruy says, has to be transformed into an effective institution.

The law of the 21st of June of last year is designed so to
transform it. On the one hand, say the authors of that law,
to balance the old so-called liberal professions, for which a
classical education was supposed to be the best preparation,
there have arisen in modern society a number of industrial,
commercial, and agricultural professions, which did not exist
a hundred years ago, and which require a different preparation from that for the old professions. On the other hand,
the superior primary instruction of 1833, with a course of
study not ill adapted to the requirements of these new
claimants, did not take, because it had an air of inferiority
about it from its connection with the primary schools, and
'on veut rarement,' says the reporter to one of the commissions which examined the new law, 'avoir l'air d'être au
niveau des humbles.' So out of social vanity boys flocked
into the Latin and Greek classes for whom these classes were
not suitable; but the vanity, as M. Duruy shrewdly enough
says, which sets people against non-classical studies, does not
carry them so far as to make them pursue classical studies
with any success.

It was required, for the sons of a new class of professional
men not socially inferior to the members of the liberal professions, to provide schools of equal rank with the classical
schools. To effect this, two parallel courses of secondary
instruction have been formed; a secondary instruction in
arts and sciences, for boys destined to agriculture, commerce,
or manufactures; a secondary instruction in classics for boys
destined to the so-called liberal professions. The two courses
are to be of equal rank, held in the same institutions, and
furnished with the same encouragements. The teachers of
the one are to enjoy an equal position and to offer equal
guarantees with those of the other.

The new legislation, therefore, unites in the public schools
the classical and non-classical pupils in the same buildings,
under the same government, but gives the non-classical

pupils separate lessons, and separate professors. It establishes a normal school, occupying the old Benedictine abbey of Cluny, for the training of the latter. It provides a distinct aggregation for them, as the professors of classics, mathematics, and modern languages have a distinct aggregation. It fixes for them a scale of payment. It provides a separate supply of scholarships for their pupils, and it draws out a separate set of programmes for the new instruction. It institutes a local body, with the title of *conseil de perfectionnement,* in connection with each establishment where the new instruction is given, and a *conseil supérieur de perfectionnement* to advise the minister in Paris. Finally, it extends to private schools giving the new instruction that power of obtaining, if judged worthy, from the communes, departments, or state, a building and a subvention, which the law of 1850 bestowed on the private secondary schools.

It is the French theory that the State's duty is to establish models and so improve private institutions. M. Duruy has certainly taken great pains to adapt his model to the purpose for which it is wanted. The pupils of the new instruction are likely to have time for only a three or four years' course, instead of the seven or eight years' course of the classical school; and the new instruction, therefore, is arranged for four years, and for boys from about the age of 12 to 16. Even this shorter course is more likely than the classical course to be abridged by the boy's sudden withdrawal; it has been attempted, therefore, to make as far as possible each year's plan of study complete in itself. Neither for the professor, nor for the pupil, has the culture to be carried so far as in the classical school; for both, therefore, the highest class of payments is cut off. In Paris the rate of payment to the professors of the new instruction is about the rate of payment to classical professors in the provinces; out of Paris, something below this; but then these new teachers will often come from the class where only primary instruction at present goes recruiting for teachers, and to this class the rate of salary will appear good. The boys, whether boarders or day scholars, pay as in the elementary division and the grammar division of the classical school; the higher rates of *philosophie* and *mathématiques spéciales* are cut off. Provision is made for drafting into the classical school boys who show aptitudes which make the prolonged training, classical, or mathematical, of that school, desirable for them.

The name of the new instruction was rather a matter of difficulty. It had got that of 'professional,' but this word gives the idea of a school where particular trades and businesses are learnt, and this is not the design of the new schools. 'We do not,' say their promoters, 'put the workshop in the school; in these new establishments the teaching is still a means, not an end, and when the pupil leaves them, the knowledge he possesses will be general knowledge. The true professional school comes later; it is such a school as the School of Commerce, or the School of Agriculture, or the School of Woodcraft.' Others proposed the name 'French;' we in England have inclined to that of 'modern;' but the name actually adopted is that of 'special,' not a very good one as it seems to me. *Enseignement secondaire spécial* is the authorised description of the new instruction.

Leaving out Latin and Greek altogether, it comprehends the mother tongue and its literature, history, geography, mathematics, natural sciences, modern languages, information of common use about the government, laws, administration, commerce, industry, and agriculture of France; accounts, book-keeping, drawing, music, and gymnastics. Mathematics and physics are taught with a direct view to application; the three great classes of professions, industrial, commercial, and agricultural,—for one or other of which every pupil is supposed to be destined,—being had in mind. Instruction in morals and religion forms, as in all the public schools, part of the course. The new and elaborate programmes for the whole course are drawn with great care, and are well worth studying. They are contained in a volume which has recently issued from the department of public instruction at Paris.* Taking the boy on his leaving the primary school at 11 or 12, when he is supposed (and

---

* *Enseignement secondaire spécial ; décrets, arrêtés, programmes et documents relatifs à l'exécution de la loi du* 21 *juin* 1865. Paris: Imprimerie Impériale, 1866.

this is worth remarking) besides his religious instruction, reading, and writing, to possess the elements of grammar, the four rules of arithmetic both in whole numbers and in vulgar and decimal fractions, and the metric system, it gives him, first, a preparatory year, in which what he possesses is perfected, his slight smattering of history and geography exchanged for a methodical foundation of those studies, a modern language, geometry, and natural history begun. Then, by a regular gradation, which yet leaves the instruction of each year as far as possible a complete whole in itself, it carries him through a four years' course in the matters named by the law. The attention paid to teaching the mother tongue, and not only its history and literature but how to write it, is as remarkable in this course as in that of the classical schools. But perhaps the greatest novelty is the information on common subjects, as it may in brief be called. The choice and arrangement of this information, simple matter as it seems when it stands in the programme, must have cost much thought and pains, there being such a lack of models to follow; and it seems to me most successful. The programme headed *législation usuelle*, giving the outline of a course on the public and private law and the administrative organisation of France,—how the government is composed, what are the functions of its different departments, how the municipalities are constituted, how the army is recruited, how taxes are raised, what is the legal and judicial system of the country, how in the most important relations of civil life, marriage, inheritance, holding property, buying, selling, lending, borrowing, partnership, the laws affect the citizen,—this programme in particular seems to me quite admirably composed, both for what it inserts and what it omits. The programmes on the legislation of commerce and industry, and on rural, industrial, and commercial economy, are also very interesting; but each of these is more particularly designed for a single division of pupils, according to the class of profession to which they are destined; whereas 'the programme for *législation usuelle* is designed for all, containing what it is important for all alike to know; and therefore this latter programme is not so easy a programme to prepare, and has a more general interest when prepared.

It is as yet too soon to judge of the success of this important addition of M. Duruy's to the public secondary instruction of France, but the correspondent of the *Museum*,—an English educational periodical deserving to be more widely known than it is,—seems to me not far from the truth, when he says that to find a population for these new schools is the difficulty, as the rich class of people wanting to use them is small, and the large class of people wanting to use them is poor. The loud demand for them comes chiefly from a certain number of rich industrialists, with views about education, and opposed to the tyranny of Latin and Greek, who yet wish their sons' school to be a school of as high social rank as the classical school. This has been done by giving the new instruction the title and apparatus of secondary instruction, and its cost, of course, along with them. A boarder in one of the new schools pays from 40*l.* to 45*l.* a year; a day scholar pays from 8*l.* to 10*l.* The rich industrialist with views about education is of course enchanted to pay this, and give his boy the prestige of a *lycée* at the same time that he gets rid of what he thinks its rubbish of Latin and Greek; but these rich industrialists are not very numerous. An immense class of well-to-do parents, whom M. Duruy would gladly see relieving the classical school of what he calls its *non-valeurs*, boys *sans aptitude pour les belles-lettres*, and sending them to the modern school, have still, and for some time are likely to have, the notion that a social stamp is put upon a youth by a classical education, and they continue sending their boys to the classical school to obtain this stamp. On the other hand, the instruction of the modern school is the very thing which the artisan class, the higher portion of it at any rate, desires; it is the supreme object, in the way of education, of the ambition of this class, which is quite free from any genteel weakness for Latin and Greek; but here the rates of payment form an insuperable obstacle.

Nevertheless, as one may say of flogging, that the set of the modern spirit is so decisively against it that it is doomed, whatever plausible arguments may be urged on its behalf, so is the set of the modern spirit so decisively in favour of the new instruction, that M. Duruy's creation, whatever reasons may be given why it should not succeed, will probably in the end succeed in some shape or other. This current of opinion is, indeed, on the Continent, so wide and strong as to be fast growing irresistible; and it is not the work of authority. Authority does all that can be done in favour of the old classical training; ministers of state sing its praises; the reporter of the commission charged to examine the new law is careful to pay to the old training and its pre-eminence a homage amusingly French.* Men of the world envy us a House of Commons where Latin quotations are still made, school authorities are full of stories to show how boys trained in Latin and Greek beat the pupils of the new instruction even in their own field. Still in the body of society there spreads a growing disbelief in Greek and Latin, at any rate as at present taught; a growing disposition to make modern languages and the natural sciences take their place. I remark this in Germany as well as in France; and in Germany too, as in France, the movement is in no wise due to the school authorities, but is rather in their despite, and against their advice and testimony. I shall have an opportunity, by-and-by, to say a few words respecting what appears to me the real import of this movement, and the part of truth and of error in the ideas which favour it. All I wish now to lay stress upon is its volume and irresistibility.

* 'On ne saurait trop exalter l'importance sociale des lettres classiques. *Ce sont elles qui ont assuré depuis des siècles la suprématie intellectuelle de la France.'* —*Enseignement secondaire spécial*, p. 438.

CHAPTER VIII.

SUPERIOR OR UNIVERSITY INSTRUCTION IN FRANCE.

SUPERIOR INSTRUCTION—FACULTIES—LETTERS AND SCIENCES—THEOLOGY—LAW— MEDICINE—OTHER INSTITUTIONS IN FRANCE FOR SUPERIOR INSTRUCTION—USE OF SUCH INSTITUTIONS—CONCLUSION.

I HAVE incidentally said something of the superior instruction of France as I went along, and at the outset I disclaimed all pretension to treat it fully; but a very short notice of it as a whole ought to be given before I pass elsewhere. The superior instruction of France consists of the faculties, and of certain other institutions,—such as, for instance, the College of France, the Museum of Natural History, the School of Living Oriental Languages,—where the studies and lectures are of a pitch which presupposes that the student's secondary instruction is completed. The students of French superior instruction are not, like our undergraduates at Oxford or Cambridge, boarded in colleges, they only attend lectures. There were in 1862 no less than 23,371 students in the French faculties; 14,364 of this number were in those of Paris. There are five faculties: theology, law, medicine, sciences, and letters. The faculties are attached to the academies, of which by the law of 1854 there are, as I have more than once said, sixteen.* It is only sciences and letters which are represented in every academy. For each of these, therefore, there are 16 seats of faculties in France, with a total of 97 chairs for sciences, 86 for letters. Large towns, not the seat of a faculty of sciences or letters, have the power of establishing auxiliary schools† of superior instruction, attendance at the lectures

---

* Two more, Chambéry and Algiers, have been added, but neither of them is as yet the seat of any faculty.

† *Écoles préparatoires à l'enseignement supérieur des sciences et des lettres.*

of which is allowed to count, within certain limits, as attendance at faculty lectures. To pass beyond the degree of bachelor it is necessary to have attended certain courses of professors' lectures. Of course the chairs of a faculty in Paris are almost always much more numerous than in the provincial academies, and in the more important of these they are more numerous than in the less important. The faculty of sciences has in the academy of Paris, for example, 18 chairs; in the academies of Clermont, Nancy, and Poitiers it has but four. These four, which may be taken as representing the absolute necessary for a faculty of sciences, are the following: physics, chemistry, pure and applied mathematics, natural history. In letters the Paris faculty has eleven chairs, the provincial faculties have five each, which in all of them, except that of Toulouse, are the same: ancient literature, French literature, foreign literature, philosophy, history. Toulouse substitutes for chairs of ancient and of foreign literature chairs of Greek and of Latin literature.

Theology has seven seats of faculties, five for the Catholics and two for the Protestants. The seats of the two Protestant faculties are Montauban and Strasburg. The chairs of these faculties are nowhere more than seven or fewer than five. The subjects common to them all are dogmatic theology, ecclesiastical history, and (here I use the French titles) *éloquence sacrée*, and *morale évangélique*. The faculty of theology, which has in all 42 chairs, is the least important of all the faculties in France, because the Church of Rome does not recognise its degrees, and they have no canonical validity. Of course, for those who aspire to be professors in this faculty, its degrees and attendance at its lectures are indispensable; and by an ordinance of the Government of 1830 its degrees are required for all ecclesiastical preferment down to the post of *curé de chef-lieu de canton* inclusive; but as a certain number of years' pastoral service was to be accepted as an equivalent for these degrees, and they were not to be required of anybody who when the ordinance appeared was more than twenty-one years old, they have not come to much. The French church is not eminent at present for theological learning, and what theological learning it has does not come to it from the University.

Law has eleven seats of faculties, with 98 chairs. The great chairs in this faculty are those for the *Code Napoléon*, Roman law, civil procedure, commercial law, administrative law. The *Code Napoléon* has to itself six chairs at Paris and three in each of the other ten seats of faculties. Two of these ten, Nancy and Douai, have been recently added, and the reader may like to know how an additional faculty, when wanted, is provided. The town of Nancy, already the seat of an academy, of a faculty of sciences, and of a faculty of letters, desired a faculty of law also, Lorraine having formerly, under its old sovereigns, possessed one. The State agreed to establish one there, the municipality of Nancy undertaking on its part to raise every year and pay to the treasury a sum reimbursing the State for its outlay on the new faculty, its professors, *agrégés*, and courses of lectures. Douai got its faculty of law on the same terms. The State gives the character of a national institution, the guarantee of publicly appointed teachers, and the privilege of conferring degrees; and the town is abundantly willing to pay for this.

No one in France can practise as a barrister (*avocat*) without the degree of licentiate of law. No one can practise as a solicitor (*avoué*) without the *certificat de capacité en droit*. Let us see what the possession of these two diplomas implies.

A licentiate of law must first have got the degree of bachelor of law. To get this he must have the degree of bachelor of letters, have then attended two years' lectures in a faculty of law and undergone two examinations, one in Justinian's *Institutes*, the other in the *Code Napoléon*, the Penal Code, and the Codes of Civil Procedure and Criminal Instruction. Dues for lectures, examinations, and the diploma, make the diploma of bachelor of law cost, when the candidate has obtained it, nearly 25*l.** The new bachelor must then, in order to become licentiate, follow a third year's lectures in a faculty of law, undergo two more examinations, the first on

---

* To be exact, 620 fr.

the *Institutes* of Justinian again, the second on the *Code Napoléon*, the Code of Commerce, and Administrative Law, and must support theses on questions of Roman and French Law. The degree of licentiate costs 24*l.*

A solicitor, to obtain the 'certificate of capacity in law,' must for one year have attended lectures in a faculty of law, embracing in this one year both the first and the second year's course of lectures on the *Code Napoléon*, and on Civil and Criminal Procedure, and undergoing an examination on the subject of each course. The cost of this certificate, all fees for lectures, &c., included, is from 11*l.* to 12*l.**

The professors in the faculty of law are men eminent in the knowledge of their several branches. English readers will do well to compare this regular and educative course of legal instruction with the way in which a barrister is left, with us, to pick up the trick of his trade as he likes; and they may bear in mind at the same time the resources of our universities and Inns of Court for legal education, and how our universities and Inns of Court apply them.

Medicine has three great seats of faculties, with 61 chairs. The faculties are at Paris, Montpellier, and Strasburg. To be a physician or surgeon in France, a man must have the diploma of doctor either in medicine or in surgery. To obtain this, he must have attended four years' lectures in a faculty of medicine, and had two years' practice in a hospital. When he presents himself for the first year's lectures, he must produce the diploma of bachelor of letters; when for the third, that of bachelor of sciences, a certain portion of the mathematics generally required for this degree being in his case cut away. He must pass eight examinations, and at the end of his course he must support a thesis before his faculty. His diploma, by the time he gets it, has cost him a little over 50*l.*†

A medical man with a doctor's degree may practise throughout France. To practise without it, a man must have the diploma of *officier de santé*. To practise without the diploma either of doctor or of *officier de santé* is penal. The

---

* The exact sum is 285 fr.
† 1,260 fr. is the exact sum.

officier de santé must have attended three years' lectures in a faculty and had two years' practice in a hospital, and he must pass five examinations and write a paper bearing on one of the subjects of his instruction. Before he can be admitted to attend lectures in a faculty of medicine he must produce a *certificat d'examen de grammaire*, a sort of minor bachelor of arts degree, turning on the matters taught in *quatrième*, the highest class in the grammar division of the *lycées*. Thus his having learnt some Latin and Greek is, our British Association will be shocked to hear, rendered necessary. His diploma costs him altogether about 32*l.*, but it only authorises him to practise in the department where he has been received *officier de santé*, and he may not perform any great operation except in the presence of a doctor.

A kind of branch of the faculties of medicine is formed by the *Écoles supérieures de Pharmacie*, three in number, with nineteen chairs. These schools, too, are at Paris, Montpellier, and Strasburg. Chemistry, toxicology, pharmacy, and natural history are the main matters of instruction. For medicine and pharmacy there are, as for sciences and letters, auxiliary schools * in a number of the large towns of France, with professors only a grade below the faculty professors, with lectures allowed to count, to a certain extent,† as faculty lectures, and with the right of examining for some of the lower diplomas and granting them. No one can practise as a druggist or apothecary in France without getting either a first or a second class diploma. A first class diploma necessitates three years' study in an *École supérieure de Pharmacie*, three years' practice with a regularly authorised apothecary, and the passing eight examinations, the last of which cannot be passed before the age of twenty-five. The cost of obtaining this diploma comes to nearly

---

* *Écoles préparatoires de médecine et de pharmacie.* There are twenty-two of them.

† For instance; for a doctor of medicine's diploma, three years' and a half attendance on lectures in an *école préparatoire*, and one year's in a faculty, is accepted in lieu of four years' attendance on faculty lectures. For a druggist's second class diploma, a year and a half's instruction in an *école préparatoire* is accepted in lieu of a year's instruction in one of the three *écoles supérieures de pharmacie*.

56*l*.   A *pharmacien* with this first class diploma may practise anywhere in France.   A second class diploma only entitles its holder to practise in the department chosen by him when he entered his name for lectures.   But to hold this second class diploma he must have attended faculty lectures for one or two years, have practised six or four * years with a regular *pharmacien*, and passed four or five examinations, for the last of which he must be twenty-five years old.   The candidate for the first class diploma must have the degree of bachelor of sciences before he can enter himself to follow the lectures of the pharmacy school ; the candidate for the second class diploma must have the *certificat d'examen de grammaire* mentioned above.

I must add that our whole regulation, or rather non-regulation, of the teaching and practice of pharmacy strikes the best judges on the Continent with perfect astonishment, and is condemned there with one voice.   I see that an eminent English physician declared last year, at the meeting of the British Association, that while the practitioner whom in England, where he knows less of chemistry than anywhere else, we are pleased to call a chemist, can in France or Germany perform any analysis which the physician may require of him, in this country he is in nine cases out of ten quite incompetent for such a task.   This exactly corresponds with what I have heard on the Continent.   Here, at any rate, we can trace a clear practical inconvenience from our educational shortcomings.   Signor Matteucci, whom I have already quoted, a most favourable judge of England, who, though he says Oxford and Cambridge are but *hauts lycées*, hopes we shall long keep them, told me that he considered the strengthening of our superior instruction, especially in the direction of the sciences, our most pressing need of all in the matter of public education.

In Paris the seat of the faculties of theology, sciences, and letters is at the Sorbonne ; of the faculty of medicine, at the *École de Médecine* ;† of that of law, at the *École de Droit*.‡   There

---

* A second year's attendance on lectures is accepted in lieu of two years' practice.

† In the *Place de l'École de Médecine*.   ‡ In the *Place du Panthéon*.

are eight inspectors of superior instruction,—four for letters, four for sciences, one for medicine, and one for law. Six of the eight are members of the Institute, and their names will probably be familiar to many English readers: M. Ravaisson, M. Nisard, M. Dumas (the chemist), M. Le Verrier, M. Brongniart, and M. Charles Giraud. Their salary, like that of the faculty professors in Paris, is 12,000 fr. a year, a high salary for France; and the posts of inspector-general and professor of superior instruction form a valuable body of prizes for science and literature. Each faculty has an aggregation, similar in plan to that which exists for the professors of secondary instruction, and which I have described; but, for aggregation in a faculty, very high and complete studies are necessary. In general, the course of promotion is this: the intending *agrégé* first obtains the degree of doctor in his faculty; after being admitted *agrégé* he becomes assistant professor, and finally full professor. A full faculty professor must be thirty years old. The Dean of Faculty is chosen by the Minister of Public Instruction from among the professors of his faculty. While the minister has power to dismiss of his own authority the functionaries of secondary instruction, those of superior instruction can only be dismissed by imperial decree.* The faculties have also the right of proposing candidates for their vacant chairs, though the Emperor, who nominates, is not bound to adopt their proposal.

Free or private courses on the matters of superior instruction cannot be publicly given, in France, without the authorisation of the Minister of Public Instruction, who, before granting it, takes the advice of the prefect and the academic rector for the locality where it is proposed to open them.

Outside the faculties are a number of important State-establishments, all of them contributing to what may be called the higher instruction of the country. The most remarkable of these is the College of France, founded at the Renaissance, to make up, one may say, for the short-comings of the mediæval universities, and which has grown in scale,

* *Décret organique du 9 mars 1852 sur l'instruction publique*, art. 3.

value, and consideration till it now has thirty-one professors, covering with their instruction all the most important provinces of human culture, and many of them among the most distinguished men * in France. The *École des Chartes*, the pupils of which have laboured so fruitfully among the archives of France and the early documents of her history, has seven professors. The Museum of Natural History has sixteen. The School of Living Oriental Languages has nine. The School of Athens is designed to give to the most promising of the young professors, from the age of about twenty-five to thirty, of French public instruction, the opportunity of for two years studying on the spot the language and antiquities of Greece. All who have made these a special object of study know what sound and useful memoirs have proceeded from pupils of the French School of Athens. I may mention, as a specimen, the memoir on the Island of Euboea, by M. Jules Girard. All these establishments, with the *Bureau des Longitudes*, and the public libraries of the capital,—the great library in the Rue Richelieu, the Mazarine Library, the Sainte Geneviève Library, the Arsenal Library, and the Sorbonne Library,—are under the Minister of Public Instruction. Other ministers have special schools, some of which I have already mentioned, attached to their department. The Minister of War has thus the Polytechnic, Saint Cyr, and the Cavalry School of Saumur; the Minister of Marine has the Naval School and the Schools of Hydrography; the Minister of Finance has the School of Woodcraft (*École forestière*) ; the Minister of the Household has the School of Fine Arts; the Minister of Agriculture, Commerce, and Public Works has the Schools of Agriculture, the Veterinary Schools, the Schools of Arts and Trades, the Central School of Arts and Manufactures, the School of Commerce, the Schools of Mines and Miners, and the *École Impériale des Ponts et Chaussées*. The grants to the Institute and to the Academy of Medicine (a sort of medical institute) come into the estimates of the

---

* Among them at the present moment are MM. Élie de Beaumont, Flourens, Coste, Franck, Laboulaye, Michel Chevalier, Alfred Maury, Munk, Caussin de Perceval, Jules Mohl, Stanislas Julien, Sainte Beuve, and Paulin Paris. The salary of a professor at the College of France is 7,500 fr. a year.

Minister of Public Instruction. Into his estimates come also all grants, whether for pensions, gratuities, missions,* publications, or subscriptions, which fall under the head of grants for literature, science, and art. For 1865 these grants amounted to 680,000 fr. (27,200*l.*). The grants to the Institute and Academy of Medicine, grants which really come under the same category as the preceding, amounted to above 26,000*l.* more. These figures have an eloquence which I will leave the English reader, acquainted with our national expenditure for the advancement of literature, science, and art, to appreciate for himself.

Public establishments such as these which I have enumerated serve a twofold purpose. They fix a standard of serious preparation and special fitness for every branch of employment; a standard which acts on the whole intellectual habit of the country. To fix a standard of serious preparation is a very different thing, and a far more real homage to intelligence and study, than to demand,—as we have done since the scandal of our old mode of appointment to public functions grew too evident,—a single examination, by a single board with a staff of examiners, as the sole preliminary to all kinds of civil employment. Examinations preceded by preparation in a first-rate superior school, with first-rate professors, give you a formed man; examinations preceded by preparation under a crammer give you a crammed man, but not a formed one. I once bore part in the examinations for the Indian Civil Service, and I can truly say that the candidates to whom I gave the highest marks were almost without exception the candidates whom I would not have appointed. They were crammed men, not formed men; the formed men were the public school men, but they were ignorant on the special matter of examination,—English literature. A superior school forms a man at the same time that it gives

---

* It may be worth mentioning how, in France, a public department usually proceeds with a report like mine to the Schools' Enquiry Commission, for instance. It sends its reporter and receives his report, but it does not print and publish it in an official volume. It leaves its author to publish it as an ordinary book, the department, however, subscribing for 200 or 300 copies, which it distributes among institutions or individuals that it wishes to inform on the matter to which the book relates.

him special knowledge. The reader may have seen, probably, a correspondence published last year respecting some appointments to the British Museum. Whatever we may think of the points in dispute between Mr. Panizzi and the Civil Service examiners, it will hardly be maintained that the certificate of these examiners is an adequate guarantee for the fitness of an archivist or librarian for his functions. In France a public archivist or librarian does not go before one or two gentlemen of general education, and satisfy them on their general questions; he must have the diploma of *archiviste paléographe*. To possess this he must have for three years attended lectures at the *École des Chartes,*—free lectures, by men masters of their subject. At the end of each year he is examined, and if he cannot pass, is set aside; success in the third year's examination, and a thesis publicly supported on some matter of palæography, bring him his diploma and his appointment.

Again: we have Eastern possessions and interests compared with which those of all other European nations are insignificant, but France has a public school of living Oriental languages and we have none. Professors, among whom are M. Stanislas Julien, M. Garcin de Tassy, and M. Caussin de Percival, teach there Arabic, Persian, Turkish, Armenian, Hindustani, modern Greek, Chinese, Malay, and Japanese. And pupils from all parts of Europe come to their instruction.

A second purpose which such public establishments serve is this. They represent the State, the country, the collective community, in a striking visible shape, which is at the same time a noble and civilising one; giving the people something to be proud of and which it does them good to be proud of. The State is in England singularly without means of civilisation of this kind. But a modern state cannot afford to do without them, and the action of individuals and corporations cannot fully compensate for them; the want of them has told severely on the intelligence and refinement of our middle and lower class. It makes a difference to the civilisation of these classes whether it is the Louvre which represents their country to them, or the National Gallery; and whether the

State consecrates in the eyés of the people the great lines of intellectual culture by national institutions for them, or leaves them to take care of themselves. What the State, the collective permanent nation, honours, the passing people honour; what the State neglects, they think of no great consequence. It is in this point of view that the national institution, on the Continent, of all that interests human culture seems to me especially important. In France, in her superior and still more in her secondary instruction, there is undoubtedly too much regulation by the central government, too much prescribing to teachers the precise course they shall follow, too much requiring of authorisations before a man may stir. If the professors were left free to arrange their programmes by concert among themselves, if any one, not ἄτιμος, and with proper guarantees of capacity (for to a rigorous demand for these there ought to be no objection) were free to open a school or to deliver public lectures without any further check whatever, thought and learning in France would in my opinion be great gainers. This change, however, would but remove what is an excrescence upon the public establishment of education, a noxious excrescence due to political causes, and to their predominance in France as with us (only with us they have operated in another way by preventing the public establishment of education altogether) over intellectual interests. All the salutary and civilising effects of the public establishment of education are to be had without this excrescence. When I come to Germany I will show them so existing.

II.

ITALY.

CHAPTER IX.

DEVELOPMENT AND HISTORY OF THE ITALIAN SECONDARY SCHOOLS.

MEDIÆVAL SCHOOLS OF ITALY—THE RENAISSANCE AND THE ITALIAN UNIVERSITIES—THE CATHOLIC REACTION—LONG TORPOR OF THE ITALIAN SCHOOLS—EFFORTS AT IMPROVEMENT—PIEDMONTESE ADMINISTRATION—THE FRENCH IN ITALY; THEIR IMPROVEMENTS—REACTION AFTER 1815.

I HAVE said that the early history of secondary and superior instruction might be traced in France as in a kind of representative country, because France was the main centre, of that great movement of the eleventh and twelfth centuries, in which the seats of this instruction,—seats where it took the character which it everywhere still keeps more or less, and in England keeps to a remarkable degree,—had their origin. These seats were the universities, and the University of Paris was in early times the most important of them. But Italy has universities which for antiquity and early importance run the University of Paris very hard. Tradition attributes the first beginnings of the University of Pavia to Charlemagne, and our Lanfranc, William the Conqueror's Archbishop of Canterbury, studied in the school of law there. But in the twelfth century the law school of the University of Bologna eclipsed all others in Europe. The two great branches of legal study in the middle ages, the Roman law and the canon law, began in the teaching of Irnerius and Gratian at Bologna in the first half of the twelfth century. At the beginning of this century the name of university first replaces that of school; and it is said that the great university degree, that of doctor, was first instituted at Bologna, and that the ceremony for conferring it was devised there. From Bologna the degree and its ceremonial travelled to Paris. A bull of Pope Honorius, in 1220, says that the study of *bonæ literæ* had at that time made the city of Bologna famous throughout the world. Twelve thousand students from all parts of Europe are said to have been congregated there at once. The different nations had their colleges, and of colleges at Bologna . there were fourteen. These were founded and endowed by the liberality of private persons; the university professors, the source of attraction to this multitude of students, were paid by the municipality, who found their reward in the fame, business, and importance brought to their town by the university. The municipalities of the great cities of northern and central Italy were not slow in following the example of Bologna; in the thirteenth century Padua, Modena, Piacenza, Parma, Ferrara, had each its university. Frederick II. founded that of Naples in 1224; in the fourteenth century were added those of Pavia, Perugia, Pisa, and Turin. Colleges of examiners, or, as we should say, *boards*, were created by Papal bull to examine in theology, and by imperial decree to examine in law and medicine.

It was in these studies of law and medicine that the Italian universities were chiefly distinguished. The medical school of Salerno carries back its origin to the most remote antiquity, and boasts the same priority for its teaching of medicine which Bologua boasts for its teaching of law. The statutes of foreign universities regulate their studies *ad instar studii Bononiensis*, just as they so often regulate them by the example of Paris. But Paris had the pre-eminence in theology and philosophy, and as these were the great studies of the mediæval universities, the university which took the lead in them surpassed all others in importance. So complete . was the lead of Paris in the study which swallowed up all others,—the so-called philosophy of the schoolmen,—that the technical style of this philosophy was called by the humanists of the Renaissance, who inveighed against it: ' the style of Paris.'

To Italy we owe the Renaissance, and in the fourteenth century she took the intellectual lead which in the twelfth century belonged to France. But the movement of the Renaissance did not in Italy any more than in France possess itself of the universities and schools, and make these its grand channels. The Renaissance was a literary movement, and the great men of the Renaissance were the humanists. The grand business of the universities was the scholastic philosophy, and this governed all the rest of their teaching, even their teaching of letters. The humanists were men, like Petrarch, outside of the established school-teaching of their day, and hostile to it; but this teaching went on in spite of them. There were isolated efforts by men of genius to bring education too into the movement of the Renaissance, and to give the guiding of education to humanists and the humanities; such an effort was that of Vittorino di Feltre with his school at Mantua, and very interesting the history of such efforts is. But they did not succeed. The organised official teaching of Italy remained mediæval and barbarous long after her great writers and artists had launched their country, and Europe along with her, on the line of modern ideas and modern civilisation.

The last phase of the scholastic philosophy was Averroism, —Aristotle interpreted through the *Great Commentary* of Averroes. What this second or third hand Aristotle was,— an Aristotle that had passed through Syriac, Arabic, Hebrew, and Latin translation, with blunders in each, and was then studied by the light of his Arabian commentator, and with the uncritical spirit of the Middle Age, with a view to find in him a philosophy of the universe,—is now well known. Averroism ruled in the Italian universities down to the seventeenth century, long after it had disappeared from the French schools, its earlier stronghold, and when the humanities, which Italy herself had had so large a share in introducing, and the new philosophy of Descartes, had extinguished it everywhere else. The extraordinary number of copies of certain Averroist professors' lectures, still preserved in manuscript in the libraries of northern Italy, shows the popularity of this teaching, and enables us to trace its duration.* Cremonini, who is called the last schoolman, was professor at Padua in 1631. This countryman of Galileo, after the dis-

---

* See *Averroès et l'Averroïsme*, par M. Renan, p. 324.

covery of Jupiter's satellites, judging that this discovery contradicted Aristotle, would never consent to look through a telescope again. One could not have a better incident to end the career of the scholastic philosophy.

The Averroist doctrines, in this later phase in which the Italian universities received them, were at wide variance with Catholic orthodoxy, and the Lateran Council of 1512 condemned them. Still the theologians were, at bottom, not ill-disposed to the routine, the respect for authority, the clinging to established texts, which the Averroist teaching shared with their own, and which both of them had learned in the same uncritical school of the Middle Age. The Averroist professors, on their part, made connivance easy by drawing the distinction, so often drawn since, between philosophy and religion. According to philosophy, they always said, according to Aristotle and Avérroes, this is so and so; if the Church says otherwise, we are obedient sons of the Church, and we submit our opinion to hers. On the other hand, it was not the arid jargon and barren formulas of the Averroist schoolman, it was his free canvassing of problems such as the unity of the intellect and the immortality of the soul, which drew the Italian students, full of the scepticism and intellectual agitation of that time, to their lectures. ' Tell us about the soul,' was the cry with which, at Padua and Bologna, the crowd of students is said to have received a new professor. By this side Averroism might also win some indulgence from the school of positive and experimental science which was rising beside it, the creation of that scientific intellect of Italy, which is one of her chief glories, and, perhaps, her chief force; and which, through the worst times of the last three centuries, has never failed her.

Nothing, indeed, could be more surely fatal to scholasticism, in all it forms, than the growth of positive and experimental science, and nothing could seem a more certain means to have swept it, in the end, out of the Italian universities. But Averroism and all the philosophical and literary movement, both of the Italian universities and of the Italian nation, fell by another cause. It fell by the Catholic reaction which followed the abortive attempts to bring about a reform of religion in Italy. The intellectual development which the England of Elizabeth seemed to promise was in like manner checked by the triumph of Puritanism; but the triumph of Catholicism in Italy was far more complete, was the triumph of a far more unprogressive and anti-intellectual influence, and far more fatal. Boards of reform, as they were called, were instituted for the supervision of studies; religious orders, like the Jesuits, the Barnabites, and the *Padri Scolopi*, took to school-keeping, and many pious foundations for education date from this period; but education was by the promoters of this movement not valued for its own sake, as the liberal culture of the human spirit, but was applied as an auxiliary to promote the authority of the old religion, and as a preventive against heresy.

Thus the soul was taken out of it, and with education and government well matching each other, the brilliant Italy of the Renaissance settled down into the frivolity and torpor of its eighteenth century. The number of professors' chairs at Bologna, which in the seventeenth century had been 166, had in 1737 fallen to 62. The communes which had disputed eagerly the possession of a distinguished professor, and bidden against one another for his services, sunk into apathy. The boards of examiners, distinct from the regular teachers of the students, which in the earlier and flourishing times of the universities had made examinations independent, honest, and searching, fell into disuse. Universities came to be regarded not as seats of learning, but as mere instruments for conferring degrees, and their examinations were a farce. At Naples, the noble family of Avellino had the privilege assigned to it of giving, after a pretence of examination, the diploma of doctor in law and medicine, and of exacting the fees for it. It is remarkable, however, that through all this period of apathy and decline, the scientific tradition of Italy was never broken; a continuous chain of great names carries on this tradition uninterrupted from the sixteenth century to our own : Falloppio, Galileo, Torricelli, Malpighi, Valisnieri, Spallanzani, Galvani, Volta, Scarpa. In letters and philosophy, on the other hand, Italy has, perhaps, from the seventeenth century to the nineteenth, only one truly great name to set against this illustrious list,—the name of Vico. It shows how insufficient are the natural sciences alone to keep up in a people culture and life, that the Italians, at the end of a period with the natural sciences alone thriving in it, and letters and philosophy moribund, found themselves, by their own confession, with ' a poverty of general culture, and in an atmosphere unpropitious to knowledge,' which they sorrowfully contrast with the condition of other and happier nations.

Two efforts after life and improvement break this long period of deadness in the education of Italy. The first is the endeavour of the princes of the House of Savoy to make the organisation of public instruction in their own states more efficient. The Royal Constitutions of 1729 and 1772 were the fruit of such an endeavour. By these constitutions the control of secondary instruction was taken away from the religious orders, and the *Collegio delle Provincie*, with 100 free studentships, was established with the aim of preparing, in connection with the University, teachers qualified to give this instruction. Schools of method were established to prepare teachers for primary schools, and with the title of *Magistrato della Riforma* the germ of a well-composed Council of Public Instruction appeared. The regulations of this Council gave strictness to the lax university examinations, and thus braced the University studies. Inspired by a political interest rather than by a love for culture and science, these reforms of the Turin Government had, probably, for their main design to give the State the control of so powerful an instrument as public education; but in certain circumstances such a design may prove to be patriotic and useful. The Turin Government imported into education the ideas which the Italy of that time so greatly needed, and which have made Piedmont's fortune in Italy; the ideas of public spirit, effective administration, honest work, and rigid discipline. These alone are not enough to form what the Italians well call an *atmosfera intellettuale propizia agli studi*, but they form character, and prepare the indispensable foundations for a people's greatness: and even in that sub-alpine soil where, as Peyron, the celebrated Piedmontese hellenist, contemptuously said: 'The thyme of Attica refuses to strike root,' their application produced a system of schools the best worked and managed, on the whole, in Italy.

The second effort was due to the French occupation. We in England, impressed with their faults because it was our lot to meet them as enemies, do not in general know the true merits either of the French Revolution or of the first Napoleon. Their faults are palpable and undeniable; their merits are equally undeniable, but it needs some knowledge of the Continent, and some reflection, to make them palpable to an Englishman. The great merit of the French Revolution, the great service it rendered to Europe, was *to get rid of the Middle Age;* very few Englishmen yet perceive even that. The great merit of the first Napoleon, the great service he rendered to Europe, was *to found a civil organisation for modern society.* With all his faults, his reason was so clear and strong that he saw, in its general outline at least, the just and rational type of civil organisation which modern society needs, and wherever his armies went, he instituted it.

That the French Revolution's merit and service was a real one is shown by all the world, as it improves, getting rid more and more of the Middle Age. That Napoleon's merit and service was a real one is shown by the bad governments which succeeded him having always got rid, when they could, of his work, and by the progress of improvement, when these governments become intolerable, and are themselves got rid of, always bringing it back. Where governments were not wholly bad and did not get rid of Napoleon's good work, this work turns out to have the future on its side, and to be more likely to assimilate the institutions round it to its pattern than to be itself assimilated by them. The Rhine province of Prussia has the *Code Napoléon* and Westphalia has not; but there is far more likelihood of Westphalia's having one day the *Code Napoléon* than of the Rhine province having the law of Westphalia.

The absurdities and abuses of which the old education of Europe was full, and nowhere so full as in Italy, the French reformed with unsparing vigour. Convents were turned into schools, and in the half-barbarous district of Southern Italy Joseph Bonaparte's government planted *licei* in the towns, while it extirpated brigandage in the country. The now existing public schools at Bari and Lecce were then established. Medical study in the kingdom of Naples having declined from the diplomas of the school of Salerno to those of the Princes of Avellino, the French restored it by founding the *Collegio Medico-chirurgico Napolitano*, in which medical students were boarded, lodged, and taught by special professors of their own; to this day, I am told, one of the best institutions in Europe for its purpose. Faculties and universities, of which it is easy to have,—and Italy had and has,—too many, were suppressed, and the expenditure on them turned to better account for the interests of public instruction. Thus at Ferrara the feeble and unneeded university was closed, and a *liceo*, which the city up to that time did not possess, and a school of hydraulics, for which Ferrara by its situation offers special advantages, substituted for it. Other universities, like Pavia, strong already, were strengthened still more; indeed, such a constellation of famous names as is seldom seen was to be found at Pavia under Napoleon's rule: Volta, Spallanzani, Frank, Scarpa, Foscolo, and Monti, were all professors there at the same time. The exact sciences, which stir the whole man less than letters and philosophy, are better suited than letters and philosophy to a political system like the first Napoleon's; and his own special turn, too, was for the exact sciences; so in Italy, as in France, these throve and shone far more than letters. Yet for letters, too, and general culture, Napoleon did the very best thing, perhaps, that any government could do for them, by founding the Normal School of Pisa, on the model of, and in connection with, the Normal School of Paris, of which I have said so much. At the present moment the Pisa school is the sheet anchor of Italian secondary instruction.

With the fall of the first French Empire all this improvement stopped. The Normal School of Pisa was closed. I have mentioned the French reforms in medical study at Naples. Besides reforming this, the French Government had reorganised the whole University, established new chairs, museums, a botanic garden, &c. But 'the Bourbon restoration,' says Signor Matteucci, 'struck particularly at the University, reducing the number of students as much as possible by creating in the provinces university faculties, which had often only a nominal existence, and by confiding all instruction to the Jesuits and to the clergy.' As it was at Pisa and Naples, so it was everywhere. At Turin itself, the early seat of reform of a certain kind, the University was in 1821 closed. The attempts of the better Italian governments to do something for education were but half-hearted attempts, made without light and faith. In Tuscany the Grand-Ducal Government reopened in 1846 the Normal school of Pisa; but so languid was this effort at revival, and so unfavourable were the circumstances for it, that in 1862 there was not a single pupil left.

CHAPTER X.

THE ITALIAN SECONDARY SCHOOLS SINCE 1859.

THE NEW KINGDOM OF ITALY—THE LEGGE CASATI—THE ITALIAN SECONDARY SCHOOLS AT THE PRESENT TIME—LAXITY IN WORKING THE LEGGE CASATI.

MEANWHILE those events happened which consolidated Italy and placed the Piedmontese Government at its head. Count Cavour well knew how necessary an agent in the regeneration of Italy was a good system of public instruction. He knew too that in modern times the State cannot remain a stranger to this instruction. The first Piedmontese Minister of Public Instruction had been appointed in 1847. The first Council of Public Instruction was nominated at the same time. Piedmont was at that time only Piedmont. It began at once to organise and improve instruction within its own borders, and the Piedmontese habits of discipline, regular work, and honest administration, produced, as I have said, excellent results in the Piedmontese schools, though the literary and scientific genius of Italy, and her love for all humane culture, do not come to her from Piedmont. The moment the first annexation had taken place, the Turin Government hastened to provide for the now enlarged requirements of its public instruction by a new law. This law was the education law of the 13th of November, 1859,—the *Legge Casati*, as, from the name of the Minister of Public Instruction who introduced it, it is generally called. As fresh portions of Italy came under King Victor Emmanuel's rule, this law was extended to them also,* with some slight modifications. From that time to

---

* To Tuscany by the Tuscan Government's law of March 10th, 1860; to the Neapolitan provinces by the law of the Government of the Lieutenancy, February 10th, 1861 ; to Sicily by the decree of the Prodictatorial Government, October 17th, 1860.

this, ministries have rapidly succeeded one another in Italy; no Minister of Public Instruction has held his post long, and from each, while he held it, numerous regulations and re-arrangements have proceeded. There is, therefore, a certain want of unity in what has been hitherto done. But the law of 1859 imposed on the Council of Public Instruction the duty of making a report to the Minister at the end of every five years on the state of all parts of public instruction in the Italian Kingdom. The first quinquennial period expired in November, 1864, and in May, 1865, the Council, through their Vice-President, Signor Matteucci,—himself at that time an Ex-Minister of Public Instruction,—addressed to the Minister, Baron Natoli, a report full of interest on the actual condition of superior, secondary, and primary education in the kingdom of Italy, with recommendations for dealing with them. The Council had prepared itself for its task by sending inspectors through the kingdom, by addressing questions to the university and school authorities, and by collecting statistics. To ascertain the progress made since 1859 was of course the immediate object of the Council's inquiry; but in elucidating this, they threw clear light on the condition of studies which the law of 1859 found existing. I begin with secondary instruction; and my notice of superior instruction, except at its point of contact with secondary, will, as before when I was speaking of France, be very brief.

In 1865 there were in the northern provinces of the Italian kingdom 40 *licei*, in the central provinces 19, in the southern provinces 14, in Sardinia 2, in Sicily 7; 82 in all. The *licei* are established in the principal towns; the State has one, at the least, in each province, and there are 59 provinces. Sixty-two of the 82 *licei* are State establishments. The course in a *liceo* is of three years only, and they correspond with the superior division of the French *lycées*. With the grammar division and elementary division correspond the *ginnasi*, or gymnasiums, with a five years' course, answering to the two classes of the French elementary division and the three of the grammar division. Only in the Neapolitan pro-vinces is the *ginnasio* a part of the *liceo*; the united institu-tion there takes the name of *liceo-ginnasiale*. In other provinces they are separate schools under separate management and often in separate premises. A certain number of *ginnasi*, are, like the *licei*, at the State's charge; * one, at least, in each province is so; but in every chief town of a province, or district of a province (*circondario*, the French *arrondissement*) where the State has not a *ginnasio*, the municipality is bound by the law of 1859 to provide and superintend one. Many municipalities prefer to provide the requisite funds and to hand over the task of superintendence to the State; and this is permitted by the law. There were, in 1865, 117 *ginnasi* in the northern provinces, 43 in the central, 17 in the southern, 12 in Sardinia, and 29 in Sicily; 218 in all. Ninety-five of these are State establishments. After the *licei* and the *ginnasi* come the *scuole tecniche*. These are a creation of that modern desire for schools not exclusively classical which has founded the *Real-Schulen* in Germany, and is founding the *enseignement secondaire spécial* of France. In Piedmont the first attempt to satisfy this desire was made in 1840, when Latin was struck out of the programme of the primary schools, and arithmetic, geography, and history, introduced into that of the secondary. A step further was taken in 1848, when there was instituted ('by way of experiment,' as the law said †) a special course in the public schools for boys whose studies were not to be classical. This special course embraced the usual matters,—the mother-tongue and modern languages, modern history, mathematics and natural sciences, drawing, account-keeping, &c.,—which we have seen it embrace elsewhere. A bifurcation was thus established, not as in France, in the middle of secondary instruction, but at its outset, and immediately after primary instruction; and the technical course, like the gymnasial, was of five years. Subventions were offered by the State to provinces and communes which would establish special courses of this kind, and the law of 1859 allowed the municipalities which were under the obligation of providing a

* Of the *liceo*, however, the material as well as the personal expenses (as they are called) are at the State's charge; that is, the State pays for buildings, repairs, fittings, &c., as well as for teachers; of its *ginnasi* and *scuole tecniche* only the personal expenses, the teachers' salaries, are defrayed by the State.

† *Legge del* 4 *Ottobre* 1848, *sui collegi nazionali,* art. 25.

ginnasio to provide a *scuola tecnica* instead of it. The same law entirely separated the technical from the classical schools, and divided the technical or special course into two grades: the first of three years in the *scuola tecnica;* the second of two years in the *istituto tecnico.* The *scuola tecnica* remained in connection with the department of Public Instruction, and its teaching was made gratuitous. The *istituto tecnico* was attached to the department of Agriculture and Commerce, and became a special or trade school, rather than a school of general secondary instruction, classical or non-classical.

Of *scuole tecniche* there were, in 1865, 85 in the northern provinces, 44 in the central, 7 in the southern, 3 in Sardinia, and 18 in Sicily; 157 in all. A certain number of these schools,* too, are State establishments, having been originally founded by the State, or transferred to its care by the municipalities. Every State school takes the prefix of ' royal ' (*regia*).

The schools which are not State institutions are divided into *pareggiate* and *non-pareggiate. Pareggiate* means assimilated. In the assimilated schools the course is the same as in the State schools; the pupils are classified in the same way, and the programmes which the Minister of Public Instruction, as in France, issues, and which differ little from the French programmes which I have already described, are followed. The non-assimilated schools regulate their course, classify their scholars, and fix their studies, as they please.

The vast majority of the boys frequenting these schools are day-scholars. Italy, however, has a great many foundations for the free board and lodging of a certain number of scholars in connection with the schools of the place where the foundation exists. An establishment where scholars are boarded and lodged is in Italy called a *convitto.* It may happen that pupils who pay for their board and lodging are received there as well as scholars proper, or bursars, but the *convitto* exists for the sake of the latter. Many of these foundations are in the hands of the religious, many in those of the munici-

---

* 45 out of the 157.

palities ; the State has nine of them, and these State foundations are called *convitti nazionali.*

The expenditure of the State on these nine *convitti*, and on the 62 lyceums, 95 gymnasiums, and 45 technical schools, with which it has charged itself, was, in the school-year 1863–64, 2,194,634 fr. ; in round numbers, 88,000*l.* The rest of the public secondary schools are maintained by local expenditure on the part of the provinces and communes, of which no complete accounts have yet been collected and published.

The population of the public secondary schools of the Italian kingdom * is 24,492.† It is divided as follows. The *licei* have 3,362 scholars; the *ginnasi*, 12,862 ; the *scuole tecniche*, 8,268. To divide it in another way : the classical public schools have 16,224 pupils, the non-classical, 8,268. For the body of 24,492 scholars there are 2,342 teachers, of whom 905 are ecclesiastics.

This is extravagant work on the face of it, for we have here a teacher to every ten scholars and a fraction. The more we examine the school statistics the more clearly does the extravagance of the present order of things come out. The best frequented schools by far are those of the northern provinces, the old dominions of the throne of Sardinia ; but even in these schools the supply of pupils reaches on an average only 19 and a fraction per class for the *licei*, 15 and a fraction per class for the *ginnasi*, and 24 pupils and a fraction per class for the *scuole tecniche.*‡ But in the new provinces of the Italian kingdom the proportion is very much lower. In central Italy the *licei* have on the average only 9 pupils per class, the *ginnasi* 10, and the *scuole*

---

* The kingdom of Italy contained, by the census of 1861, 21,747,334 inhabitants.

† These numbers are taken from the recent report of the Superior Council of Public Instruction to the Minister. The statistics, however, collected with so much pains for that most valuable document, are not absolutely complete ; the returns from some places either could not be procured, or arrived too late to be used. See *Sulle Condizioni della pubblica Istruzione nel Regno d'Italia ; Relazione generale presentata al Ministro dal Consiglio Superiore di Torino* (Milan, 1865), p. 245.

‡ As in France, the *class*, in Italy, represents a year of the school course, and the school has as many classes as it has years of course. The *licei* and *scuole techniche* have thus a three-year course and three classes ; the *ginnasi*, a five-year course and five classes.

tecniche only 8. As we go farther south the proportion becomes lower still. It is calculated by the Council of Public Instruction that in northern Italy and Sardinia there are at present twice as many *licei* as are wanted, in central Italy four times as many as are wanted, in southern Italy and Sicily more than four times. The pupils are wanting to the schools, they say, not the schools to the pupils; and it is in the classical schools that the deficiency of pupils is greatest and increases, while the non-classical schools are continually getting fuller.

The Council do not recommend the suppression, at present, of any of the existing *licei*, but, to diminish a source of needless expense, they propose to put the literary and mathematical instruction of the *licei* into the two first years of the course there, and the instruction in natural sciences into the third year, and that in all those *licei* which are unprovided with the proper outfit for giving the latter instruction, the course shall be restricted to two years, and the third year's course suppressed.

A more efficacious retrenchment is proposed in the case of the lower secondary schools. It is proposed to strike Latin and Greek out of the first three years of the gymnasial course, to fill these three years with the modern and practical studies of the technical school, to make the first three years' course gratuitous, and to amalgamate the technical school with the lower part of the gymnasium. Latin and Greek are not to come till the two last years of the gymnasial course. This seems a very sensible proposal. The separation established by the law of 1859 between the technical school and the gymnasium was costly and unnecessary. It had more inconveniences than the old French bifurcation, because it separated the boys younger. It is in general premature to decide for a boy, the moment his primary instruction is finished, whether his secondary instruction shall be classical or non-classical. In any case, whether it is to be classical or non-classical, much of his instruction,—arithmetic, geography, history, and so on,—must be the same; and to have two schools and two sets of teachers for the same thing, is to double your expenses needlessly. Communes and munici-

palities, with funds and population really but for one secondary
school, were obliged, by the law of 1859, to make their school
either altogether classical or non-classical; they were pulled
different ways between an influential minority of their inhabitants who wanted a classical school, and the bulk of their
middle class who wanted a non-classical; and they often
ended by establishing two schools, a *ginnasio* and a *scuola
tecnica*, both of which could not be maintained properly,
though one might have been. The practical studies, as they
are called, of the earlier years of the *ginnasio*, were besides
insufficient, especially if it be considered how few boys,
comparatively, pass on from the *ginnasio* to the *liceo*; for
how many, therefore, the five gymnasial years of Latin and
Greek, and nothing else, are time misused. Nor are even
Latin and Greek properly learned in the *ginnasio* during
these five years, as the examinations at the end of the course
show; they might be better learned in two years, a good
substratum of modern instruction having preceded them.
So the Council propose, as I have said, ' the unification of
the first triennium of the *ginnasio* with the first grade of the
scuola tecnica.' If the united pupils exceed 40 or 50 per
class, a second teacher is to be provided. But with the present school population the unification, if adopted, will, in a
very great number of cases, enable three teachers to do what
six are now employed for, and effect an important saving.
The two last years of the *ginnasio* will remain devoted, as
before, to classical instruction and to preparation for the
liceo. The boy who does not want this will go, after his three
years of modern instruction, either straight into business,
or to one of the *istituti tecnici*, the special schools under the
Minister of Agriculture and Commerce.

The Council foresee that this recommendation may expose
them to the charge of discouraging Latin and Greek, and
they meet this anticipated accusation by drawing a picture
of the study of Latin and Greek, as this study exists at present in the Italian schools. Everything that I myself observed
entirely confirms the faithfulness of the Council's picture; but
the testimony of Italians is more weighty in this case than
that of any foreigner. ' What fruits,' the Council ask, ' do

we obtain from our classical studies at present? After a youth has spent seven or eight years in the study of Latin, five or six in that of Greek, is he in a condition to read with pleasure and without effort a Latin author, to write correctly a short piece of Latin prose, to make out by himself one of the easiest Greek authors? The Latin compositions which the Council have had before them, the entrance examinations at the University,* in which one or more members of this Council have since 1860 constantly borne part, the competitive examinations for the studentships in the *Collegio delle Provincie*, the accounts we have received from the inspectors, and for the southern provinces the detailed reports of the Visiting Commission of 1862, afford convincing proof that Latin is neither studied nor liked by our youth, and that there is a notable going back in the knowledge of it in the last twenty-five years. What shall we say of Greek? The study of Greek in our schools leads to such scanty result, our young men, the moment they leave school, forget so utterly all the little Greek they have ever learned, that it is impossible not to consider as lost the time and labour which pupils and masters have spent on it.'

And elsewhere the Council speak of the inferiority of Italy to other countries in secondary instruction, and above all in the literary and classical part of it,† as a matter too clear for doubt or concealment.‡ This inferiority is indeed patent. It is often said, and with truth, that in English classical schools there is a great disproportion between the amount of time and labour spent in teaching Latin and Greek, and the result obtained; the same might be said everywhere; still no one who knew the work in the highest forms of the great public schools of England, Germany, or France, would draw such a picture of classical instruction in those three countries as the Italian reporter draws of it in Italy.

The state in which the law of 1859 found it, accounts for its present deficiencies. The relative superiority of the schools

---

* Of Turin, where the candidates come from schools which, compared with those of other parts of Italy are, as I have said, well worked.

† *Sulle Condizioni della pubblica Istruzione nel Regno d' Italia*, p. 258.

‡ *Sulle Condizioni*, &c., p. 236.

in the north of Italy I have already mentioned.   Elsewhere
(I quote again the Italian reporter) 'secondary instruction
had lost the organisation given to it under the French empire, and was reduced to Latin, a little Italian, and, in the
last years of the school course, elementary mathematics,
physics, and the reading of certain treatises of philosophy.'
As the proper means of teaching physics were in general
wanting, this bill of fare may certainly be pronounced
scanty.   With this instruction the scholars managed, however, nearly always to pass the University examinations;
'but' (says the reporter again) 'the Government delegates
who inquired into their examinations, and had not only the
registers but the candidates' papers before them, could not
but come to the conclusion that the examinations were
nothing but a pure form, so great was the laxity used in
passing one and all of the candidates.'   The attendance in
the secondary schools was irregular to an inconceivable degree.
In many of the new provinces from one-third to one-half of
the pupils absented themselves daily.

The law of 1859 introduced programmes, mainly after the
French model; a staff of inspectors-general at head-quarters,
and, in each province, a *provveditore* to represent the State, and
a Provincial School Council to represent the local authority.
It required guarantees of capacity from teachers.   It exacted
for admission to the *liceo* the production of the *licenza ginnasiale*, a certificate showing that the candidate had passed
with success an examination in the studies of the *ginnasio*;
for admission to the University, the production of the *licenza
liceale*, showing the same thing with respect to the studies of
the *liceo*.   It introduced greater strictness into the university
examinations, providing that they should be given by boards
of examiners named by the universities or by the Minister of
Public Instruction.

But many causes combined to impair the effectual operation of this law.   It was extended to other parts of the kingdom as they were annexed.   Having been made for one part
of the kingdom, it could not be extended to others without
some modification; the principle of modification having been
once admitted, relaxations and exceptions were conceded to

importunity, and by these the sound provisions of the original law were in many cases made a dead letter. The programmes were pitched too high; for instance, geometry and algebra were in the programme of the *ginnasio*, and these were so evidently beyond the pupils' state of preparation, that they had to be struck out and arithmetic by itself substituted for them. For arithmetic the law had provided that there should be separate teachers, but it had omitted to impose any test of fitness on them. Unqualified persons were therefore appointed, and arithmetic was ill taught. The degree of bachelor, obtainable after three years of university study, was made the condition of admission to the higher masterships of secondary schools, and a certificate of capacity, obtainable by examination (*esame d'abilitazione*), was required for the lower; but by admitting *equipollent titles*, as they are called, that is, titles of admission allowed to count instead of the degree or the certificate, a door was opened to great abuse, and the law was continually evaded. The school authorities were out of humour with changes which interrupted the easy life they had hitherto led, and which gave them a great deal of fresh work and trouble. In the *ginnasi*, arithmetic having been assigned to a special master, one master was to be charged with all the other work,—Latin, Italian, history, and geography,—of his class; it having been found that when there was a master for each subject, the pupil learnt next to nothing from any one of them, as they had no firm hold on him. When, however, one master had the four subjects, it soon appeared that he taught none of these subjects but Latin. In the *licei*, the pupils, accustomed to lax discipline, without thorough grounding in classical studies, and borne, by what inclination for knowledge they had, anywhere rather than in the direction of these studies, showed themselves entirely averse to the Latin and Greek lessons, and it needed vigorous measures to prevent their absenting themselves from them. The *licenza ginnasiale* is indispensable for a number of Government employments, the *licenza liceale* is indispensable for admission to the university, the degrees of which are required for the exercise of law and medicine; so through the school the pupil must go; but he manifests, it is said, a febrile impatience to get through as fast as possible, he is nearly always pushed into a class above his real attainments, cannot profit by its teaching, and passes out of it by an examination which is illusory. With this pressure on the part of pupils and parents, and the general low standard of studies, the school authorities are apt to be slack and indulgent; two-thirds of those presented for the *licenza ginnasiale* and the *licenza liceale* now pass, but it is calculated by the Council that hardly one-third of them ought to pass. The same reasons make the provincial school councils also,—coming, as they do, within the influence of local feelings,—slack and indulgent. The *provveditore* and the one or two central inspectors representing the State, have had no staff through which to exercise an efficient inspection or control; for the law of 1859, while providing that the inspection of the secondary schools should be entrusted to two inspectors-general *and their representatives*, had omitted to say who or what these representatives should be. Nor did the university examinations, as remodelled by the legislation of 1859, suffice to raise the standard of instruction throughout the country. In the first place, the most important articles of that legislation were, as regards many universities, withdrawn or suspended. The change they introduced was too sweeping, the opposition they provoked too strong. Thus, in the great University of Naples, a university with some 5,000 students, there still continues to be no obligatory matriculation, and therefore no obligatory examination of the student at entrance. In the second place, high pitched examinations are the result, not the cause, of a high condition of general culture, and examinations tend, in fact, to adjust themselves to studies. So long, therefore, as the Italian secondary schools are what they are, the standard of university examinations in Italy, even when they are enforced, is irresistibly dragged down below the point at which the reformers of education try to fix it. The prescribed strictness is not maintained; in the university year 1862-63 the rejected candidates for degrees in the Italian universities were not more than six for every hundred who passed; in similar trials in France, Belgium, Germany, and England, the proportion rejected is far larger, though no one will say that the candidates in these countries present themselves worse prepared than in Italy. The admission examinations show the same over-indulgence, nearly every candidate being admitted in some Italian universities, while for the corresponding examinations in France,—those for the degree of bachelor,—the number of rejections is on an average 20 per cent. at least, and sometimes rises as high as 50 per cent.

CHAPTER XI.

THE ITALIAN UNIVERSITIES.

PAUCITY OF STUDENTS IN ARTS—GREAT NUMBER OF UNIVERSITIES IN ITALY.

FROM 1858 to the present time there has been in Italy a slight but steady falling off in the attendance at the universities. From the want of admission registers at Naples it is impossible to determine with accuracy the total number of students in the Italian Universities in a given year; 10,000, however, is not far from the mark. In the French faculties, in 1862, 23,371 students were entered; 14,364 of them in Paris alone. In the nineteen universities of Germany, exclusive of Austria, there are about 30,000 students.* It is calculated that France has about one university student for every 1,900 inhabitants, Germany one for every 1,500, Italy one for every 2,200. But the great difference between Italy and these countries is in the character of studies followed by the university students. While a fourth of the German students study letters and philosophy, the proportion of Italian students who study these is utterly insignificant. The prevalence of the study of letters is a good test of a country's general condition of culture and civilisation; and that it is so is strikingly confirmed by Turin,—the centre not, certainly, of the most gifted part of Italy, but of the best governed, trained, and civilised part,—having in its university incomparably more students in letters than any other university

---

* So says Signor Matteucci, and I leave his numbers for the sake of the remarks he founds on them; but in 1864 there were only (in round numbers) 20,000 *matriculated* students in all the German universities, including those of Austria. It is possible Signor Matteucci reckons unmatriculated attendants at lectures, and so gets his high number of students, but I have been able to find no statistics corroborating the high number he assigns.

town of the kingdom. The greater part of the universities have next to none. Pavia, out of 1,200 students in the year 1864, had only eight of them in the faculty of letters. The principal of the Normal School at Pisa reports that his pupils are often the sole attendants at the lectures in the faculty of letters at Pisa, and he adds that in several universities, and notably in that of Naples, there are years in which not a single degree in letters, or, as we should say, *arts*, is given. Nor is this because of the greater popularity of the natural sciences. It is not the faculty of mathematical and natural sciences,—a faculty which, like that of letters and philosophy, the student in general follows simply for purposes of education,—it is not this faculty that is frequented at the expense of the faculty of letters. The throng of students is in the faculties where *Brodstudien*, as the Germans say, are prosecuted,—in medicine and laws. This is especially the case at Naples, where I have seen in the lecture-rooms of these faculties a concourse of students said, and I can well believe it, to number not less than 400.

The Italian universities had, in 1862–63, 714 professors, of whom 542 are full or regular professors (*ordinarii*). It is the abundance of supplementary professors which shows intellectual life and movement in a university; through means of their lectures a subject gets treated on all its sides, the regular professors are kept up to the mark by a competition which stimulates them, and men fitted to be, when their turn comes, regular professors, are enabled to show themselves. The extra-professors and the *Privat-docenten* are thus the life of the German universities. The smaller universities there have nearly as many regular professors as the greater; what distinguishes Berlin or Heidelberg is the multitude of able men, who, as extra-professors or as *Privat-docenten*, are swelling the volume of university instruction there, and developing their own powers at the same time. The University of Freyburg in the Duchy of Baden has only seven regular professors less than Heidelberg; one has 34, the other 27; but Heidelberg has 53 extra-professors and *Privat-docenten*, while Freyburg has only 14. Berlin, in like manner, has 111 extra-professors and *Privat-docenten* to its 55 regular professors. In this way not only is the teaching augmented and stimulated, but the State, which pays the regular professors, is saved expense by having to provide fewer of them, and is enabled to pay them better and to make their chairs, as they should be, valuable prizes. Neither the stimulus nor the economy are to be found in the Italian university system. The university professors are,— for Italy, where officials are in general paid miserably, and none more miserably than those of secondary instruction,— not ill paid. A law passed in 1862 fixes the salaries of professors in the principal universities at 200*l.* and 240*l.* a year; of those in the less important ones at 120*l.* and 144*l.* But the burden of all these salaries has to be borne by the State. Nor does it get full work out of this host of regular professors. The same laxity and want of discipline which astonish us in the secondary schools prevail generally in the universities. The students are in the habit of departing when they think term (as we should say) has lasted long enough ; as vacation time approaches, which is when the students please, and not when the *Regolamento* pleases, ' the whole body of students with one accord,' says the official report, ' sometimes leave the schools deserted.'* Here again Turin forms an exception to the other Italian universities, and is exempt from their irregularity. Again, in France and Germany there are from thirty-two to thirty-seven weeks of lectures in the university year, with four lectures a week from all lecturers charged with the principal matters of study ; a professor's yearly course, therefore, contains from 90 to 120 lectures. From 60 to 70 lectures, or even less, is all that the Italian professors give a year. Finally, the students are in the habit of migrating from the university where they have studied to take their degree in some other university where the examinations are reported to be easier.

Italy has 15 universities,† which, with the *Istituto Superiore* of Florence, an establishment with a part of the teaching and of the degrees of a university, are all of them State institu-

---

* *Sulle Condizioni, &c.,* p. 197.

† They are the following: Bologna, Pisa, Pavia, Turin, Naples, Palermo, Modena, Parma, Genoa, Catania, Siena, Cagliari, Messina, Sassari, Macerata. To these will now be added the universities of Venetia.

tions. She has also four free universities,* as they are called ;
municipal institutions supported by their own funds, and,
when these fall short, by the municipality. Thus, for instance,
the free university of Camerino has property of the value of
35,469 francs a year; like several of the other universities, it
has not the complete number of faculties, it has only two,—
law and medicine. The municipality is bound, in return for
the privilege of possessing a body which gives. instruction
and degrees in law and medicine, to make good to the two
faculties their expenses, so far as they are not covered by
what their property and their fees bring them in.

The fifteen universities of the State are a heavy burden to
it. The State has taken their property, but their property and
their fees together represent an annual sum not approaching
that which the State spends upon them. Bologna had property which now lets at 15,000 francs a year, but the State
spends 490,000 francs on Bologna. Naples had a charge on
the *Gran Libro* of 19,591 francs a year ; this is now handed
over to the Clinical Institute, and the State spends 670,000
francs a year on the University of Naples. Palermo had
nearly 145,000 francs a year, which is now received by the
Treasury ; but the Treasury pays back to Palermo more than
420,000 francs. The University of Turin is still the nominal
possessor of its own property ; but this property is administered by the State, and what it brings in is treated as
ordinary State revenue, not as revenue to be specially applied
to the university, which, however, gets from the State nearly
620,000 francs a year. In short, the fourteen or fifteen millions of francs which is what the total property of the Italian
universities, when they became State establishments, was
worth, represent in annual value less than an eighth part of
the annual sum which the State now spends on the universities. Italy is spending yearly on her faculty-instruction
the prodigious sum of 5,500,000 of francs ; France spends
3,500,000 ; Prussia 3,000,000. But of the 3,500,000 of francs
which the French Treasury spends on faculty-instruction, it
gets back in fees, which are high and collected with regularity,
more than 2,500,000 ; so that the real cost of this instruction

* Urbino, Perugia, Camerino, and Ferrara.

to the State does not exceed 800,000 francs. In Prussia the fees are low, but the State outlay on faculty-instruction is in the first instance £100,000 less than that of Italy; and the State has for low fees this compensation, that what the student thus saves he spends on extra instruction, and at least the culture of the nation is a gainer. In Italy the fees are so low and so irregularly collected that they produce to the State less than 500,000 francs. Nor has the State the consolation of seeing its students, as in Germany, by paying extra-teachers who supplement the regular instruction, turn the cheapness of this to the best account.

As the municipal liberality, the vigorous organisation, the intellectual stir, of which in the Middle Age the Italian universities had the benefit, have died out, so has the college system of the Middle Age. Only a few years ago there were still left at Bologna one or two foreign colleges for free students; 'remains,' says Signor Matteucci, 'of the so many and famous colleges of the various nations which individuals and governments had founded in this celebrated university.' They are gone; and the college system of the mediæval university is no doubt unsuited to meet the general requirements of those who seek university instruction in our own time. The *Collegio delle Provincie,* which I have already mentioned, a foundation of comparatively modern date, still exists at Turin; and in connection with the university of this city there are not less, in all, than 170 free maintenances for students. Pavia has still the *Collegio Ghislieri,* with 66; some of the holders of these enjoy them at the University of Pavia, others at the Normal School of Pisa, others at the special schools of Turin and Milan. Pavia has also the *Collegio Borromeo,* with 28 free studentships. But the whole yearly sum which the State now disposes of for bursarships and exhibitions at the universities amounts to no more than 153,063 francs.*

* *Sulle Condizioni, &c.,* p. 161.

CHAPTER XII.

PRIVATE SCHOOLS AND ECCLESIASTICAL SCHOOLS.

STATE UNIVERSITIES AND SCHOOLS BETTER THAN ANY OTHERS IN ITALY—RELIGIOUS
CONGREGATIONS AND THEIR SCHOOLS—THE SECULAR CLERGY AND THEIR SEMINARIES
—TRENCHANT REFORMS IN THE SCHOOLS OF THE RELIGIOUS.

THERE seems no doubt that the free universities are the laxest in passing candidates ; as Turin, with its traditions of a strict public service, and Naples, with the life and competition created by its 5,000 students, are the strictest. There seems no doubt, too, that the secondary schools of the State are in general better than the private schools ; that the laxity, too great in the public schools, is yet greater in the private, which have also remained untouched by what improvement and progress have, since 1859, appeared in the public schools. ' The great danger of our private teaching,' say the Italian reports, ' consists in this; that blind and ignorant parents suffer themselves to be misled by the usurped reputation of a master who, knowing nothing, takes upon himself to teach everything, from *a*, *b*, *c*, to philosophy.' The same danger attends unregulated private schools in all countries; only in England we always console ourselves with our favourite maxim that the parents who send their children to these schools are ' acting in the spirit of self-respect and independence.'* In the same independent spirit, parents and boys like to cut as short as they can the period given to schooling. ' We find a febrile impatience ' (say the Italian reports again) ' to shorten the term of study ; and to gratify this impatience a number of private schools have sprung up, in which the

* See in the *Times*, of October 30th, 1866, the letter of Mr. Flint, Registrar to the Royal Commission on Popular Education.

getting through the work well is sacrificed to the getting through it quick.' These schools profess to do in two years what the public schools do in three; and as examinations have hitherto been very lax in Italy, and as in the assimilated or semi-private schools, which have been allowed to examine all comers, and which for the sake of the fees were glad to attract as many examinees as possible, they have been laxest of all, the half-prepared private school boy presented himself at an *istituto pareggiato* to pass the examination for the gymnasial licence or the lyceal licence, and generally managed to scramble through. This abuse became so flagrant that the minister has been obliged to take away from the *istituti pareggiati* the right of examining for the licence any pupils but their own.

In Upper Italy rather less than a fifth of the candidates for the gymnasial licence, and rather more than a fourth of the candidates for the lyceal licence, come from private schools. In Central Italy private school teaching, if estimated by the number of candidates it presents for these examinations, would appear next to nothing; its candidates are not six per cent. of the whole number presented. In Southern Italy, where education of all kinds is wanting, the whole number of candidates is, to be sure, insignificant; but of what there are the private schools send a better proportion; they send about a third of the candidates for the gymnasial licence, about a sixth of those for the lyceal.

As regards lay private schools, anything like complete statistics and information is not at present to be had. As regards ecclesiastical private schools it is different. These are of two kinds, the schools of the religious corporations and the seminaries or schools under episcopal control. In the report of the Superior Council of Public Instruction, from which I have quoted so much, no account is given of these schools. But at the end of 1865 the Minister of Public Instruction, Baron Natoli, having first instituted the necessary inquiries, drew up two reports* on them, which have

---

* *Statistica del Regno d'Italia: Istruzione data da Corporazioni religiose*; and *Statistica del Regno d' Italia: Istruzione data nei Seminari.* Florence, 1865.

since been printed, and which are full of curious and interesting matter.

All through Italy, in the Catholic reaction which followed the stoppage of the Reformation there, religious congregations were formed which took the management of education. The Jesuits have a world-wide celebrity, but the names at least of other congregations are not wholly unfamiliar to most of us; the Barnabites (authorised in 1533), the *Scolopi*, or *Scuole Pie* (1621), the Theatines (1524), the Redemptorists (1732), the Christian Brothers, of French origin, but extended to Italy (1600). Pious persons left money to build and endow schools in connection with these. societies. There were societies of each sex, with schools for each sex, for primary instruction and for secondary, for boarders and for day scholars. Anti-civil and anti-modern tendencies are generally imputed by the friends of progress to these corporations, and at the end of the last century they had fallen into disfavour. The reforms of the Emperor Joseph II. were hostile to them in his Italian dominions. The French rule, with its resolute maxims of lay and civil organisation, was more hostile still; but the governments which were restored in 1815 made alliance with them. Austria persisted for some time in the Josephine traditions, but after 1848 events forced her into the policy which led to the Concordat of 1856, and to the religious corporations this policy was, of course, favourable. Piedmont began the decisive change in this as in other things. The Piedmontese law of the 29th of May, 1855, suppressed a number of religious corporations. Then came 1859 and the annexation of the new provinces. These provinces, the moment they expelled their old governments, adopted the Piedmontese law, carrying it a little further. The Piedmontese law assigned for the benefit of the poorer and underpaid clergy the property of the corporations which were suppressed. The new provinces assigned a certain proportion to lay instruction and to charitable institutions. The Piedmontese law, however, had suffered the teaching corporations to subsist, while it abolished other religious corporations; and this exemption was maintained in the new provinces in order to keep their legislation at once with that of Piedmont. The party of progress regarded this as a mere temporary compromise, and demanded a far more radical reform. The government brought before the Italian Parliament a bill for the dissolution of all religious corporations. Baron Natoli says that the majority in the country desired such a measure. But the time was, at all events, not fully ripe for it, and the bill was, as we all remember, withdrawn.

Regarding, however, the respited corporations as certainly doomed, and their dissolution as only adjourned for a little while, the minister has taken the inventory of his victims' effects. It appears that there are 63 institutions in which secondary instruction is given by religious corporations. These institutions have 462 teachers and 5,752 boys. The girls are much more numerous. Of the boys 30 per cent. are boarders. Primary instruction, with which I am not now concerned, is given by the religious corporations to a far larger body of pupils, and among these, again, the girls far outnumber the boys.*

The minister speaks unfavourably of the instruction given by the religious. Attentively read, however, his criticisms point rather to disaffection in these teachers than to ignorance and incompetence. He says that their teaching tends to make bad citizens, and to keep up a spirit of resistance to the new order of things in Italy. He relates that when a royal inspector asked a girl in a school of the Ursuline nuns at Benevento who was the king of Italy, the girl, to avoid acknowledging the lawful sovereign, answered: *Il nostro re è Gesù Cristo.* He maintains that letters and sciences get a peculiar and illiberal tinge when taught in the cloister. He adds, going to more indisputable ground, that the management of their property by the religious corporations is in the highest degree wasteful and injudicious, and that in many cases funds once ample have by this management been rendered insufficient for the proper maintenance of the schools. In other cases funds still ample are abused; and he cites the instance of a college for girls at Milan, where with a revenue

---

* The numbers are as follows: total number of pupils of the religious corporations, 97,440; 62,901 girls and 18,712 boys. Of the latter, 12,960 are receiving primary instruction; 5,752 (as I have said) secondary.

of 8,000*l.* a year a band of 37 governesses and lay sisters maintain and teach 30 pupils.

The minister has been able to deal with the seminaries more effectually than with the schools of the religious corporations. The seminaries were instituted by the Council of Trent to train young men for holy orders without exposing them to the influence of the universities. These schools were placed in every diocese; they were governed by a rector whom the bishop nominated; they were subsidised out of the bishop's revenues, and entirely under his control. At first they confined themselves to their original design of solely training for the priesthood, and even exacted repayment from those who after benefiting by their endowments did not proceed into orders. Soon, however, their character changed. It was according to the notions of those days that education should be under clerical direction; persons desirous to found an endowment for the instruction of the lay youth in their locality founded it in connection with the seminaries. Municipalities, too poor to establish schools of their own, assigned grants to the seminaries on condition of their undertaking the instruction of those children who required it. The governments of the old time, looking upon the clergy as their natural and useful allies, not only did their best to get lay schools attached to the seminaries,—augmenting their property from the State domains, or diverting lay and communal foundations for their benefit,—but they also tried to put under the bishops' rule the schools of the religious corporations. The bishops were glad of the additional influence which an extended control over education placed in their hands. So it comes to pass that the kingdom of Italy, which has the prodigious number of 231 dioceses, has 260 seminaries or episcopal schools, one for each diocese and 29 to spare. These schools have 13,174 scholars, of whom 9,726 are boarders. There are 1,208 of their pupils under 12 years of age; the vocation of these, therefore, cannot be supposed to be yet very strongly declared. As many as 1,297 boys wear the lay costume and make no profession of any intention to go into orders; 8,429 wear the clerical habit, but numbers of these wear it for a time only, for the sake of a host of small exhibitions given by the seminaries to youths professing to prepare for orders, and for the sake of exemption from military service. When their object has been gained, when they have enjoyed their exhibition and escaped the conscription, they renounce their intention of going into orders. The recruitment for the clergy is becoming difficult in Italy, and this with 260 seminaries to serve as a field for it.

In fact not more than 52 of these institutions are real theological colleges. The mass of them are very indifferent secondary schools, too numerous to be well off either in good teachers or in pupils. They have on an average but 57 pupils to each institution, and 12 pupils to each class. The inquiries made by the minister convinced him of the general weakness of seminary instruction. The theological studies themselves are in a very depressed condition; with these, however, the State assumes no right to meddle. It leaves the care of these to the bishops, to whom the Council of Trent gave it. But the legislation of 1859 gives to the government in Italy the right of inspecting all establishments of secondary instruction, of exacting certain guarantees of capacity from those who conduct them, and of satisfying itself that nothing in their teaching or management violates morality or the laws. It was notorious that the seminaries openly preached disaffection. Two of them had become a public scandal from proved immorality. In most of them the teaching, consisting of Latin, a little Italian,—not the Italian of the classics of Italy, but an Italian false in taste and false in style,—very little arithmetic or mathematics, still less geography and history, and no study of the natural sciences at all, was quite unsuited to the wants of the present day. The schools of the religious associations had at least admitted inspection and satisfied the law by providing their teachers with the requisite certificates (*patenti d' idoneità*). But the ordinaries of the Italian dioceses maintained that State inspection of the seminaries was contrary to the laws of the church, which gives to the bishops the sole superintendence of the instruction and education in the seminaries. Employing a line of argument familiar to the clergy everywhere, they asked who but the bishops ought to exercise this superintendence, since they were to answer before God for the learning and virtue of those on whom they at ordination laid their hands. The government replied that of the learning and virtue of those whom they were going to ordain it left them the sole guardians, but that it had to satisfy itself about the learning and virtue of that great majority of their pupils who were destined to lay callings. A very few bishops accepted inspection with a good grace; many submitted reluctantly; some broke up their seminaries sooner than admit it; others shut their school-doors against it. The government persisted, and ordered the closing of all seminaries which would not admit the State inspector.

Eighty-two were closed by the middle of the year 1865. Then, by a decree dated the 1st of September in that year, the government ordered the reopening of all the seminaries which had been closed. But they were to reopen far other than they had closed. The State sequestrated their whole revenues. One-third it gave back, in each seminary, to the ordinary for a strictly theological college; the other two-thirds it assigned to the municipality for the purposes of public and lay secondary instruction. The task of seeing the work of partition and transformation carried into effect was committed to a gentleman who has many friends in this country, Signor Fusco. He accomplished his commission during the spring of 1866.

CHAPTER XIII.

REFORMS PROPOSED FOR SCHOOLS AND UNIVERSITIES IN ITALY.

THE EXECUTIVE SUPPORTED IN ITS REFORMS BY PUBLIC OPINION— EXTENSIVE REFORMS PROPOSED FOR THE UNIVERSITIES AND LAY SCHOOLS—NEED OF THE REFORMS PROPOSED—INTELLIGENCE OF ITALIAN STATESMEN.

THE Italian reformers of public instruction consider, however, that they have thus made only a beginning in what needs to be done with the seminaries. The minister announces a plan for reducing the 231 dioceses of the Italian kingdom at one blow to 59, a diocese for each province. Each diocese is to have one real theological college, *alto istituto seminaristico,* for training its clergy. This institution is alone to enjoy that exemption from State inspection which the seminaries claim. Schools for the laity are to be under laymen ; or, if ecclesiastics wish to conduct such schools, they must conduct them on the same conditions as laymen, by providing themselves with the legal guarantees of capacity, and by admitting State inspection.

The English jealousy of the executive, and reverence for vested interests, would probably incline us to designate these proceedings (at least it would if they were not employed against Papists) as tyrannical. I will only observe that in every single instance where a seminary has been closed, the local municipality has declared its satisfaction with the measure; in every single instance where endeavours have been made to get a closed seminary reopened, the local municipality has petitioned the government not to reopen it. The executive in Italy is in fact at this moment much stronger than even in France. It represents the lay and civil elements in society ; and the Italians, or that part of them which really determines the national policy, know that to make this element triumph is the necessity of the present moment for them. Thus the right of inspection of private schools, which in France is construed not to extend to their instruction, and therefore, except in the case of some signal offence against health, morality, or the law of the land (the three matters which the inspection of private schools is defined as regarding), remains practically unexercised,* and could not be exercised without exciting discontent and opposition, is in Italy construed, and with acquiescence and applause on the part of the public, to extend to the instruction, and to authorise the same examination as is practised by the State in the public schools. Unless we see what the lessons are, say the government authorities, how are we to satisfy ourselves that they do not contravene morality or the laws? A similar argument might be used in France; but in truth it is public opinion, and the national sense of what the wants of the nation are, that determines, for such a State right as the right of school inspection, the exact limits of its exercise. Only, if this right itself is not written in the laws, abuses of the gravest kind may prevail in the education of a country, and things may even come to a dead lock, whatever the wants of the nation may meanwhile be, without the possibility of applying a remedy.

The Superior Council recommends, for the universities and lay schools, reforms hardly less thorough than those which the minister recommends for the seminaries. The Council insists, in the first place, on the necessity of one organic education law for the kingdom,—*una legge universalmente accettata, e non derogata con provvedimenti transitori e particolari.* Recognising the expediency of interesting the provinces and communes in the secondary and primary schools by giving them a share in the supervision and management of them, it yet maintains that with the State, represented by the Minister of Public Instruction, rests the supreme duty of seeing that the whole concern of national education is properly and efficiently worked. It proposes to reduce the 59 *provveditori* to 10 or 14, to make the 59 provinces into 10 or 14 school

---

* It must be remembered, however, that the preliminary guarantee is taken of requiring titles of his capacity from every head of such schools.

districts by grouping several provinces together for each district, and to put at the disposal of each *provveditore* two or more visitors, or, as we should say, inspectors. These *provveditori* are the delegates of the State in the provinces, and, with their inspectors, answer in the main to the rectors and academy inspectors of France. As in France, there is to be at head-quarters a body of inspectors general, who are to make annual tours of inspection and annual reports. Their reports are to be published. It is calculated that this organisation, while it will enable the government to have for its ten or fourteen provincial delegates men of real weight and reputation, and while it will provide what is wanting at present, an effective inspection, will cost only half as much as the present system. The delegates who exercise inspection on behalf of the local powers, the Provincial School Council and the communes, are to be appointed by them and unpaid.

The Council further proposes that all teachers in the secondary schools shall be required to hold a diploma from a normal school. The only exceptions are teachers of arithmetic, who are to undergo an *esame d'abilitazione* before appointment. No equipollent titles are in future to be admitted, except works of approved merit published by the candidate on the subjects he is to teach, and recognised as of approved merit by the Superior Council of Public Instruction.

New programmes are to be drawn up by different commissions for the different branches of instruction, and after being adjusted to one another, and revised by a single commission formed by representatives from all the separate commissions, are to replace the present programmes, thrown together piecemeal, from different quarters and different hands, and without unity of aim.

For text-books used in the public schools approval by the Superior Council is to be strictly required. Only one grammar is to be used; for other matters more than one text-book may be used, but no text-book which has not had the Council's sanction.

The leaving examination at the *ginnasio** is to have for a counterpart and check to it an entrance examination at the

* *Licenza ginnasiale.*

liceo turning on exactly the same matters* and of exactly the same degree of difficulty. In like manner, the sincerity of the leaving examination at the *liceo*† is to be tested by an exactly corresponding entrance examination at the university.‡ The candidate must get seven-tenths of the allotted number of marks in each matter on which he proposes to follow lectures at the university. An attentive study of German schools and universities is visible in this and other parts of the Italian report.

Finally, to check cram for single examinations, and to check, in general, the scamped and hurried work which is laid to the charge of private schools, the Council proposes that the boy who comes from a private school or a private tutor to try for the *licenza liceale* shall undergo, besides the leaving examination for the licence itself, the two examinations which the public school boy has had to undergo at the end of his first and second school years.

Abroad far more than in England, where university instruction is the privilege of comparatively few, secondary instruction leads to superior or university instruction. For good superior instruction, says Signor Matteucci most truly, the two great requisites are, first, good secondary schools; secondly, first-rate men in the university chairs. It is the professor and not the charter which really makes the university,—*il successo di siffatti istituzioni riposa interamente sulla celebrità degli insegnanti.* Only the presence of such men can create that interest, that glow of intellectual life, which constitutes what the Italians, with their love of fine culture, happily call an *atmosfera intellettuale propizia agli studi.* To have their chairs filled by first-rate professors the Italian universities are at present far too numerous. The Council proposes to retain but three faculties of letters for all Italy. These faculties are at the same time to be normal schools to

---

* These are, on paper, translation from Latin, and composition in Italian; *viva voce*, Latin, Greek, and Italian grammar, elementary mathematics, history, and geography.

† *Licenza liceale.*

‡ These are, on paper, translation from Greek into Latin, and an Italian essay; *viva voce*, Greek, Latin, and Italian authors, philosophy, mathematics, physics, and natural history.

form schoolmasters for secondary instruction; their degrees are to be the schoolmaster's certificate, and the special examination for *agrégation* and the title of *agrégé*, of which I have spoken at length in my account of France, are to be introduced, and are to form, in Italy as in France, the schoolmaster's *honours*, and his title to the higher posts in his profession. The universities of Turin, Pisa, and Naples are to be the seats of these faculties. Pisa already possesses a normal school, which now in fact comprises, one may say, the whole body of students following the faculty of letters at Pisa. Turin has in its *Collegio delle Provincie* an institution just suitable to be amalgamated, for normal school purposes, with the faculty of letters at the university. Naples is so great a university that the literary normal school for southern Italy must clearly be placed there; and the new institution may probably awaken some of that zeal for the study of letters which at present is wanting in the Neapolitan university.

Similarly there are to be but three high faculties or superior normal schools for the mathematical and natural sciences. These are to be in connection with the universities of Naples and Turin and the Museum of Florence. These three schools will alone examine and give degrees in mathematics and natural sciences, as the three schools or faculties of Turin, Pisa, and Naples will alone examine and give degrees in letters.

The remaining universities will only preserve two faculties, those of law and medicine. The government will maintain eleven of each; it will maintain faculties both of law and medicine at Naples, Turin, Bologna, Pisa, Pavia, Palermo, Genoa, Catania, Parma, and Modena; a faculty of law at Sassari, and one of medicine at Cagliari.

The reorganisation of theological study is left for a future occasion. At present the seminaries have possession of this study. It will be desirable, say the authorities, to connect it, in part at least, with the universities, the dogmatic part being still left to the seminary, the auxiliary parts of a theological training being committed to the university, and university degrees being required in them. But this connection of the clergy with the universities,—from the point

of view of a nation's civil interests, at any rate, so desirable,
—has not yet been accomplished even in France.

Provinces, communes, and private associations are still to
be at liberty to maintain free universities; and the Council
recommends that the government should cede to them, on
application, the buildings, collections, and scientific apparatus
of the faculties which it abandons. These free universities,
however, are only to admit students who pass the entrance
examination to be fixed by an organic law for the whole
kingdom, which examination is henceforth to be required of
every university student; and they are not to confer degrees,
which will only be conferred by examining commissions in
connection with the faculties maintained by the State.

These examining commissions are to be named by the
Minister of Public Instruction, and to consist of university
professors and members of the principal literary and scientific bodies of the kingdom. The programmes of examination
are to be approved by the Superior Council of Public Instruction.

English university men will be astonished at hearing that
an Italian student's average yearly cost for maintaining himself at the university is calculated at 800 fr. (32*l.*) It is
proposed that the State should found a certain number of
scholarships of this value, and of half this value, to be obtained by competitive examination. These scholarships are
to be in connection with free universities, as well as with
those of government. The fees for university lectures are to
be raised. These fees have been reduced very low, without
any corresponding increase in the number of students frequenting the lectures. The duration of the university courses,
the number of lectures in them, the periods at which the
preparatory examination and the final degree examination
for the *laurea,* or doctorate, shall occur, are all to be fixed by
the organic law. All university examinations are to be *per
materia,* and not, like ours at Oxford and the old examinations
in Italy, in several matters lumped together.

The Council proposes, in order to complete the organisation of superior instruction for the kingdom, certain high
schools for practical and professional instruction also. The

present *scuole d'applicazione* at Turin, Milan, and Naples, are to form three high schools of engineering, civil and military. Six clinical institutes, to receive pupils who have completed their studies in a faculty of medicine, are to be established in connection with the great hospitals of Bologna, Florence, Milan, Naples, Palermo, and Turin. The seven or eight observatories of the kingdom, following the plan of strengthening by suppression and amalgamation which the establishments of Italy so generally need, are to be reduced to three or four. It is even recommended that in this country of local academies and municipal spirit one representative academy should be formed, to take the lead as embodying the science and culture of Italy. There are at present, in the kingdom of Italy, 54 literary or scientific institutions with the name or nature of an academy.

These are sweeping reforms to propose,* but then education in Italy needs to be reconstructed from the very bottom. We must remember from what a state of neglect, laxity, and bad government the start has to be made. Nearly three quarters of the population of Italy, over five years of age, are *analfabeti*,† as the Italians call it,—unable to read and write. The old government of Naples opposed the establishment of even infant schools ; there were actually but four of them in the city of Naples before the revolution. Primary schools hardly existed ; the municipality of Palermo has set on foot 140 of them since 1859. There were hardly any public secondary schools ; bad schools kept by the monks and Jesuits, in which some Latin was taught, but scarcely anything else,—no Greek, no modern languages or modern history, and no natural history,—were the substitute. Since 1859 there has been a great movement of school opening and school organising ; but this movement has to work with the instruments it finds ready to its hand, and these instruments have the slack and easy-going habits which so many Italians seem to have contracted from the conditions of their national life during the last two centuries. One or two men of genius in important

---

* They have not yet (at the end of 1867) been carried into effect.

† The exact rate is 746·82 of *analfabeti* for each 1,000 of population. The proportion is greater for the female sex than the male : 812·66 for the former to 680·90 for the latter.

posts work themselves nearly to death, but to get day after day a fair day's work out of every one of her citizens who has an employment, public or private, to discharge, seems at present, to a stranger, the great want for Italy. Her school system is very much modelled on that of the French; and this makes the slack habits of so many of the Italian schools, those in the south particularly, the more conspicuous, because one is reminded of France, where a similar school organisation has all done for it that hard work, discipline, and exactitude can do. The professors in the Italian secondary schools are underpaid; 2,000 fr. (80*l.*) a year is at present their highest salary; but they are also in general underworked, some of them not having more than three hours' work a week, and most of them giving you the impression that what they really require is an iron system which shall get five or six hours of steady work every day out of them. I find in my notes this entry respecting a great Italian public school which I will not name: 'Good building, bad smells, unsatisfactory *proviseur*, weak professors, and inaccurate Latin and Greek.' The same entry would more or less apply to far too large a number of the public schools in Italy.

The schools under ecclesiastical management were in some respects the best of those I saw in Italy. Nowhere on the Continent have I seen such good accommodation, according to our English notions, for boarders, as at the *Collegio Nazareno* in Rome and at the Barnabites' School at Moncalieri. The boys have rooms to themselves, and excellent rooms. Nowhere in Italy did I find the Greek so good (but a lesson was not more than three or four lines of Homer) as at Moncalieri. Nowhere in Italy did I find such good Latin as that which the *Collegio Romano* at Rome, in its *Virgil* lesson and its boys questioning one another in prosody, showed me. Very likely he who has been reared in an English public school has in general a certain prepossession for schools conducted by ecclesiastics, and has, from his own training, a stronger satisfaction at finding Latin and Greek properly learnt than at finding anything else. But there is no doubt that the current which is bearing the Italians away from clerical schools, and carrying them towards public and lay schools, is the main current of modern civilisation. Perhaps even in the aversion of her students for the old classical studies, in their strong preference for studies which are scientific, modern, and positive, Italy is again showing that quick instinct of a change in the forms and conditions of the higher culture, that tact for a new phase of intellectual life, which she has so decisively shown before. The most animated and effective lessons, as regards both teachers and pupils, that I saw given in Italy, were lessons to a large class in the *liceo Parini* at Milan, on the sense of hearing and on magnetism.

The Italian schools may, possibly, flourish without the Latin or Greek of the great German or English or French schools, but without their steadiness and genuine work they cannot. They are themselves beginning to see this, and at the Normal School of Pisa,—where, in 1862, at the first competitive examination, out of 31 candidates who presented themselves, 20 were admitted,—at last year's examination only 7 candidates were admitted out of 27, the diminution being due, not to a falling off in the candidates' attainments, but to a rise in the examiners' standard. If the distinguished statesmen who now direct public instruction in Italy can but get this bracing and stringent treatment resolutely applied and strictly followed, their direction will soon show excellent fruits. Intelligent this direction is sure to be ; for no statesmen can perceive more clearly than the statesmen of this *terre des sentiments humains*, that a government's duty in education is not to fear and flatter ignorance, prejudice, and obstructiveness, but *comprendere, e insinuare nello spirito pubblico, che una buona organizzazione degli studi, e la grandezza intellettuale di una nazione, sono i più saldi fondamenti della potenza degli stati e della vera e ordinata libertà dei popoli.*

III.

GERMANY.

CHAPTER XIV.

DEVELOPMENT OF THE GERMAN SECONDARY SCHOOLS.

THE RENAISSANCE AND THE REFORMATION—THE GERMAN SCHOOLS AND THE REFOR-
MATION—DECLINE OF THE GERMAN SCHOOLS AND THEIR RECOVERY.

THE schools of France and Italy owed little to the great
modern movement of the Renaissance. In both these
countries that movement operated, in both it produced mighty
results ; but of the official establishments for instruction it did
not get hold. In Italy the mediæval routine in those establishments at first opposed a passive resistance to it; presently
came the Catholic reaction, and sedulously shut it out from
them. In France the Renaissance did not become a power
in the State, and the routine of the schools sufficed to exclude
the new influence till it took for itself other channels than
the schools. But in Germany the Renaissance became a
power in the State; allied with the Reformation, where the
Reformation triumphed in German countries the Renaissance
triumphed with it, and entered with it into the public schools.
Melanchthon and Erasmus were not merely enemies and
subverters of the dominion of the Church of Rome, they were
eminent humanists ; and with the great but single exception
of Luther, the chief German reformers were all of them
distinguished friends of the new classical learning, as well
as of Protestantism. The Romish party was in German
countries the ignorant party also, the party untouched by the
humanities and by culture.

Perhaps one reason why in England our schools have not
had the life and growth of the schools of Germany and
Holland is to be found in the separation, with us, of the
power of the Reformation and the power of the Renaissance.
With us, too, the Reformation triumphed and got possession

of our schools; but our leading reformers were not at the
same time, like those of Germany, the nation's leading spirits
in intellect and culture.   In Germany the best spirits of the
nation were then the reformers; in England our best spirits,
—Shakspeare, Bacon, Spenser,—were men of the Renaissance,
not men of the Reformation, and our reformers were men of
the second order.   The Reformation, therefore, getting hold
of the schools in England was a very different force, a force
far inferior in light, resources, and prospects, to the Reformation getting hold of the schools in Germany.

But in Germany, nevertheless, as Protestant orthodoxy
grew petrified like Catholic orthodoxy, and as, in consequence,
Protestantism flagged and lost the powerful impulse with
which it started, the school flagged also, and in the middle
of the last century the classical teaching of Germany, in spite
of a few honourable names like Gesner's, Ernesti's, and
Heyne's, seems to have lost all the spirit and power of the
16th century humanists, to have been sinking into a mere
church appendage, and fast becoming torpid.   A theological
student, making his livelihood by teaching till he could get
appointed to a parish, was the usual schoolmaster.   'The
schools will never be better,' said their great renovator,
Friedrich August Wolf, the well-known critic of Homer, 'so
long as the schoolmasters are theologians by profession.   A
theological course in a university, with its smattering of
classics, is about as good a preparation for a classical master
as a course of feudal law would be.'*   Wolf's coming to Halle
in 1783, invited by Von Zedlitz, the minister for public
worship under Frederick the Great, a sovereign whose civil
projects and labours were not less active and remarkable
than his military, marks an era from which the classical
schools of Germany, reviving the dormant spark planted in
them by the Renaissance, awoke to a new life, which, since

---

* See a most interesting article on Wolf in the *North British Review* for June
1865.   Not only for its account of Wolf, but for its sketch of the movement in the
higher education of Germany at a very critical time, this article well deserves
studying; and having been obliged to make myself acquainted with many of the
matters which its writer touches, I may perhaps be allowed, without appearing
guilty of presumption, to add that it seems to me as trustworthy as it is interesting.

the beginning of this century, has drawn the eyes of all students of intellectual progress upon them. Prussia was the scene of Wolf's labours, and the Prussian schools, both from their own excellence and from the preponderating importance of Prussia at the present time, are naturally the first in Germany to attract the observer's attention. Having begun with France, and then proceeded to Italy, which it was desirable to visit before the full heats of summer set in, I could not reach Germany till the beginning of July, when it wanted but a fortnight of the annual school vacation. This fortnight I spent in Berlin, and before the schools closed I visited all the more important of them, and attended their classes as I had attended those of the schools in France and Italy. Then came the holidays, longer than ours because the foreign schools have in their school year only this one break of any importance; at Christmas and Easter they have only a few days' vacation. The holidays not beginning at the same time in North and South Germany, I was enabled, after leaving Berlin, to see some schools at work in the Rhine Province, and later I visited the famous establishment of Schulpforta, and other establishments both in Prussian and in non-Prussian parts of Germany. In general, however, though everywhere I was obligingly received and furnished with all possible information, the holidays, either in prospect, actual, or just ended, interfered so much with my seeing the schools in full operation, that the fortnight I passed at Berlin remained the most valuable part, by far, of my experience in German schools. This being so, and it being evidently convenient to select the school system of some one country of Germany for particular description, and for a representative of that of others where the schools follow, in general, the same course, I will choose that of Prussia for this purpose. As a rule, the secondary schools of Northern and Central Germany are better than those of Southern, and those of Protestant Germany better than those of Catholic. This will hardly be disputed; yet the school system all through Germany is in its main features much the same, and is, in its completeness and carefulness, such as to excite a foreigner's admiration. In Austria this excellent school system is not wanting; what is wanting there is the life, power, and faith in its own operations which animate it in other parts of Germany. Nowhere has it this life and faith more than in Prussia. It has them, indeed, in other and smaller German territories as well; a Prussian will himself readily admit that the schools of Frankfort,* or of the kingdom of Würtemberg, are as good as his own. But it is in countries of the scale and size of Prussia that a living and powerful school system bears the most noteworthy fruits; and it is in Prussia, therefore, that I now proceed to trace them.

* This was written before Frankfort became Prussian.

CHAPTER XV.

PRESENT ORGANISATION OF THE SECONDARY OR HIGHER SCHOOLS IN PRUSSIA.

THE PRUSSIAN SCHOOLS REPRESENTATIVES OF THOSE OF GERMANY—HIGHER SCHOOLS OF PRUSSIA—GYMNASIEN—PROGYMNASIEN—REALSCHULEN—HÖHERE BÜRGERSCHULEN —VORSCHULEN, OR PREPARATORY SCHOOLS—NUMBERS OF TEACHERS AND SCHOLARS.

THE schools with which we are concerned, the secondary schools as the French call them, the higher schools (*höhere Schulen*) as the Germans call them, are in Prussia thus classed: Gymnasiums, Progymnasiums, Real Schools, Upper Burgher Schools (*Gymnasien, Progymnasien, Realschulen, höhere Bürgerschulen*). Above these are the universities, below them the primary or elementary schools.*

At the head of these secondary schools, and directly leading to the universities, are the *Gymnasien*. The uniform employment of this term *Gymnasium* to designate them, dates from a government instruction of 1812. Before this they were variously called by the names of Gymnasium, Lyceum, Pædagogium, College, Latin School, and others.

A gymnasium has properly six classes, counted upwards from the sixth, the lowest, to the first (*prima*), the highest. But, in fact, in all large schools the classes have an upper part and a lower part, and each part has, if necessary, two parallel groups (*cœtus*). The sixth and fifth classes form the lower division of the school, the fourth and third the middle division, the second and first the upper division. In former times the *Fachsystem*, or system by which the pupil was in

---

* The middle school (*Mittelschule*), variously called *Stadtschule, Bürgerschule, Rectoratschule*, is in truth only an elementary school of a higher grade, and in France is called *école élémentaire supérieure*, in Switzerland, *höhere Volkschule, Secundarschule*. A description of a school of this kind will be found in my account of the schools of Canton Zurich.

different classes for the different branches of his instruction, was prevalent; since 1820 this system has been gradually superseded by the *Classensystem*, which keeps the pupil in the same class for all his work. The course in each of the three lower classes is of one year, in each of the three higher of two years, making nine in all; it being calculated that a boy should enter the gymnasium when he is nine or ten years old, and leave it for the university when he is eighteen or nineteen.

The *Lehrplan,* or plan of work, is fixed for all *Gymnasien* by ministerial authority, as in France and Italy. It is far, however, from being a series of detailed programmes as in those countries. What it does is to fix the matters of instruction, the number of hours to be allotted to them, the gradual development of them from the bottom of the school to the top. Within the limits of the general organisation of study thus established, great freedom is left to the teacher, and great variety is to be found in practice.

Some years ago the hours of work were 32 in the week. This was found too much, and since 1856, in the lowest class of a gymnasium there are 28 hours of regular school work in the week, in the five higher classes there are 30 hours. The school hours are in the morning from 7 to about 11 in summer, from 8 to about 12 in winter; in the afternoon they are from 2 to 4 all the year round. As in France, there is but one half-holiday in the week, and it is in the middle of the week.

Latin has ten hours a week given to it in all five classes below *prima,* and eight in *prima.* Greek begins in *quarta,* and thenceforward has six hours a week in each class, by which the reader will at once see that we are no longer in France or Italy, but in a country whose schools treat the study of Greek as seriously as the best schools among ourselves. The mother tongue (and here we quit the practice of English schools) has two hours a week in all classes below *prima,* and three in *prima.* But in the two lowest classes it is always taught in connection with Latin and by the same teacher, and time may, if necessary, be taken from Latin to give to it. Arithmetic or mathematics have four hours a week in *secunda* and *prima*, three in *quinta*, *quarta*, and *tertia*, and four again in the lowest class. French begins in *quinta*, and is the only modern language except their own which the boys learn as part of the regular school work; it has three hours a week in *quinta*, and two in all the classes above. Many gymnasiums offer their pupils the opportunity of learning English or Italian, but as an extra matter. Geography and history have two hours a week in *sexta* and *quinta*, and thenceforward three hours. The natural sciences get two hours in *prima* and one in *secunda*; in the rest of the school they are the most movable part of the work, the school authorities having it in their power to take time from them to give to arithmetic, geography, and history, or to add time to them in places where there is no *Realschule* and the boys in the middle of the gymnasium wish to study the natural sciences in preference to Greek. Drawing is a part of the regular school work in the three lower classes of the school, and has two hours a week. *Sexta* and *quinta* have three hours a week of the writing master.

Every class has religious instruction; *sexta* and *quinta* for three hours a week, the four higher classes for two. All the boys learn singing and gymnastics, and all who are destined for the theological faculty at the university learn in *secunda* and *prima* Hebrew; but these three matters do not come into the regular school hours.

I have said that in places where there is no *Realschule* boys in the middle division of a gymnasium may substitute other studies for that of Greek. Where there is a *Realschule* accessible, this is not permitted; and in the upper division of a gymnasium it is nowhere permitted. In general, the gymnasium is steadily to regard the *allgemeine wissenschaftliche Bildung* of the pupil, the formation of his mind and of his powers of knowledge, without prematurely taking thought for the practical applicability of what he studies. It is expressly forbidden to give this practical or professional turn to the studies of a pupil in the highest forms of a gymnasium, even when he is destined for the army.

Progymnasiums are merely gymnasiums without their higher classes. Most progymnasiums have the lower and middle divisions of a gymnasium, four classes; some have only the lower division and half of the middle, three classes some, again, have all the classes except *prima*. The progymnasium follows, so far as it has the same classes, the *Lehrplan* of the gymnasium. In the small towns, where it is not possible to maintain at once a progymnasium and a *Realschule*, the progymnasium has often parallel classes for classical and for non-classical studies. But in general the tendency within the last five years has been for the progymnasium to develope itself into the full gymnasium, and when I was at Berlin Dr. Wiese, a member of the Council of Education there, to whom I am indebted for much valuable assistance,* pointed out to me on the map a number of places, scattered all about the Prussian dominions, where this process was either just completed or still going on.

To reform the old methods of teaching the classics, to reduce their preponderance, to make school studies bear more directly upon the wants of practical life, and to aim at imparting what is called 'useful knowledge,' were projects not unknown to the seventeenth and eighteenth century as well as to ours. Comenius, a Moravian by birth, who in 1641 was invited to England in order to remodel the schools here, and in the following century Rousseau in France and Basedow in Germany, promulgated, with various degrees of notoriety and success, various schemes with one or other of these objects. The Philanthropinum of Dessau, an institution established in pursuance of them, was an experiment which made much noise in its day. It was broken up about 1780, but its impulse and the ideas which set this impulse in motion, continued, and bear fruit in the *Realschulen*. The name *Realschule* was first used at Halle; a school with that title was established there by Christoph Semler, in 1738. This *Realschule* did not last long, but it was followed by others in different parts of the country. They took a long time to hit their right line and to succeed; it is said to be

---

* Dr. Wiese has written an interesting work on the English public schools, but his book on those of Prussia, *Das höhere Schulwesen in Preussen*; Berlin, 1864 (pp. 740), is a mine of the fullest, most authentic information on the subject of which it treats, and is indispensable for all who have to study this closely.

only from 1822 that the first really good specimen dates. This one was at Berlin, and though it did not begin to work thoroughly well till 1822, it had been founded in 1747, and had been in existence ever since that time. Its founder's name was Johann Hecker, who was a Berlin parish-clergyman. The Government began to occupy itself with the *Realschulen* in 1832, and as the growth of industry and the spread of the modern spirit gave them more and more importance, a definite plan and course had to be framed for them, as for the *Gymnasien.* This was done in 1859.* *Realschulen* were distinguished as of three kinds ; *Realschulen* of the first rank, *Realschulen* of the second rank, and higher Burgher Schools. For *Realschulen* of the first rank the number and system of classes was the same as that for the *Gymnasien*; the full course was of nine years. The *Lehrplan* fixes a rather greater number of hours of school work for them than the *Gymnasien* have ; 30 for the lowest class, 31 for the class next above, 32 for each of the four others.

All three kinds of *Realschulen* are for boys destined to callings for which university studies are not required. But Latin is still obligatory in *Realschulen* of the first rank, and in the three lower classes of these schools it has more time allotted to it than any other subject. In the highest class it comes to its minimum of time, three hours ; and in this class, and in *secunda*, the time given to mathematics and the natural sciences amounts altogether to eleven hours a week. As the *Realschule* leads, not to the university, but to business, English becomes obligatory in it as well as French. French, however, has most time allotted to it. Religious instruction has the same number of hours here as in the *Gymnasien.* Drawing, which in the *Gymnasien* ceases after *quarta* to be a part of the regular school work, has in the *Realschule* two hours a week in each of the five classes below *prima*, and three in *prima*.

It is found that after *quarta*, that is, after three years of school, many of the *Realschule* boys leave ; and an attempt

* By the *Unterrichts- und Prüfungsordnung für die Realschulen und die höheren Bürgerschulen*, of the 6th of October in that year.

is therefore made to render the first three years' course as substantial and as complete in itself as possible.

The *Realschulen* of the second rank have the six classes of those of the first; but they are distinguished from them by not having Latin made obligatory, by being free to make their course a seven years' course instead of a nine, and, in general, by being allowed a considerable latitude in varying their arrangements to meet special local wants. A *general*, not professional, mental training, is still the aim of the *Realschule* of the first rank, in spite of its not preparing for the university. A lower grade of this training, with an admixture of directly practical and professional aims, satisfies the *Realschule* of the second rank.

Where a gymnasium and a *Realschule* are united in a single establishment, under one direction, the classes *sexta* and *quinta* may be common to both, but above *quinta* the classes must be separate.

The term *Bürgerschule* was long used interchangeably with that of *Realschule*. The regulations of 1859 have assigned the name of higher Burgher School to that third class of *Realschulen*, which has not the complete system of six forms that the *Gymnasien* and the other two kinds of *Realschulen* have. The higher Burgher School stands, therefore, to the *Realschule* in the same relation in which the *Progymnasium* stands to the *Gymnasium*. Some Burgher Schools have as many as five classes, only lacking *prima*. The very name of the *Bürgerschulen* indicates that in the predominance of a local and municipal character, and in the smaller share given to classics, they follow the line of the *Realschulen* of the second order. Still Latin has three or four hours a week in all the best of these schools. They are, however, the least classical of all the higher schools; but several of them, in small places where there cannot be two schools, have gymnasial classes parallel with the *real* classes, just as certain *Gymnasien*, in like circumstances, have real classes parallel with their classical classes.

As the elementary schools pursue a course of teaching which is not specially designed as a preparation for the higher schools, it has become a common practice to establish

Vorschulen, or preparatory schools, as in France, to be appendages of the several higher schools, to receive little boys without the previous examination in reading, writing, arithmetic, grammar and Scripture history, which the higher school imposes, and to pass them on in their tenth year, duly prepared, into the higher school. These *Vorschulen* have in general two classes.

These are the higher or secondary schools of Prussia. Before the recent war, the population of Prussia was 18,476,500. The latest complete school returns are those for the year 1863. In 1863, Prussia possessed 255 higher schools, with 3,349 teachers in them, and 66,135 scholars. She had 84 *Vorschulen*, or public preparatory schools, with 188 teachers, and 8,027 scholars. Of the 255 higher schools, 172 were classical schools, gymnasiums or progymnasiums, with 45,403 scholars; 83 were non-classical schools, belonging to one or other of the three orders of *Realschulen*, with 20,732 scholars.

All these schools have a public character, are subject to State inspection, must bring their accounts to be audited by a public functionary, and can have no masters whose qualifications have not been strictly and publicly tried. The reader will recollect that we found in the public schools of France 65,832 scholars in the year 1865. He will recollect also that we found, I will not say in the public schools of England, but in all the schools which by any straining or indulgence can possibly be made to bear that title, 15,880 scholars. In the public higher schools and preparatory schools of Prussia we find 74,162 scholars.

I will not now press this comparison, but will pass on to show in what way the higher schools of Prussia have a public character.

CHAPTER XVI.

GOVERNMENT AND PATRONAGE OF THE PRUSSIAN PUBLIC SCHOOLS.

COMMON LAW OF PRUSSIA—STATE-ACTION AND REGULATION—ORIGIN AND HISTORY OF THE CENTRAL EDUCATION DEPARTMENT—ORIGIN AND HISTORY OF THE PRO-VINCIAL SCHOOL AUTHORITIES—PROVINCIAL SCHOOL BOARDS AND DISTRICT SCHOOL BOARDS—EXAMINING COMMISSIONS—LOCAL AND MUNICIPAL SCHOOL AUTHORITIES—ENDOWMENTS AND CHARITIES ; THEIR MANAGEMENT—PATRONAGE OF SCHOOLS.

THERE is no organic school-law in Prussia like the organic school-law of France, though sketches and projects of such a law have more than once been prepared. But at present the public control of the higher schools is exercised through administrative orders and instructions, like the minutes of our Committee of Council on Education. But the administrative authority has in Prussia a very different basis for its operations from that which it has in England, and a much firmer one. It has for its basis these articles of the *Allgemeine Landrecht*, or common law of Prussia, which was drawn up in writing in Frederick the Great's reign, and promulgated in 1794, in the reign of his successor :—

' Schools and universities are State institutions, having for their object the instruction of youth in useful information and scientific knowledge.

' Such establishments are to be instituted only with the State's previous knowledge and consent.

' All public schools and public establishments of education are under the State's supervision, and must at all times submit themselves to its examinations and inspections.

' Whenever the appointment of teachers is not by virtue of the foundation or of a special privilege vested in certain persons or corporations, it belongs to the State.

' Even where the immediate supervision of such schools

and the appointment of their teachers is committed to certain
private persons or corporations, new teachers cannot be
appointed, and important changes in the constitution and
teaching of the school cannot be adopted, without the previous knowledge or consent of the provincial school authorities.

'The teachers in the gymnasiums and other higher schools
have the character of State functionaries.'

To the same effect the Prussian Deed of Constitution (*Ver-
fassungs-Urkunde*) of 1850 has the following :—

'For the education of the young sufficient provision is to
be made by means of public schools.

'Every one is free to impart instruction, and to found and
conduct establishments for instruction, when he has proved
to the satisfaction of the proper State authorities that he
has the moral, scientific, and technical qualifications requisite.

'All public and private establishments are under the supervision of authorities named by the State.'

With these principles to serve as a basis, administrative
control can be exercised without much difficulty. These
principles, however, may with real truth be said to form part
of the common law of Prussia, for they form part of almost
every Prussian citizen's notions of what is right and fitting
in school concerns. It would be a mistake to suppose that
the State in Prussia shows a grasping and centralising
spirit in dealing with education; on the contrary, it makes
the administration of it as local as it possibly can; but it
takes care that education shall not be left to the chapter of
accidents.

Up to the middle of the last century, however, the higher
schools were so far left to this chapter of accidents, that the
State practised little or no interference with the free action
of patrons. But it is important to observe that the State
was always, in Prussia, an important school patron itself,
and exercised its rights of patronage, while in England
these rights slipped from its hands. Royal foundations for
schools are in Prussia very numerous, and in all Prussian
schools of royal foundation the patronage remains vested in

the Crown till this day. Schools like Eton and Westminster, like King Edward's School at Birmingham, like the grammar schools of Sherborne, of Bury St. Edmunds, and so many others, would have been in Prussia 'Crown patronage schools,' with a public, responsible, disinterested authority nominating their masters. So far, therefore, even without any assertion of the 'right of the State to control private patrons, the higher schools of Prussia have a security which ours have not. The assertion of such a State right, beyond the mere rights of the Crown as a patron, appears in the reign of Friedrich Wilhelm I., and gains definiteness and purpose from that time forth. The *General-Directorium* created by this sovereign, in 1722, was a ministerial body with a department for spiritualities (*Geistliches Departement*) to which the exercise of the Crown rights of control over churches and schools were entrusted. This department was in a few years attached to that of the Minister of Justice, and as such it was held by an able minister, formed in Frederick the Great's school, Von Zedlitz, who in 1787 separated the church and school affairs of the *Geistliches Departement*, and committed the school affairs to a High Board of Schools (*Ober-Schulcollegium*). In the great movement of reconstruction which between 1806 and 1812 renewed the civil and military organisation of Prussia, the Board of Schools was abolished, and the Education Department was made, in 1808, a section of the Home Office. Wilhelm von Humboldt was placed at its head.* Finally, in 1817, this Education section became an independent ministerial department, and its chief took the title of Minister for Spiritualities and Education (*Minister der geistlichen und Unterrichtsangelegenheiten*). The first minister was Freiherr von Altenstein. Medicine having been added to the affairs over which this department has supervision, the minister's full style now is *Minister der geistlichen Unterrichts- und Medicinal-Angelegenheiten*. The present minister is Dr. von Mühler.

When the Education Department was made a section of

---

* In June 1810, Wilhelm von Humboldt went as Prussian envoy to Vienna, and the rest of his public life was chiefly passed, as is well known, in the diplomatic service of his country.

the Home Office, Wilhelm von Humboldt had two functionaries with the title of *technische Räthe*, technical counsellors,
placed with him.   These *technische Räthe* have now grown
into eight, and they, with the Minister and the under Secretary of State for the department, constitute the central
authority for the affairs of education.

But in Prussia it is not the central minister who has the
most direct and important action on the schools, it is the
authorities representing the State in the several parts of the
country.   It is from Wilhelm von Humboldt's accession to
office in 1808 that the establishment of a fruitful relation
between these two authorities, the schools and the central
power, really dates.   Before that time, in accordance with
the notions which closely connected the School with the
Church, the provincial authorities with an action upon the
schools were the consistories.   These were, indeed, State
authorities, for their members are named by the Crown, or
head of the State; the head of the State being in Prussia far
more practically than in England the head of the Church
also, inasmuch as in Prussia the Crown is actually *summus
episcopus*, the powers of supervision and discipline vested of
old in the bishops, and in England, where we have kept our
bishops, still vested in them, having gone, in Protestant Germany, straight to the Crown.   The Crown as *summus episcopus*
exercises its rights through consistories, and the members of
the consistories are in consequence nominees of the State.
The consistories therefore supplied a provincial State authority for dealing with schools.   But the employment of
them for this purpose had two evident administrative inconveniences, to say nothing of other objections to it.   In the
first place, the consistories were in relation at the centre of
Government not with the Education Department but with
the High Consistory.   In the second place, it is only as a
Protestant sovereign that the King of Prussia is head of the
Church and represented throughout the country by consistories.   As a Catholic sovereign he is not head of the
Church, and has in the provinces no consistory or ecclesiastical authority which is also a State authority.   But Prussia
has nearly seven millions of Catholic subjects.   For Catholic

schools, therefore, as well as for Protestant, a provincial State authority was required, and this authority the consistory could not supply.

The administration of 1808 established in each of the *Regierungen*, or governmental districts, into which Prussia was divided, a deputation for worship and public instruction (*Deputation für Cultus und öffentlichen Unterricht*). These deputations were in immediate connexion with the Education Department at Berlin, they represented, in the supervision of the schools in the provinces, the State authority, and exercised for the most part the Crown patronage. In 1810 were added three Scientific Deputations (*Wissenschaftliche Deputationen*), one at Berlin, one at Königsberg, one at Breslau, to examine teachers for the secondary schools and to advise the Government on all important matters relating to these. The Berlin deputation had for its members the two *technische Räthe* of the Education Department, Süvern and Nicolovius, and besides these, Ancillon, Friedrich August Wolf, and Schleiermacher. The English reader will observe the sort of persons who in Prussia were chosen for the management, at a critical moment, of the State's relations with education.

The higher schools of Prussia feel to this day the benefits of that management. Variations took place in the organisation of the provincial authority, as the different divisions of the Prussian monarchy were constituted afresh, but its general character remained the same, and has remained so till this day. Prussia is now divided into eight provinces,* and these eight provinces are again divided into twenty-six governmental districts, or *Regierungen*. There is a Provincial School Board (*Provinzial-Schulcollegium*) in the chief town of each of the eight provinces, and a Governmental District Board in that of each of the twenty-six *Regierungen*. In general, the State's relations with the higher class of secondary schools are exercised through the Provincial Board, its relations with the lower class of them, and with the primary schools, through the District Board. In Berlin, the

---

* I speak throughout of Prussia as she was before her late war with Austria.

relations with these also are managed by the Provincial
Board. A *Provinzial-Schulcollegium* has for its president the
High President of the province, for its director the vice-
president of that governmental district which happens to
have for its centre the provincial capital. The Board has
two or three other members, of whom, in general, one is a
Catholic and one is a Protestant; and one is always a man
practically conversant with school matters. The District
Board has in the provincial capitals the same president and
director as the Provincial Board; in the other centres of
Regierungen it has for its president the President of the
Regierung, and three or four members selected on the same
principle as the members of the Provincial Board.

The provincial State authority, therefore, is, in general,
for gymnasiums, the larger progymnasiums, and *Realschulen*
of the first rank, the Provincial School Board; for the
smaller progymnasiums, *Realschulen* of the second rank, the
higher Burgher Schools, and the primary schools of all kinds,
the Governmental District Board. Both boards are in continual communication with the Education Minister at Berlin,
and every two or three years they have to draw up for him a
general report on the school affairs of their province or
district.

The Scientific Deputations are now replaced by seven Examination Commissions (*Wissenschaftliche Prüfungscommissionen*).* The most important business of these Commissions
being to examine teachers for the secondary schools, they
have seven members, one for each of the main subjects in
which teachers are examined,—philology, history, mathematics, pædagogy, theology, and the natural sciences. These
Commissions report to the Minister every year.

Besides the central and provincial administration there is
a local or municipal administration for schools that are not
Crown patronage schools. Matters of teaching and discipline,
—*interna* as they are called,—do not in any public schools,
even when their patrons are municipalities or private persons,

* The seats of these seven Commissions are the towns of Berlin, Königsberg,
Breslau, Halle, Münster, Bonn, and Greifswald. These towns are also the seats of
the Prussian universities.

come within the jurisdiction of the local authority; they are referred to the provincial and district boards. The local authority administers *externa*,—that is, it manages the school property, fixes the school fees, gives free admissions to poor scholars, and the like; and it nominates, when the patronage is private or municipal, the teacher; but for his confirmation recourse must be had to the State authority, provincial or central. Thus, if local or municipal patrons chose to appoint a master who had not got his certificate from one of the Examination Commissions, the appointment would be quashed. In most towns the local authority for schools of municipal patronage is the town magistracy, assisted by a *Stadtschulrath*; sometimes the local authority is a *Curatorium* or *Schulcommission*. To take one case as a specimen. The two town gymnasiums at Breslau are under a *Curatorium*, of which the composition is as follows: a member of the magistracy (who must be a lawyer), president; two members chosen by the representative body of the commune, and the rectors of the two gymnasiums. This body draws up the school estimate, of which presently; looks after the administration of the school property, sees that the school premises are kept in order and properly supplied with what they want, represents the town at the leaving examinations, or other public solemnities in which the gymnasiums are concerned, has a consultative voice as to any change in the mode of regulating the free admissions, receives from the rector, when he and the majority of the masters are agreed on a boy's expulsion, notice that a boy has been expelled, with the grounds for it; if the rector and a majority of his *Lehrercollegium* differ as to the propriety of expelling, the *Curatorium* decides. It is not the *Curatorium* that nominates the masters, but the town magistracy, subject to approval by the proper State authority. The teaching and all that relates to it are in each gymnasium under the rector's control, who is responsible on this head to the Provincial Board and not to the *Curatorium*.

In cases where the Crown has had a share in endowing a school, or has made a grant to it, it acquires joint rights of patronage with the local patrons, and for the exercise of these rights it is represented by a commissioner, who is always, as such, a member of the *Curatorium*.

Only a few Prussian schools, such as those of Schulpforta and Rossleben, or the Joachimsthal School at Berlin, have so large an endowment that it can fully support them. But a very large number have endowments of some sort, or else grants from some school charity or other, such as the *Marienstift* at Stettin for schools in Pomerania, the *Sacksche Stiftung* in Silesia for schools in the principalities of Glogau, Wohlau, and Liegnitz, and many other such foundations. The Provincial or District Boards supervise the *externa*, the property concerns, as well as the *interna*, the teaching concerns, of all schools of Crown patronage; but by the Prussian law, wherever there is an endowment there is a public right to see that this endowment is properly employed; so that there is a public control for the management of all endowments of private as well as of Crown patronage. The school appoints a man of business (*Rendant, Rechnungsführer*) charged with the financial administration (*Cassenführung*) of the school; the authority in whom the patronage of the school is vested (*Patronatsbehörde*) draws out a school estimate (*Schul-Etat*) every three years, showing in detail the school's income, actual and estimated, for the three years about to commence, and its estimated expenditure. In every government district, or *Regierung*, there is a public functionary whose business it is to review these estimates, and who addresses to the *Rendant* his remarks and requirements (*Revisionserinnerungen, Revisionsforschungen*), which the *Rendant* has to lay before the *Patronatsbehörde*, whatever this may be, *Curatorium, Schulcommission,* &c., and to which this authority must pay attention. An abusive application of trust funds, or of grants from a charity, is thus checked: all expenses not in the estimate have to be accounted for, and all improper expenses are disallowed. The local patrons can only resist by applying to the administrative authority next above that which has dealt with them (*vorgesetzte Instanz*), and this appeal they will never make when they know they have a bad case.

The State has part in the patronage of more than half of the secondary schools in Prussia; in 72 of them as absolute patron, in 74 of them as part patron. The immense majority of the schools of which it is absolute patron belong to the category of *Gymnasien*, the highest and most expensive class of secondary schools. There were, in 1864,* 145 gymnasien in Prussia; of 65 of these the Crown had the exclusive patronage. At the same date there were 28 *Progymnasien*, 49 *Realschulen* of the first rank, 16 of the second, and 21 higher Burgher Schools. Of only seven of these had the Crown the exclusive patronage; of three progymnasiums, two *Realschulen* of the first rank, one of the second, and one higher Burgher School. Under municipal patronage were 26 gymnasiums, 11 progymnasiums, 35 *Realschulen* of the first rank, 10 of the second, and 13 higher Burgher Schools. The municipalities thus show that leaning towards *real* instruction which might be expected from them; of the 49 *Realschulen* of the first rank they have 35. What is most striking to an Englishman is the small number of public schools under patronage neither royal nor municipal, but under the patronage of some church, or corporation, or private person; there are but 12 of them altogether, five *Gymnasien*, two *Progymnasien*, one *Realschule* of the first order, and four higher Burgher Schools. The question therefore as to the rights and interests of private patrons of public schools does not take, so far as the number of their schools goes, very important dimensions. The total expenditure on the higher schools and their *Vorschulen* was, in 1864, 2,580,684 thalers (in round figures, about 387,100*l.*). Of this sum the scholars' fees contributed 1,193,055 thalers; the State 526,722 thalers, the municipalities, 401,046 thalers; school property produced 384,224 thalers, and benefactions not under public administration, 75,637 thalers. The State is therefore, after the scholars themselves, the great supporter of the public schools, as well as the principal patron of them.

But the reader will ask, in what sense are the schools with private patrons to be called public schools? They are public schools because they fulfil the requirements, adopt the title

---

* A year later than the year for which there are complete returns, and for which I gave, as the total of Prussian higher schools open in that year, 255. In 1864 there were 259.

and constitution, and follow the *Lehrplan*, fixed by public authority for the five classes of public secondary schools, and by so doing obtain the *status* and privilege of such schools. Are there not a great many important establishments, then, the reader may next ask, which do not care to get this status, but prefer to be independent? I answer: No school in Prussia can be *independent*, in the sense of owing no account to any one for the teacher it employs, or the way in which it is conducted; for every school there is a *verord-nete Aufsichtsgewalt*, an ordained authority of supervision. But private persons are no doubt free to open establishments of their own, give them a constitution of their own, and follow a *Lehrplan* of their own. There are ten large private schools in Berlin for the class of boys who go to secondary schools; these private schools, however, have the public schools in view, and take boys whose parents do not like to send them very young to the great public schools, classical or non-classical; but when these boys are ready for the middle division of the public Gymnasium or *Realschule*, they pass on there. These private schools are merely preparatory schools for the public schools, and accordingly they are organised as progymnasiums and as higher Burgher Schools. They represent no anti-public-school feeling, no rival line in education. Two remarkable institutions which did not prepare for the public schools, which gave a complete course of secondary instruction of their own arranging, and which were private schools, *écoles libres*, in the full sense of the term,—the *Plamannsche Anstalt* and the *Cauersche Anstalt*,—existed at Berlin not long ago, but they exist there no longer. Experiments of the same kind are being tried elsewhere. The *Victoria Institut*, at Falkenberg, is a prominent specimen of them; it is a regular private boarding school, charging 400 thalers (60*l.*) a year, and it professes to give the training either of the gymnasiums or of the *Real-schulen*, whichever the pupil prefers. The English generally know more of schools of this kind than of the public schools in Germany, because this kind of private school has a boarding establishment and the public schools have not, and a foreign parent generally looks out for a school with a boarding establishment. For the most part he is no judge at all of schools on their real merits; he sends his son to a foreign school that he may learn the modern languages, and the boy will learn these at a private school just as much as at a public one. But the Germans themselves undoubtedly prefer their public schools. An attendance in the public secondary schools of 74,000 pupils, in a population of 18,500,000, which is Prussia's population, shows that the Prussians prefer them. And it is the same in other German countries.

CHAPTER XVII.

PREPONDERANCE OF PUBLIC SCHOOLS.   THE ABITURIENTEN-
EXAMEN.

I BELIEVE that the public schools are preferred, in Prussia, on their merits.   The Prussians are satisfied with
them, and are proud of them, and with good reason; the
schools have been intelligently planned to meet their intelligent wants.   But the preponderance of the public schools is
further secured by the establishment in connexion with
them of the 'leaving examinations' (*Abiturientenprüfungen,
Maturitätsprüfungen, Entlassungsprüfungen, Abgangsprüfun-
gen*), on which depends admission to the universities, to
special schools (*Fachschulen*) like the *Gewerbe-Institut* or the
Bauakademie, and to the civil and military service of the
State.   The learned professions can only be reached through
the universities, so the access to these professions depends on
the leaving examination.   The pupils of private tutors or
private schools can present themselves for this examination,
but it is held at the public schools, it turns upon the studies of
the upper forms of the public schools, and it is conducted in
great part by their teachers.   A public schoolboy undoubtedly
presents himself for it with an advantage; and its object undoubtedly is, not the illusory one of an examination-test as
in our public service it is employed, but the sound one of
ensuring as far as possible that a youth shall pass a certain
number of years under the best school-teaching of his country.
This really trains him, which the mere application of an examination-test does not; but an examination-test is wisely
used in conjunction with this training, to take care that a

youth has really profited by it. No nation that did not
honestly feel it had made its public secondary schools
the best places of training for its middle and upper classes,
could institute the leaving examination I am going to describe;
but Prussia has a right to feel that she has made hers this,
and therefore she had a right to institute this examination.
It forms an all-important part of the secondary instruction of
that country, and I hope the reader will give me his attention
while I describe it.

Before 1788 admission to the Prussian universities was a
very easy affair. You went to the dean of the faculty in
which you wished to study; you generally brought with you
a letter of recommendation from the school you left; the
dean asked you a few questions and ascertained that you
knew Latin; then you were matriculated. The *Ober-Schulcollegium*, which was in 1788 the authority at the head of
Prussian public instruction, perceiving that from the insufficiency of the entrance examination the universities were
cumbered with unprepared and idle students, determined to
try and cure this state of things. In December of that year
a royal edict was issued to the public schools and universities
directing that the public schools should make their boys
undergo an examination before they proceeded to the university; and that the universities should make the boys who
came up to them from private schools undergo an examination corresponding to that of the public schoolboys.
Every one who underwent the examination was to receive a
certificate of his ripeness or unripeness for university studies
(*Zeugniss der Reife, Zeugniss der Unreife*). The candidates
declared to be unripe might still enter the university if their
parents chose; but it was hoped that, guided by this test,
their parents would keep them at school till they were properly prepared, or else send them into some other line. No
plan of examination was prescribed, but the certificate was to
record, under the two heads of *languages* and *sciences*, the
candidate's proficiency in each of these matters.

The *Allgemeine Landrecht*, promulgated in 1794, after
complaints had been rife that the universities had still a
number of unprofitable students, and that young men went

there merely to escape military service, made yet stricter regulations. It ordered the examination held at the university for boys coming from private schools to be conducted by a Commission; and it forbade the matriculation of any one who did not obtain a certificate of his ripeness.

But the omitting to prescribe a definite plan for the examination, and the entrusting them to two different bodies, the schools and the universities, caused the intentions of the Government to be in great measure frustrated. There was no uniform standard of examination. The schools made the standard high, the universities made it low; and numbers of young men, leaving the public schools without undergoing the *Abiturientenexamen* there, waited a little while, and then presented themselves to be examined at the university, where the examination was notoriously much laxer than at the school.

The great epoch of reform for the higher schools of Prussia is Wilhelm von Humboldt's year and a half at the head of the Education Department. The first words of a memorandum of this date on a proposal not to require Greek except of students for orders : *Es ist nicht darum zu thun, dass Schulen und Universitäten in einem trägen und kraftlosen Gewohnheitsgange blieben, sondern darum, dass durch sie die Bildung der Nation auf eine immer höhere Stufe gebracht werde,** —might be taken as a motto for his whole administration of public instruction. It was Wilhelm von Humboldt who took the most important step towards making the *Abiturientenprüfung* what it now is. He was the originator of a uniform plan of examination obligatory on all who examined candidates for entrance to the university. Schleiermacher, who, as I have said, was a member of the Education Council, wished to take away this examination from the universities, and to give it entirely to the schools. This was not done, but the course of examination was strictly defined, and a form of certificate, fully indicating its results, was prescribed. The certificate was of three grades; No. 1 declared its possessor to be

* 'The thing is *not*, to let the schools and universities go on in a drowsy and impotent routine; the thing is, to raise the culture of the nation ever higher and higher by their means.'

thoroughly qualified for the university, No. 2 declared him to be partially qualified, No. 3 to be unqualified (*untüchtig*). But this plan of reform, which was brought into operation in 1812, could not produce its due fruits so long as the double examination was maintained. After the peace of 1815 there was a great flow of students to the universities; many of them were very ill prepared; but the universities, with the natural desire to get as many students as possible, eased the examinations to them as much as they could, and admitted the holders of any certificate at all, even of No. 3, to matriculation. At Bonn, in 1822, out of 139 certificates for that year, 122 were of No. 3, declaring the holder unqualified for the University; 16 were of No. 2, declaring him partially qualified; only one was of No. 1, declaring him thoroughly qualified. The Provincial School Boards reported to the minister that the efforts of the schools were frustrated by the laxity of the university commissions, which got more and more candidates. The schools in their turn were inclined to make the first grade of certificate a reward of severe competitive examination, which was by no means what those who instituted it intended. The admission to the universities of young men declared to be unqualified, the two kinds of examining bodies with differing views and standards, and the threefold grade of certificate, were found fatal obstacles to the successful working of the reform of 1812.

All three obstacles have been removed. The regulations at present in force date from 1834 and 1856.* The leaving examination is now held at the *Gymnasien* only. The threefold grade of certificate is abolished, and the candidate is, as in old times, certified to be either *reif* or *unreif*. No one, as a general rule, can without a certificate attend university lectures at all; and no one without a certificate of ripeness can be regularly matriculated in any faculty. The examining body is thus composed : the director of the gymnasium and the professors who teach in *prima*; a representative of the *Schul-Curatorium*, where the gymnasium has a *Curatorium*; the Crown's *Compatronats Commissarius* (joint patronage

---

* *Reglement vom* 4. *Juni* 1834, completed by *Verfügung vom* 12. *Jan.* 1856.

commissary) where there is one ; and a member or delegate of the Provincial School Board. The representative of the Provincial School Board is always president of the examining commission. The *Abiturient*, or leaving boy, must have been two years in *prima*. The examination work is to be of the same pitch as the regular work of this class, though it must not contain passages that have been actually done in school. But neither, on the other hand, must it be such as to require any *specielle Vorstudien*. It embraces the mother tongue, Latin, Greek, and French ; mathematics and physics, geography, history, and divinity. An *Abiturient* who is going to enter the theological faculty at the University is examined in Hebrew. The examination is both by writing and *viva voce*. The paper work lasts a week,* and the candidate who fails in it is not tried *viva voce*. The examination papers are prepared by the director and teachers, but several sets have to be in readiness, and the president of the examining commission, who represents the Provincial School Board and the State, chooses each paper as it is to be given out. He also, at the *viva voce* examination, chooses the passages if he likes, and himself puts any question he may think proper. The Provincial School Board have at any time the power to direct that the same examination papers shall be used for all the gymnasiums of the province. Each performance is marked *insufficient, sufficient, good,* or *excellent,* and no other terms, and no qualifications of these, are admitted. A candidate who is fully up to the mark in the mother tongue and in Latin, and considerably above it either in classics or mathematics, is declared *reif,*—passes,—though he may fall below it in other things. If the commission are not unanimous about passing a candidate, they vote ; the youngest member voting first and the president last. If the votes are equal the president has a casting vote. But the president may refuse

* Specimens of the subjects set for the German and Latin essay at these examinations are the following. For the German essay :—' How did Athens come to be the centre of the intellectual life of Greece ?'—' From Goethe's *Götz von Berlichingen* draw out a picture of the social state of Germany at the time in which the action of the play is laid.' For the Latin essay :—*P. Clodio, cum, ut Ciceronem in exilium ejiceret, in animum induxisset, quæ res fuerint adjumento?— Hannibal quibus de causis, quod sibi proposuerat, Italiam subigere, non potuit?*

to pass a candidate though the majority have voted for him. In this case, however, the candidate's papers must go to the highest examining authority, the *Wissenschaftliche Prüfungs-commission* in whose district the province is, for their decision upon them. To this same High Commission all the papers of half the gymnasiums of each province are each half year referred for their remarks; their remarks, if they have any to make, are addressed by them to the Provincial School Board, and by the Provincial School Board transmitted to the gymnasiums concerned.

The examination takes place about six weeks before the end of the half. The certificates are given out to the successful candidates at the solemnity * which takes place in the *Aula* of a German public school at the end of a half year, or *Semester*. Each member of the examining commission signs the certificate, which, besides defining the candidate's proficiency in each of the matters of examination, has three additional rubrics for *conduct, diligence,* and *attainments,* which are filled up by the school authorities as he deserves.

The candidate who is considered *unreif,* and not passed, is recommended, according to his examination and his previous school career, either to stay another half-year at school and then try again, or to give up his intention of going to the university. If he still persists in going there at once he may; but he must carry with him a certificate of his present unfitness (*Zeugniss der Nichtreife*), a certificate with the same rubrics as the other, and signed in the same way. With this certificate he holds an exceptional, incomplete position at the university; he cannot enter himself in any faculty except that of philosophy, and then he is entered in a special register, and not regularly matriculated. He can, therefore, attend lectures; but his time does not count for a degree, and he

---

† At this solemnity a dissertation is read by the director or one of the professors, and every European student knows how much valuable matter has appeared in these dissertations. I have before me the dissertations held in the last year or two at several of the schools I visited. The following are specimens of their subjects:—*De Sallustii dicendi genere commentatio.—Criticarum scriptionum specimen.—Der Prediger Salomo.—Die Erziehung für den Staatsdienst bei den Athenern. —Untersuchungen über die Cissoide (mathematische Abhandlung).*

can hold no public benefice or exhibition. He may be examined once more, and only once, going to a gymnasium for that purpose ; the three or four years' course required in the faculty which he follows only begins to count from the time when he passes.

The reader will recollect that for the learned professions, —the church, the law, and medicine,—and for the post of teachers in the high schools and universities, it is necessary to have gone regularly through the university course and to have graduated.

Candidates who have not been at a public school, but who wish to enter the university, must apply to the Provincial School Board of their province for leave to attend a certificate examination. They have to bring testimonials, and a *curriculum vitæ* written by themselves in German, and are then directed by the school board to a gymnasium where they may be examined. They have to pay an examination fee of 10 thalers. If they fail, the examining commission of the gymnasium is empowered to fix a time within which they may not try again, and they may only try twice. They may, however, if they fail to pass, go up to the university on the same condition as the public school boys who fail. These *externi*, as they are called, are not examined along with the *Abiturienten* of the gymnasium, though they are examined by the same examining commission; but the boys who come from private instruction are by the minister's directions to have allowance made for their not being examined by their own teachers, and, so far, to be more leniently treated in the examination than the *Abiturienten*. On the other hand, boys who have been at a gymnasium and who have left it in order to prepare themselves with a private tutor, are not entitled to any special indulgence. Indeed a public school boy, who to evade the rule requiring two years in *prima*, leaves the gymnasium from *secunda*, goes to a private school or private tutor, and offers himself for examination within two years, needs a special permission from the minister in order to be examined. So well do the Prussian authorities know how insufficient an instrument for their object,—that of promoting the national culture and filling the professions with fit men,

—is the bare examination-test; so averse are they to cram; so clearly do they perceive that what forms a youth, and what he should in all ways be induced to acquire, is the orderly development of his faculties under good and trained teaching.

With this view all the instructions for the examination are drawn up. It is to tempt candidates to no special preparation and effort, but to be such as 'a scholar of fair ability and proper diligence, may at the end of his school course come to with a quiet mind and without a painful preparatory effort tending to relaxation and torpor as soon as the effort is over.' The total cultivation (*Gesammtbildung*) of the candidate is the great matter, and this is why the two years of *prima* are prescribed, 'that the instruction in this highest class may not degenerate into a preparation for the examination, that the pupil may have the requisite time to come steadily and without overhurrying to the fulness of the measure of his powers and character, that he may be securely and thoroughly formed, instead of being bewildered and oppressed by a mass of information hastily heaped together.' All *tumultuarische Vorbereitung* and all stimulation of vanity and emulation is to be discouraged, and the examination, like the school, is to regard *das Wesentliche und Dauernde*—the substantial and enduring.* Accordingly, the composition and the passages for translation are the great matters in German examinations, not those papers of questions by which the examiner is so led to show his want of sense, and the examinee his stores of cram.

That a boy shall have been for a certain number of years under good training is what, in Prussia, the State wants to secure; and it uses the examination test to help it to secure this. We leave his training to take its chance, and we put the examination test to a use for which it is quite inadequate, to try and make up for our neglect.

The same course is followed with the *Realschulen* and with the higher Burgher Schools. For entrance to the different branches of the public service, the leaving certificate of the classical school had up to 1832 been required. For certain

---

* *Perverse studet qui examinibus studet*, was a favourite saying of Wolf's.

of these branches it was determined in 1832 to accept henceforth the certificate of the *Realschule* or the higher Burgher School instead of that of the gymnasium. Different departments made their own stipulations; the Minister of Public Works, for instance, stipulated that the certificate of the candidate for the *Bauakademie* (School of Architecture) should be valid only when the candidate's *Realschule* or higher Burgher School had been one of the first class, or with the full number of six classes, and when he had passed two years in each of the two highest classes. I mention a detail of this kind to show the English reader how entirely it is the boy's school and training which the Prussian Government thinks the great matter, and not his examination. Since 1832 the tendency has been to withdraw again from the *Realschule* certificate its validity for the higher posts in the scientific departments of the public service; for these posts, the gymnasial leaving certificate is now again required. But for a very great number of posts in the public service the certificate of the *Realschule* is still valid, and for a still greater number of posts in the pursuits of commerce and industry employers now require it. The Education Department issued in 1859 the rules by which the examination for this certificate is at present governed. They are the same, *mutatis mutandis*, with those for the *Maturitätsprüfung* at the gymnasium. The examining commission is composed in precisely the same way; the examination and the issue of the certificates follow the same course. The subjects are : divinity, the mother tongue and its literature, the translation of easy passages from Latin authors, but, in general, no Latin writing; French and English, in translation, writing, and speaking; ancient history; the history of Germany, England, and France, for the last three centuries; geography; physics and chemistry; pure and applied mathematics, and drawing. Excellence in one subject may counterbalance shortcomings in another, but no candidate can pass who absolutely fails in any. *Externi* who want the certificate are admitted to examination on the same terms, and at the same fee, as in the *Gymnasien*. In *Realschulen* of the second rank the examination is easier than in those of the first, but the certificate has not the same value. The *Abgangsprüfung* and *Abgangszeugniss* of a higher Burgher School, again, are still more easily passed and won, but still less valuable. The *Abgangszeugniss* of a higher Burgher School entitles the holder to enter the *prima* of a first-rate *Realschule*; often a very important opening to a clever boy in a small country place, who for one year can afford to go to a school away from home, but could not have afforded to get all his schooling there.

To the passage from the *tertia* and *secunda* of the gymnasium or of the *Realschule*, examinations are also attached, for which certificates, if the boy leaves after passing one of them, are given, declaring his ripeness at that stage. For many subordinate employments in the civil service these certificates are accepted. To be a teacher of drawing in a public school, for instance, a certificate of ripeness for *secunda* of a gymnasium or of a first rank *Realschule* or higher Burgher School is required; this if the candidate has not been at a public school and has to be examined as an *externus*;* if he has been at a public school, the certificate of his having passed the examination out of *secunda* at a second rank *Realschule* is sufficient. One important employment of school certificates is to entitle the holder to shorter military service (*Zulassung zum einjährigen freiwilligen Militairdienst*). Young men who volunteer to serve for one year, arming and clothing themselves, the term of military service to be then at an end, must, to be accepted, produce a certificate of a certain value, either from a gymnasium or a *Realschule*.

It shows how many more gymnasium boys there are who go through the full school course than *Realschule* boys, that whereas from the *Gymnasien* in 1863 there were 1,765 *Abiturienten* from *prima*, from the *Realschulen* in the same year there were but 214. Adding to the 1,765 *Abiturienten* 40 *Externen* who passed at the same time, we have 1,805 boys who got the classical certificate of ripeness in 1863. Of this number 1,563 went in that year to the Prussian universities. Of the 214 *Abiturienten* from the *Realschulen* (to whom are to be added three *Externen*, making 217), 124 went into the

---

* For the examination of *externi* for this lower kind of certificate, the fee is four thalers.

public service, 92 into the pursuits of commerce or industry; one went to prepare for the gymnasial leaving examination, that he might go into a learned profession. Evidently the mass of those who go into business leave the *Realschule* before *prima,* and the majority of those who stay for *prima* stay with the hope of public enployment. But the minor certificates accessible to those who leave *secunda* and *tertia* promote an attendance at school longer than that which boys going into business would without the attraction of these certificates be willing to give; and they promote, too, a wholesome return upon the school work done, and a mastering of it as a whole, which tend, the school work having in the first instance been sound and well given, to make culture take a permanent hold upon the future tradesmen or farmer. Accordingly, it is common to meet in Germany with people of the tradesman class who even read (in translations, of course) any important or interesting book that comes out in another country, a book like Macaulay's *History of England,* for instance; and how unlike this state of culture is to that of the English tradesman, the English reader himself knows very well.

CHAPTER XVIII.

THE PRUSSIAN SCHOOLMASTERS; THEIR TRAINING, EXAMINA-
TION, APPOINTMENT, AND PAYMENT.

EXAMINATION FOR SCHOOLMASTERS—ITS HISTORY—PRESENT PLAN OF EXAMINATION
FOR SCHOOLMASTERS — NORMAL SEMINARIES FOR SCHOOLMASTERS — PROBATION
AND PRACTISING LESSONS OF SCHOOLMASTERS—APPOINTMENT OF SCHOOLMASTERS,
AND JURISDICTION OVER THEM—INTERVENTION OF THE EDUCATION MINISTER —
RELIGIOUS INSTRUCTION—DENOMINATIONAL CHARACTER OF THE PRUSSIAN SCHOOLS
—WIDE ACCEPTATION OF THE DENOMINATION EVANGELISCH — EXCLUSION FROM
SCHOOL POSTS OF CERTAIN DISSENTERS AND OF JEWS — RANK AND TITLE OF
SCHOOLMASTERS—PAYMENT OF SCHOOLMASTERS.

TO insure that the school work, which so much is done to encourage, shall indeed be sound and well given, it is not in Prussia thought sufficient to test the schoolboy and the candidate for matriculation ; the candidate for the office of teacher is tested too.   This test is the famous *Staatsprüfung* for schoolmasters (*Prüfung der Candidaten des höheren Schul-amts*), and is the third great educational reform I have enumerated (the *Lehrplan* and the *Maturitätsprüfung* being the other two) which owes its institution to Wilhelm von Humboldt.   Before 1810 a certificate of having proved his fitness was not required of a candidate for the post of school-master.   Municipal and private school patrons in particular made their nomination with little regard to any test of the kind.   There was generally in their school a practice of promoting the teachers by seniority to the higher classes, and this practice had very mischievous results.   A project was canvassed for giving to the authorities of public instruc-tion the direct appointment to the more important posts in schools even of municipal or private patronage.   This project was abandoned.   'But,' said Wilhelm von Humboldt, 'the one defence we can raise against the misuse of their rights by patrons, is the test of a trial of the intending school-master's qualifications.'

This test was established in 1810. An examination and a trial lesson were appointed for all candidates for the office of teacher. It was made illegal for school patrons to nominate as teachers any persons who were not *geprüfte Subjecte*. As time went on, the security thus taken was gradually made stronger. The trial lesson was found to be an inutility, as any one who has heard trial lessons in our primary Normal Schools can readily believe, and a trial year in a school (*Probejahr*) was in 1826 substituted for it. In the following year it was ruled that the *pädagogische Prüfung*, which forms part of the examination of candidates for orders, and which had hitherto been accepted in lieu of the new test, was insufficient; and that persons in orders, as well as others, must go through the special examination for schoolmasters. This regulation gave full development to a policy which had been contained in the reform of 1810, a policy which Wolf had long before done his best to prepare and had declared to be indispensable if the higher schools of Prussia were to be made thoroughly good,—the policy of making the schoolmaster's business a profession by itself, and separating it altogether from theology.

The rules now in force for this examination date in the main from 1831. It is held by the High Examining Commissions (*Königliche Wissenschaftliche Prüfungscommissionen*) of which I have already described the composition, and which are seven in number. The candidate sends in his school-certificate of fitness for university studies, and his certificate of a three years' attendance at university lectures. With these certificates he forwards to the commission a *curriculum vitæ*, such as used to be required from candidates for the Oriel fellowships. The candidate for the gymnasium writes this in Latin; the candidate for the *Realschule* may write it in French. The certificate given takes the form of a *facultas docendi*, or leave to teach; and this is *bedingte* or *unbedingte*,—conditional or unconditional. The matters for examinations are grouped under four main heads (*Hauptfächer*): first, Greek, Latin, and the mother tongue; secondly, mathematics and the natural sciences; thirdly, history and geography; fourthly, theology and Hebrew. This last *Hauptfach* concerns especially those who are to give the religious instruction in the public schools; if they have been examined for orders before a theological board and have passed well, an oral examination is all the divinity examination they have to undergo before the Commission. Those who are to give the secular instruction have likewise only an oral examination in divinity, and are not examined in Hebrew; but they must satisfy the Commission as to their acquaintance with Scripture and with the dogmatic and moral tenets of Christianity. Candidates weak in their divinity have this weakness noted in their certificate, and the Provincial School Boards are directed not to appoint any teacher weak in this particular till he has been re-examined and has passed satisfactorily; and the *curriculum vitæ* of every candidate has in the first instance to state what he has done at the university to keep up and increase his knowledge of divinity (*seine religionswissenschaftlichen Kenntnisse zu erweitern und tiefer zu begründen*). These latter regulations date from within the last twenty years.

The unconditional *facultas docendi* is only given to that candidate who in his *Hauptfach* shows himself fit to teach one of the two highest forms, and sufficiently acquainted with the matters of the other *Hauptfächer* to be useful to his class in them. The candidate who in one *Hauptfach* is strong enough for any class up to *secunda* inclusive, but falls altogether below the mark in other sciences, receives a *bedingte* 'facultas docendi,' for the middle or the lower forms, according as his capacity and the extent of his performance and of his failure seem to merit.

All candidates are required to be able to translate French with ease, and they must know its grammar. All must show some acquaintance with philosophy and pædagogic,* candidates for the unconditional *facultas docendi* a very considerable acquaintance; and all must satisfy the examiners that they have some knowledge of the natural sciences.

---

* The Germans, as is well known, attach much importance to the science of pædagogic. That science is as yet far from being matured, and much nonsense is talked on the subject of it; still, the total unacquaintance with it, and with all which has been written about it, in which the intending schoolmaster is, in England, suffered to remain, has, I am convinced, injurious effects both on our schoolmasters and on our schools.

The candidate for a *Realschule* or a higher Burgher School need not take Greek, but he must pass in Latin. His *Hauptfächer* are : mathematics, natural sciences, history and geography, the mother tongue, modern languages. His examination in all the non-classical matters is even more stringent than that of candidates for the gymnasium, because of his comparative exemption from classics.

The trials *pro loco* and *pro ascensione* are examinations imposed when the nominee to a place has not yet proved his qualifications for that place. For instance, the holder of a conditional *facultas docendi* cannot be appointed to a class in the highest division without being re-examined, and the holder of an unconditional *facultas docendi* cannot teach another matter than the *Hauptfach* in which he has proved his first-class qualification, without being re-examined.

A special *facultas docendi* is given to the foreign teacher of modern languages; but even he, besides the modern language he is to teach, must know as much Latin, history, geography and philosophy as is required of candidates who are to teach in the middle division of a gymnasium. This provision guards against the employment of subjects so unfit by their training and general attainments to rule a class, as those whom we too often see chosen as teachers of modern languages.

The High Commissioners send yearly to the Provincial School Board of each province a report of these examinations for that province, with the necessary remarks. The candidates for masterships present themselves, with their certificates, to the School Board of the province in which they wish to be employed. In certain exceptional cases candidates may be employed two half-years running without a certificate; but at the end of that time, if they have not passed the examination, they must be dismissed.

Those who at the university have taken, after examination, the degree of doctor, and have published the Latin dissertation required for that degree, are excused from the written part of the schoolmaster's examination. When this examination was first instituted, both Schleiermacher and Wolf, being then members of the Education section, declared themselves strongly against allowing any university title to exempt candidates for the *höhere Schulamt* from going through the special examination. Probably they were right, for the seriousness of the degree examination, and the value of the degree, is not the same in every German university. They were over-ruled, however; but little or no inconvenience does in fact arise from the allowance, in this case, of an equipollent title; because if a candidate brings the degree of doctor from a university whose degrees are not respected, and if he inspires any suspicion, the patrons who are to nominate him, or the Provincial Board which is to confirm him, invite him to go through the special examination first; and if he refuses, or if he cannot pass, his appointment is not proceeded with.

The *Probejahr*, or year of probation, must, as a general rule, be passed at a gymnasium or a *Realschule*, not at a pro-gymnasium or a higher Burgher School. In this way the schoolmaster of the lower class of secondary schools is a man who has known the working and standards of the higher. The probationer is commonly unpaid, but if he is used in the place of an assistant master the school which so uses him must pay him. The schools are, however, expressly directed not to treat the probationer as a means of relieving an over-tasked staff, but to give him an opportunity of learning, in the best way for himself, the practice of his business, and to let him therefore work with several different classes in the course of his year. At the end of his year he receives a certificate from the school authorities as to the efficiency which he shows.

The time passed in a Normal seminary counts instead of the *Probejahr*; but these seminaries have not in Prussia, any of them, the importance of the *École Normale* in France. There is not the same need of the institution in Germany as in France, and no German professor is obliged to pass through it. The *École Normale* is of much more use in giving its student the thorough possession of what he knows and the power of independent application of it, than in teaching him to teach; and these more valuable functions of a Normal school are performed in Germany by the *Gymnasien* and the

universities, to an extent to which the *lycées* and faculties in
France by no means perform them. Hence in France the
need and utility of the *École Normale*. The normal seminaries in Germany are connected with the different universities,
and designed, in general, to give the future schoolmaster a
more firm and thorough grasp on the matters he studies
there. The pædagogical seminaries have not been so important or so fruitful to him as the philological seminaries, where
this design has been applied to what has hitherto been the
grand matter of his studies,—*Alterthumswissenschaft*, the systematic knowledge of classical antiquity. It was as the head
of the philological seminary at Halle that Wolf gave that
impulse to the formation of a body of learned and lay schoolmasters of which Germany has ever since felt the good
effects. This seminary was opened in 1787, and Wolf was
its director for nearly twenty years, till the University of
Halle was closed by Napoleon after the battle of Jena, and
Wolf went to Berlin to be a member of the Department of
Education there. During the latter part of Wolf's time at
Halle, he was assisted in the seminary by Immanuel Bekker.
There were 12 seminarists, with a small exhibition of 40
thalers (6*l*.) a year each ; the exhibition was tenable for two
years. No one was admitted to an exhibition who had not
already completed his first year's course in the university,
but students from any of the faculties might attend the seminary lectures. They attended in great numbers, and for the
exhibitions themselves there were at the first examination 60
candidates. The seminary lessons were interpretation lessons
and disputation lessons, the former being, as the name implies, the interpretation of a given author ; the latter being
the discussion, between two or more of the seminarists, either
of a thesis set long beforehand and treated by them in written
exercises, or of a thesis set by Wolf at the moment and then
and there treated orally, in Latin, by his pupils. Wolf's
great rule in all these lessons was that rule which all masters
in the art of teaching have followed,—to take as little part as
possible in the lesson himself ; merely to start it, guide it,
and sum it up, and to let quite the main part in it be borne
by the learners. The more advanced seminarists had some

practice in the Latin school of the Orphan House at Halle. The more recent statutes of this philological seminary have set forth in express words, as the object of the institution, the design which Wolf always had in his mind in directing it;—the design to form effective classical masters for the higher schools. Every Prussian university has a philological seminary, or group of exhibitioners much like that which I have described at Halle, not more than 12 in number, with a two years' course following one year's academical study, and *Alterthumswissenschaft* being the object pursued. There are generally two professors specially attached to the seminary, one for Greek, the other for Latin. Besides the ordinary members or seminarists, a good number of extraordinary members, and a yet much larger number of *Auscultanten*, attend the lessons. The staff of the philological seminary at Berlin has this constellation of names, from 1812, when this seminary was founded, to the present time :—Boeckh, Buttmann, Bernhardy, Lachmann, Haupt. The philological seminary of the University of Bonn was founded in 1819, and has had on its staff Professors Näke, Welcker, Ritschl, Otto Jahn. The mouth of the student of *Alterthumswissenschaft* in other countries may indeed water, when he reads two such lists as these.

At the University of Bonn there is also a *Naturwissenschaftliches Seminar*, founded in 1825, on the express ground that qualified teachers of the natural sciences in the secondary schools were so much wanting. Bonn has, too, a *historisches Seminar* founded in 1861 for the promotion of historical studies, and also to provide good history-teachers for the secondary schools. Dr. von Sybel, the well-known historian, is at present one of its professors. The Universities of Breslau, Greifswald, Königsberg, have likewise historical seminaries, serving either by statute or in practice the same end, of preparing specially qualified teachers of history for the public schools. Berlin, Königsberg, and Halle have also seminaries either for mathematics, or for mathematics and the natural sciences together; these, too, serve, in their line of study, the same end as the philological and historical seminaries serve in theirs. Berlin has also travelling fellowships of a year's duration, to enable Germans, who are to teach French in the public schools, to study the French language and literature in France itself. Two exhibitions of 45*l.* a year each are attached to the Royal French School in Berlin, with the like object of enabling the future teacher of French to learn French practically and thoroughly. These are Crown foundations; the Crown, associations, and private individuals, are all founders of seminaries. The estimate of none of those which I have named exceeds 1,000 thalers (150*l.*) a year. It is astonishing how much is done in Prussia with small supplies of money.

Special pædagogic seminaries (*pädagogische Seminarien*) exist at Berlin, Königsberg, Breslau, Stettin, and Halle. Of these the assigned business with their seminarist is ' to introduce him to the practical requirements of the profession of schoolmaster;' but this introduction is still to be carefully accompanied by a continuance of his general intellectual culture. In general, the seminarist here must have passed the examination *pro facultate docendi*, and instead of the *Probejahr* in a school he spends two or three years in the pædagogic seminary. Each seminarist has a certain number of hours' practice (six hours a week at Berlin) in a secondary school; he is present at the conferences, or teachers' meetings, of the school to which he is attached, and he lives with one of its older masters. The Berlin *pädagogische Seminar* was founded in 1787, at first with a single gymnasium (the *Friedrich-Werdersche*) assigned as its practising school; since 1812 all the gymnasiums of Berlin have served in common for this purpose. There are now ten regular exhibitioners, but the exhibitions here are good, and the estimate for the seminary is much larger than that for any other seminary I have named; it is 2,390 thalers a year. Dr. Boeckh is the director of this seminary as well as of the philological one, and this joint direction well illustrates the close relation at present, in Germany as elsewhere, of the schoolmaster with philology. At Stettin the seminary has only four regular exhibitioners; they have good exhibitions, lasting for two or three years. This seminary is for the benefit in the first instance of the province of Pomerania, and the seminarists have to engage themselves to take, when their exhibition expires, any mastership the Provincial School Board offers them, and to keep it three years.

It is evident from what I have said that these exhibitions do not exist in sufficient number to provide seminary training for anything like the whole of that large body of teachers which the secondary schools of Prussia employ. It is found too that the directors and masters of great schools in large towns, who have a great deal to do and constant claims upon their attention, do not like being saddled with the care of seminarists either at their homes or in their classes. The same difficulties tell against their giving to probationers in their trial year due supervision. But it is the living for a time with an experienced teacher and the making the first start in teaching under his eye, that is found to be so especially valuable for promising novices. It is proposed therefore, instead of founding fresh pædagogic seminaries, to make arrangements for selecting a certain number of good schoolmasters, who will take charge, for payment, of a batch of novices (not more than three) for a two years' probationary course before launching them independently; and a *stipendium*, or exhibition, such as is given in the seminaries, is to be bestowed on those probationers whose circumstances require it. It is hoped in this way to provide a preliminary training of two years for all the most deserving subjects who go into the profession.

At the end of his term of probation the probationer gets his appointment. I have said before that for all appointments to masterships in the secondary schools the intervention of the State authority is necessary. In schools of Crown patronage the appointment is called *Bestallung*; in schools not of Crown patronage it is called *Vocation*; the State can give *installation*, absolute occupation; other patrons can only nominate, and their nominee, if an improper person, is rejected, with reasons assigned, by the State authorities. The Crown, exercising its patronage through the Education Minister, appoints, in all Crown patronage gymnasiums and *Realschulen*, the director. The Provincial Boards, in the minister's name and by commission from him, appoint the

upper masters (*Oberlehrer*) in these schools, and the rector in
all Crown patronage progymnasiums and higher Burgher
Schools. The other masters in Crown patronage schools the
Provincial Board appoints by its own authority. The nomination of a director in schools of municipal or private patronage
requires the Crown's assent and the minister's confirmation.
The nomination of an *Oberlehrer* in such schools requires the
minister's assent and the Provincial Board's confirmation.
The nomination of other masters in such schools the Provincial Board is empowered to confirm without the assent
of the minister. All directors and masters, whether appointed
by the State or only confirmed by it, take an *Amtseid*, or oath
of office, by which they swear obedience to the Crown. In
schools of Crown patronage, when the minister directs, on
special grounds, the appointment, promotion, or transference,
of a master, the Provincial Board must comply.

The minister, however, has in Prussia a far less immediate
and absolute action upon the secondary schools than the
minister has in France. In France the minister can dismiss
any functionary of secondary instruction; in Prussia he can
reprimand him and stop his salary for a month, but he cannot
of his own authority dismiss him. Directors and upper
masters are under the jurisdiction of the Court of Discipline
for the Civil Service (*Disciplinarhof*) at Berlin; this court is
a judicial body, four of its members belonging to the Supreme Court of Berlin; and any complaint requiring the
dismissal of a director or upper master must be tried before
it. From the sentence of this court there is an appeal to the
minister; but he is bound to appoint, for hearing the appeal,
two referees, one of whom must be a member of the Department of Justice; and their decision is final. Complaints of
like gravity against other masters (*ordentliche Lehrer*) are
tried by the Provincial Board, which like the Court of Discipline hears counsel, and examines witnesses on oath; from
the sentence of the board there is also an appeal to the
minister, who appoints in this case one referee only, but the
referee, before deciding the appeal, has to take the opinion
of the Court of Discipline. Everywhere in Prussia and in all
German countries we shall find a disposition to take security

against that immediate and arbitrary action of the executive
which we remark in France; and though the Germans give
effect in a very different way from ours to this innate disposition of the Teutonic race, yet they give such effect to it
as to establish a notable difference,—the more manifest the
more one examines the institutions of the two countries,—
between the habit and course of administration in Germany
and in France.

I cannot but think an Education Minister a necessity for
modern States, yet I know that in the employment of such
an agency there are inconveniences, and I do not wish to
hide any of them from the English reader. I have said that
in France political considerations are in my opinion too
much suffered to influence the whole working of the system
of public education. In Prussia the minister is armed with
powers, and issues instructions showing how he interprets
those powers, which in England would excite very great
jealousy. He tells the provincial authorities that no reproach
must attach to the private and public life, any more than to
the knowledge or ability, of a candidate for school employment; he tells them that they are to take into consideration
the whole previous career, extra-professional as well as professional (*das gesommte bisherige amtliche und ausseramtliche
Verhalten*), of such a candidate; and that schoolmasters
should be men who will train up their scholars in notions of
obedience towards the sovereign and the State.

I know the use likely to be made, in England, of the
admission that a Prussian Education Minister uses language
of this kind; and I will be candid enough to make bad worse
by saying that the present minister, Dr. von Mühler, is what
we should call in England a strong Tory and a strong Evangelical. It is not, indeed, at all likely that in England, with
the forces watching and controlling him here, a minister
would use language such as I have quoted; and even if it
were, I am not at all sure that to have a minister using such
language, though it is language which I cordially dislike, is
in itself so much more lamentable and baneful a thing than
that anarchy and ignorance in education matters, under
which we contentedly suffer. However, what I wish now to

say is, that in spite of this language, the political influence which has such real effect upon the public education of France, has no effect, or next to none, upon that of Prussia. I do not believe that it has more on that of Prussia than it has on that of this country. I took great pains to inform myself on this head. The last few years have been a time of great political pressure in Prussia; I arrived there when this pressure was at its height, and I conversed mainly with persons opposed, some of them bitterly opposed, to the Government. They all told me that the State administration of the schools and universities was in practice fair and right; that public opinion would not suffer it to be governed by political regards, or by any but literary and scientific regards; and that public opinion would always, in this particular, find strong sympathies among the ministers themselves. I heard of one director to whom Dr. von Mühler had refused confirmation because his politics, which had been very strongly declared, were unacceptable. This director I had the pleasure of seeing; he told me himself, what I heard also from others, that his case was an isolated one; and that it had caused such strong dissatisfaction, not only among the public, but to the school authorities who represent the State in the provinces and consider themselves responsible for the march and efficiency of secondary instruction, that the minister had found himself obliged to appoint him, within a very few months, to a Crown patronage school of greater importance than the municipal school for which he had refused him confirmation. The director added, and this too was confirmed by others, that such an intrusion of political feeling as had prevented his confirmation, was in the case of a *Lehrer* or teacher,—either an upper teacher or an ordinary teacher,—absolutely unknown.

The truth is, that when a nation has got the belief in culture which the Prussian nation has got, and when its schools are worthy of this belief, it will not suffer them to be sacrificed to any other interest; and however greatly political considerations may be paramount in other departments of administration, in this they are not. In France neither the national belief in culture nor the schools themselves are sufficiently developed to awaken this enthusiasm; and politics are too strong for the schools, and give them their own bias.

I have spoken several times of the religious instruction as forming part of school work and of examinations. The two legally established forms of religion in Prussia are the Protestant (*evangelisch*) and the Catholic. All public schools must be either Protestant, Catholic, or mixed (*Simultananstalten*). But the constitution of a mixed school has not been authoritatively defined, and though the practice has grown up, especially in *Realschulen*, of appointing teachers of the two confessions indifferently, yet these *Simultananstalten* retain the fundamental character of Christian schools, and indeed usually follow the rule either that the director and the majority of the masters shall be Catholic or that they shall be Protestant. In general, the deed of foundation or established custom determines to what confession a school shall belong. The religious instruction and the services follow the confession of the school. The ecclesiastical authorities,—the consistories for Protestant schools, the bishops for Catholic schools,—must concur with the school authorities in the appointment of those who give the religious instruction in the schools. The consistories and the bishops have likewise the right of inspecting, by themselves or by their delegates, this instruction, and of addressing to the Provincial Boards any remarks they may have to make on it. The *ordinarius*, or class-master who has general charge of the class, as distinguished from the teachers who give the different parts of the instruction in it, is generally, if possible, the religious instructor. In Protestant schools the religious instructor is usually a layman; in Catholic, an ecclesiastic. The public schools are open to scholars of all creeds; in general, one of the two confessions, evangelical or Catholic, greatly preponderates, and the Catholics, in especial, prefer schools of their own confession. But the State holds the balance quite fairly between them; where the scholars of that confession which is not the established confession of the school are in considerable numbers, a special religious instructor is paid out of the school funds to come and give them this religious instruction at the school.

Thus in the gymnasium at Bonn, which is Catholic, I heard a lesson on the Epistle to the Galatians (in the Greek) given to the Protestant boys of one of the higher forms by a young Protestant minister of the town, engaged by the gymnasium for that purpose. When the scholars whose confession is in the minority are very few in number, their parents have to provide by private arrangements of their own for their children's religious instruction.

Prussia has 11,289,655 Protestant inhabitants, 6,901,023 Catholic inhabitants. She has nearly 300,000 inhabitants who are classed neither as *evangelisch* nor as Catholic, and these are principally Jews. In her public higher schools, out of 66,135 boys, 46,396 are Protestant (*evangelisch*), 14,919 are Catholic. The rest, 4,820, are Jews.

The wide acceptation which the denomination *evangelical* takes in the official language of Prussia prevents a host of difficulties which occur with us in England. Under the term *evangelisch* are included Lutherans, Calvinists, and the United Church formed on the basis of what is common to Lutherans and Calvinists ; Baptists also, Independents, Wesleyans (for there are Wesleyans in Prussia) are included by it, and, in short, all Protestants who are Christians, in the common acceptation of that word. The State, however, in Prussia, not only declares itself Christian (*der Preussische Staat ist ein christlicher,* says the *Unterrichtsverfassung* of 1816) but it expressly disclaims the neutral, colourless, formless Christianity of the Dutch schools and of our British schools (*der Religionsunterricht darf durchaus nicht in einen allgemeinen Religionsunterricht hinübergespielt werden*). So the Protestant schools as well as the Catholic employ a dogmatic religious teaching. In all schools of the evangelical confession Luther's Catechism is used, and all Protestant boys of whatever denomination learn it. Not the slightest objection is made by their parents to this. It is true that Luther's Catechism is perhaps the very happiest part of Lutheranism, and therefore recommends itself for this common adoption, while our Catechism can hardly be said to be the happiest part of Anglicanism.

The various denominations of Protestant Christians are

thus harmoniously united in a common religious teaching. But the State, keeping in view the *christlichen Grundcharakter* of itself and its public schools, refuses to employ any masters who are not either Catholics, or, in the wide sense assigned to the term *evangelisch*, Protestants. Dissenters who are not Christians, and specially the *Lichtfreunde*, as they call themselves (they would with us generally go by the name of Unitarians or Socinians), are thus excluded from the office of public teacher, and so are Jews. In a country where the Jews are so many and so able, this exclusion makes itself felt. A Jew may hold a medical or mathematical professorship in the Prussian universities, but he may not hold a professorship of history or philosophy. France is in all these matters a model of reason and justice, and as much ahead of Germany as she is of England. The religious instruction in her schools is given by ministers of religion, and the State asks no other instructor any questions about his religious persuasion.

Restrictions such as that which I have just described are said to be contrary to the provisions of the Prussian Constitution of 1850. The Prussian Parliament has begun to occupy itself with them, and it is probable they will not long be maintained.

A master on his appointment takes the title of *ordentliche Lehrer*, ordinary master (the title of under-master is not used in the Prussian schools), or of *Oberlehrer*, upper master. The *Oberlehrer* is so either by post or by nomination. The posts conferring the title of *Oberlehrer*, posts in the upper part of the school, can only be held by a teacher whose certificate entitles him to give instruction in one of the two highest classes. *Oberlehrer* by nomination are masters of long standing, who as *ordinarii* or general class-masters have done good service, and have the title of upper-master given to them in acknowledgment of it; but the title so conferred does not enable them to give instruction in any class for which their certificate does not qualify them. The regulations direct that there shall be not more than three *Oberlehrer*, exclusive of the director, for every seven *ordentliche Lehrer*; but in schools with a larger staff of *ordentliche Lehrer* than this, the proportion of *Oberlehrer* to *ordentliche Lehrer* may become much larger. The minister confers the title of professor upon masters distinguished by their attainments and practical success. The directors rank as full professors of the universities, the masters with the title of professor rank as assistant professors of the universities. It should be said that in Germany the title of professor confers on its holder a fixed rank, as a few official titles do here in England. The director is more like one of our head-masters than he is like a French *proviseur*, but he does not, like our head-masters, give the whole of the instruction, or even the whole of the classical instruction, to the head class. Often he is not its *ordinarius*. He, like other masters, cannot give any part of the instruction for which he has not at some time proved his qualification. In general he has some special branch in which he is distinguished, and in this branch he gives lessons in *prima*, and usually in other classes too; governing also, as his name implies, the whole movement of the school, and appearing, much oftener than our head-masters, in every class of it.

Formerly few masterships had fixed incomes assigned to them, but it has more and more become a rule of administration in Prussia to give to all directors and teachers fixed incomes, and to do away with their sharing the school fees. Neither the proceeds of these, nor the proceeds of foundations, are in any case abandoned to the school staff, to do what they like with. On the school estimates which I have described, all salaries appear, and all receipts from endowments or from school fees; the surplus of receipts over salaries and other school expenses is funded, and becomes available for enlarging or improving the school. There are few large endowments; in one or two cases, as at Schulpforta, the endowment is allowed to create for the director and the teachers a position above the average, and at Berlin, where the proceeds of the school-fees are very great, the masters of the public schools have also a position above the average; but all this is kept within strict regulation, and is settled, as I have said, by administrative boards of public composition, or under public supervision, and is not left to the disposition of the school staff itself. Schulpforta has a yearly income of more than 8,000*l.*, but of this sum, less than 2,000*l.* goes in salaries to the rector and masters. The yearly sum funded, after all the expenses of this noble foundation are paid, is not much smaller than the sum spent in salaries.

By a *Normaletat,* or normal estimate, there is fixed for the staff of State gymnasiums the following scale of payments, which is above rather than below the average scale in *Real-schulen,* or in any kind of secondary school not of State patronage. The scale has three classes : the first class is for nine places in Prussia, exclusive of Berlin and Schulpforta, which stand on an exceptional footing of their own; the second class is for thirty-four places; the third class for fifty-eight. Of course the nine places in the first class, being the principal towns in Prussia except the capital, have far more than nine gymnasiums. In all the State gymnasiums of these nine places, the scale of salaries is, for the director, 270*l.* a year ; for the masters, according to their post and their length of standing, from 90*l.* a year to 195*l.* In the thirty-four places of the second class, the scale is, for a director, 240*l.* a year ; for the masters, from 82*l.* 10*s.* to 172*l.* 10*s.* In the fifty-eight places of the third, for a director, 195*l.* ; for the masters, from 75*l.* to 150*l.* The salaries thus fixed are meant to represent the whole emoluments of the post ; when a house is attached to a post, the rule is that a deduction of 10 per cent. shall be made from the salary to balance the gain by the house. In some places there are special endowments for augmenting masters' salaries; thus the *Streitsche Stiftung* gives 455*l.* a year to augment the masters' salaries at the Greyfriars gymnasium, in Berlin ; but nowhere probably in Prussia does a school salary reach 350*l.* a year, and the rector of Schulpforta, whose post is perhaps the most desirable school post in the Prussian dominions, has, I understand, about 300*l.* a year, and a house. To hold another employment (*Nebenamt*) along with his school post, is not absolutely forbidden to the public teacher ; thus Dr. Schopen, the excellent Latin scholar at the head of the Bonn gymnasium, is at the same time professor in the philosophical faculty of the University there ; but the *Nebenamt* must not interfere with his school duty,

and the supervising authorities take good care that it shall
not.   So far as it does not interfere with his school duty, the
public teacher may give private tuition, and in this manner
increase his income; but to give private tuition for fee to the
pupils of his own form in the public school, he needs the
director's consent.   Even when every possible addition to it
has been allowed for, the salary of a Prussian schoolmaster
will appear to English eyes very low.

The whole scale of incomes in Prussia is, however, much
lower than with us, and the habits of the nation are frugal
and simple.   The rate of schoolmasters' salaries was raised
after 1815, and has been raised again since; it is not
exceptionally low as compared with the rates of incomes in
Germany generally.   The rector of Schulpforta with his
300*l.* a year and a house, has in all the country round him,—
where there is great well-doing and comfort,—few people
more comfortably off than himself; he can do all he wants to
do, and all that anybody about him does, and this is wealth.
The schoolmasters of the higher school enjoy, too, great consideration; and consideration, in a country not corrupted, has
a value as well as money.   As a class, the Prussian schoolmasters are not, so far as I could find out, fretting or discontented; they seem to give themselves heartily to their work,
and to take pride and pleasure in it.

What I have yet to say about Prussian schools, their
scholars, and their teachers, may perhaps be best said in connection with two or three of those institutions which I visited.
In this manner I shall have an opportunity of rendering, by
the help of particular illustrations, general results and state-
ments more interesting to the English reader, and more in-
telligible to him.

CHAPTER XIX.

THE PRUSSIAN SYSTEM SEEN IN OPERATION IN PARTICULAR SCHOOLS.

THE BERLIN SCHOOLS—THE FRIEDRICH-WILHELMS GYMNASIUM—ITS HISTORY—ITS CONFESSIONAL CHARACTER, TEACHERS AND CHARGES—ITS CLASSES—ITS LESSONS —SCHOOL-BOOKS—THE GREYFRIARS GYMNASIUM—ITS HISTORY AND ENDOWMENT —DAY SCHOLARS AND BOARDERS IN GERMAN SCHOOLS—THE JOACHIMSTHALSCHE GYMNASIUM—SCHULPFORTA—THE STUDIENTAG AT SCHULPFORTA—GAMES AND GYMNASTICS—THE FRIEDRICH-WILHELMS GYMNASIUM AT COLOGNE—STUDIES OF THE GYMNASIUM AND OF THE REALSCHULE—CONFLICT BETWEEN THEIR PARTISANS.

BERLIN has four royal gymnasiums, one with a *Realschule* annexed; four municipal gymnasiums, one with a *Realschule* annexed; four other municipal *Realschulen*, and one higher Burgher School. All these are full; there were, in 1863, 6,874 scholars in them, without counting the children in the *Vorschulen* or preparatory schools which several of them have as appendages; but the supply of higher schools in Berlin is not sufficient for the demand, and the municipality, which was spending in 1863 more than 40,000*l.* a year on the secondary and primary schools of the city, is about to provide several higher schools more. All through Prussia one hears the same thing: the secondary schools are not enough for the increasing numbers whom the widening desire for a good education (*der weiter verbreitete Bildungstrieb*) sends into them. The State increases its grants, and those grants are met by increased exertions on the part of the communes, but still there is not room for the scholars who come in, and the rise which has taken place in the rate of school-fee has in no degree stopped them. To obtain the State's consent to the formation of a new school with the name and rights of a public secondary school, a commune must satisfy the State authority both that its municipal schools for the poor will not be pinched for the sake of the new establishment, and also that it can provide resources to carry on the new establishment properly, and in conformity with the requirements of the *Lehrplan.* This is being done in all directions.

Perhaps the most remarkable of the higher schools at Berlin is the *Friedrich-Wilhelms Gymnasium.* The Grey-friars gymnasium (*Gymnasium zum grauen Kloster*) has about the same number of scholars, but with the *Friedrich-Wilhelms Gymnasium* is connected a *Realschule*; a *Vorschule*, or preparatory school, common to the gymnasium and the *Realschule* both; and a girls' school, called from the then Crown Princess of Prussia who gave it her name in 1827, the *Elisabet-schule.* There were, at the end of 1863, 2,200 scholars in the whole institution together; 581 in the Gymnasium, 601 in the *Realschule,* 522 in the preparatory school, and 496 in the girls' school. The gymnasium is remarkable as being the only higher school in Prussia, except the *Realschule* on the Franck foundation at Halle, where the receipts from the scholars cover the expenditure of the school. The annual expenditure for the gymnasium, *Realschule,* preparatory school, and *Elisabetschule* together, is in round figures 65,000 thalers; the receipts from the scholars' fees are in round figures 53,000 thalers. The property of the institution is very small, producing about 400*l.* a year only, so the deficiency is made up by a State grant of about 10,000 thalers; this deficiency, however, arises not in the gymnasium, where the school-fees more than cover the expenses, but in the schools allied with it.

The history of this institution is the history of many public schools in Prussia. It owes its origin to the Church, and has then in course of time passed under the superintendence of the State. I have mentioned the establishment by Johann Hecker in 1747 of the first *Realschule* at Berlin. Hecker was preacher at the Trinity Church in the Friedrichsstadt, and he grouped together several small schools in his parish under the name of a *Realschule.* The institution throve from the first; in 1748 it had 808 scholars, and 20 years after-wards it had 1,267. It was governed by the curators of the Trinity Church and by inspectors of their appointment; and it was supported, having no endowment except a very trifling house-property, by voluntary contributions and by school-fees. The Latin school, which was one of the grouped schools, grew in importance, and at the fiftieth anniversary of the institution it received the name of *Friedrich-Wilhelms Gymnasium*, and in 1803 was rebuilt with a grant from the king of nearly 10,000*l.* towards the rebuilding. At the great reforming epoch of 1809 it passed with the other public secondary schools of Berlin under the administration of the Education Department; this change being sanctioned, not only by public opinion, but by the governing bodies of the schools themselves, with the view of giving to these great and important metropolitan establishments the benefit of a common and intelligent direction. The *Friedrich-Wilhelms Gymnasium* is now, therefore, both for *interna* and *externa*, under the School Board of the province of Brandenburg, to which, as soon as the School Boards were constituted, the central department transferred its direct charge of the public schools.

The gymnasium is by foundation Protestant, and out of the 600 boys whom I found there, only 20 were Catholics and 15 were Jews. The united schools have a joint director and a joint administration of their affairs. They have altogether 66 teachers, of whom 21 are for the gymnasium. Of these 21, 11 are *Oberlehrer*, and of these 11, six or seven have the title of professor. The director is Dr. Ferdinand Ranke, a brother of the historian; he has been nearly twenty-five years director here, and more than forty years in the profession. He and seven of the upper masters of the gymnasium are lodged in the school buildings, which are very plain; but in the school-court is one of those relics of the past, so far more common in the German schools, as in ours, than in the French,—the inscription on Hecker's original school-house : *Scholæ Trinitatis ædes in Dei honorem, regis gaudium, civium salutem, juventutis institutioni dicatæ.* There are no boarders, a boarding establishment which originally formed part of the institution having been done away with in 1832. The scholars all through the school pay the same fee, 26 thalers a year (3*l.* 18*s*). In the *Vorschule* the fee is the same; in the *Real-*

schule it is only two thalers a year lower. In one gymnasium at Berlin the scholars pay four thalers a year more than in the *Friedrich-Wilhelms Gymnasium*; in all the others they pay one thaler less. There is very considerable variety in the rate of school-fees in Prussia, the circumstances of the school and locality being always taken into account in fixing it. The rate in the metropolitan schools is of course a comparatively high one, low as it seems to us. Many schools have a rate rising with the class or .division; thus in the gymnasium at Wetzlar the boys in *sexta* and *quinta* pay 16 thalers, those in *quarta* and *tertia* pay 10 thalers, those in *secunda* and *prima* pay 20 thalers. In some schools the rate is as low as eight or ten thalers for the lower classes, and 14 or 16 thalers for the higher. As an average rate for all the gymnasiums of Prussia, 20 thalers (3*l.*) a year, would certainly be rather above the mark than under it. The rates in the *Realschulen* and the higher Burgher Schools do not in general range below those of the classical schools. Moderate as these present rates appear to us, they are much higher than they used to be; in the *Friedrich-Wilhelms Gymnasium* the school-fee twenty years ago was only 16 thalers in *sexta* and *quinta*, and 20 thalers in the other classes. In many provincial schools it was astonishingly low, as low as two, two and a half, and three thalers. In a gymnasium I have already mentioned, the *Magdalenen-Gymnasium* at Breslau, there was, in 1824, a uniform fee of 8 thalers, and there is now a uniform fee of 24 thalers.

In the *Friedrich-Wilhelms Gymnasium* I found that 10 per cent. of the 600 scholars had free schooling. The number of free posts as they are called (*Freistellen*) varies in different schools; in some it goes up to 25 per cent., but I think 10 per cent. may be taken as a fair average. These free posts are given on the ground of need and public claim. There are also a few exhibitions in the *Friedrich-Wilhelms Gymnasium*, but it will be best to notice the subject of exhibitions when I am speaking of some older and richer establishment.

Of course in the very large schools it is not possible to actually group and teach the scholars in six classes, nor yet is it always possible to observe the rule which enjoins that there shall not be more than forty scholars in either *secunda* or *prima*, or more than fifty in any of the other classes. The supply of class-rooms falls short, even more than the supply of teachers. The highest class, however, always remains *prima*, as in our great schools it always remains the *sixth*; and in the higher classes the Germans, as I have already mentioned, follow, when it is necessary, the plan of having an upper and lower division (*oberprima, unterprima*), and in other classes both this plan and the plan of having two groups or assemblages (*cœtus*) at the same stage of school work, and advancing parallel to one another.

The first lesson I heard was Dr. Ranke's own lesson to *prima*, on the *Philoctetes* of Sophocles. He spoke Latin to his class and his class spoke Latin in answer; this is still a common practice in the German schools, though not so common as formerly. The German boys have certainly acquired through this practice a surprising command of Latin; Dr. Schopen's lessons at Bonn to his *prima* in extemporaneous translation into Latin,—a lesson which has a deserved celebrity,—I heard with astonishment; a much wider command of the Latin vocabulary than our boys have, and a more ready management of the language, the Germans certainly succeed in acquiring. On the other hand, the best style of the best authors is not, to my mind, so well caught in Latin composition by their boys as by ours. This is more particularly the case in verse, where their best scholars often show, I cannot but think, not only a want of practical skill (that of course is nothing), but a want of tact for what is uncouth and inadmissible, which one would not have expected of people who know the Latin models so well. The same is true, in a less degree, of their prose; the best scholars in the best schools of England or France, if set to write a speech or a character in the style of Cicero or Tacitus, would, I think, in general acquit themselves of the task more happily than the corresponding boys of a German school.

But the feeling which was strongest with me in the Berlin *Philoctetes* lesson was the feeling that one seemed to be back in the sixth form at Rugby again, as I remember it nearly thirty years ago. After the lecture rooms at Oxford, and the

French *lycées*, and the Italian *licei*, here was at last a body of pupils once more who had worked at their lessons, had learnt Greek, and were at home in a Greek play. What the Berlin boys knew about the scope of the play, its chief personages, and the governing idea and character of each, was more than the Rugby boys would have known; but the quantity of lines done, the style of doing them, and the extent of scholarship expected in the boys and found in them, seemed to me as nearly as possible the same thing at Berlin and at Rugby. I thought the same in the afternoon when I heard Professor Zumpt (a son of the famous Latin scholar) take *unterprima* in Cicero's speech *Pro Sex. Roscio Amerino*. The boys had been through the oration during the early part of the half-year; they were now going very rapidly through it again, translating into fluent German without taking the Latin words. The master let the boys be the performers, and spoke as little as possible himself, but every good or bad performance was noticed. Just the same with lessons in Thucydides, Livy, and Horace, which I heard at other gymnasiums in Berlin. The lessons had been well prepared by the pupils, the master made few comments, and only on really noteworthy matters, or to cite some parallel passage which was not likely to have come within his pupils' reading; in general, when he spoke it was to question, and he questioned closely. I was struck with the exact knowledge of the Horatian metres which the *unterprima* boys at Greyfriars showed when questioned on them. I found that the practice was to begin by taking eleven odes as specimens of metre, and carefully studying these before proceeding further. Then they commence the *Odes* at the beginning and go right through them. The portion of a Latin or Greek author got through at a lesson is about the same as in the corresponding form in one of the best English schools, but either in school or by private study the boys have certainly read more than our boys or the French; it is the general rule that a boy who goes in for the leaving examination has read Homer all through. A larger number of the boys, too, seem to have really benefited by the instruction, and to be in the first flight of their class, than with us. But the great superiority of the Germans, and where they show how much farther they have gone in *Alterthumswissenschaft* than we have, is in their far broader notion of treating, even in their schools, the ancient authors as *literature*, and conceiving the place and significance of an author in his country's literature, and in that of the world. In this way the student's interest in Greek and Latin becomes much more vital, and the hold of these languages upon him is much more likely to be permanent. This is to be set against the superior finish and elegance of the best of our boys in Latin and Greek composition; above all, in Latin and Greek verse. Greek verse, indeed, can scarcely be said to be a school exercise at all, so far as I could see or hear, in the foreign schools.

Instead of having to write Greek iambics, the boys in *prima* at the *Friedrich-Wilhelms Gymnasium*, on one of the days when I was there, had had to write a summary of Lessing's essay on the epigram. The summaries were handed to the professor, who then made a boy stand up and give in his own words the substance of Lessing's essay, beginning at the beginning, the professor commenting and asking questions as the boy proceeded. Presently another boy was set on, and in this way they went through the essay. The lesson was as much out of the range of my English school experience as the lessons on the *Femmes Savantes* of Molière, which I heard, as I have already said, with so much interest in the *École Normale* at Paris. The Berlin lesson, like the Paris one, was very interesting.

In the lower division of *tertia* (about the middle of the school) I had another opportunity of observing a way, not, I think, in use in England, of practising the boys in Latin. The lesson was Ovid; the boys had had to translate at home a certain portion of Ovid into German, and then to bring their translation with them to school. This they had then, in school, to turn back into Latin, not metrical. After this, boys were called upon one after another, as in England, to say a few lines of Ovid by heart; but then, again, each boy had also to say in German prose the passage he had just recited in Ovid's verse.

In *quinta* I heard the religious instruction. For boys still so near the primary school stage, religious instruction, as a part of the school lessons, seems to me to be still, as in the primary school, in place, and still useful; in the higher classes of the secondary school it seems to me, I confess, unprofitable and inappropriate. Anything more futile and useless than the lesson in the *Galatians* which I heard given to *secunda* at Bonn cannot possibly be imagined. In *quinta* here at Berlin, it was different; the boys were first questioned in Bible narratives from a text-book; a good text-book and good questioning; then they said Luther's Short Catechism, and then they repeated hymns. The two or three Catholic and Jewish boys belonging to the class did not come to this lesson.

The mention of a text-book reminds me to say a word about the rule in the Prussian public schools for schoolbooks. The masters choose the books, but the approval of the Provincial Board must be obtained for their choice; before approving for the first time any new book, the Provincial Board must refer to the Education Minister and his Council. When a book has once been approved for a gymnasium, it may be used in any other gymnasium or progymnasium of the same province; but approval for a gymnasium does not count for a *Realschule,* and *vice versa.*

I must in passing observe how greatly some intelligent censorship like that of the Provincial Boards and the Minister in Prussia, or that of the Council of Public Instruction in France, is needed for school-books in England. Many as are the absurdities of our state of school anarchy, perhaps none of them is more crying than the book-pest which prevails under it. Every school chooses at its own discretion; many schools make a trade of book-dealing, and therefore it is for their interest to have books which are not used elsewhere, and which the pupil will not bring with him from his last school; so that a boy who has been at three or four English schools has often had to buy a complete new set of school-books for each. The extravagance of this is bad enough; but then, besides, as there exists no intelligent control or selection of them, half at least of our school-books are rubbish, and to the other defects of our school system we may add this, that in no other secondary schools in Europe do the pupils spend so much of their time in learning such utter nonsense as they do in ours.

I have mentioned the Greyfriars gymnasium, where I also heard lessons, and where they were of the same character as at the *Friedrich-Wilhelms Gymnasium*, a character much more like that of the lessons in our best English public schools than of the lessons in the French *lycées*. The history of Greyfriars is this. It occupies the site of a Franciscan convent abolished at the Reformation; in 1574 the third part of the convent premises was assigned by the elector, at the instance of the town magistracy, for use as a public school. The magistracy endowed it, and the elector made it over to them, but with an electoral *Schulordnung*. Here from the earliest times of the school there was a *convictorium* (the Italian *convitto*). The robust appetite of the sixteenth century for the humanities appears in the original plan of work; Greek had thirteen hours a week, Latin ten, logic two, arithmetic two, singing five. In 1655 the school had 400 scholars. In the second quarter of the eighteenth century the mother-tongue and its literature first appear as part of the school course; the German public schools having thus the start of ours, in this particular, by about 125 years. In 1793 the school got the benefit of a great endowment which I have already mentioned, the *Streitsche Stiftung*; the capital of this endowment is now 33,000*l*. It is administered by a *Directorium* composed, not of Sigismund Streit's descendants, but as follows: the provost of St. Nicholas (parish minister), the director and the prorector of the school, a councillor of the Education Department, a merchant or tradesman, and a lawyer. The financial administration of this *Directorium* is controlled, in the manner I have already described, by the public finance officers of the *Regierung* or governmental district in which Berlin stands.

Streit's endowment maintains at Greyfriars teachers of the modern languages, of astronomy, and of music, provides a *Wohncommunität* (lodging, bedding, fire and lights) for twelve scholars, and a *Freitisch* (board) for twenty-four more; and keeps improving the school library (now 20,000 volumes), the

observatory, collections, &c. It also augments the salaries
of the director and a number of the masters. Other benefactions provide the widows of masters who die in office with
a sum for their husbands' funeral expenses, and a pension of
45*l.* a year. There is an endowment of nearly 450*l.* a year
for exhibitions to be enjoyed at the school, and of 150*l.* a
year for exhibitions at the universities. Every two years is
held a school-festival in honour of founders and benefactors.
The school premises had an important enlargement by Crown
grants of land in 1819 and 1831, and great additions have
since that time been made to the buildings. I found about
550 boys, with a director and twenty-five masters. On an
average, twenty-five boys pass the *Abiturientenexamen* from
this school every year. Here, too, as at the *Friedrich-
Wilhelms Gymnasium*, the number of free posts is ten per
cent. They are provided by the municipality. The school
gets a grant of about 100*l.* a year from the State and 1,000*l.*
a year from the city of Berlin.

By original foundation and by endowment this school too
is Protestant. Hardly any Catholic boys are here, but of
Jewish boys there are seventy or eighty. About a third of
the whole number of the scholars are *auswärtige*, boys who
come from a distance, and cannot, therefore, live with their
parents. The great *internats* of the French *lycées* are unknown in Germany; the *Alumnate* or *Convicte* of the German
schools are properly establishments like *college* at Eton or
Winchester, and are for foundationers; for establishments
like the School House and the masters' boarding-houses at
Rugby, or Commoners at Winchester, the strict designation
would in Germany be *Pensionat*, *Pensionsanstalt*, and not
Alumnat. The practice of having one's son live at home
and go to school for his lessons only, obtains much more
widely in Germany than with us; 40,000 of the 66,000 boys
in the Prussian higher schools are day scholars. Still this
leaves 26,000 who are not; and of these the vast majority
live with some respectable family in the place where they go
to school. The household with which their son is to board
or lodge is designated by the parent, but must, by the school
regulations of Prussia, be approved by the director of the

boy's school, who holds the householder responsible for the boy's conduct out of school. ·The family life in North Germany is in general decent, kindly, and God-fearing ; and a boy is, I think, much better placed as a boarder in this way than as an *interne* of a French *lycée*. Still the school authorities in Prussia are of opinion that the provision of boarding establishments in immediate connection with the public schools needs increasing, and they design to increase it.

The patron at Greyfriars, for matters that do not come within the province of the *Directorium* of Streit's charity, is still, as the elector John George originally appointed, the city of Berlin, the municipality. The reader will remember that for the *interna* of a Prussian gymnasium the intervention of the Provincial Board always subsists.

I must give a word in passing to the great *Alumnat* of Berlin, the *Joachimsthalsche Gymnasium.* Here I found 404 scholars; 120 of them were collegers (*Alumnen*), 12 were boarders in the establishment (*Pensionaire*) ; the rest were boys who came for the lessons only (*Hospiten*). Ten per cent of these have free schooling. The *Pensionaire* pay only 24*l.* a year; the *Alumnen* are not all of them free of all cost; 25 of them pay 8*l.* 14*s.* a year, 75 of them pay 4*l.* 10*s.* There are 20 places with board, lodging, and instruction all entirely free, for 20 proved scholars of the highest forms.

The *Joachimsthalsche Gymnasium* is a royal foundation, endowed with lands by the elector Joachim Frederick in 1607. It is Protestant. The school has now an income of over 3,000*l.* a year from land, and of over 2,000*l.* a year from money in the funds. The Crown is the patron ; the property is administered, owing to its connection with the Crown domain, by the *Regierung* at Potsdam.

This is an interesting school, for the list of its masters contains the names of Buttmann, Schneider, Passow, Zumpt, Krüger, and Bergk. The director is Dr. Kiessling, a son of the editor of Theocritus. Constantly in the rolls of the German schools one is coming upon a well-known name of this kind ; on the roll of former teachers at Greyfriars are to be found the names of Heindorf, Spalding, Droysen. Nor are other recollections, as interesting as any school in the·

world can boast, wanting to the Prussian schools. The
Joachimsthal School had a scholar of *quarta* who, like so
many German schoolboys, joined the army in the great
uprising against the French in 1813. This boy was wounded
at Leipzig, made the campaign of France, was at Waterloo,
received the decoration of the Iron Cross, and finally, with
the decoration on his breast, took his place again on his old
school-bench as a scholar of *quarta*.

But no *Alumnat* in Prussia, or indeed in Germany, can
compare with Schulpforta, which by its antiquity, its beauty,
its wealth, its celebrity, is entitled to vie with the most
renowned English schools. The Cistercian abbey of St.
Mary's, Pforta, dates from 1137. It was secularised in 1540;
and Duke Maurice of Saxony, in 1543, established in its
place and endowed with its revenues a Protestant school
for 100 scholars. It stands near the Saal, in the pleasant
country of Prussian Saxony; and the venerable pile of buildings rising among its meadows, hills, and woods, is worthy of
the motto borne on the arms of the old abbey : ' *Hier ist nichts
anderes denn Gottes Haus, und hier die* Pforte *des Himmels.*' *
It has a beautifully restored chapel, regular commemorative
services, and a host of local usages. A Latin grace is sung
in hall every day before dinner by the whole body of scholars.
Every scholar has by ancient institution his *tutor*, every
master his *famulus*. This is the German school where Latin
verse has been most cultivated, and the *Musæ Portenses*, like
those of Eton, have been published.

The property is very large, and considerable Church
patronage is attached to it. Up to 1815, when it passed
into the possession of Prussia, the old abbey estate had still
its feudal privileges, and enjoyed full civil and criminal jurisdiction. The property is now entirely under the superintendence of the School Board of the province of Saxony,
which appoints a procurator for it. The revenues of Pforta
are from 8,000*l.* to 9,000*l.* a year.

The great head-master of Schulpforta was Ilgen, whose
name every one who has read the Homeric Hymns ought to

* 'This is none other but the house of God, and this is the gate (*porta, Pforte*)
of heaven.'— *Gen.* xxviii. 17.

respect. Ilgen was rector for nearly thirty years, from 1802
to 1831, and his reforms make this period an epoch in the
school's history. Few schools can show such a list of old
scholars. Grœvius, Ernesti, Klopstock, Böttiger, Mitscherlich,
Fichte, Dissen, Thiersch, Spitzner, Döderlein, Spohn, were
all of them schoolboys here.

There are now about 205 pupils: 180 *Alumnen* proper, or
collegers, 20 boarders (*Pensionaire, Extraneer*), and four or
five half-boarders (*Semi-Extraneer*). These half-boarders have,
in fact, all the advantages of collegers, except board, for
a payment of 7*l.* 10*s.* a year; their board they get at a
master's. The real *Extraneer* board and lodge with a master;
they pay him about 45*l.* a year for their board and lodging,
and the school 5*l.* 8*s.* a year for their instruction.

The *Alumnen* proper have all of them certain payments to
make; those exacted, however, from the 140 who hold *Freistellen* are very trifling. There are 30 old *Koststellen*, or
posts with board, the holders of which pay about 3*l.* a year
each, and 20 new *Koststellen*, the holders of which pay 7*l.*
As a general rule, a boy is not admitted at once to a *Freistelle.*
The right of nominating to about half the posts on the foundation belongs to the Crown, that to the other half to different
municipalities. Of the Crown appointments a certain number
is reserved, by convention with the Saxon Government when
Pforta passed into Prussia's possession, for natives of the
duchy of Saxony. The rest are given, on grounds of public
claim, by the Minister of Justice and the Home Secretary.
No boy is admitted till he is twelve years old; he must be able
to pass for *tertia.* The school begins with *tertia,* but it has
six forms, because there is an upper and a lower division of
each class. There are 77 boys in the two divisions of *tertia,*
79 in the two of *secunda,* 49 in the two of *prima.* For some
of the posts several boys are nominated, and the one who
passes the best examination gets admitted; but the candidates here, the English reader will observe, must all of them
be over twelve years of age. The school is well provided with
exhibitions, in general of from 10*l.* to 15*l.* a year in value, to
the universities.

There is a noteworthy usage here of making one day in

the week a *Studientag*, in which the boy is free from all
school lessons that he may pursue his private studies. In the
same spirit, in the *Gymnasien* generally, promising boys in
prima are excused certain of the school lessons, that they
may work at matters which specially interest them. Results
of this private study are to be produced at the *Abiturientenexamen*, and are taken into account for the leaving
certificate. Nothing could better show the freedom of Germany, as compared with France, in treating school matters,
than a practice of this kind, which to the French authorities
would appear monstrous. In England the school authorities
would have a belief, in general too well justified, that hardly
any one of our boys has any notion of such a thing as
systematic private study at all.

At Schulpforta they are very proud of their playing-field,
which is indeed, with the wooded hill rising behind it, a
pleasant place ; but the games of English playing-fields do
not go on there : instead of goals or a cricket-ground, one
sees apparatus for gymnastics. The Germans, as is well
known, now cultivate gymnastics in their schools with great
care. Since 1842, gymnastics have been made a regular part
of the public-school course ; there is a *Central-Turnanstalt* at
Berlin, with 18 civilian pupils who are being trained expressly
to supply model teachers of gymnastics for the public schools.
The teachers profess to have adapted their exercises with
precision to every age, and to all the stages of a boy's growth
and muscular development. The French are much impressed
by what seems to them the success of the Germans in this
kind of instruction, and certainly in their own *lycées* they
have not at present done nearly so much for it. Nothing,
however, will make an ex-schoolboy of one of the great
English schools regard the gymnastics of a foreign school
without a slight feeling of wonder and compassion, so much
more animating and interesting do the games of his remembrance seem to him. This much, however, I will say: if
boys have long work-hours, or if they work hard, gymnastics
probably do more for their physical health in the comparatively short time allotted to recreation than anything else
could. In England the majority of public schoolboys work

far less than the foreign schoolboy, and for this majority the English games are delightful; but for the few hard students with us there is in general nothing but the *constitutional*, and this is not so good as the foreign gymnastics. For little boys, again, I am inclined to think that the carefully taught gymnastics of a foreign school are better than the lounging shiveringly about, which in my time used often at our great schools to be the portion of those who had not yet come to full age for games.

All the schools I have hitherto described are denominational schools. Before I conclude, I must describe a mixed (*simultan*) school, or the nearest approach to it to be found. Such a school is the *Friedrich-Wilhelms Gymnasium* at Cologne. Cologne, as every one knows, is Catholic; up to 1825 it had only one gymnasium, a Catholic one. It has now two Catholic gymnasiums, one with 382 scholars, the other with 281; it has also a *Realschule* of the first rank, with 601 scholars.* Besides these schools it has a Protestant gymnasium, with *real* classes; as we should say, with a modern school forming part of it. This is the *Friedrich-Wilhelms Gymnasium*. An old Carmelite college, which had become the property of the municipality, was in 1825 made into a public gymnasium, in order to relieve the overcrowding in the Catholic gymnasium and to provide special accommodation for the Protestants. In 1862 this school was, by the subscriptions of friends, both Catholic and Protestant, provided with *real* classes up to *secunda*, the two lowest classes (*sexta* and *quinta*) being common to both classical and *real* scholars. There are, therefore, in fact, three special classes for *real* scholars; or, as we should say, a modern school of three classes. There are 356 boys in the classical school, and about 100 in the modern school. Of the boys in the classical school 125 only are Protestants, though the school is by foundation *evangelisch*; 215 are Catholics and 16 are Jews. Nothing could better show how little the 'religious difficulty' practically exists in Prussian schools, than this abundance of Catholic scholars in a Protestant school, where the director and the majority of the 15 masters are Pro-

* Cologne is a town of 120,570 inhabitants.

testants.   The regular religious instruction of the school is of course Protestant; but the Catholics being in such numbers, a special religious instructor has been provided for them, as, too, there is a special religious instructor provided for the Protestants in the two Catholic gymnasiums. It will be remembered that where the boys not of the confession for which the school is founded are very few in number, the parents have to make private arrangements for their religious instruction, and the school does not provide it. The school-fee is from 18 to 22 thalers a year, according to the form a boy is in.

The property of the school brings in less than 200*l.* a year. The State contributes about 900*l.* a year. School-fees produce almost exactly the same sum. The municipality gave in the first instance the school premises, and now contributes about 50*l.* a year to keep them up. It is a Crown patronage school, but the *externa,* or property concerns, of this school, as of all the gymnasiums and school endowments of Cologne, are managed by a local *Verwaltungsrath,* or council of administration.   This *Verwaltungsrath* is thus composed: a representative of the Provincial School Board, the directors of the three gymnasiums, with a lawyer, a financier, an administrator, and two citizens of Cologne; these last five chosen, on the presentation of the Common Council, by the Provincial School Board.   For the *Studienfonds,* which are endowments general for education in Cologne, and not affected to particular institutions, a Catholic ecclesiastic is added to the *Verwaltungsrath.*   These *Studienfonds* are very considerable, producing close upon 60,000 thalers a year (9,000*l.*).   The *Verwaltungsrath* has a staff of seven clerks, office-keepers, &c., and both council and staff are paid for their services.

The director was the personage already mentioned, whose nomination to a school* the Education Minister had refused to confirm, because of the nominee's politics.   I had much conversation with him, and he struck me as a very able man.. He said, and his presence in this Cologne school confirmed it, that the Government found it impossible to treat their

---

* The school was the gymnasium at Bielefeld.

school patronage politically, even so far as the directors or head-masters were concerned.   The appointment of the professor and teachers, he declared, it never even entered into the Government's head to treat politically. We went through the school admission-book together, that I might see to what class in society the boys chiefly belonged.   We took a class in the middle of the school, and went through this boy by boy, both for the classical school and the modern school. As it happened, the social standing of the *real* scholars was on the whole somewhat the highest, but there was very little difference.   There were a few peasants' children, picked boys from the elementary schools in the neighbourhood, but these were all of them bursars.   There were a good many sons of Government officials.   But the designation I found attached to by far the greater number of parents' names was *Kaufmann,*—'trader.'   I heard several lessons, and particularly noticed the English lesson in the third class of the modern school.   This lesson was given by a Swiss, who spoke English very well, and who had been, he told me, a teacher of modern languages at Uppingham.   I thought here, as I thought when I heard a French lesson at Bonn, that the boys made a good deal more of these modern language lessons in Germany than in England; the Swiss master at Cologne said this impression of mine was quite right.   Even in France I thought these lessons better done,—with better methods, better teachers, and more thoroughly learned,— than in England.   In Germany they were better than in France.   The lessons in the natural sciences, on the other hand, which in France seemed to me inferior to the mathematical lessons, I thought less successfully given in Germany than even in France.   But of this matter I am a very incompetent judge, and England, besides, supplied me here with no standard of comparison, for in the English schools, when I knew them, the natural sciences were not taught at all.   The classical work in the Cologne gymnasium was much the same that I had seen in other Prussian gymnasiums, and calls for no particular remark.

Dr. Jäger, the director of the united school,—well placed, therefore, for judging, and, as I have said, an able man,—

assured me it was the universal conviction with those competent to form an opinion, that the *Realschulen* were not, at present, successful institutions. He declared that the boys in the corresponding forms of the classical school beat the *Realschule* boys in matters which both do alike, such as history, geography, the mother-tongue, and even French, though to French the *Realschule* boys devote so far more time than their comrades of the classical school. The reason for this, Dr. Jäger affirms, is that the classical training strengthens a boy's mind so much more.

This is what, as I have already said, the chief school authorities everywhere in France and Germany testify: I quote Dr. Jäger's testimony in particular, because of his ability and because of his double experience. In Switzerland you do not hear the same story, but the regnant Swiss conception of secondary instruction is, in general, not a liberal but a commercial one; not culture and training of the mind, but what will be of immediate palpable utility in some practical calling, is there the chief matter; and this cannot be admitted as the true scope of secondary instruction. Even in Switzerland, too, there is a talk of introducing Latin into the *Realschule* course, which at present is without it; so impossible is it to follow absolutely the commercial theory of education without finding inconvenience from it. But I reserve my remarks on this question for my conclusion.

CHAPTER XX.

SUPERIOR OR UNIVERSITY INSTRUCTION IN PRUSSIA.

PASSAGE FROM SECONDARY TO SUPERIOR INSTRUCTION—SPECIAL SCHOOLS AND UNI-
VERSITIES — UNIVERSITIES OF PRUSSIA — PROPORTION OF UNIVERSITY STUDENTS
TO POPULATION — GERMAN UNIVERSITIES STATE ESTABLISHMENTS — UNIVERSITY
AUTHORITIES — UNIVERSITY TEACHERS—1. FULL PROFESSORS—2. ASSISTANT PRO-
FESSORS—3. PRIVATDOCENTEN—STUDENTS—FEES—CERTIFICATES OF ATTENDANCE
AT LECTURES — DEGREES — THE STAATSPRÜFUNG — CHARACTER OF THE GERMAN
UNIVERSITY SYSTEM.

THE secondary school has essentially for its object a general liberal culture, whether this culture is chiefly pursued
through the group of aptitudes which carry us to the humanities, or through the group of aptitudes which carry us to the
study of nature. It is a mistake to make the secondary school
a direct professional school, though a boy's aims in life and
his future profession will naturally determine, in the absence
of an overpowering bent, the group of aptitudes he will seek
to develope. It is the function of the special school to give
a professional direction to what a boy has learnt at the secondary school, at the same time that it makes his knowledge,
as far as possible, systematic,—developes it into science. It
is the function of the university to develope into science the
knowledge a boy brings with him from the secondary school,
at the same time that it directs him towards the profession in
which his knowledge may most naturally be exercised. Thus,
in the university, the idea of science is primary, that of the
profession, secondary; in the special school, the idea of the
profession is primary, that of science, secondary. Our English
special schools have yet to be instituted, and our English
universities do not perform the function of a university, as
that function is above laid down. Still we have, like Germany, great and famous universities, and those universities
are, as in Germany, in immediate connection with our chief
secondary schools. It will be well, therefore, to complete

my sketch of the Prussian school system by a sketch of the university system with which it is co-ordered.

Prussia has now six complete universities, with all the four faculties of theology, law, medicine, and philosophy; and two incomplete universities, with only the faculties of theology and philosophy. The complete universities are Berlin, Bonn, Breslau, Greifswald, Halle, and Königsberg; the incomplete ones are Münster and Braunsberg. In both of these last the faculty of theology is Catholic.

These eight Prussian universities had, in 1864, 6,362 students and 600 professors. But this number does not represent the number of Prussians who come under university instruction, because many Prussians go to German universities out of Prussia, such as Heidelberg, Göttingen, Leipzig, Jena. There is very free circulation of the German students through the universities of the fatherland; and to estimate the proportion, in any German State, who come under superior instruction, the fairest way is to take the proportion which the whole number of students in Germany bears to the whole population. For else, while we get for Prussia but about one student to every 2,800 inhabitants, we shall get for Baden, and for the three Saxon duchies, Weimar, Coburg, and Altenburg, about one student to every 1,100 inhabitants; yet it is not that in these territories more of the population go to the university than in Prussia, but Baden has the University of Heidelberg, and the three Saxon duchies have in common the University of Jena, and to these two universities students from all parts of Germany come. Taking, therefore, the whole of Germany, exclusive of the non-German States of Austria, we get about one matriculated student for every 2,600 of population; and this proportion is probably pretty near the truth for Prussia, and for most of the single States. In England the proportion is about one matriculated student to every 5,800 of the population.

The universities of the several German States differ in many points of detail, but in their main system and regulations they are alike. I shall continue, in speaking of universities, to have Prussia in immediate view; but the English reader will understand that what I say of the Prussian university system may be applied in general to that of all Germany.

The German university is a State establishment, and is maintained, so far as its own resources fall short, by the State. A university's own resources are both the property it has and the fees it levies. The two most important of the Prussian universities, Berlin with its 2,500 students and Bonn with its 1,000, date from this century, and foundations of this century are seldom very rich in property. For the year 1864, the income of the University of Berlin was 196,787 thalers (29,518*l*.); of this sum, the real and funded property of the university produced 161 thalers, fees produced 7,557 thalers. The State gave all the rest,—189,069 thalers (about 28,842*l*.). And the State which does this is the most frugal and economical State in Europe.*

The Minister of Public Instruction appoints the professors of a university, the academical senate having the right of proposing names for his acceptance; and he has also his representative in each university,—the *curator*,—who acts as plenipotentiary for the State, and whose business it is to see to the observance of the laws and regulations which concern the universities. Thus, for instance, a full professor (*professor ordinarius*) is bound by regulation to give throughout the *Semester*, or half-year, at least two free lectures a week on his subject; if he tried to charge fees for them, it would be the curator's business to interfere. And the university authorities cannot make new regulations for the government of the university without obtaining for them the sanction of the minister and of Parliament. Still the university authorities practically work, in Germany just as much as in this country, their own university; the real direction of the university is in their hands, and not, as in France, in those of the minister.

These university authorities are the following. First comes

* For further details respecting the University of Berlin see the Appendix. I have there given, also, a list of all the universities of Germany, with the numbers of their students and teachers. For valuable information on this subject, and for excellently composed tables in which that information is exhibited, I am indebted to M. Minssen's clear and useful *Étude sur l'Instruction secondaire et supérieure en Allemagne* (Paris, Librairie Internationale, 1866). M. Minssen was sent by M. Duruy to see the universities and gymnasiums of Germany, and was in that country at the same time that I was.

the rector, or, in cases where the sovereign is the titular rector, as at Halle and Jena, the pro-rector, who answers to our vice-chancellor, only he is elected for one year only, instead of four. His electors are the full professors. The rector or pro-rector is the visible head of the university, and is charged with its discipline. Like our vice-chancellor, he has an assessor, or judge, who sits with him whenever there is a question of inflicting fines, or whenever one of the parties appearing before him is not a member of the university. The academical senate is also chosen by the full professors, and for one year, its members consisting of the actual rector (or pro-rector), the outgoing rector, and a full professor of each faculty. In some universities all the full professors are members of the academical senate. The rector is president, and the internal affairs of the university are brought before it for its discussion and regulation of them.

Next come the faculties. The faculties in nearly all German universities are four in number :* theology, law, medicine, and philosophy. Philosophy embraces the humanities, and the mathematical and natural sciences. As a university authority, a faculty consists only of its full professors, headed by the dean, whom these professors elect for one year. It is the business of the faculty thus composed to see that the students attend regularly the courses of lectures for which they are entered, to summon defaulters before it, to reprimand them, and to inflict on them, if it think proper, a slight penalty.

The last university authority to be mentioned is the *quæstor.* He has to collect from the students the fees for the courses for which they have entered themselves, and to pay those fees to the professors to whom they are due, a small deduction being made for the quæstor's salary and for the university chest.

And now to take the university, not as an administrative but as a teaching body. Of the university, considered in this capacity, the *faculty* is a very different thing from the limited

---

* In one or two universities there is a separate faculty for political economy ; in general this science is comprehended in the faculty of philosophy.

faculty above described. The university faculty, as a teaching body, comprehends not only all the full professors of that faculty, but all its professors extraordinary, or assistant professors, and all its *Privatdocenten*. The dean of faculty ascertains from all the full professors, all the professors extraordinary, and all the *Privatdocenten* of his faculty, what subject each of them proposes to treat in the coming *Semester*: there is perfect liberty of choice for each lecturer, but by consent among themselves they so co-order their teaching that the whole field of instruction proper to their faculty may be completely covered. Then the dean calls together the full professors, who make the administrative faculty; and the programme of lectures is by them drawn up from the data collected by the dean, and is promulgated by their authority.

All full professors must have the degree of doctor in their faculty. Each of them is named for a special branch of the instruction of his faculty; and in this branch he is bound, as I have said, to give at least two public lectures a week without charging fees. He receives from the State a fixed salary which is sometimes as much as 350*l.*, or even 400*l.*, a year; he has also a share in the examination fees, and he has the fees for what lectures he gives besides his public lectures. The regular number of full professors in each university is limited, but the State can always, if it thinks fit, nominate an eminent man as full professor in a faculty, even though the faculty may have its complement of full professors; and the State then pays him the same salary as the other full professors. Both from the consideration which attaches to the post and from its emolument, a full professor's place is in Germany the prize of the career of public instruction, and no schoolmaster's place can compare with it. At Heidelberg several professors have, I am told, an income, from fixed salary and fees together, of 1,000*l.* a year, and one an income of 1,500*l.*

The professors extraordinary, or assistant professors, are also named by the State, but they have not in all cases a fixed salary. Their main dependence is on fees paid by those who come to their lectures. They are in general taken from the most distinguished of the *Privatdocenten*, and they rise through the post of professor extraordinary to that of full professor.

Other countries have full professors and professors extraordinary. France, for instance, has her *professeurs titulaires* and her *professeurs suppléants*; but the *Privatdocent* is peculiar to Germany, and is the great source of vigour and renovation to her superior instruction. Sometimes he gives private lessons, like the private tutors of our universities; these lessons have the title of *Privatissima*. But this is not his main business. His main business is as unlike the sterile business of our private tutors as possible. The *Privatdocent* is an assistant to the professorate; he is free to use, when the professors do not occupy them, the university lecture-rooms, he gives lectures like the professors, and his lectures count as professors' lectures for those who attend them. His appointment is on this wise. A distinguished student applies to be made *Privatdocent* in a faculty. He produces certain certificates and performs certain exercises before two delegates named by the faculty, and this is called his *Habilitation*. If he passes, the faculty names him *Privatdocent*. The authorisation of the minister is also requisite for him, but this follows his nomination by the faculty as a matter of course. He is then free to lecture on any of the matters proper to his faculty. He is on his probation, he receives no salary whatever, and depends entirely on his lectures; he has, therefore, every motive to exert himself. In general, as I have said, the professors and *Privatdocenten* arrange together to parcel out the field of instruction between them, and one supplements the other's teaching; still a *Privatdocent* may, if he likes, lecture on just the same subject that a professor is lecturing on; there is absolute liberty in this respect. The one precaution taken against undue competition is, that a *Privatdocent* lecturing on a professor's subject is not allowed to charge lower fees than the professor. It does honour to the disinterested spirit in which science is pursued in Germany, that with these temptations to competition, the relations between the professors and the *Privatdocenten* are in general excellent; the distinguished professor encourages the rising *Privatdocent,* and the *Privatdocent* seeks to make his teaching serve science, not his own vanity. But it is evident how the neighbourhood of a rising young *Privatdocent* must tend to keep a professor up to the mark, and hinder him from getting sleepy and lazy. If he gets sleepy and lazy, his lecture-room is deserted. The *Privatdocent*, again, has the standard of eminent men before his eyes, and everything stimulates him to come up to it.

In the faculty of philosophy at Berlin the number of *Privatdocenten* is about exactly the same as the number of full professors. There are 28 full professors and 29 *Privatdocenten.* The professors extraordinary are more numerous than either. They are 33 in number. The whole number of teachers in the University of Berlin is 183.

Now I come to the students. The university course in theology, law, and philosophy, takes three years; in medicine it takes four or five. A student in his *triennium* often visits one or two universities, seldom more. Lachmann (to take an eminent instance) first went for half-a-year to Leipzig to hear Hermann; then he passed on to Göttingen, where he afterwards got his *Habilitation.* To become a member of a university, the student has to be entered on the university register (*Matrikel*), and then on the register of the faculty in which he means to follow lectures; for inscription on the university register the production of the school leaving certificate (*Maturitätszeugniss*), of which I have already said so much, is indispensable. You may get leave to attend lectures without being a member of the university, and without any school certificate; but such attendance counts nothing for any purpose for which a university course is by law or official rule required. The university entrance fee is about 18*s.* The matriculating student signs an engagement to observe the laws and regulations of the university. The penalties for violating them are enforced by the rector. These penalties are, according to the nature of the offence, reprimand; fine; imprisonment for a period not exceeding one month in the university *carcer*; *consilium abeundi*, or dismissal from the particular university to which the student belongs, but with liberty to enter at another; and finally, *Relegation*, or absolute expulsion, notice being sent to the other universities, which then may not admit the student expelled.

The lecture fees range from 16*s.* to 1*l.* 14*s.* for every course which is not a public and gratuitous one. They are somewhat higher at Berlin than in most German universities. In the faculty of medicine they are highest; here they go as high as 1*l.* 14*s.* a *Semester* for a course of about five hours a week. A course of the same length in theology or philosophy costs at Berlin about 17*s.* a *Semester.* The fees are collected, as I have said, by the university quæstor, and they must be paid in advance. But every professor has the power to admit poor auditors to his lectures without fee, and often he does so. Poor students are also, by a humane arrangement, suffered to attend lectures on credit, and afterwards, when they enter the public service,—which in Prussia means not only what we in England call the public service, but the learned professions as well,—their lecture fees are recovered by a deduction from their salary. Each university has besides, for the benefit of poor scholars, a number of exhibitions ranging from 12*l.* to 60*l.* a year; and it is common to allow the holders of school exhibitions, which are of smaller amount, and range from 6*l.* to 30*l.* a year, to retain them at the university.

Certificates of having followed certain courses of lectures are required both for the university degree and for the subsequent examination for a public career (*Staatsprüfung*) which almost every university student has in view. It is said that the professors whose lectures are very numerously attended have difficulty in ascertaining who is there and who is not, and that they give the certificates with too much laxity. In general, however, it is certain that a student who has his way to make, and who is worth anything, will attend regularly the lectures for which he has entered himself and paid his money. There are, of course, many idlers; the proportion of students in a German university who really work I have heard estimated at one-third; certainly it is larger than in the English universities. But the pressure put upon them in the way of compulsion and university examinations is much less than with us. The paramount university aim in Germany is to encourage a love of study and science for their own sakes; and the professors, very unlike our college tutors, are constantly warning their pupils against *Brodstudien*, studies pursued with a view to examinations and posts. The examinations within the university course itself are far fewer and less important in Germany than in England. It is Austria, a country which believes in the things of the mind as little as we do, which is the great country for university examinations. There they are applied with a mechanical faith much like ours, and come as often as once a month; but the general intellectual life of the Austrian universities is lower, though Vienna and Prague are good medical schools, than that of any other universities of Germany. ' *Le pays à examens, l'Autriche,*'—exclaims an eminent French professor, M. Laboulaye, who has carefully studied the German university system with a view to reforming that of France,—' *Le pays à examens, l'Autriche, est précisément celui dans lequel on ne travaille pas*; ' and every competent authority in Germany will confirm what M. Laboulaye says. I do not say that in countries like Austria and England, where there is next to no real love for the things of the mind, examinations may not be a protection from something worse.* All I say is that a love for the things of the mind is what we want, and that examinations will never give it.

Each faculty in a German university examines for degrees in that faculty and confers them. The *Maturitätszeugniss* which the student brings with him from school answers to our grade of bachelor of arts. The degree of licentiate, answering to our degree of master, is only given in theology and philosophy, and is not often sought for. The great faculty degree is the degree of doctor. For this a certificate of university studies, an oral examination, and a written dissertation, are required. The dissertation is in Latin or German, and is usually published. A doctor's degree in philosophy costs 17*l.* at Berlin; there are faculties and uni-

---

* Although I am no very ardent lover of examinations, I am inclined to think the non-Austrian universities of Germany might with advantage make a somewhat greater use of them.

versities in which a doctor's degree costs as much as 22*l.* 10*s.*
A poor student who passes a brilliant examination has sometimes his degree given him without fees. I have already said
that the degree of doctor is given much more easily and
carelessly in some German universities than in others. But
in none is the degree examination in itself such as to make it
what the degree examination is with us,—the grand final cause
of the university life. '*Der Zweck des Lebens ist das Leben
selbst,*' says the German poet; and this is certainly true, in
Germany, of the university life.

The *Staatsprüfung*, however, supplies a bracing examination
test; but this examination falls outside the sphere of the
university itself. As I have again and again begged the
English reader to remark, the examination test is never used
in Prussia as sufficient in itself; it is only used to make the
assurance of a really good education doubly sure; the really
good education is regarded as the main assurance, and no
one who has not had this may present himself for the *Staatsprüfung*. The student who leaves a university receives from
the rector a certificate mentioning what lectures he has
attended, and what the character of his university career has
been. With this certificate, and with the leaving certificate
of his school, the future civil servant, clergyman, lawyer, or
doctor, presents himself before an examining commission
(*Prüfungscommission*) such as I have described in an earlier
part of this volume. He is then examined, having three or
four days of paper work, and six or eight hours of *viva voce.*
For lawyers and for clergymen there is a double examination,
the second coming three years after the first.

Such, sketched in the briefest possible outline, is the system of the German universities. *Lehrfreiheit* and *Lernfreiheit*,
liberty for the teacher and liberty for the learner; and *Wis-
senschaft*, science, knowledge systematically pursued and
prized in and for itself, are the fundamental ideas of that
system. The French, with their ministerial programmes for
superior instruction, and their ministerial authorisations
required for any one who wants to give a course of public
lectures,—authorisations which are by no means a matter of
form,—are naturally most struck with the liberty of the

German universities, and it is in liberty that they have most need to borrow from them. To us, ministerial programmes and ministerial authorisations are unknown; our university system is a routine, indeed, but it is our want of science, not our want of liberty, which makes it a routine. It is in science that we have most need to borrow from the German universities. The French university has no liberty, and the English universities have no science; the German universities have both.

IV.

SWITZERLAND.

CHAPTER XXI.

THE SCHOOLS OF SWITZERLAND.

WHAT is most important in the Swiss secondary schools is so closely akin to what is to be found in Germany, that the sketch I have given of the higher schools of Prussia might serve in the main for those of the most notable Swiss cantons also. But I will take the opportunity which Switzerland gives me to notice the secondary schools, which in Germany I have chiefly noticed by their classical side, by that side of them which is not classical, and also in connection with the primary schools.

Nowhere is the continuity between the primary and the higher schools so complete as in Canton Zurich, which I therefore will take as a representative of Switzerland, in the same way that I took Prussia as the representative of Germany. Zurich is, no doubt, an eminently favourable representative to take; it is on the whole the best provided with schools of all the Swiss cantons. Its schools, however, are scarcely better, even as a whole, than those of Canton Aargau and Canton Basle; in the classical school, Canton Basle probably surpasses Canton Zurich. Even in cantons which are generally spoken of as backward, Lucern, for instance, my astonishment was, and the astonishment of every Englishman accustomed to the unhappy deficiencies of our own school system must be, not to find the Lucern schools no better than they are, but to find them so good as they are. Zurich, therefore, though a very favourable specimen, is not unique, is still representative; and every day, as the great movement of education goes on which has for the last thirty years made the force of Switzerland, the cantons which are behind Zurich are more and more exerting themselves to emulate her example.

Canton Zurich has about 260,000 inhabitants, the immense majority of whom are of German stock and Protestants. Nearly a third of the whole public expenditure of the canton is directed to education, and one in five of the population are in school.

The schools in the canton are communal, cantonal, or federal. The system begins with the communal school. By the school law of the canton, instruction is obligatory on all children between the ages of six and sixteen. The communal day-school takes the child at six. It is a school of six classes, three of them *Elementarclassen,* and three of them *Realclassen*; each class takes the child a year to pass through it. By the time he has passed through the communal day-school he has, therefore, completed his twelfth year. He has still three years more of obligatory instruction before he arrives at his confirmation;—this, which answers to the *première communion* of the Catholics, being for Zurich Protestants the epoch to which the term of obligatory school-attendance is reckoned, and this epoch being reached when the child is sixteen. If he does not pass from the communal day-school into a school of a higher order, two courses are open to him. Either he attends the *Ergänzungsschule,* or finishing school, which is in fact a department of the communal day-school for his benefit and that of others like him, with eight hours' instruction a week, the eight being generally taken in two mornings; or, if he cannot spare time for even so much as this, he becomes a *Sing- und Unterweisungsschüler.* He is a pupil of the *Singschule,* to keep up by one hour's practice in the week that knowledge of church music and singing which in Protestant Germany is thought so important; and he is a pupil, for *Unterweisung,* or religious instruction, of the pastor of the place, who has him for an hour and a half in the week to keep up his religious instruction preparatory to his confirmation. The instruction comes to much the same in amount as the instruction of our Sunday-schools. One of these two courses is obligatory, from the age of thirteen to the age of sixteen, upon every child who does not go to some higher school.

I have seen many of the Swiss primary day-schools, and think them in general better than even the inspected schools of this class with us now are. The programme of work for them is fixed by the Education Council of the canton, and embraces religious instruction, the mother-tongue, arithmetic and geometry, the elements of natural philosophy, history and geography, singing, handwriting, drawing, gymnastics; and, for girls, needlework. Needlework is taught in the day-school to the three elementary classes only; for girls in the *real* classes of the day-school, and for girls in the *Ergänzungsschule,* there are special schools, *weibliche Arbeitschulen,** to which they have to go for their instruction in needlework. The needlework of girls in the elementary schools of Germany and Switzerland is very much better than that of girls in ours. The *Arbeitschulen* are of course taught by women, but the immense majority of the Zurich day-schools are mixed schools, and taught by men. The canton has a Normal School at Küssnacht to train its teachers, who have of course to pass an examination and to obtain a certificate.

From seven to thirteen, therefore, every child in Canton Zurich has the instruction of such a day-school as I have described. In 1864 there were 365 day-schools in the canton, with 515 departments under separate teachers (*Einzelnschulen*). The moment the number of scholars in a school exceeds 100, the law compels the school to have a second teacher and a second school-room. But the Education Council may order this relief when there are more than 80 scholars, and, in fact, as soon even as there are more than 40 or 50, the commune of its own motion frequently bestows it; providing, if not a second schoolmaster, at least a trained

* There were, in 1864, 322 *Arbeitschulen* of this kind in Canton Zurich.

assistant with the title of *Adjunct*. The school hours in the day-school are from 18 hours a week in the lowest classes to 27 hours a week in the highest, and there are eight weeks of holidays in the year.

I have said that every child in Canton Zurich has, from the age of seven to that of thirteen, the instruction of such a day-school as I have described. Not that every child is obliged to go to the communal day-school; but at the beginning of every school year the pastor of the commune furnishes a list of all the children of the commune who have reached the legal school age; the school committee of the commune issues a notice that all such children must be brought to school; and if any of them are taught at home or sent to private schools, their parents must satisfy the school committee that they receive an instruction at least equal to that of the communal day-school, and meanwhile must pay to this school the fee for them just the same as if they attended. This being so, and the public day-schools being really good, few children go elsewhere, and one finds all classes of society mixed in them. In the school district of Zurich, comprising the city itself and its environs, there were in 1864 only two private schools for boys, with forty boys of school age divided between the two establishments.

The 365 communal day-schools of Canton Zurich had, in 1864, 25,797 scholars between the ages of seven and thirteen. The number of school absences in the year was 13·12 per scholar. But school absences are distinguished into *verant-wortete*, those of which a satisfactory explanation (illness, death in the family, &c.) is given, and *strafbare*, those which are unallowed and punishable. The latter were only 1·04 per scholar. In different places the mode of dealing with punishable absences differs. In the town of Zurich the school authority warns the offending parent or guardian after three punishable absences, cites him after three more, fines him after three more. This applies to absences from the day-school; for absences from the *Ergänzungsschule* or *Sing-schule* the warning is after the second punishable absence, the citation after the fourth, the fine after the sixth. But in all cases the law which makes non-attendance penal is enforced, the Education Council repaying to the local school authorities the costs of any proceedings against defaulters. The same authorities are also empowered to see that the half-timers, as we might call them, of their locality, the pupils of the *Ergänzungsschule,* are not overtaxed out of school hours by their employers, or rendered unfit for the school work still required of them.

Of children between thirteen and sixteen, 10,441 attended in 1864 the *Ergänzungsschulen* of Canton Zurich, and 11,428 were only *Sing- und Unterweisungsschüler.* It is noteworthy that almost one-half of the scholars whose day-school obligation had ended took the greater rather than the less amount of schooling assigned for their last three years of educational nonage. The law fixes three francs a year as the school fee* of a day-scholar, and a franc and a half as the fee of all scholars not day-scholars. No distinction is made between a scholar of the *Ergänzungsschule* and a scholar of the *Singschule.* This of course constitutes an inducement to the parent to send his son if he can to the finishing school rather than the singing school, to get as much as he can for his school money.

I have several times spoken of the school authorities. These form a closely connected series. The authority nearest to the elementary school (*Allgemeine Volksschule*) is the *Schul-genossenschaft,* or school partnership, composed of the school's immediate tributaries. Each school has its own *Schulge-nossenschaft,* to abridge or to extend the limits of which, or to unite it with another *Schulgenossenschaft,* the intervention of the Council of State, the high governing body of the canton, is requisite. Each school has likewise its own *Schulfond,* or school fund, and *Schulverwalter,* or steward of this fund. The school partnership elects its steward, who is then its representative in the management of the school finances. It also elects, if it pleases, its schoolmaster; fixes, within the limits left to it by the law, the rate of school fee; and decides what poor scholars shall be admitted gra-

---

* The local school authority may increase this up to double the amount. In the great communal day-school of Zurich, with nearly 1,400 scholars, and with fifteen or sixteen teachers in each of its two departments, the school fee is six francs a year.

tuitously, and what at reduced rates. Pauper children are paid for out of the poor's fund of that whole commune of which the *Schulgenossenschaft* forms a part.* The school partnership is charged with providing, fitting, maintaining, and warming the school premises, with the payment of 8*l.* a year towards the schoolmaster's salary, and with finding him a house, ground, and firing, or an equivalent in money. The schoolmaster takes half the school fees; the other half goes into the school chest. If the schoolmaster's half of the school fees, with his fixed salary from the school partnership, does not reach a certain minimum, the State, if necessary, makes his income up to that minimum. But the school partnership, or the whole commune, often provides out of its own resources schoolmasters' salaries much above the legal minimum; in the more important communes this is more particularly the case. In the town of Zurich the fifteen teachers of the boys' division of the elementary school all receive an income from the commune of from 80*l.* to 104*l.* a year. In the small country communes 40*l.* is about the average of a teacher's salary. The revenues from the *Schulfond*, which consists of the landed or funded property with which the school is endowed, of settlement dues paid by all new settlers in the commune, and of dues paid on all marriages in the commune, are, with the proceeds of school fines and of half the school fees, with what the school partnership raises among its own members and with what the State grants, the means of providing for the yearly support of the school. In the town of Zurich the commune rates itself to make up the sum it requires for its schools; in the country, the school partnerships raise by voluntary contributions among their members the amount they need. The *Schulfonds* of the elementary schools of Canton Zurich amount altogether to nearly 5,550,000 francs; to the yearly income from this source

---

* Though our English National schools date from George the Third's reign only, their constitution has a mediæval character. But in some parts of England the supporters of a Methodist day-school afford a specimen of a genuine *Schulgenossenschaft*, providing, maintaining and managing the school they require for their own children. But they are not, as in Switzerland, co-ordered with a regular graduated series of school authorities; they have nothing between them and the central Education Department in London.

the State adds about 300,000 francs,—35,000 francs for school buildings in poor communes, and 275,000 francs for teachers' salaries; for the rest of the expenditure on the elementary schools, school-fees and the contributions of the local bodies provide.

The school partnership is not charged with the duty of superintending the discipline and teaching of its school. This duty belongs to the next authority in the series, to the school administration of the commune (*Gemeindeschulpflege*). This body represents the whole *Schulkreis*, or school circle, in which the school partnership falls; it represents the commune in fact, for the school circles of Canton Zurich coincide as a general rule with its communes. The canton has 162 school circles, and 367 school partnerships. The school administration of the school circle or commune is a body of four or more members elected by the commune; the *Pfarrer*, or parson,* being *ex officio* their president. The other members are elected by universal suffrage, but no one under twenty-five may be on the *Schulpflege*, and two near relations or connections may not be on it together. The meetings of this *Gemeindeschulpflege* are attended by all the teachers of the school circle, but they have a consultative voice only. Whenever the financial affairs of a school are under consideration by the *Schulpflege*, the steward representing the school partnership of that school attends. The duties of the communal *Schulpflege* are to see that in all the elementary schools of the *Gemeinde*, or commune, the school law is properly obeyed, the teacher properly paid, the rules issued from time to time by the Education Council of the canton properly followed, the teaching and discipline properly maintained. The members inspect by rotation the schools of their commune, and make a yearly report to the body next above

---

* In Canton Geneva the lay tendencies of modern democracy have so far prevailed that the pastor, or the curé, is not *ex officio* a member of the communal school committee; but all the communal schools have a dogmatic religious instruction, Catholic or Protestant. Many people in England seem to have a notion that a State system of education must of necessity be undenominational and secular. So far is this from being the case, that in all the countries to which the present work relates,—France, Italy, Germany, and Switzerland,—there is a State system of education, and that system is both denominational and religious. Only the different denominations are not suffered to persecute one another.

them in the chain of school authorities,—the school administration of the district (*Bezirksschulpflege*).

Canton Zurich has eleven *Bezirke*, or districts. Each district, like each commune, has its *Schulpflege*. The district *Schulpflege* is composed of from nine to thirteen members, of whom three are chosen by the teachers of the *Bezirk*, the rest by the inhabitants of the district by universal suffrage. The members choose their own president and secretary. This higher *Schulpflege* sees that the communal *Schulpflege* properly fulfils its functions, that the law and the Education Council's rules are observed, that the children are sent regularly to school, and the school premises kept in good condition. Plans for new school buildings have to be submitted to this *Schulpflege* for approval, with appeal from its decision to the Education Council. It names each of its members visitor (*Visitator*) for certain schools for a certain period; the visitor has to visit twice a year each of the schools assigned to him, to be present at the yearly examination by which in every school the pupils pass from one class to another, and to report to his *Schulpflege*. The district *Schulpflege* itself reports annually to the Education Council.

A small allowance of from three to six francs is made to the visitors of this *Schulpflege* for days on which they are actually employed in inspecting, and the school partnerships generally pay their stewards; with these exceptions, all the functions I have been describing are performed gratuitously.

The supreme authority, to which we now come, is the Education Council (*Erziehungsrath*). This represents the State. The Director of Education for the canton, who is president of the Education Council, is a member of the government of the canton, the Council of State. The Education Council has six members besides its president. Four of the six are chosen by the Great Council of the canton, that is, by universal suffrage; two are chosen by the School Synod, a body which consists of all the teachers of the canton, those of the higher schools as well as those of the popular schools. One teacher elected must be chosen from among the masters of the higher schools, the other from among those of the popular schools. The members of this Council are appointed for four years, and half of them go out every two years ; the other bodies I have been describing, and in general all public councils and committees in Canton Zurich, follow the like course.

The superintendence and promotion of education, higher and lower, throughout the canton, is the business of the *Erziehungsrath*. It is the centre to which the reports of the district committees and the communal committees converge, and to which appeals are brought. It selects the commissions of superintendence for the cantonal schools, of which I have yet to speak; of each of these commissions the Director of Education is president, if he chooses; if not he, then some other member or members of the Education Council must be on each commission. The Council has also the power of ordering special inspections, and has a credit opened to it for this purpose. It can, also, suspend or interdict teachers.

Such is the series of authorities by which popular education in Canton Zürich is managed. The spirit in which they have been contrived, balanced, and organised, is, as the English reader will perceive, an intensely democratic and an intensely local spirit ; yet not insanely democratic, so that the idea of authority, nor insanely local, so that the idea of the State, shall be lost sight of.

But the obligatory three years of the finishing school or the singing school, are not the proper completion of the six years of the elementary or common popular school (*allgemeine Volksschule*), though they are a completion which the law accepts. The proper completion is three years of the higher popular school (*höhere Volksschule*), or, as it is also called (the school nomenclature of Switzerland being somewhat different from that either of Germany or of France), the secondary school (*Secundarschule*). This is the *Mittelschule* of Germany, the *école élémentaire supérieure* of M. Guizot's law; but what is important to be observed is that it is still a school for the people, or *Volksschule*, and also a school which the public provides for them. The Council of State divides the canton into *Secundarschulkreise*,—school circles for the higher popular school, as the commune is the school circle for the common popular school. Of these *Secundarschulkreise* there are 57; the communes which compose each circle undertaking to maintain, with aid from the State, a secondary school in it. Each of these schools, too, has its *Schulfond*; the aggregate value of their property was in 1864, in round numbers, 470,000 francs. The school-fee is 24 francs a year, but the school is bound to take one scholar in eight as a free scholar. The regular State grant to each of the 57 secondary schools is 42*l.* a year; this is increased, however, when the school is considerable enough to need more than one teacher. These teachers are trained, like the primary teachers, in the Normal school at Küssnacht, which has special lessons for them, and special certificates. In 1864 there were 74 teachers in the 57 secondary schools, and 2,398 scholars. The studies are in general the same as those of the primary school, but each branch is carried further, and French is added. The school has a three years' course, is held for about twenty-eight hours in each week, and there are eight weeks of holidays in the year. It is evident, therefore, that this is no supplementary or half-time school, and can take no children who are not able to give their whole time to it. None are admitted who have not passed the examination which guards the exit from the primary school. Some special preparation for the business of agriculture or of trade is attempted in the secondary school.

The master of a secondary school gets on an average about 60*l.* a year, with house, ground, and firing. In the town of Zurich, where the secondary school, established, like the primary school, in a really splendid building, is excellent, his position is far better than this; the income of the five or six masters in the boys' department averaging there from 100*l.* to 110*l.* a year. I saw both departments of this school at work; the girls were more numerous than the boys, about 250 to the boys' 150. In both schools almost all the teaching is done by masters; nor, indeed, does the American preference of women as teachers get in general any sanction from the practice of the Continent.* I found in this Zurich girls'

* I may say that competent foreign observers who have studied the American schools, report that, as a general rule, though something is to be learnt from them as to providing and maintaining schools, little or nothing is to be learnt from

school ten masters employed and nine mistresses, but eight
of the nine mistresses were for needlework. The children
were of the class that one finds in the better British or
Wesleyan schools in England, but they receive an instruction
such as can be got in no British or Wesleyan school. I was
particularly struck with the thorough way in which French
was taught and learnt. · The introduction of a foreign language, as an obligatory part of the school course for every
scholar, marks sufficiently the broad difference between the
instruction in the Zurich secondary school and that in any
British or Wesleyan school of ours ; but the essential difference is in the abundance of teachers, and in their training
and culture. Scholars who show eminent promise are passed
on, with free posts if necessary, into the higher schools of the
canton.

Every secondary school has its *Schulpflege*, of from seven
to eleven members, two of whom are chosen by the *Bezirksschulpflege* of the district in which the school stands, the rest
by the *Schulpflegen* of the communes which make up the
secondary school circle. Their functions for the secondary
school are like those of the communal *Schulpflege* for the
primary school, and they report to the *Bezirksschulpflege*.

The child who after completing his twelfth year goes
neither to the finishing school (*Ergänzungsschule*), nor to
the singing school (*Singschule*), nor to the secondary school
(*Secundarschule*), has still three years of *Schulzwang*, or obligation to be under instruction. But such a child must be of a
class to do more than satisfy this obligation, and he goes to the
gymnasium, where the school course lasts six years and a half,
or to the *Industrieschule* (so at Zurich a *Realschule* is called),
where it lasts five years and a half. These are *cantonal* schools,
at the charge of the whole canton. Each of them has its
own *Aufsichtscommission*, or commission of superintendence,
of nine members, chosen, as I have said, by the Education
Council. A delegate from this commission attends and
controls, as in Prussia, the yearly examinations at which

them as to teaching. Nor is this the slightest reproach to America, which has
inherited from us our preference of business to learning, and up to the present time
has had a thousand reasons more than we for following this preference.

leaving certificates are issued. The rectors of the cantonal
schools are always members of the commission of superintendence, but they never, of course, represent it at examinations. Nor do they represent it at inspections, which the
other members of the commission perform by monthly rotation, the inspector having to visit each class and hear lessons
given in it, in the course of the month. The rectors are
nominated by the Council of State ; the masters by the
Education Council, reinforced by a certain number of members of the commission of superintendence for the school
concerned. The commission for the gymnasium and that
for the *Industrieschule* have a joint meeting once a quarter,
to ensure the harmonious working of the two schools.

The instruction in the gymnasium is classical, and the
passage to the university lies through it. It is in all important respects modelled on a German gymnasium such as
those which I have so fully described in speaking of Prussia.
It is divided into a lower gymnasium (*unteres Gymnasium*),
with a course of four years, and an upper gymnasium (*oberes
Gymnasium*), with a course of two and a half years. In the
lower gymnasium the school-fee is thirty francs a year. A
boy passes the sixth year's examination of the elementary
school, and then enters at the bottom of the gymnasium.
He cannot,—and this is the general rule in the Swiss and
German schools,—be put above his age. If for any reason
he does not come to the gymnasium till he is fourteen or
fifteen, he is still not placed by examination, but goes to the
form which at fourteen or fifteen he would have reached had
he entered the gymnasium in due course after twelve. He
is not admitted at all unless he is up to the work of the class
to which his age assigns him. The graduation of the school
programme, according to which the fit work is supposed to
be assigned for each age in fit proportions, is the ground
for these rules, which seem to me to be on the whole judicious.

In the lower gymnasium the boys have religious instruction,* Latin, Greek, French and the mother tongue, history,

* The regulations with respect to this are in Canton Zurich, and in Protestant
German countries generally, as in Prussia,

geography and natural history, arithmetic and mathematics, free-hand drawing, writing, singing, gymnastics, and military exercising. In the upper gymnasium the fee is forty-eight francs a year. Here they of course carry the studies of the lower gymnasium further, and they add to them Hebrew besides, and logic. Enumerations of this kind are not in themselves very instructive; the English reader will get a clearer notion of the Zurich gymnasium by bearing in mind that whereas in Prussia the *Volksschule* is, as I mentioned, not regarded as the right preparation for the gymnasium, the Swiss law expressly assigns to both sides, the classical as well as the *real*, of the cantonal school, an immediate connection with the popular school. Then for scholars who enter above the second class of the lower gymnasium, and for all scholars in the upper gymnasium, Greek is not obligatory. But what is most noteworthy is that not only is no Latin or Greek verse done in the gymnasium at all, but no original Latin or Greek composition in prose is done there; a translation once a week,—into Greek one week and into Latin another,—is all the Greek and Latin composition done; and this translation is little more than a grammatical exercise. Composition in French is carried as far as the essay, and much beyond composition in the old classical languages. Greek, however, gets from five to eight hours a week in every class of the gymnasium above the lowest, and Latin ten hours in the lowest class, and from six to eight hours in the rest. It may be noticed that in the highest class of the gymnasium Greek gets only five hours a week, an hour less than it gets in the *prima* of a Prussian gymnasium.

There are about 180 scholars in the Zurich gymnasium, and fourteen of them in 1864 obtained the certificate of ripeness (*Zeugniss der Reife*) which here, as in Germany, is required for matriculation at the university.

The *Industrieschule* is more fully attended than the gymnasium, and has about 250 scholars. Like the gymnasium, it has an upper and a lower division. The lower division has a three years' course, and the fee, thirty francs a year, is higher than in the corresponding division of the gymnasium.

There is not, as in the German *Realschule*, Latin. Latin and Greek being left out and geometrical drawing added, the list of matters of instruction is nearly identical with that of the lower gymnasium, and it is in the proportion of time allotted and the development given to the several matters of instruction, that the two schools, the one designed to lead to the university, the other to what the school law calls 'technical and business lines,' differ. The school course of the lower *Industrieschule* is, as a general rule, the same for all scholars there, and is obligatory in all its parts for all of them. In the upper division it is not so; there is one programme, but no scholar goes through the whole of it; the lessons composing it fall into three groups, that for the mechanical line, that for the chemical line, and that for the business line; and each boy, according to the line of life he intends to follow, is assigned by the rector to the group of lessons suitable for him. Of eighty-four scholars in the upper *Industrieschule* in 1864, thirty-four were in the mechanical group, thirteen in the chemical, and thirty-seven in the business group. The Education Council urges the masters not to let the school be turned into a place for mere professional study; but this organisation gives, of course, a bias which it is hard to resist. English and Italian make part of the regular school course in this division.

The moment instruction becomes professional it becomes saddled with special expenses, and in the upper *Industrieschule* the school-fee is 60 francs a year, a high school-fee for Switzerland. The pupils who follow the chemical line pay 60 francs a year for the expenses of the laboratory.

The lessons in the upper *Industrieschule* are excellent, and qualified pupils from other public establishments are allowed, if the rector of the *Industrieschule* and their own master consents, to attend particular lessons which are better given at the *Industrieschule* than anywhere else. Young men who have left school, but are following an occupation for which these lessons are useful, are also allowed, if properly qualified for profiting by them, to attend. Such hearers take the title of *Auditoren*, and pay five francs a week for each lesson they follow. Of the 84 pupils in the three groups of the upper *Industrieschule* in 1864, 12 were *Auditoren* of this kind.

There are ten weeks' holiday for the cantonal schools in the year. These holidays were going on when I was at Zurich; but the town of Winterthur has established higher schools both for boys and girls,* which, though not cantonal but municipal, emulate the higher schools of Zurich in their organisation and far excel them in their school buildings; these I saw at work, and I saw also those of Basle. Winterthur is, I think, for its school establishments the most remarkable place in Europe. It is the second town for importance in Canton Zurich, and thrives by its manufacture of muslins; but it has not more than 8,000 inhabitants. The schools of this small place recall the municipal palaces of Flanders and Italy. They are the objects of first importance in the town, and would be admirable anywhere; besides the elementary schools there is a *Mittelschule,* an *Industrieschule,* and a gymnasium, all built within the last twenty-five years, and which have cost the town not less than 100,000*l.* I found about eighty scholars in the gymnasium, about two-thirds of them Winterthur boys; the rest come from a distance, and board, under regulations similar to those in Prussia, with the masters or with families in the town. I heard a lesson in Livy in the class which with us would have been the fifth form; the performance was quite as good as that which I remember in the fifth form of Winchester or Rugby. In the *Industrieschule* I found about 200 scholars; in the upper division of this there is the same grouping of scholars for different lines (*Richtungen*) which obtains at Zurich. The teaching is said by competent judges to be

* I have found it impossible to include in this work an account of the girls' schools of the Continent. I visited several of them, but in the boys' schools I had already more on my hands than I could well manage, and the girls' schools well merit a separate enquiry, and by an enquirer who has first thoroughly acquainted himself, as I have not, with the working of our girls' schools at home. I will just mention, as places where the girls' schools will richly reward the future enquirer's attention, Naples, Weimar and Zurich. And I will add, that Italian girls seem to me those in all Europe who are best suited for school education as distinguished from home education; who derive most benefit from it, and with the fewest drawbacks of any kind. On the other hand, I doubt whether there is any German or English girl for whom there are not grave drawbacks to balance its benefits.

particularly well organised in these higher *Realschulen* of
Switzerland. The Winterthur higher schools, though not
cantonal schools, have, and deservedly, an exceptional
position ; they are under the inspection of a cantonal
commission, and in immediate relation with the Education
Council. The burghers of Winterthur seek competent advice
and superintendence with as much zeal as in England a batch
of local people show in resisting it. Nor is it to get money
that they have recourse to the State; the grant from the
State to these Winterthur establishments is 80*l.* a year, and
the town of Winterthur itself spends 3,200*l.* a year on them.
This sum is supplied from the *Bürgergut* or communal property, and it is to be observed that generally in a Swiss parish
it is the commune that is the great proprietor, as in England
it is the squire. The sons of Winterthur burghers have free
schooling; others pay much the same rates as at Zurich.
As at Zurich, too, half of the school-fees is divided among
the teachers; the other half goes to the school chest.

The teachers in Canton Zurich form a sort of guild, and
exercise considerable influence. I have already said how
they are represented on the local *Schulpflegen*. In the higher
schools they form *Convente* and *Specialconvente,* the *Convent*
being for each school, the *Specialconvent* for each division,
upper or lower, of each school. They are in fact masters'
meetings, as at Rugby we used to call them; but in Switzerland they have a legal status, and report regularly to the
commissions of superintendence. They are said to be of
great service in keeping the school work properly graduated,
and in maintaining uniformity of standard. New rules they
can only make for points which the school law and the regulations of the Education Council have not already settled,
but changes cannot be introduced without their opinion
being taken upon them. In the same way, the teachers of
the primary and secondary schools of each *Bezirk,* or district,
form a *Schulcapitel,* or school chapter, which meets four times
a year, forms sections for the discussion of any special matters
in which schools and teachers are interested, reports to the
Education Council, and has a right to be heard before any
change in the work-plan or in the regulations of the popular

schools are adopted. These chapters, again, unite with the whole body of teachers of the higher schools of the canton to form a School Synod, having for its business the promotion of education in the canton, and to convey the wishes and proposals of the teaching body to the authorities. This Synod meets once a year, its business and method of proceeding being always prepared beforehand by a Pro-Synod.

I have already said that private schools must, if they are schools for popular education, give an instruction at least equal to that of the public popular school. All private schools are entirely open to State inspection and must furnish yearly reports of themselves to the authorities. But besides this, for the opening of any private school the consent of the State, and an official approval of the work-plan, are necessary. The great development of the public schools in the last thirty years, however, and the increasing favour they enjoy, tend to make the Swiss private schools of less and less importance, so far as the Swiss themselves are concerned. The better status of the public school teacher is an attraction for masters; the better guarantees of the public school are an attraction for parents. I met at Basle an excellent teacher, the son of a Swiss private schoolmaster of European celebrity; the son had given up his father's establishment when it came, at his father's death, into his hands, in order to take the more interesting and honourable functions of a public teacher. I was told by Swiss gentlemen of authority and standing, who had themselves been brought up in Fellenberg's famous school at Hofwyl, that they would not send their own sons to any but a public school, and that even a man of Fellenberg's special gifts could not now, since the improvement of the public schools, establish a private school to vie with them successfully. When it was the habit of the young Swiss cadet of family to enter into foreign service, he had a special inducement to go to a famous school like that at Hofwyl, where, by meeting Austrians or Bavarians who had been attracted thither by Fellenberg's reputation, he formed connections which were useful to him in after life. This habit having been stopped, a considerable attraction which a private school like Fellenberg's offered to the Swiss of the last generation has ceased ; and the best informed Swiss will tell you that the Swiss private schools, of which we hear so much in England, now exist mainly *pour exploiter les Anglais*, who do indeed invite *exploitation*.

At the apex of the school system of Canton Zurich stands the *Hochschule*, or university. This is in all important respects a German university, and many of the professors come from Germany ; the famous Dr. Strauss was, as is well known, a professor here. The canton pays the professors, of whom there are five for each of the three faculties of theology, law and medicine, and fourteen for that of philosophy. Here, as in Germany, the professors are divided into *ordinarii* and *extraordinarii*, full professors and assistant professors; and their teaching is powerfully supplemented by that of the *Privatdocenten*. The Education Council proposes professors, the Council of State appoints them, the opinion of the faculty concerned being always taken. That of the Church Council (*Kirchenrath*) is also taken on the appointment of a theological professor. The professors, *ordinarii* and *extraordinarii*, of each faculty, form a body who elect their own dean ; the deans of faculty and the ordinary, or full, professors compose the *senatus academicus*, which chooses the rector, who must be confirmed by the Council of State. The academical senate is charged with the discipline of the university, and has a right to be heard before the Education Council can introduce any changes in academical matters.

. At the end of 1864 there were in the *Hochschule* of Zurich 200 matriculated students, besides seven who were not matriculated. Of the 200, twenty-seven were in the faculty of theology, thirty-seven in that of law, seventy-eight in that of medicine, and fifty-eight in that of philosophy. The Swiss students were 138 out of the 200; of these 138 the Zurichers were sixty-three. But of the fifty-eight students in philosophy the Swiss numbered only twenty-six, and of these twenty-six the Zurichers were only eight. The remaining thirty-two came chiefly from Germany and Russia ; two were from England.

But more noteworthy than the university at Zurich is the Polytechnicum, or high school for forming civil engineers, for teaching the applied sciences, and for training teachers for all departments of technical instruction. This is a federal and not a cantonal institution. It was established by the Federal Council for the benefit of the whole of Switzerland, and a commission appointed by the Federal Council administers it. It was placed at Zurich, where it occupies a commanding position on a slope above the town, and is one of the first objects that attracts a stranger's notice.

This Polytechnicum was in vacation when I visited Zurich, but I saw at work another admirable institution of the same kind, the Polytechnicum at Stuttgardt, of which the object and the methods are very much the same. That of Zurich has six divisions; the school of construction, the school of civil engineering, the school of mechanics, the school of chemistry, the school of woodcraft, and the school of mathematical and natural sciences, of literature, and of moral and political sciences. The course in the different divisions varies in length from two to three years. The fees are low, and the staff of professors excellent; some of the most distinguished scientific men of Germany have been brought here by the Swiss Government. A professor may in his lessons use the German, French, or Italian language, as suits him best. The yearly cost of the institution is about 340,000 francs (13,600*l.*), of which 16,000 fr. are given by the town of Zurich, 10,000 fr. come from the *Schulfond*, 64,000 fr. from the students' fees, and the ' remaining 250,000 fr. from the Swiss Confederation. There are about fifty professors and five hundred students.

The Polytechnicum, though not specially belonging to Canton Zurich, worthily crowns by its presence the astonishing series of schools which this canton exhibits, and which I have endeavoured to describe to the English reader. A territory with the population of Leicestershire possesses a university, a veterinary school, a school of agriculture, two great classical schools, two great *real* schools, a normal school for training primary and secondary teachers, fifty-seven secondary schools, and three hundred and sixty-five primary schools; and many of these schools are among the best of their kind in Europe.

The primary, secondary, and *real* schools, are those of which this can be affirmed most decidedly. I can well understand that M. Baudouin, who was sent by the French Minister of Public Instruction to see the schools for the middle and trading classes in countries which have any such schools to show, and who has published an elaborate and invaluable report* of what he saw, should have imagined himself in Paradise when he came to Zurich, and should have thought no words too strong to express his admiration. The *Realstudien* of the Swiss schools are prosecuted without any of the misgivings and hesitations which hang about them in Germany. Switzerland does not much trouble her head with ideas such as haunt a German Education Minister in genuine Germany, that '*die unwissenschaftliche Praxis des Nützlichkeitsprincips den Charakter einer allgemeinen höheren Bildungsanstalt aufhebe;*' or share his concern because, do what he will, the programme of a *Realschule* possesses less *innere Geschlossenheit* than that of a gymnasium. The aim which Swiss education has before it, is not, I think, the highest educational aim. The idea of what the French call *la grande culture* has not much effect in Switzerland, and accordingly it is not in her purely literary and scientific high schools, and in the line of what is specially called a liberal education, that she is most successful. Her highest teachers are Germans from Germany; but large as are the salaries paid to draw these distinguished foreigners to Zurich, a genuine German, I am told, does not much like the atmosphere in which he finds himself there; he sighs for the more truly scientific spirit, the *wissenschaftliche Geist*, of the universities of his own country, and will not in general stay long at Zurich. The spirit which reigns at Zurich, and in the thriving parts of German Switzerland, is a spirit of intelligent industrialism, but not quite intelligent enough to have cleared itself from vulgarity. At Lausanne and Geneva the French language and the traditions of a high intellectual life introduce other elements; but even at Lausanne and Geneva, the effect of the great movement of the last thirty

* *Rapport sur l'état actuel de l'enseignement spécial en Belgique, en Allemagne et en Suisse*, par J. M. Baudouin. Paris, Imprimerie Impériale, 1865.

years, has been to develop, as the principal power there, the same sort of intelligent industrialism as is the principal power in German Switzerland. The representatives of the old high culture and intellectual traditions of French Switzerland are not now masters of the situation there, and the course of events pushes them more and more aside.

But the grand merit of Swiss industrialism, even though it may not rise to the conception of *la grande culture*, is that it has clearly seen that for genuine and secure industrial prosperity, more is required than capital, abundant labour, and manufactories; it is necessary to have a well-instructed population. So far as instruction and the intelligence developed by instruction are valuable commodities, the Swiss have thoroughly appreciated their market worth, and are thoroughly employing them.

They seem to me in this respect to resemble the Scotch. The Scotch, too, as the state of their universities shows, have at present little notion of *la grande culture.* Instead of guarding, like the Germans, the *wissenschaftliche Geist* of their universities, they turn them into mere school-classes; and instead of making the student, as in Germany, pass to the university through the *prima* of a high school, Scotland lets the University and the High School of Edinburgh, with a happy spirit of independence worthy of their neighbours south of the Tweed, compete for schoolboys; and the University recruits its Greek classes from the third or fourth forms of the High School. Accordingly, while the aristocratic class of Scotland is by its bringing up, its faults, its merits, much the same as the aristocratic class in England, the Scotch middle class is in *la grande culture* not ahead of the English middle class. But so far as intellectual culture has an industrial value, makes a man's business-work better, and helps him to get on in the world, the Scotch middle class has thoroughly appreciated it and sedulously employed it, both for itself and for the class whose labour it uses; and here is their superiority to the English, and the reason of the success of Scotch skilled labourers and Scotch men of business everywhere. In this they are like the Swiss, though the example and habits of England have, as was inevitable, prevented the Scotch from developing their school institutions, even for their limited purpose, with the method and admirable effectiveness shown by the Swiss.

What I admire in Germany is, that while there too industrialism, that great modern power, is making at Berlin, and Leipzig, and Elberfeld, the most successful and rapid progress, the idea of culture, culture of the only true sort, is in Germany a living power also. Petty towns have a university whose teaching is famous through Europe; and the King of Prussia and Count Bismark resist the loss of a great *savant* from Prussia, as they would resist a political check. If true culture ever becomes at last a civilising power in the world, and is not overlaid by fanaticism, by industrialism, or by frivolous pleasure-seeking, it will be to the faith and zeal of this homely and much ridiculed German people, that the great result will be mainly owing.

Meanwhile let us be grateful to any country, which, like Switzerland, prepares by a broad and sound system of popular education the indispensable foundations on which a civilising culture may in the future be built; and do not let us be too nice, while we ourselves have not even laid the indispensable foundations, in canvassing the spirit in which others have laid them.

CHAPTER XXII.

GENERAL CONCLUSION. SCHOOL STUDIES.

THE reader will probably expect that at the end of this
long history I should offer some opinion as to the lessons
to be drawn from all which I have been describing. This I
shall attempt to do; although I can hardly hope, perhaps, to
communicate to him the weight of conviction with which I
myself am left by what I have seen. Two points, above all,
suggest matter for reflection: the course of study of foreign
schools, and the way in which these schools are established
and administered. I begin with the first.

Several times in this volume I have touched upon the conflict between the gymnasium and the *Realschule*, between the
partisans of the old classical studies and the partisans of
what are called real, or modern, or useful studies. This conflict is not yet settled, either by one side crushing the other
by mere violence, or by one side clearly getting the best of
the other in the dispute between them. We in England,
behindhand as our public instruction in many respects is,
are nevertheless in time to profit, and to make our schools
profit, by the solution which will certainly be found for this
difference. I am inclined to think that both sides will, as is
natural, have to abate their extreme pretensions. The modern spirit tends to reach a new conception of the aim and
office of instruction; when this conception is fully reached,
it will put an end to conflict, and will probably show both

the humanists and the realists to have been right in their main ideas.

The aim and office of instruction, say many people, is to make a man a good citizen, or a good Christian, or a gentleman; or it is to fit him to get on in the world, or it is to enable him to do his duty in that state of life to which he is called. It is none of these, and the modern spirit more and more discerns it to be none of these. These are at best secondary and indirect aims of instruction; its prime direct aim is to enable a man *to know himself and the world*. Such knowledge is the only sure basis for action, and this basis it is the true aim and office of instruction to supply. To know himself, a man must know the capabilities and performances of the human spirit; and the value of the humanities, of *Alterthumswissenschaft*, the science of antiquity, is, that it affords for this purpose an unsurpassed source of light and stimulus. Whoever seeks help for knowing himself from knowing the capabilities and performances of the human spirit, will nowhere find a more fruitful object of study than in the achievements of Greece in literature and the arts during the two centuries from the birth of Simonides to the death of Plato. And these two centuries are but the flowering point of a long period, during the whole of which the ancient world offers, to the student of the capabilities and performances of the human spirit, lessons of capital importance.

This the humanists have perceived, and the truth of this perception of theirs is the stronghold of their position. It is a vital and formative knowledge to know the most powerful manifestations of the human spirit's activity, for the knowledge of them greatly feeds and quickens our own activity; and they are very imperfectly known without knowing ancient Greece and Rome. But it is also a vital and formative knowledge to know the world, the laws which govern nature, and man as a part of nature. This the realists have perceived, and the truth of this perception, too, is inexpugnable. Every man is born with aptitudes which give him access to vital and formative knowledge by one of these roads; either by the road of studying man and his works, or by the road of studying nature and her works. The business of instruction is to seize and develope these aptitudes. The great and complete spirits which have all the aptitudes for both roads of knowledge are rare. But much more might be done on both roads by the same mind, if instruction clearly grasped the idea of the entire system of aptitudes for which it has to provide; of their correlation, and of their *equipollency*, so to speak, as all leading, if rightly employed, to vital knowledge; and if then, having grasped this idea, it provided for them. The Greek spirit, after its splendid hour of creative activity was gone, gave our race another precious lesson, by exhibiting, in the career of men like Aristotle and the great students of Alexandria, this idea of the correlation and equal dignity of the most different departments of human knowledge, and by showing the possibility of uniting them in a single mind's education. A man like Eratosthenes is memorable by what he performed, but still more memorable by his commanding range of studies, and by the broad basis of culture out of which his performances grew. As our public instruction gets a clearer view of its own functions, of the relations of the human spirit to knowledge, and of the entire circle of knowledge, it will certainly more learn to awaken in its pupils an interest in that entire circle, and less allow them to remain total strangers to any part of it. Still, the circle is so vast and human faculties are so limited, that it is for the most part through a single aptitude, or group of aptitudes, that each individual will really get his access to intellectual life and vital knowledge; and it is by effectually directing these aptitudes on definite points of the circle, that he will really obtain his comprehension of the whole.

Meanwhile neither our humanists nor our realists adequately conceive the circle of knowledge, and each party is unjust to all that to which its own aptitudes do not carry it. The humanists are loth to believe that man has any access to vital knowledge except by knowing himself,—the poetry, philosophy, history which his spirit has created; the realists, that he has any access except by knowing the world,—the physical sciences, the phenomena and laws of nature. I, like so many others who have been brought up in the old routine, imperfectly as I know letters,—the work of the human spirit

itself,—know nothing else, and my judgment therefore may
fairly be impeached.   But it seems to me that so long as the
realists persist in cutting in two the circle of knowledge, so
long do they leave for practical purposes the better portion
to their rivals, and in the government of human affairs their
rivals will beat them.   And for this reason.   The study of
letters is the study of the operation of human force, of human
freedom and activity; the study of nature is the study of the
operation of non-human forces, of human limitation and passivity.   The contemplation of human force and activity tends
naturally to heighten our own force and activity; the contemplation of human limits and passivity tends rather to
check it.   Therefore the men who have had the humanistic
training have played, and yet play, so prominent a part in
human affairs, in spite of their prodigious ignorance of the
universe; because their training has powerfully fomented the
human force in them.   And in this way letters are indeed
runes, like those magic runes taught by the Valkyrie Bryn-
hild to Sigurd, the Scandinavian Achilles, which put the
crown to his endowment and made him invincible.

Still, the humanists themselves suffer so much from the
ignorance of physical facts and laws, and from the inadequate
conception of nature, and of man as a part of nature,—the
conduct of human affairs suffers so much from the same cause,
—that the intellectual insufficiency of the humanities, con-
ceived as the one access to vital knowledge, is perhaps at the
present moment yet more striking than their power of practical
stimulation; and we may willingly declare with the Italians*
that no part of the circle of knowledge is common or unclean,
none is to be cried up at the expense of another.   To say that
the fruit of classics, in the boys who study them, is at present
greater than the fruit of the natural sciences, to say that the
realists have not got their matters of instruction so well adapted
to teaching purposes as the humanists have got theirs, comes
really to no more than this : that the realists are but newly

---

* 'Essendo diverse le parti dell' insegnamento, nessuno mostri di spregiare le
altre, esaltando troppo quella cui è addetto.   Nessun ramo del sapere è meno neces-
sario; di tutte le scienze si avvantaggia l'umana società; tutte cospirano al suo
bene.'—*Sulle Condizioni,* &c. p. 384.

admitted labourers in the field of practical instruction, and that while the leading humanists, the Wolfs and the Buttmanns, have been also schoolmasters, and have brought their mind and energy to bear upon the school-teaching of their own studies, the leaders in the natural sciences, the Davys and the Faradays, have not. When scientific physics have as recognised a place in public instruction as Latin and Greek, they will be as well taught.

The Abbé Fleury, than whom no man is a better authority, says of the mediæval universities, the parents of our public secondary schools: *Les universités ont eu le malheur de commencer dans un temps où le goût des bonnes études était perdu.* They were too late for the influences of the great time of Christian literature and eloquence, the first five centuries after Christ; they were even too late for the influences of the time of Abelard and Saint Bernard. And Fleury adds: *De là* (from these universities founded in a time of inferior insight) *nous est venu ce cours réglé d'études qui subsiste encore.* He wrote this in 1708, but it is in the main still true in 1867. All the historical part of this volume has shown that the great movements of the human spirit have either not got hold of the public schools, or not kept hold of them. What reforms have been made have been patchwork, the work of able men who into certain departments of school study which were dear to them infused reality and life, but who looked little beyond these departments, and did not concern themselves with fully adjusting instruction to the wants of the human mind. There is, therefore, no intelligent tradition to be set aside in our public schools; there is only a routine, arising in the way we have seen, and destined to be superseded as soon as ever that more adequate idea of instruction, of which the modern spirit is even now in travail, shall be fully born.

That idea, so far as one can already forecast its lineaments, will subordinate the matter and methods of instruction to the end in view;—the end of conducting the pupil, as I have said, through the means of his special aptitudes, to a knowledge of himself and the world. The natural sciences are a necessary instrument of this knowledge; letters and *Alter-*

thumswissenschaft are a necessary instrument of this knowledge. But if school instruction in the natural sciences has
almost to be created, school instruction in letters and *Alterthumswissenschaft* has almost to be created anew. The prolonged philological discipline, which in our present schools
guards the access to *Alterthumswissenschaft*, brings to mind the
philosophy of Albertus Magnus, the mere introduction to which,
—the logic,—was by itself enough to absorb all a student's
time of study. To combine the philological discipline with
the matter to which it is ancillary,—with *Alterthumswissenschaft* itself,—a student must be of the force of Wolf, who used
to sit up the whole night with his feet in a tub of cold water
and one of his eyes bound up to rest while he read with the
other, and who thus managed to get through all the Greek
and Latin classics at school, and also Scapula's Lexicon and
Faber's Thesaurus ; and who at Göttingen would sweep clean
out of the library shelves all the books illustrative of the
classic on which Heyne was going to lecture, and finish them
in a week. Such students are rare; and nine out of ten,
especially in England, where so much time is given to Greek
and Latin composition, never get through the philological
vestibule at all, never arrive at *Alterthumswissenschaft*, which
is a knowledge of the spirit and power of Greek and Roman
antiquity learned from its original works.

But many people have even convinced themselves that the
preliminary philological discipline is so extremely valuable
as to be an end in itself; and, similarly, that the mathematical discipline preliminary to a knowledge of nature is so
extremely valuable as to be an end in itself. It seems to me
that those who profess this conviction do not enough consider the quantity of knowledge inviting the human mind,
and the importance to the human mind of really getting to
it. No preliminary discipline is to be pressed at the risk of
keeping minds from getting at the main matter, a knowledge
of themselves and the world. Some minds have such a
special aptitude for philology, or for pure mathematics, that
their access to vital knowledge and their genuine intellectual
life lies in and through those studies; but for one whose
natural access to vital knowledge is by these paths, there

will be ten whose natural access to it is through literature, philosophy, history, or through some one or more of the natural sciences. No doubt it is indispensable to have exact habits of mind, and mathematics and grammar are excellent for the promotion of these habits; and Latin, besides having so large a share in so many modern languages, offers a grammar which is the best of all grammars for the purpose of this promotion. Here are valid reasons for making every schoolboy learn some Latin and some mathematics, but not for turning the preliminary matter into the principal, and sacrificing every aptitude except that for the science of language or of pure mathematics. A Latin grammar of thirty pages, and the most elementary treatise of arithmetic and of geometry, would amply suffice for the uses of philology and mathematics as a universally imposed preparatory discipline. By keeping within these strict limits, absolute exactness of knowledge,—the habit which is here our professed aim,—might be far better attained than it is at present. But it is well to insist, besides, that all knowledge may and should, when we have got fit teachers for it, be so taught as to promote exact habits of mind; and we are not to take leave of these when we pass beyond our introductory discipline.

But it is sometimes said that only through close philological studies and the close practice of Greek and Latin composition, can *Alterthumswissenschaft* itself, the science of the ancient world, be truly reached. It is said to be only through these that we get really to know Greek and Latin literature. For all practical purposes this proposition is untrue, and its untruth may be easily tested. Ask a good Greek scholar, in the ordinary English acceptation of that term, who at the same time knows a modern literature,—let us say the French literature,—well, whether he feels himself to have most seized the spirit and power of French literature, or of Greek literature. Undoubtedly he has most seized the spirit and power of French literature, simply because he has read so very much more of it. But if, instead of reading work after work of French literature, he had read only a few works or parts of works in it, and had given the rest of his time for study to the sedulous practice of French composition and to minutely learning the structure and laws of the French language, then he would know the French literature much as he knows the Greek; he might write very creditable French verses, but he would have seized the spirit and power of French literature not half so much as he has seized them at present. No doubt it is well to know French philology like M. Littré, and to know French literature too; or to write Italian verse like Arthur Hallam, and to know Italian literature too; just as it is well to know the Greek lexicographers and grammarians as Wolf did, and yet to know, also, Greek literature in its length and breadth. But it needs a very rare student for this; and as, if an Englishman is to choose between writing Italian sonnets and knowing Italian literature, it is better for him to know Italian literature, so, if he is to choose between writing Greek iambics and knowing Greek literature, it is better for him to know Greek literature. But an immense development of grammatical studies, and an immense use of Latin and Greek composition, take so much of the pupil's time, that in nine cases out of ten he has not any sense at all of Greek and Latin literature as *literature*, and ends his studies without getting any. His verbal scholarship and his composition he is pretty sure in after life to drop, and then all his Greek and Latin is lost. Greek and Latin *literature*, if he had ever caught the notion of them, would have been far more likely to stick by him.

I was myself brought up in the straitest school of Latin and Greek composition, and am certainly not disposed to be unjust to them. Very often they are ignorantly disparaged. Professor Ritschl, I am told, envies the English schools their Latin verse, and he is no bad judge of what is useful for knowing Latin. The close appropriation of the models, which is necessary for good Latin or Greek composition, not only conduces to accurate verbal scholarship; it may beget, besides, an intimate sense of those models, which makes us sharers of their spirit and power; and this is of the essence of true *Alterthumswissenschaft*. Herein lies the reason for giving boys more of Latin composition than of Greek, superior though the Greek literature be to the Latin; but the power of the Latin classic is in *character*, that of the Greek is in *beauty*. Now character is capable of being taught, learnt, and assimilated; beauty hardly; and it is for enabling us to learn and catch some *power* of antiquity, that Greek or Latin composition is most to be valued. Who shall say what share the turning over and over in their mind, and masticating, so to speak, in early life as models for their Latin verse, such things as Virgil's

> 'Disce, puer, virtutem ex me, verumque laborem '—

or Horace's

> 'Fortuna sævo læta negotio '—

has not had in forming the high spirit of the upper class in France and England, the two countries where Latin verse has most ruled the schools, and the two countries which most have had, or have, a high upper class and a high upper class spirit? All this is no doubt to be considered when we are judging the worth of the old school training.

But, in the first place, dignity and a high spirit is not all, or half all, that is to be got out of *Alterthumswissenschaft*. What else is to be got out of it,—the love of the things of the mind, the flexibility, the spiritual moderation,—is for our present time and needs still more precious, and our upper class suffers greatly by not having got it. In the second place, though I do not deny that there are persons with such eminent aptitudes for Latin and Greek composition that they may be brought in contact with the spirit and power of *Alterthumswissenschaft*, and thus with vital knowledge, through them,— as neither do I deny that there are persons with such eminent aptitudes for grammatical and philological studies, that they may be brought in contact with vital knowledge through *them*,—nevertheless, I am convinced that of the hundreds whom our present system tries without distinction to bring into contact with *Alterthumswissenschaft* through composition and philology almost alone, the immense majority would have a far better chance of being brought into vital contact with it through literature, by treating the study of Greek and Latin as we treat our French, or Italian, or German studies. In other words, the number of persons with aptitudes for being carried to vital knowledge by the literary, or historical, or philosophical, or artistic sense,—to each of which senses we give a chance by treating Greek and Latin as literature, and not as mere scholarship,—is infinitely greater than the number of those whose aptitudes are for composition and philology.*

I cannot help thinking, therefore, that the modern spirit will deprive Latin and Greek composition and verbal scholarship of their present universal and preponderant application in our secondary schools, and will make them, as practised on their present high scale, *Privatstudien,* as the Germans say, for boys with an eminent aptitude for them. For the mass of boys the Latin and Greek composition will be limited, as we now limit our French, Italian, and German composition, to the exercises of translation auxiliary to acquiring any language soundly; and the verbal scholarship will be limited to learning the elementary grammar and common forms and laws of the language with a thoroughness which cannot be too exact, and which may easily be more exact than that which we now attain with our much more ambitious grammatical studies. A far greater quantity of Latin and Greek literature might, with the time thus saved, be read, and in a far more interesting manner. With the Latin and Greek classics, too, might be joined, as a part of the literary and humanistic course for those whose aptitude is in this direction, a great deal more of the classics of the chief modern languages than we have time for with our present system.

We have still to make the mother tongue and its literature a part of the school course; foreign nations have done this, and we shall do it; but neither foreign nations nor we have yet quite learnt how to deal, for school purposes,

---

* Since the above remarks were in print they have received powerful corroboration from the eminent authority of Mr. Mill, in his inaugural address at St. Andrews. The difference of my conclusions on one or two points from Mr. Mill's only makes the general coincidence of view more conspicuous; Mr. Mill having been conducted to this view by independent reflection, and I by observation of the foreign schools and of the movement of ideas on the Continent.

Mr. Farrar's very interesting lecture has still more recently come to show us this movement of ideas extending itself to the schools of England, and to distinguished teachers in the most distinguished of these schools.

with modern foreign languages. The great notion is to
teach them for speaking .purposes, with a view to practical
convenience. This notion clearly belongs to what I have
called the commercial theory of education, and not the liberal
theory; and the faultiness of the commercial theory is well
seen by examining this notion and its fruits. Mr. Marsh,
the well-known author of the *History of the English Language,*
who has passed his life in diplomacy and is himself at once
a *savant* and a linguist, told me he had been much struck by
remarking how, in general, the accomplishment of speaking
foreign languages tends to strain the mind, and to make it
superficial and averse to going deep in anything. He in-
stanced the young diplomatists of the new school, who, he said,
could rattle along in two or three languages, but could do
nothing else. Perhaps in old times the young diplomatists
could neither do that nor anything else, so in their case there
may be now a gain; but there is great truth in Mr. Marsh's
remark that the speaking several languages tends to make
the thought thin and shallow, and so far from in itself carrying us to vital knowledge, needs a compensating force to
prevent its carrying us away from it. But the true aim of
schools and instruction is to develop the powers of our mind
and to give us access to vital knowledge.

Again: if the speaking of foreign languages is a prime school
aim, this aim is clearly best reached by sending a boy to a
foreign school. Great numbers of English parents, accordingly,
who from their own want of culture are particularly prone to
the more obvious theory of education,—the commercial one,
—send their boys abroad to be educated. Yet the basis of
character and aptitudes proper for living and working in
any country is no doubt best formed by being reared in that
country, and passing the ductile and susceptible time of
boyhood there; and in this case Solomon's saying applies
admirably : ' *As a bird that wandereth from her nest, so is a
man that wandereth from his place.*' That, therefore, can
hardly be a prime school aim, which to be duly reached
requires from the scholar an almost irreparable sacrifice.
So the learning to speak foreign languages, showy as the
accomplishment always is, and useful as it often is, must be

regarded as a quite secondary and subordinate school aim. Something of it may be naturally got in connection with learning the languages; and above all, the instructor's precept and practice in pronunciation should be sound, not, as in our old way of teaching these languages through incompetent English masters it too often was, utterly barbarous and misleading; but all this part is to be perfected elsewhere, and is not to be looked upon as true school business. It is as literature, and as opening fresh roads into knowledge, that the modern foreign languages, like the ancient, are truly school business; and far more ought to be done with them, on this view of their use, than has ever been done yet.

To sum up, then, the conclusions to which these remarks lead. The ideal of a general, liberal training is, to carry us to a knowledge of ourselves and the world. We are called to this knowledge by special aptitudes which are born with us; the grand thing in teaching is to have faith that some aptitudes of this kind everyone has. This one's special aptitudes are for knowing men,—the study of the humanities; that one's special aptitudes are for knowing the world,—the study of nature. The circle of knowledge comprehends both, and we should all have some notion, at any rate, of the whole circle of knowledge. The rejection of the humanities by the realists, the rejection of the study of nature by the humanists, are alike ignorant. He whose aptitudes carry him to the study of nature should have some notion of the humanities; he whose aptitudes carry him to the humanities should have some notion of the phenomena and laws of nature. Evidently, therefore, the beginnings of a liberal culture should be the same for both. The mother tongue, the elements of Latin and of the chief modern languages, the elements of history, of arithmetic and geometry, of geography, and of the knowledge of nature, should be the studies of the lower classes in all secondary schools, and should be the same for all boys at this stage. So far, therefore, there is no reason for a division of schools. But then comes a *bifurcation*, according to the boy's aptitudes and aims. Either the study of the humanities or the study of nature is henceforth to be the predominating part of his instruction. Evidently there are some advantages in making one school include those who follow both these studies. It is the more economical arrangement; and when the humanistic and the real studies are in the same school, there is less likelihood of the social stamp put on the boy following the one of them, being different from that put on a boy following the other. Still the *bifurcation* within one school, as practised in France, did not answer. But I think this was because the character of the one school remained so overwhelmingly humanistic, because the humanist body of teachers was in general much superior to the realist body, and because the claims of the humanities were allowed to pursue a boy so jealously into his *real* studies. In my opinion, a clever *Realschüler*, who has gone properly through the general grounding of the lower classes, is likely to develop the greater taste for the humanities the more he is suffered to follow his *real* studies without let or stint. The ideal place of instruction would be, I think, one where in the upper classes (the instruction in the lower classes having been the same for all scholars) both humanistic and *real* studies were as judiciously prosecuted, with as good teaching and with as generous a consideration for the main aptitudes of the pupil, as the different branches of humanistic study are now prosecuted in the best German *Gymnasien*; where an attempt is certainly made, by exempting a pupil from lessons not in the direction of his aptitudes, and by encouraging and guiding him to develope these through *Privatstudien*, to break through that Procrustean routine which, after a certain point, is the bane of great schools. There should, after a certain point, be no cast-iron course for all scholars, either in humanistic or naturalistic studies. According to his aptitude, the pupil should be suffered to follow principally one branch of either of the two great lines of study; and, above all, to interchange the lines occasionally, following, on the line which is not his own line, such lessons as have yet some connection with his own line, or, from any cause whatever, some attraction for him. He cannot so well do this if the *Gymnasium* and the *Realschule* are two totally separate schools.

His doing it at all, however, is, it will be said, only an

ideal. True, but it is an ideal which the modern spirit is, more and more, casting about to realise. To realise it fully, the main thing needful is, first, a clear central conception of what one can and should do by instruction. It is, secondly, a body of teachers, in all the branches of each of the two main lines of study, thoroughly masters of their business, and of whom every man shall be set to teach that branch which he has thoroughly mastered, and shall not be allowed to teach any that he has not.

CHAPTER XXIII.

GENERAL CONCLUSION CONTINUED. SCHOOL ESTABLISHMENT.

ENGLAND AND THE CONTINENT—CIVIL ORGANISATION IN MODERN STATES—CIVIL ORGANISATION TRANSFORMED NOT ONLY IN FRANCE BUT ALSO IN OTHER CONTINENTAL STATES—NOT IN ENGLAND—A RESULT OF THIS IN ENGLISH POPULAR EDUCATION—ENGLISH SECONDARY AND SUPERIOR INSTRUCTION NOT TOUCHED BY THE STATE—INCONVENIENCES OF THIS—THE SOCIAL INCONVENIENCE—THE INTELLECTUAL INCONVENIENCE — THEIR PRACTICAL RESULTS — SCIENCE AND SYSTEMATIC KNOWLEDGE MORE PRIZED ON THE CONTINENT THAN IN ENGLAND—EFFECT OF THIS ON OUR APPLICATION OF THE SCIENCES, AND ON OUR SCHOOLS AND EDUCATION IN GENERAL — A BETTER ORGANISATION OF SECONDARY AND SUPERIOR INSTRUCTION A REMEDY FOR OUR DEFICIENCIES—PUBLIC AND PRIVATE SCHOOLS—NECESSITY FOR PUBLIC SCHOOLS—WITH PUBLIC SCHOOLS, AN EDUCATION MINISTER NECESSARY—A HIGH COUNCIL OF EDUCATION DESIRABLE — FUNCTIONS OF SUCH A COUNCIL — PROVINCIAL SCHOOL BOARDS REQUISITE — HOW TO MAKE PUBLIC SCHOOLS—DEFECTS OF OUR UNIVERSITY SYSTEM—OXFORD AND CAMBRIDGE MERELY *HAUTS LYCÉES*—LONDON UNIVERSITY MERELY A BOARD OF EXAMINERS—INSUFFICIENT NUMBER OF STUDENTS UNDER SUPERIOR INSTRUCTION IN ENGLAND—SPECIAL SCHOOLS WANTED, AND A REORGANISED UNIVERSITY SYSTEM, TAKING SUPERIOR INSTRUCTION TO THE STUDENTS, AND NOT BRINGING THESE STUDENTS TO OXFORD AND CAMBRIDGE FOR IT—CENTRES OF SUPERIOR INSTRUCTION TO BE FORMED IN DIFFERENT PARTS OF ENGLAND, AND PROFESSORS TO BE ORGANISED IN FACULTIES—OXFORD, CAMBRIDGE, AND LONDON TO REMAIN THE ONLY DEGREE-GRANTING BODIES—EDUCATION MINISTER SHOULD HAVE THE APPOINTMENT OF PROFESSORS—PROBABLE CO-OPERATION OF EXISTING BODIES WITH THE STATE IN ORGANISING THIS NEW SUPERIOR INSTRUCTION—HOW, WHEN ESTABLISHED, IT SHOULD BE EMPLOYED—FINAL CONCLUSION.

I COME next to the second point for consideration: the mode of establishing and administering schools. I have now on two occasions, first in 1859 and again in 1865, had to make a close study, on the spot and for many months together, of one of the most important branches of the civil organisation of the most civilised states of the Continent. Few Englishmen have had such an experience. If the convictions with which it leaves me seem strange to many Englishmen, it is not that I am differently constituted from the rest of my countrymen, but that I have seen what would certainly give to them too, if they had seen it with their own eyes as I have, reflections which they never had before. No one of open mind, and not hardened in routine and prejudice, could observe for so long and from so near as I observed it, the civil organisation of France, Germany, Italy, Switzerland, Holland, without having the conviction forced upon him that these countries have a civil organisation which has been framed with forethought and design to meet the wants of modern society; while our civil organisation in England still remains what time and chance have made it. The States which we really resemble, in this respect, are Austria and Rome. I remember I had the honour of saying to Cardinal Antonelli, when he asked me what I thought of the Roman schools, that for the first time since I came on the Continent I was reminded of England. I meant, in real truth, that there was the same easy-going and absence of system on all sides, the same powerlessness and indifference of the State, the same independence in single institutions, the same free course for abuses, the same confusion, the same lack of all idea of *co-ordering* things, as the French say,—that is, of making them work fitly together to a fit end; the same waste of power, therefore, the same extravagance, and the same poverty of result, of which the civil organisation of England offers so many instances. To the like effect a French publicist said the other day with great truth to the Austrian Government:—' La cour de Vienne comprendra-t-elle qu'il n'y a point de salut pour les états européens en dehors des idées modernes, c'est-à-dire des libres institutions populaires *et des organisations administratives positives et strictement contrôlées?*' We have in England the *libres institutions populaires*, so for us the point is in the last words of the sentence. Modern States cannot either do without free institutions, or do without a rationally planned and effective civil organisation. Unlike in other things, Austria, Rome, and England are alike in this, that the civil organisation of each implies, at the present day, a denial or an ignorance of the right of mind and reason to rule human affairs. At Rome this right is sacrificed in the name of religion; in Austria, in the name

of loyalty; in England, in the name of liberty. All respectable names; but none of them will in the long run save its
invoker, if he persists in disregarding the inevitable laws
which govern the life of modern society.

Every one is accustomed to hear that France paid the
horrors of her great Revolution as the price for having a
tabula rasa upon which to build a new civil organisation.
But what one learns when one goes upon the Continent and
looks a little closely into these things, is, that all the most
progressive states of the Continent have followed the example
of France, and have transformed or are transforming their
civil organisation. Italy is transforming hers by virtue of
the great opportunity which the events of the last eight
years have given her. Prussia transformed hers from 1807
to 1812, by virtue of the stern lesson which her disasters and
humiliation had then read her. Russia is at this moment
accomplishing a transformation yet more momentous. The
United States of America came into the world, it may be
said, with a *tabula rasa* for a modern civil organisation to be
built on, and they have never had any other. What I say
is, that everywhere around us in the world, wherever there
is life and progress, we find a civil organisation that is
modern; and this in States which have not, like France,
gone through a tremendous revolution, as well as in France
itself.

Who will deny that England has life and progress? but
who will deny also that her course begins to show signs of
uncertainty and embarrassment? This is because even an
energy like hers cannot exempt her from the obligation of
obeying natural laws; and yet she tries to exempt herself
from it when she endeavours to meet the requirements of a
modern time and of modern society with a civil organisation
which is, from the top of it to the bottom, not modern.
Transform it she must, unless she means to come at last to
the same sentence as the Church of Sardis: ' *Thou hast a
name that thou livest, and art dead.*' However, on no part of
this immense task of transformation have I now to touch,
except on that part which relates to education. But this
part, indeed, is the most important of all; and it is the part

whose happy accomplishment may render that of all the rest, instead of being troubled and difficult, gradual and easy.

About popular education I have here but a very few words to say. People are at last beginning to see in what condition this really is amongst us. Obligatory instruction is talked of. But what is the capital difficulty in the way of obligatory instruction, or indeed any national system of instruction, in this country? It is this: that the moment the working class of this country have this question of instruction really brought home to them, their self-respect will make them demand, like the working classes on the Continent, *public* schools, and not schools which the clergyman, or the squire, or the mill-owner, calls 'my school.' And what is the capital difficulty in the way of giving them public schools? It is this: that the public school for the people must rest upon the municipal organisation of the country. In France, Germany, Italy, Switzerland, the public elementary school has, and exists by having, the commune and the municipal government of the commune, as its foundations, and it could not exist without them. But we in England have our municipal organisation still to get; the country districts, with us, have at present only the feudal and ecclesiastical organisation of the Middle Ages, or of France before the Revolution. This is what the people who talk so glibly about obligatory instruction, and the Conscience Clause, and our present abundant supply of schools, never think of. The real preliminary to an effective system of popular education is, in fact, to provide the country with an effective municipal organisation ; and here, then, is at the outset an illustration of what I said, that modern societies need a civil organisation which is modern.*

* France has now 37,500 communes, and nearly 37,500,000 inhabitants; about one commune, therefore, to every 1,000 inhabitants. The mayor of the commune is named by the Crown, and represents the State, the central power; the municipal council, of which the mayor is president, is elected by universal suffrage of the commune.

We have in England 655 unions and about 12,000 parishes; but our communes, or municipal centres, ought at the French rate to be 20,000 in number. Nor is this number, perhaps, more than is required in order to supply a proper basis for the national organisation of our elementary schools. A municipal organisation being once given, the object should be to withdraw the existing elementary schools from their present private management, and to reconstitute them on a municipal basis.

We have nearly all of us reached the notion that popular education it is the State's duty to deal with. Secondary and superior instruction many of us still think should be left to take care of themselves. Well, this is what was generally thought, or at any rate practised, in old times, all over Europe. I have shown how the State's taking secondary instruction seriously in hand dates, in Prussia, from Wilhelm von Humboldt in 1809; in the same year, a year for Prussia of trouble and anxious looking forward, he created the University of Berlin. In Switzerland the State's effective dealing with all kinds of public instruction dates from within the last thirty years; in Italy it dates from 1859. In all these countries the idea of a sound civil organisation of modern society has been found to involve the idea of an organisation of secondary and superior instruction by public authority, by the State.

The English reader will ask: What inconvenience has arisen in England from pursuing the old practice? The investigations of the Schools Enquiry Commission, I feel sure, will have made it clear that we have not a body of 65,000 boys of the middle and upper classes receiving so good an instruction as 65,000 boys of the same classes are receiving in the higher schools of Prussia, or even of France. The English reader will not refuse to believe, though no Royal Commission has yet made enquiries on this point, that we have not a body of 6,300 university students in England receiving so good an instruction as the 6,300 matriculated students in the Prussian universities, or even as the far more numerous students in the French faculties, are receiving. Neither is the secondary and superior instruction given in England on the whole so good, nor is it given, on the whole, in schools of so good a standing. Of course, what good instruction there is, and what schools of good standing there are to get it in, fall chiefly to the lot of the upper class. It is on the middle class that the inconvenience, such as it is, of getting indifferent instruction, or

This is not the place to enter into details as to the manner in which such a withdrawal is to be effected; I will remark only that all reforms which stop short of such a withdrawal and reconstitution are and must be mere patchwork.

getting it in schools of indifferent standing, mainly comes. This inconvenience, as it strikes one after seeing attentively the schools of the Continent, has two aspects. It has a social aspect, and it has an intellectual aspect.

The social inconvenience is this. On the Continent, the upper and middle class are brought up on one and the same plane. In England the middle class, as a rule, *is brought up on the second plane.* One hears many discussions as to the limits between the middle and the upper class in England. From an educational point of view these limits are perfectly clear. Half-a-dozen famous schools, Oxford or Cambridge, the army or navy, and those posts in the public service supposed to be posts for gentlemen ; these are the schools all or any one of which give a training, a stamp, a cast of ideas, which make a sort of association of all those who share them, and this association is the upper class. Except by one of these modes of access an Englishman does not, unless by some special play of aptitude or of circumstances, become a vital part of this association, for he does not bring with him the cast of ideas in which its bond of union lies. This cast of ideas is naturally for the most part that of the most powerful and prominent part of the association, the aristocracy. The professions furnish the more numerous but the less prominent part ; in no country, accordingly, do the professions so naturally and generally share the cast of ideas of the aristocracy as in England. This cast of ideas, judged from its good side, is characterised by a high spirit, by dignity, by a just sense of the greatness of great affairs,— all of them governing qualities; and the professions have accordingly long recruited the governing force of the aristocracy, and assisted it to rule. Judged from its bad side, this cast of ideas is characterised by its indisposition and incapacity for science, for systematic knowledge. The professions are on the Continent the stronghold of science and systematic knowledge ; in England, from the reason above assigned, they are not. They are also in England separate, to a degree unknown on the Continent, from the commercial and industrial class with which in social standing they are naturally on a level. So we have amongst us the spectacle

of a middle class cut in two in a way unexampled anywhere
else; of a professional class brought up on the first plane,
with fine and governing qualities, but without the idea of
science; while that immense business class, which is becoming so important a power in all countries, on which the
future so much depends, and which in the leading schools of
other countries fills so large a place, is in England brought
up on the second plane, cut off from the aristocracy and the
professions, and without governing qualities.

If only, in compensation, it had science, systematic knowledge! The stronghold of science should naturally be in a
nation's middle class, who have neither luxury nor bodily
toil to bar them from it. But here comes in the intellectual
inconvenience of the bad condition of the mass of our secondary schools. On the Continent, if the professions were as
aristocratic in their indifference to science as they are here,
the business class, educated as it is, would at once wrest the
lead from them, and would be fit to do so. But here in
England, the business class is not only inferior to the professions in the social stamp of its places of training, it is
actually inferior to them, maimed and incomplete as their
intellectual development is, in its intellectual development.
Short as the offspring of our public schools and universities
come of the idea of science and systematic knowledge, the
offspring of our middle class academies probably come, if
that be possible, even shorter. What these academies fail
to give in social and governing qualities, they do not make
up for in intellectual power.

If this is true, then that our middle class does not yet itself see the defects of its own education, perceives no practical inconvenience to itself from them, and is satisfied with
things as they are, is no reason for regarding this state of
things without disquietude. '*He that wandereth out of the
way of understanding shall remain in the congregation of the
dead;*' sooner or later, in spite of his self-confidence, in spite
of his energy, in spite of his capital, he must so remain, by
virtue of nature's laws. But if the English business class
can listen to testimonies that in the judgment of others, at
any rate, its inferior education is beginning to threaten it

with practical inconvenience, such testimonies are formidably plentiful. A diplomatist of great experience, not an Englishman but much attached to England, who in the course of the acquisition and the construction of the Italian lines of railroad, had been brought much in contact with young men of business of all nations, told me that the young Englishman of this class was manifestly inferior, both in manners and instruction, to the corresponding young men of other countries. That is, he had been brought up, as I say, on a lower plane. And the Swiss and Germans aver, if you question them as to the benefit they have got from their *Realschulen* and Polytechnicums, that in every part of the world their men of business trained in those schools are beating the English when they meet on equal terms as to capital; and that when English capital, as so often happens, is superior, the advantage of the Swiss or the German in instruction tends more and more to balance this superiority. M. Duruy, the French Minister of Public Instruction, confirms this averment, not as against England in especial, but generally, by saying that all over the Continent the young North German, or the young Swiss of Zurich or Basle, is seizing, by reason of his better instruction, a confidence and a command in business which the young men of no other nation can dispute with him. This confidence, whether as yet completely justified or not by success, is a force which will go far to ensure its own triumph.

But the idea of science and systematic knowledge is wanting to our whole instruction alike, and not only to that of our business class. While this idea is getting more and more power upon the Continent, and while its application there is leading to more and considerable results, we in England, having done marvels by the rule of thumb, are still inclined to disbelieve in the paramount importance, in whatever department, of any other. And yet in Germany every one will tell you that the explanation of the late astonishing achievements of Prussia is simply that every one concerned in them had thoroughly learnt his business on the best plan by which it was possible to teach it to him. In nothing do England and the Continent at the present moment more strikingly differ than in the prominence which is now given to the idea of science there, and the neglect in which this idea still lies here; a neglect so great that we hardly even know the use of the word science in its strict sense, and only employ it in a secondary and incorrect sense. The English notion,—for which there is much to be said if it were not pushed to such an excess,—is, that you come to do a thing right by doing it, and not by first learning how to do it right and then doing it. The French, who in the extent and solidity of their instruction are, as a nation, so much behind the Germans, are yet in their idea of science quite in a line with the Germans, and ahead of us. That is because there is in France a considerable highly instructed class into whose whole training this idea of science has come, and whose whole influence goes to procure its application. We have no considerable class of this kind. We have, probably, a larger reading class than the French, but reading for amusement, not study; occupied with books of popular reading that leave the mind as inaccurate, as shallow, and as unscientific as it was before. The French have a much more considerable class than we have which really studies. A good test of this is the description of foreign books which get translated. Now the English reader will perhaps be surprised to hear that a German scientific book of any sort,—on philosophy, history, art, religion, &c.,—is much more sure of being translated into French than it is into English. A popular story or a popular religious book is sure enough of being translated into English; there is a public for a translation of that; but in France there is a public, not large certainly, but large enough to take an edition or two, for a translation of works not of this popular character.* In Germany, of course, there is a yet far larger public of such a kind. The very matter of public instruction suggests an illustration on this point, and an illustration at my own expense. It has been quite the order of the day

* There is nothing like an illustration, so let me name these three standard works, Creuzer's *Symbolik*, Preller's *Römische Mythologie*, and Von Hammer's *Geschichte des Osmanischen Reichs*, of each of which there is a translation in French, and none in English.

here, for some years past, to discuss the subject of popular education. This is a subject which can no more be known without being treated comparatively, than anatomy can be known without being treated comparatively. When it was under discussion in foreign countries, these countries procured accounts of what was done for popular education elsewhere, which were published, found a public to study them for their bearing on the general question, and went through two or three editions. But I doubt whether two hundred people in this country have read Mr. Pattison's report, or mine, on the popular schools of the Continent; simply because the notion of treating a matter of this kind as a matter of scientific study hardly occurs to any one in this country; but almost every one treats it as a matter which he can settle by the light of his own personal experience, and of what he calls his practical good sense.

Our rule of thumb has cost us dear already, and is probably destined to cost us dearer still. It is only by putting an unfair and extravagant strain on the wealth and energy of the country, that we have managed to hide from ourselves the inconvenience we suffer, even in the lines where we think ourselves most successful, from our want of systematic instruction and science. I was lately saying to one of the first mathematicians in England, who has been a distinguished senior wrangler at Cambridge and a practical mechanician besides, that in one department at any rate,—that of mechanics and engineering,—we seemed, in spite of the absence of special schools, good instruction, and the idea of science, to get on wonderfully well. 'On the contrary,' said he, 'we get on wonderfully ill. Our engineers have no real scientific instruction, and we let them learn their business at our expense by the rule of thumb; but it is a ruinous system of blunder and plunder. A man without the requisite scientific knowledge undertakes to build a difficult bridge; he builds three which tumble down, and so learns how to build a fourth which stands; but somebody pays for the three failures. In France or Switzerland he would not have been suffered to build his first bridge until he had satisfied competent persons that he knew how to build it, because abroad they cannot afford our extravagance. The scientific training of the foreign engineers is therefore perfectly right. Take the present cost per mile of the construction of an English railway, and the cost per mile as it was twenty years ago; and the comparison will give you a correct notion of what rule-of-thumb engineering, without special schools and without scientific instruction, has cost the country.'

Our dislike of authority and our disbelief in science have combined to make us leave our school system, like so many other branches of our civil organisation, to take care of itself as it best could. Under such auspices, our school system has very naturally fallen all into confusion; and though properly an intellectual agency, it has done and does nothing to counteract the indisposition to science which is our great intellectual fault. The result is, that we have to meet the calls of a modern epoch, in which the action of the working and middle class assumes a preponderating importance, and science tells in human affairs more and more, with a working class not educated at all, a middle class educated on the second plane, and the idea of science absent from the whole course and design of our education.

On popular education I have already touched so far as is proper for my present purpose. Secondary, and superior instruction remain. It is through secondary instruction that the social inconvenience I spoke of is to be remedied. The intellectual inconvenience is to be remedied through superior instruction, at first acting by itself, and then, through the teachers whom it forms and its general influence on society, acting on the secondary schools. I will sketch, guided by the comparative study of education which I have been enabled to make, the organisation of schools which seems to me required for this purpose. My part is simply to say what organisation seems to me to be required; it is for others to judge what organisation seems to them possible, or advisable to be attempted. The times, however, are moving; and what is not advisable to-day, may perhaps be called for to-morrow.

But the English reader will hardly, I think, have accompanied me through my long course, without sharing the conclusion that at any rate a public system of schools is indispensable in modern communities. From the moment you seriously desire to have your schools efficient, the question between public and private schools is settled. Of public schools you can take guarantees, of private schools you cannot. Guarantees cannot be absolutely certain. It is possible for a private school, which has given no guarantees, to be good; it is possible for a public school, which has given guarantees, to be bad. But even in England the disbelief in human reason is hardly strong enough to make us seriously contend that a rational being cannot frame for a known purpose guarantees which give him, at any rate, more numerous chances of reaching that purpose than he would have without them.

If public schools are a necessity, then an Education Minister is a necessity. Merely for administrative convenience he is, indeed, indispensable, But what is yet more important than administrative convenience is to have, what an Education Minister alone supplies, *a centre in which to fix responsibility.**

The country at large is not yet educated enough, political considerations too much overbear all others, for a minister with a board of six or seven councillors, like the minister at Berlin, to be left alone to perform such a task as the reconstruction of public education in this country must at first be. A High Council of Education, such as exists in France and Italy, comprising without regard to politics the personages most proper to be heard on questions of public education, a consultative body only, but whose opinion the minister should be obliged to take on all important measures not purely administrative, would be an invaluable aid to an English Education Minister, an invaluable institution in our too political country.

One or two matters on which I have already touched in the course of this work are matters on which it would be the natural function of such a Council to advise. It would be its function to advise on the propriety of subjecting children under a certain age to competitive examination, in order to determine their admission to public foundations. It would be its function to advise on the employment of the

---

* I need hardly point out that at present, with our Lord President, Vice-President, and Committee of Council on Education, we entirely fail to get, for primary instruction, this distinct centre of responsibility.

examination test for the public service; whether this security should, as at present, be relied on exclusively, or whether it should not be preceded by securities for the applicant having previously passed a certain time under training and teachers of a certain character, and stood certain examinations in connection with that training. It would be its function to advise on the organisation of school and university examinations, and their adjustment to one another. It would be its function to advise on the graduation of schools in proper stages, from the elementary to the highest school; it would be its function to advise on school books, and, above all, on studies, and on the plan of work for schools; a business which, as I have said, is more and more inviting discussion and ripening for settlement. We have excellent materials in England for such a Council. Properly composed, and properly representing the grave interests concerned in the questions it has to treat, it would not only have great weight with the minister, but great weight, as an illustrious, unpaid, deliberative, and non-ministerial body, with the country, and would greatly strengthen the minister's hand for important reforms.

Provincial School Boards, too, we have in this country very good materials for forming, and this institution of Germany is well suited to our habits, supplies a basis for local action, and preserves one from the inconveniences of an over-centralised system like that of France. Eight or ten Provincial School Boards should be formed, not too large, five or six members being the outside number for each Board, and one member being paid. This Board would be administrative; it would represent the State in the country, keeping the Education Minister informed of local requirements and of the state of schools in each district; being the direct public organ of communication with the schools, superintending the execution of all public regulations applied to them, visiting them so far as may be necessary, and representing the State by the presence of one of its members at their main annual examinations. An elaborate system of inspection, modelled on that of primary schools, is out of place when applied to higher schools; the French school authorities complained to me that they were over-inspected, and no doubt there are evident and solid objections to putting a *lycée* on the same footing, as regards inspection, with an elementary school. The Prussian system is far better, which resolves inspection, for higher schools, mainly into a concert of the State with the school authorities in great examinations,—as effective a way of inspection, in real truth, as can be found. What special visits may happen to be required are best made, as in Prussia, by members of the Provincial Boards, or by councillors of the Central Department; and a staff of school inspectors for higher schools is neither requisite nor desirable.

Where are the English higher schools, it will be asked, with which this Minister, this Council, and these School Boards are to deal? Guided by the experience of every country I have visited, I will venture to lay down certain propositions which may help to supply an answer to this question. Wherever there is a school-endowment, there is a right of public supervision, and, if necessary, of a resettlement of the endowment by public authority. Wherever, again, there is a school endowment from the Crown or the State, there is a right, to the State, of participation in the management of the endowment, and of representation on the body which manages it. These two propositions, which in ten years' time will even in England be admitted on all hands to be indisputable, supply all that is necessary for a public system of education. School endowments will certainly be dealt with ere long; and the extraordinary immunity which from the peculiar habits and isolation of this country the corporations or private trustees administering them have hithherto enjoyed, is really a reason for applying the principles of common sense and public policy, when they are at last applied to these matters, the more stringently instead of the less stringently. Endowments enough have merited an absolute withdrawal from their present bad application, and an absolute appropriation by public authority for the purposes of a better application, to furnish the State with means for creating, as a commencement, a certain number of Royal or Public schools, to be under the direct control of the Education Department and the Provincial Boards; and in which all the regulations for management, fees, books, studies, methods, and examinations, devised by public authority as most expedient, should have force unreservedly. Other schools would be found offering to place themselves under public administration, as soon as this administration began to inspire respect and confidence; and organised rightly, it would immediately inspire respect and confidence. A body of truly public schools would thus be formed, offering to the middle classes places of instruction with sound securities and with an honourable standing. Nor would these new schools long be in antagonism with our present chief schools, and following a different line of movement from them. Some of our present chief schools, like Eton and Westminster and Christ's Hospital, are royal foundations. Here the right of the State to have a share in the whole administration of the institution, and a voice in the nomination of the masters, immediately arises. Others, like Winchester, Rugby, and Harrow, are not royal foundations, but all of them are foundation schools, and therefore to all of them, as such, a right of public supervision applies. The best form this supervision can possibly take is that of a participation, as in Germany, by the public authority represented through the Provincial School Boards or through members of the High Council of Education, in their main examinations. On these examinations matriculation at the university,* and access to all the higher lines of public employment, should be made to depend. The pupils of private schools should be admitted to undergo them. In this way every endowed school in the kingdom would have yearly an all-important examination following a line traced or sanctioned by the most competent authority, the Superior Council of Education; and with a direct or indirect representation of this authority taking part in it. The organisation of studies in our very best schools could not fail to gain by this; in all but the very best, it would be its regeneration. Even in England, where the general opinion would be opposed to requiring, as in Germany, for the appointment of all public schoolmasters the sanction of a public authority, there could be no respectable objections urged to such a mode of public

---

* But there should be a different matriculation examination for each faculty, and, except for the faculties of theology and arts, Greek should not be required.

intervention as this ; the one bulwark, to repeat Wilhelm von Humboldt's words, which we can set up against the misuse of their patronage by private trustees. And we should at the same time get the happiest check put to the cram and bad teaching of private schools, by compelling them either to adjust their studies to sound and serious examinations, or to cease to impose upon the credulity of ignorant parents.

The mention of the matriculation examination brings me to superior or university instruction. This is, in the opinion of the best judges, the weakest part of our whole educational system, and we must not hope to improve effectually the secondary school without doing something for the schools above it, with which it has an intimate natural connection.   The want of the idea of science, of systematic knowledge, is, as I have said again and again, the capital want, at this moment, of English education and of English life; it is the university, or the superior school, which ought to foster this idea. The university or the superior school ought to provide facilities, after the general education is finished, for the young man to go on in the line where his special aptitudes lead him, be it that of languages and literature, of mathematics, of the natural sciences, of the application of these sciences, or any other line, and follow the studies of this line systematically under first-rate teaching. Our great universities, Oxford and Cambridge, do next to nothing towards this end. They are, as Signor Matteucci called them, *hauts lycées*; and though invaluable in their way as places where the youth of the upper class prolong to a very great age, and under some very admirable influences, their school education, and though in this respect to be envied by the youth of the upper class abroad and if possible instituted for their benefit, yet, with their college and tutor system, nay, with their examination and degree system, they are still, in fact, *schools*, and do not carry education beyond the stage of general and school education. The examination for the degree of bachelor of arts, which we place at the end of our three years' university course, is merely the *Abiturientenexamen* of Germany, the *épreuve du baccalauréat* of France, placed in both those countries at the entrance to university studies instead of, as with us, at their close. Scientific instruction, university instruction, really begins when the degree of bachelor (*bas chevalier*, knight of low degree) is taken, and the preparation for mastership in any line of study, or for doctorship (fitness to teach it), commences. But for mastership or doctorship, Oxford and Cambridge have, as is well known, either no examination at all, or an examination which is a mere form; they have consequently nó instruction directed to these grades; no real university instruction, therefore, at all. A machinery for such instruction they have, indeed, in their possession; but it is notorious that they do not practically use it.

The University of London labours under a yet graver defect as an organ of scientific or superior instruction. It is a mere *collegium*, or board, of examiners. It gives no instruction at all, but it examines in the different lines of study, and gives degrees in them. It has real university examinations, which Oxford and Cambridge have not; and these examinations are conducted by an independent board, and not by college tutors. This is excellent; but nevertheless it falls immensely short of what is needed. The idea of a university is, as I have already said, that of an institution not only offering to young men facilities for graduating in that line of study to which their aptitudes direct them, but offering to them, also, *facilities for following that line of study systematically, under first-rate instruction.* This second function is of incalculable importance; of far greater importance, even, than the first. It is impossible to overvalue the importance to a young man of being brought in contact with a first-rate teacher of his matter of study, and of getting from him a clear notion of what the systematic study of it means. Such instruction is so far from being yet organised in this country, that it even requires a gifted student to feel the want of it; and such a student must go to Paris, or Heidelberg, or Berlin, because England cannot give him what he wants. Some do go; an admirable English mathematician who did not, told me that he should never recover the loss of the two years which after his degree he wasted without fit instruction at an English university, when he ought to have been under superior instruction, for which the present university course in England makes no provision. I dare say he *will* recover it, for a man of genius counts no worthy effort too hard; but who can estimate the loss to the mental training and intellectual habits of the country, from an absence,—so complete that it needs genius to be sensible of it, and costs genius an effort to repair it,—of all regular public provision for the scientific study and teaching of any branch of knowledge?

England has twenty millions of inhabitants, and the matriculated students in England number about 3,500. Prussia,—the Prussia of this volume,—has 18,500,000 inhabitants, and 6,362 matriculated students. France has at least as large a proportion of her population coming under superior instruction. England, with her wealth and importance, has barely one-half the proportion of her population coming, even nominally, under superior instruction, that Prussia and France have. But this comparison by no means gives the full measure of her disadvantage, because, as I have just shown, Oxford and Cambridge being in reality but *hauts lycées*, and London University being only a board of examiners, the vast majority of even the 3,500 students of superior instruction whom England nominally possesses, do not, in fact, come under superior instruction at all. This entire absence of the crowning of the edifice not only tends to give us, as I have said, a want of scientific intellect in all departments, but it tends to weaken and obliterate, in the whole nation, the sense of the value and importance of human knowledge; to vulgarise us, to exaggerate our estimate, naturally excessive, of the importance of material advantages, and to make our teachers, all but the very best of them, pursue their calling in a mere trade spirit, and with an eye to little except these advantages.

Exactly the same effect which in the field of university teaching our want of any real course of superior instruction produces, is produced, in the field of the applied sciences, by our want of special schools like the School of Arts and Trades in Paris, or the *Gewerbe-Institut* of Berlin, or the Zurich Polytechnicum. It is the same crowning of the edifice of instruction which is wanting in both cases; the same bad intellectual habits and defective intellectual action, which are in both cases fostered by this want. Our Science and Art Department at South Kensington is a new experiment in this country, and has been a mark for much obloquy here. I am totally unconnected with that department; I am barely acquainted with Mr. Cole who directs it, and I have not the special knowledge requisite for criticising its operations. But I am bound to say that everywhere on the Continent I found a strong interest directed to this department, a strong sense of its importance and of the excellent effect it had already produced on our industry, with a conviction that in the mere interests of this industry we should be obliged to go on and give to this idea of a special school greater development. I, too, believe that we must have a system of special schools; but this is a subject which well deserves a separate study, and some one to treat it who is better qualified for the business than I am. I touch on it here merely as a branch of the great subject of superior instruction,—the instruction which is properly, and in all but special cases, to be given by universities.

To extend this amongst us is the great matter. Considering the wealth and occupations of the middle and upper classes of this country, we ought to have at least 8,000 students coming under this instruction. The Education Department, by the leaving examination which I have mentioned,—an examination to be held at the different schools and to represent the present matriculation examination,—should take the admission of university students entirely out of the hands of the colleges, and thus save Oxford and Cambridge from the absolute *non-valeurs* (to use M. Duruy's term) of which at present, owing to the laches of many of the colleges, they have far too many. The degree examination should be taken out of the hands of the college tutors, and entrusted, for reasons which I will give presently, to a board of examiners named by public authority. Beyond these changes, it is not in Oxford and Cambridge that the great work to be done is to be accomplished. All around me I hear people talking of university reform, university extension; all these projects end in Oxford or Cambridge, and the most liberal of them with a year's residence there. If there is one thing which my foreign experience has left me convinced of,—as convinced of as I am of our actual want of superior instruction,—it is this: that we must take this instruction to the students, and not hope to bring the students to the instruction. We must get out of our heads all notion of making the mass of students come and reside three years, or two years, or one year, or even one month, at Oxford or Cambridge, which neither suit their circumstances nor offer them the instruction they want. We must plant faculties in the eight or ten principal seats of population, and let the students follow lectures there from their own homes, or with whatever arrangements for their living they and their parents choose. It would be everything for the great seats of population to be thus made intellectual centres as well as mere places of business; for the want of this at present, Liverpool and Leeds are mere overgrown provincial towns, while Strasburg and Lyons are European cities. Oxford and Cambridge would contribute in the noblest and most useful way to the spread of university instruction, if they placed a number of their professors,—of whom they themselves make little use owing to the college system,—in these new faculties, to be established in London or the provinces, where they might render incalculable service, and still retaining the title of Oxford or Cambridge professors, unite things new and old, and help in the happiest manner to inaugurate a truly national system of superior instruction. Oxford and Cambridge can from the nature of things be now-a-days important schools only in theology, arts, and the mathematical and natural sciences. Owing to their college system, which for certain purposes, as I have said, and for a certain class, works well, they do not really need half their professors in even these three faculties, and could spare half of them for use elsewhere. They are actually bad places for schools in law and medicine, and all their professors in these faculties they might with advantage employ where there would be a better field for their services. All future application of Oxford and Cambridge emoluments to national purposes might, with advantage to the country, and honour to Oxford and Cambridge themselves, be made in this direction of endowing chairs for professors and exhibitions for students in university faculties to be organised in the great towns of England. The University of London should be re-cast and faculties formed in connection with it, in order to give some public voice and place to superior instruction in the richest capital of the world; and for this purpose the strangely devised and anomalous organisations of King's College and University College should be turned to account, and *co-ordered*, as the French say, with the University of London. Contributions from Oxford and Cambridge, and new appointments, might supply what was wanting to fill the faculties, which in London, the capital of the country, should, as at Paris or Berlin, be very strong. London would then really have, what it has not at present, a university.

It is with our superior instruction as with so much else; we have plenty of scattered materials, but these materials need to be co-ordered, and made, instead of being useless or getting in one another's way as at present, to work harmoniously to one great design. This design should be, to form centres of superior instruction in at least ten different parts of England, with first-rate professors to give this instruction. These professors should of course be grouped in faculties, each faculty having its dean. So entirely have Oxford and Cambridge become mere *hauts lycées*, so entirely has the very idea of a real university been lost by them, that the professors there are not even organised in faculties; and their action is on this account alone, if it were not on other accounts also, perfectly feeble and incoherent. The action of professors grouped in faculties, and concerting, as the professors and *Privatdocenten* of a faculty concert in Germany, their instruction together, is quite another thing. In a place like London all the five faculties of arts, mathematical and natural sciences, theology, law, and medicine, should of course be represented; but it is by no means necessary that each centre of superior instruction should have all these five faculties. Durham, for instance, ought probably to have, as

I think a Royal Commission once proposed, but two faculties, —a faculty of theology, and a faculty of mathematical and natural sciences. The requirements of different localities, and the facilities they offer for certain lines, must be taken into account. It is evident, for example, that faculties of medicine are best placed in very large towns, where hospitals and hospital patients are numerous.

Neither is it by any means necessary, or even expedient, that each centre of faculties should have the power of conferring degrees. To maintain a uniform standard of examination and a uniform value for degrees is most important, and this is impossible when there are too many bodies examining for degrees and giving them. Germany suffers from having too many universities granting degrees, and from these degrees bearing a very unequal value. We have two old and important universities, Oxford and Cambridge; one new and important university, London, and we want no more degree-granting bodies than these. The different centres of faculties throughout the country should be in connection with one or other of the universities, according as they may have received professors from them, or may be nearest to one or the other of them; and each of these three universities should have its board of examiners, composed of professors holding chairs in its district, and with the Superior Council of Education represented on each board. Thus composing your examining board substantially of professors, you would avoid the objection urged against the present examinations of the London University, that they are *in the air*, and that their standard fluctuates; composing it from among the professors of a third part of England, you would avoid the inconveniences of letting the teachers of any set of students have the sole decision of the degrees to be granted to them. All lesser examinations, such as should at the end of each year be held in order to determine whether the student makes progress and is to be allowed to go on with his course, belong naturally, in each centre, to the professors in that centre.

Such a system as that of which I have thus given the bare outline, can be properly organised only by an Education

Minister, with the concert and advice of a Superior Council of Public Instruction, and, if necessary, with the help of a public grant. The intervention of the State becomes especially necessary in superior instruction, because here the body of public opinion educated enough to discern what is wanted gets smaller than ever, while the importance of organising your instruction well and committing it to first-rate men becomes greater than ever. It is not from any love of bureaucracy that men like Wilhelm von Humboldt, ardent friends of human dignity and liberty, have had recourse to a department of State in organising universities; it is because an Education Minister supplies you, for the discharge of certain critical functions, the agent who will perform them in the greatest blaze of daylight and with the keenest sense of responsibility. Convocation made me a professor, and I am very grateful to Convocation; but Convocation is not a fit body to have the appointment of professors. It is far too numerous, and the sense of responsibility does not tell upon it strongly enough. A board is not a fit body to have the appointment of professors; men will connive at a job as members of a board who single-handed would never have perpetrated it. Even the Crown, that is, the Prime Minister, is not the fit power to have the appointment of professors, for the Prime Minister is above all a political functionary, and feels political influences overwhelmingly. An Education Minister, directly representing all the interests of learning and intelligence in this great country, a full mark for their criticism and conscious of his responsibility to them, *that* is the power to whom to give the appointment of professors, not for his own sake, but for the sake of public education. Even if the appointment of professors at Oxford and Cambridge be left as at present, the appointment of every professor in the new faculties should be vested in the Education Minister, and he should be responsible for it; though the faculties should have the right, as they have abroad, of themselves proposing to him candidates they may think proper.

Putting Oxford and Cambridge out of the question, all other places in England, even London, would have so much to gain by a regular public organisation being given to superior instruction in them, and by their professors acquiring the status and authority of public functionaries, that I cannot doubt that bodies like the Senate of the London University, the Council of London University College, or the trustees of Owens College at Manchester, would gladly co-operate with an Education Minister in transforming and co-ordering their institution so as to give them a national character and an increased effectiveness. Several of the personages in the Senate of the London University are personages who would naturally have a place in any Superior Council of Public Instruction. Following the Prussian division of school interests into *externa* and *interna*, trustees might remain charged with *externa*, the management of property; while *interna*, the appointment of professors and the organisation of faculties, devolved upon the Education department. The great towns chosen to be the seats of the new faculties would most of them gladly charge themselves with providing a fit habitation for a public establishment adding so much to their resources and importance. Many of them would furnish an annual contribution to the expenses of the faculties. I believe there would be more chance of a brisk competition among the chief towns for the honour of being made seats of university faculties, than of their under-valuing it. At any rate, no such town would be the seat of them long without learning to value them. The important thing is to establish them.

Once established, they should be employed as in a country which relying on its good intentions, its industry, and its wealth, has too long set at nought Solomon's warning: '*They that hate instruction love death.*' The end to have in view is, that every one who presents himself to exercise any calling, shall have received for a certain length of time the best instruction preliminary to that calling. This is not, it must be repeated again and again, an absolute security for his exercising the calling well, but it is the best security. It is a thousand times better security than the mere examination-test on which with such ignorant confidence we are now, in cases where we take any security at all, leaning with our whole weight. The Civil Service Examination should

be used in strict subordination to this better and ampler
security, and with a view of keeping it real.　For some
classes of post in the public service the having passed the
leaving examination of a public school ought to be demanded ;
for others, the having gone through the appointed courses
and passed the appointed examinations in certain faculties
or in certain special schools ; for all, one or the other.　Then,
and not till then, may come in, as a confirmatory and supplementary test, a rationally regulated civil service examination.　No minister of religion, to whom, as such, any
public functions are assigned, no magistrate, no schoolmaster
of a higher school, no lawyer, no doctor, should be allowed
to exercise his function without having come for a certain
time under superior instruction and passed its examinations.
The Pharmaceutical Society should be co-ordered with the
faculties of medicine, and no druggist should be allowed to
practise without its instruction and certificates.　It is with
the industrial class that the great difficulty of applying
superior instruction arises ; this class so large, wealthy, and
important, and which needs superior instruction so much just
because it feels that it needs it so little.　Owens College at
Manchester with its 100 students, and London University with
its 450 students (even if these, who have no appointed faculty
instruction, are to be called university students at all), sufficiently show, what is well known, that practically the English
industrial class cannot be said to come under superior instruction at all.　Their present indifference to it, however, affords
no true criterion for judging of their probable willingness to
accept it if it were properly organised, brought home to their
doors, and made compatible with the necessary conditions of
their lives.

Thus I have attempted to sketch in outline the plan of
reorganisation for English instruction which is suggested
almost irresistibly by a study of public instruction in other
European countries, and of the actual condition and prospects
of the modern world.　To make that study and to render an
account of it has been a long and laborious task.　The reader
will, I hope, be indulgent to the many imperfections which
he will find in my performance of it.　It was a task for many

parts of which I was ill qualified; and it was a task almost beyond any one man's powers, however qualified. He will also pardon anything which may seem too trenchant and absolute in the manner in which I have conveyed my criticisms and suggestions. In the first place, the pressure of matter and space almost obliged me to use great plainness and shortness, and to cut off all accompaniments of deprecation and apology. In the second place, I have a profound conviction that if our country is destined, as I trust it is destined, still to live and prosper, the next quarter of a century will see a reconstruction of English education as entire as that which I have recommended in these remarks, however impossible such a reconstruction may to many now seem.

Seven years ago, having been sent by a Royal Commission to study the primary schools on the Continent, I was so much struck by all I then saw, and by the comparison of it with what I had left behind me in England, that looking beyond the immediate scope of my errand, I said to my countrymen on my return: *Organise your secondary instruction.* That advice passed perfectly unheeded, the hubbub of our sterile politics continued, ideas of social reconstruction had not a thought given them, our secondary instruction is still the chaos it was; and yet now, so urgent and irresistible is the impression left upon me by what I have again seen abroad, I cannot help presenting myself once more to my countrymen with an increased demand: *Organise your secondary and your superior instruction.*

APPENDIX.

APPENDIX:

1. TABLE showing the NUMBER and POPULATION of the French *Lycées*, with the STATE GRANTS to them, for the Years 1842, 1849, 1851, 1855, and 1865 :—

Years	Number of *Lycées*	Number of Pupils	STATE GRANTS		
			For Bursarships and Allowances	For General Expenses (Examinations, Salaries of *Agrégés*, &c.)	Fixed Expenses of *Lycées* (Staff, &c.)
			fr. c.	fr. c.	fr. c.
1842	46	18,697	584,399 91	92,277 12	1,307,103 47
1849	55	20,833	711,375 7	82,026 7	1,500,641 45
1851	57	19,037	679,244 40	80,734 60	1,535,381 87
1855	63	20,960	710,918 78	41,844 48	1,301,918 7
1865	74	32,794	830,000 0	100,000 0	1,900,000 0

2. TABLE showing the NUMBER and POPULATION of the FRENCH COMMUNAL COLLEGES, with the STATE GRANTS to them, for the Years 1849,* 1855, and 1865.

Years	Number of Colleges	Number of Pupils	State Grants
			fr. c.
1849	306	31,706	99,880 94
1855	244	28,219	98,080 86
1865	247	33,038	223,000 0

* It is only since 1845 that the State has made an annual grant to the Communal Colleges.

3. GENERAL TABLE showing the STATE EXPENDITURE in FRANCE for the Year 1865 on the whole of PUBLIC INSTRUCTION.

Object of Expense	Expenditure
Sect. 1.—Central Administration:—	fr.
Staff	570,950
Matériel	140,000
Total Sect. 1	710,950
Sect 2.—General Services of Public Instruction:—	
Inspectors-General of public instruction	268,000
General services of public instruction	226,000
Academic administration	1,216,000
Total Sect. 2	1,710,000
Sect. 3.—Superior Instruction, Normal School, Literary and Scientific Establishments:—	
High Normal School	307,610
Faculties	3,828,821
University Library	26,000
Institute of France	615,700
Academy of Medicine	43,700
College of France	277,000
Museum of Natural History	592,380
Astronomical Establishments	267,260
School of Living Oriental Languages, Algiers Library and Museum	82,800
École des Chartes	37,800
School of Athens	64,500
Imperial Library	472,500
Public libraries	197,500
Learned societies	70,000
Subvention to the *Journal des Savants*	15,000
Subscriptions to literary and scientific works	140,000
Grants to *savants* and men of letters	200,000
Grants to teachers and subscriptions to adopted school-books	60,000
Expeditions and missions for scientific purposes	75,000
Collection and publication of unedited documents for French history	120,000
Total Sect. 3	7,493,071
Sect. 4.—Secondary Instruction:—	
General expenses of secondary instruction	100,000
Lycées and communal colleges	2,173,000
Bursarships and exemptions	868,000
Total Sect. 4	3,141,000
Sect. 5.—Primary Instruction:—	
Inspection	916,400
State grants to primary schools	5,946,700
Total Sect. 5	6,863,100
Total State expenditure on public instruction	19,918,121

4. TABLE showing the NUMBER and POPULATION of the PUBLIC SECONDARY SCHOOLS of ITALY for the Years 1863–64.

Divisions of the Kingdom of Italy	Number of Provinces	Number of Communes	Population in 1861	Number of Public Schools						Number of Pupils in Public Schools			Number of Teachers in Public Schools	Number of Teachers in Public Schools who are Ecclesiastics
				Classical				Technical						
				Lyceums		Gymnasiums								
				State Lyceums	Non-State Lyceums	State Gymnasiums	Non-State Gymnasiums	State Technical Schools	Non-State Technical Schools	In Lyceums	In Gymnasiums	In Technical Schools		
Northern	21	4,391	8,616,408	28	12	43	74	21	64	2,282	7,926	6,211	1,204	490
Central .	16	1,067	4,229,987	12	7	6	37	6	38	523	1,800	1,171	619	197
Southern	13	1,532	5,920,461	13	1	13	4	0	7	326	1,327	123	201	91
Sardinia	2	371	588,064	2	0	6	6	1	2	111	714	242	103	43
Sicily .	7	359	2,392,414	7	0	27	2	17	1	120	1,095	521	215	84
Totals .	59	7,720	21,747,334	62	20	95	123	45	112	3,362	12,862	8,268	2,342	905

In 1865 the State expenditure, in Italy, on the whole of public instruction, was in round figures 576,900*l.*; on secondary instruction alone, again in round figures, 137,500*l.*

5. TABLE showing the NUMBER and POPULATION of the PRUSSIAN HIGHER SCHOOLS for the Years 1853, 1859, 1863.

Years	Number of Higher Schools						Number of Pupils	Number of Teachers	Total of	
	Gymnasiums	Progymnasiums	Realschulen of first rank	Realschulen of second rank	Higher Burgher Schools	Other *Realschulen* [*]			Gymnasial Institutions	*Real* Institutions
1853	121	28	—	—	—	51	48,780	2,505	149	51
1859	135	31	30	27	3	9	58,622	3,003	166	69
1863	144	28	47	17	13	6	66,135	3,349	172	83

[*] In 1853 the classification of the various orders of *Realschulen* did not yet exist. The schools of 1859 and 1863, which are entered under the category of ' other *Realschulen*,' are *Realschulen* of which the organisation was not finally completed when these returns were made up.

6. TABLE showing the TOTAL EXPENDITURE on the PRUSSIAN HIGHER SCHOOLS, in each Province of the Kingdom, for the Year 1864.

| Provinces | Contributions supplied by | | | | | Total Expenditure |
| | State | | Town Municipalities | Churches and Independent Endowments | Scholars' payments | |
	By direct public grant	By grant from endowments at the State's disposal				
	Thlr.	Thlr.	Thlr.	Thlr.	Thlr.	Thlr.
1. Prussia Proper . .	58,753	20,604	51,837	4,166	134,603	302,106
2. Brandenburg . .	52,292	6,721	95,583	14,706	301,810	538,688
3. Pomerania . .	12,422	13,474	42,740	11,501	101,653	188,806
4. Silesia . . .	18,980	68,598	47,324	9,839	166,083	352,899
5. Posen . . .	'33,688·	21,400	22,994	928	67,963	152,134
6. Prussian Saxony .	45,903	62,254	32,965	11,959	142,066	382,907
7. Westphalia . .	28,006	26,052	33,087	5,994	76,142	200,144
8. Rhine Province and Hohenzollern territories . .	42,874	14,701	74,516	16,544	202,735	463,000
Totals . .	292,918	233,804	401,046	75,637	1,193,055	2,580,684

7. TABLE showing the NUMBER and POPULATION of the GERMAN UNIVERSITIES, with the Distribution of their Professors, for the Year 1864.

| States | Complete Universities | Incomplete Universities * | Professors and Readers | Matriculated Students | Professors | | | | |
					Theology	Law	Medicine	Philosophy	Political Economy
Prussia	6	2	600	6,362	88	64	143	281	—
Austria	4	—	396	4,792	42	74	141	116	—
Bavaria	3	9	292	2,706	25	28	72	80	13
Hanover . . .	1	—	122	711	14	19	17	61	—
Saxony . . .	1	—	112	1,007	11	22	30	47	—
Würtemberg . . .	1	—	80	737	14	9	20	25	7
Baden	2	—	155	1,157	14	19	36	56	—
Hesse Darmstadt . .	1	—	65	386	6	8	15	33	—
Mecklenburg Schwerin .	1	—	35	147	4	5	8	16	—
Saxe Weimar . .	1	—	65	518	7	11	11	28	—
Electoral Hesse . .	1	—	61	247	9	9	13	24	—
Holstein . . .	1	—	48	201	4	7	14	19	—
Totals . .	23	11	2,031	18,971	238	275	520	786	20

* Incomplete Universities are those which have not the four facultics of Theology, Law, Medicine, and Philosophy.

8. GENERAL TABLE showing the INCOME and EXPENDITURE of the PRUSSIAN UNIVERSITIES for the Year 1861.

INCOME.

Universities	From the State	From Endowments	Interest of Capital	University Fees, &c.	Totals
	Thlr.	Thlr.	Thlr.	Thlr.	Thlr.
1. Berlin . . .	179,890	50	72	7,290	187,302
2. Bonn	115,830	170	2,420	2,580	121,000
3. Breslau . . .	85,803	—	13,462	1,420	100,685
4. Greifswald . . .	1,200	57	74,710	673	76,640
5. Halle	61,465	30,635	251	4,220	96,571
6. Königsberg. . .	84,422	40	4,020	779	89,261
7. Münster . . .	2,250	15,179	—	1,450	18,879
Total . .	530,860	46,131	94,935	18,412	690,338

(The income of the University establishments (seminaries, laboratories, collections, &c.) amounted to 287,479 thalers more.)

EXPENDITURE.

Universities	Administration and Pensions	Salaries of Professors	University Establishments	Aids to Students	Repairs and Furniture	Reserve	Totals
	Thlr.	Thlr.	Thlr.	Thlr.	Thlr.	Thlr.	Thlr.
1. Berlin .	10,619	93,350	68,095	350	2,000	12,888	187,302
2. Bonn .	8,578	69,800	32,067	3,300	4,619	2,636	121,000
3. Breslau .	7,327	49,248	29,651	5,787	5,000	3,672	100,685
4. Greifswald	5,494	37,700	27,200	3,726	—	2,020	76,640
5. Halle .	7,020	49,248	24,935	8,006	3,460	4,102	96,571
6. Königsberg	6,203	37,545	29,941	8,579	2,600	4,393	89,261
7. Münster .	430	12,500	4,692	500	—	757	18,879
Totals .	45,671	349,191	217,081	30,248	17,679	30,468	690,388

9. TABLE showing the general RECEIPTS and EXPENDITURE of the UNIVERSITY of BERLIN, with the Income, in detail, of the Establishments belonging to the University, for the Year 1865.

RECEIPTS.	Thlr.	EXPENDITURE.	Thlr.
1. From the State .	. 189,069	1. Administration . .	10,804
2. From Endowments . .	50	2. Salaries of Professors .	102,400
3. Interest of Capital . .	111	3. University Establishments	70,230
4. University Fees, &c	. 7,557	4. Aid to Students . .	350
		5. Repairs and Taxes . .	2,000
		6. Reserve	11,003
Total .	. 196,787	Total . .	196,787

UNIVERSITY ESTABLISHMENTS.

Establishments	State Grant			Interest of Capital			Endowments			Totals	
	Thlr.	sgr.	pf.	Thlr.	sgr.	pf.	Thlr.	sgr.	pf.	Thlr.	sgr.
1. Divine Service	850	0	0	—			—			850	0
2. Clinical Surgery	4,650	0	0	65	15	0	11,973	15	0	16,686	0
3. General Clinical Medicine	2,441	0	0	—			—			2,441	0
4. Clinical Midwifery	7,300	0	0	—			1,500	0	0	8,800	0
5. Widows' Pensions	1,000	0	0	7,224	0	0	4,964	0	0	13,188	0
6. Theological Seminary	830	0	0	—			—			830	0
7. Philological Seminary	500	0	0	—			—			500	0
8. Observatory	3,641	15	0	—			—			3,641	15
9. First Chemical Laboratory	1,000	0	0	—			—			1,000	0
10. Second Chemical Laboratory	500	0	0	—			—			500	0
11. Anatomical Theatre and Collections	4,297	27	6	—			—			4,297	27
12. Physiological Institution	1,129	0	0	—			—			1,129	0
13. Institution for Researches in Chemistry and with the Microscope	600	0	0	—			—			600	0
14. Pathological Institution	2,000	0	0	—			—			2,000	0
15. Mineralogical Collection	2,843	0	0	—			—			2,843	0
16. Library	2,337	0	0	—			—			2,337	0
17. Zoological and Entomological Collections	6,948	0	0	—			—			6,948	0
18. Botanic Garden	20,426	24	3	—			—			20,426	24
19. Herbarium	3,084	15	0	—			—			3,084	15
20. University Garden	1,189	0	0	—			—			1,189	0
21. Cabinet of Surgical Instruments	430	0	0	—			—			430	0
22. Establishment for Legal Medicine	150	0	0	—			—			150	0
23. Pharmacological Collection	100	0	0	—			—			100	0
24. Apparatus for Mathematical and Physical Sciences	800	0	0	—			—			800	0
25. Archæological Museum of Christian Art	300	0	0	—			—			300	0
26. Laboratory for Physical Science	500	0	0	—			—			500	0
27. Seminary for Mathematical Science	400	0	0	—			—			400	0
Total	70,229	21	9	7,289	15	0	18,434	15	0	95,953	21

10. List of the Courses of Lectures by Professors, *Privatdocenten*, and Readers, in the University of Berlin, during the Winter *Semester* of 1865-66.

I. Faculty of Theology.

Full Professors.

1. Special Dogmatics (6 hours a week)
2. Theology of the New Testament, and Life of Christ (5 hours).
3. God's Kingdom till the Coming of Christ (1 h.)
4. Introduction to the books of the Old Testament (5 h.)
5. Explanation of the Psalms (5 h.)
6. Life of Christ, and Critical History of the Gospels (2 h.)
7. History of the Church of the Reformation (6 h.)
8. Exercises in Catechisation and Preaching (2 h.)
9. The same (2 h.)
10. Practical Theology (5 h.)
11. The Creeds (1 h.)
12. Symbolical Theology, and Introduction to the Criticism of the New Testament (5 h.)

Assistant Professors.

13. The book of Judges (1 h.)
14. The book of Genesis (5 h.)
15. Life and Doctrine of Saint Paul (1 h.)
16. The Epistle to the Romans (5 h.)
17. The Circle of Knowledge and Methodology (2 h.)

18. Church History, part 1 (5 h.)
19. Archæology and Patristic Study (1 h.)
20. Homiletics, theoretical and practical (2 h.)
21. Biblical History (4 h.)
22. Dogmatics (1 h.)
23. The book of Isaiah (6 h.)
24. Introduction to the books of the Old Testament (5 h.)

Privatdocenten.

25. The book of Genesis (5 h.)
26. Prophetical Inspiration (2 h.)
27. The book of Isaiah (5 h.)
28. History of the Israelitish Worship (2 h.)
29. The book of Isaiah (5 h.)
30. Chaldaic and Syriac Grammar (2 h.)
31. Three of St. Paul's Epistles explained (2 h.)
32. History of the Christian Dogmas (5 h.)
33. Symbolical Theology (1 h.)
34. The Dogmatical Passages in the Old and New Testament explained (5 h.)
35. Church History, part 1 (5 h.)
36. History of Christian Dogmas (5 h.)

II. Faculty of Law.

Full Professors.

1. Psychology of Crimes (1 h.)
2. Natural Law, Philosophy of Law (4 h.)
3. Criminal Law (4 h.)
4. Criminal Procedure (2 h.)
5. Law of Nations (2 h.)
6. Private German Law, Commercial Law (5 h.)
7. Practical Exercises (1 h.)
8. The Pandects (1 h.)
9. Practical Law of the Pandects (6 h.)
10. History of English Law (1 h.)
11. Roman Law of Inheritance (2 h.)
12. Common and Prussian Civil Process (4 h.)
13. German and Prussian Public Law (4 h.)

14. Canon Law (4 h.)
15. Prussian Law (1 h.)
16. Methodology of Law (3 h.)
17. Prussian Civil Law (4 h.)
18. History of the German Empire and German Law (4 h.)
19. History of the Provincial Estates in Germany (3 h.)
20. The fourth book of Gaius explained (2 h.)
21. History of Roman Law (5 h.)
22. Institutes and Antiquities of Roman Law (5 h.)

Assistant Professors.

23. History and actual state of the German Confederation (3 h.)
24. Common Law of Prussia (4 h.)

25. French Civil Law (4 h.)
26. Catholic and Protestant Law of Marriage (1 h.)
27. Prussian Civil Law (4 h.)
28. Catholic and Protestant Canon Law (4 h.)
29. Ecclesiastical and Canon Law (4 h.)
30. Practice of Ecclesiastical and Canon Law (1 h,)
31. Capital Punishment (1 h.)
32. Common and Prussian Criminal Law (4 h.)
33. French Criminal Procedure (2 h.)
34. German Public Law, Rights of Sovereigns (2 h.)
35. Law of Nations (3 h.)
36. Practical Exercises on the Criminal Law (1 h.)

Privatdocenten.

37. Prussian Law (1 h.)
38. History of Roman Law (1 h.)
39. Institutes and Antiquities of Roman Law (4 h.)
40. Prussian Civil Law (4 h.)
41. Feudal Law (1 h.)
42. Private German Law (4 h.)
43. Commercial Law, Maritime Law, and Law of Exchange (4 h.)
44. History of Roman Law in Germany (1 h.)

45. History of the Empire, and of German Law (4 h.)
46. Prussian Law of Succession (1 h.)
47. Practical Exercises on the Jurisprudence of the Pandects (1 h.)
48. Institutes and Antiquities of Roman Law (5 h.)
49. Relations between Church and State (1 h.)
50. Ecclesiastical and Marriage Law (4 h.)
51. German Public Law, Private Rights of Sovereigns (2 h.)
52. Prussian Public Law (3 h.)
53. Practical Exercises on Public and Canon Law (1 h.)
54. Private Justice among the Romans (2 h.)
55. Roman Law of Succession (3 h.)
56. Modern Law of Exchange in Germany (1 h.)
57. Private Law and Feudal Law in Germany (4 h.)
58. Commercial and Maritime Law in Germany (4 h.)
59. The *Speculum Saxonicum* explained (2 h.)
60. History of the Empire, and of German Law (4 h.)
61. Interpretation of the Solutions in the Digests (1 h.)
62. Methodology of Law (3 h.)

III. FACULTY OF MEDICINE.

Full Professors.

1. On certain Discoveries of the Naturalists (1 h.)
2. Experimental Physiology (5 h.)
3. Practical Exercises in Experimental Physiology (1 h.)
4. Comparative Physiology with the Microscope (1 h.)
5. General History of Medicine (1 h.)
6. Pathology and Therapeutics (3 h.)
7. Clinical Medicine (6 h.)
8. Diseases of the Nervous System (5 h.)*
9. Medical Practice (6 h.)
10. History of Popular Maladies (1 h.)
11. General History of Medicine (3 h.)
12. Pathology and Therapeutics (5 h.)
13. Hernia (2 h.)
14. General and Special Surgery (4 h.)
15. Clinical Surgery, and Clinical Ophthalmics, Clinical Surgery (5 h.)*

16. Experiments in Surgery and Anatomy.
17. Clinical Surgery, and Clinical Ophthalmics (6 h.)*
18. Midwifery (4 h.)
19. Clinical Midwifery (6 h.)*
20. Practical Exercises in Midwifery (1 h.)
21. Excitant Drugs in Medicine (2 h.)
22. *Materia Medica* (6 h.)
23. Osteology (1 h.)
24. Anatomy of the Brain and Spinal Marrow (1 h.)
25. General Anatomy (6 h.)
26. Structure of the Human Body, with the Microscope (1 h.)
27. Practical Exercises in Anatomy (24 h.)
28. Methodology of Medicine (2 h.)
29. General Pathology and Therapeutics, and their History (4 h.)
30. *Materia Medica*, with Experiments (6 h.)

* Delivered either at one of the hospitals, or at one of the medical institutions, of Berlin.

31. Pathological Anatomy (4 h.)
32. Practical Course of Anatomy and Pathology, with the Microscope (6 h.)
33. Practical Course of Pathological Osteology (6 h.)

Assistant Professors.

34. Spectacles (1 h.)
35. Ophthalmology (2 h.)
36. The same (2 h.)
37. Clinical Ophthalmics (6 h.)
38. Practical Course of Ophthalmics, with Experiments (1 h.)
39. General Surgery (6 h.)
40. Surgical Operations on Dead Bodies
41. Diseases of Children (6 h.)
42. Errors of Modern Medicine (1 h.)
43. Hygiene (1 h.)
44. Theory and Practice of Treatment of Diseases of the Eye (4 h.)
45. Anatomy of the Organs of Sense (1 h.)
46. Osteology and Syndesmology of the Human Body (3 h.)
47. Public Hygiene (1 h.)
48. Legal Medicine (3 h.)
49. Medico-legal Dissection (6 h.)
50. The Nerves (2 h.)
51. Clinical Study of Diseases of the Nerves (6 h.)
52. Toxicology (2 h.)
53. Legal Medicine (3 h.)
54. Medico-legal Dissection (6 h.)
55. Pathology and Therapeutics (1 h.)
56. Auscultation (4 h.)
57. Clinical Lectures on Auscultation and Percussion (6 h.)*
58. Wounds (1 h.)
59. Fractures and Dislocations (2 h.)
60. Application of Bandages (3 h.)

Privatdocenten.

61. Diseases of the Teeth and Mouth (2 h.)
62. Diseases of the Teeth and their Cure, with Experiments (6 h.)
63. Surgical and Ophthalmological Experiments.
64. Drawing up of Prescriptions (2 h.)
65. Special Pathology and Therapeutics (6 h.)
66. Venereal Diseases (2 h.)
67. Cutaneous Diseases (2 h.)
68. Clinical lectures on Diseases of Children (2 h.)

69. Diseases of the Ear (1 h.)
70. Moral Responsibility (1 h.)
71. Pathology of Venereal Diseases (1 h.)
72. Surgery (6 h.)
73. Legal Medicine (2 h.)
74. Diseases of Women (2 h.)
75. Theory and Practice of Midwifery (4 h.)
76. Baths and Thermal Waters (2 h.)
77. Drawing up of Prescriptions (3 h.)
78. Physiological Effects of Gases (3 h.)
79. Toxicology (3 h.)
80. Going over previous Lectures in Physiology and Osteology (1 h.)
81. Theory and Practice of Midwifery (4 h.)
82. Operations in Midwifery (1 h.)
83. Clinical Study of Cutaneous and Venereal Diseases (3 h.)
84. Use of the Laryngoscope (1 h.)
85. Diseases of the Heart (1 h.)
86. Percussion, Auscultation, &c. (3 h.)
87. Auscultation, Percussion, and use of the Laryngoscope (4 h.)
88. General and Special Surgery.
89. Physiology of Animal Generation (1 h.)
90. Physiology of the Nerves and Muscles (4 h.)
91. Hernia (1 h.)
92. Puncture with experiments (1 h.)
93. Hereditary vices (1 h.)
94. General and Special Surgery (4 h.)
95. Auscultation, Percussion, &c. (1 h.)
96. Diagnostics (2 h.)
97. Use of Electricity in Medicine (1 h.)
98. Experimental Physiology (2 h.)
99. Going over previous lectures on different points of Physiology (1 h.)
100. Ophthalmology (3 h.)
101. Use of the Ophthalmoscope (1 h.)
102. Diagnostics of abnormal states of the Eye (1 h.)
103. Theory and Practice of Midwifery (4 h.)
104. Operations in Midwifery (1 h.)
105. Thermal Waters (2 h.)
106. Going over previous lectures on Pharmacology (1 h.)
107. Position of the *Viscera* in the Human Body (1 h.)
108. The Laryngoscope (1 h.)
109. The Laryngoscope, Auscultation, Inhalations, &c. (1 h.)
110. Cure of Insanity; the Diseases of the Brain (2 h.)

* Delivered either at one of the hospitals, or at one of the medical institutions, of Berlin.

IV. Faculty of Philosophy.

Full Professors.

1. Æschines *in Ctesiphontem* (2 h.)
2. Palæontology (5 h.)
3. Greek Antiquities (6 h.)
4. Botany (1 h.)
5. Special Botany (4 h.)
6. *Cryptogama, &c.* (1 h.)
7. Meteorology (1 h.)
8. Experimental Physics (4 h.)
9. Grecian History (4 h.)
10. Modern History, from 1780 to 1815 (5 h.)
11. Archæology (2 h.)
12. Greek Mythology (1 h.)
13. National Economy (4 h.)
14. Science of Finance (4 h.)
15. The *Persæ* of Æschylus (4 h.)
16. The *Miles Gloriosus* of Plautus (4 h.)
17. Politics and Political Economy (1 h.)
18. Principles of Political Economy (4 h.)
19. Logic and Metaphysics (4 h.)
20. Political Economy ; Theory of Finance (4 h.)
21. Organic Chemistry (1 h.)
22. Experimental Chemistry (3 h.)
23. The Speeches of Lysias (2 h.)
24. The Homeric Poems, and particularly the *Odyssey* (4 h.)
25. Surfaces of the Fourth Order (1 h.)
26. Analytical Mechanics (4 h.)
27. History of Egypt (1 h.)
28. Grammar of Hieroglyphics (3 h.)
29. Explanation of Egyptian Monuments (1 h.)
30. Physical Experiments (1 h.)
31. The 41st book of Livy, and onwards (1 h.)
32. Latin Inscriptions (4 h.)
33. Monuments of the Ancient German Language explained (1 h.)
34. History of the Ancient Poetry of Germany (4 h.)
35. The *Germany* of Tacitus (4 h.)
36. Analysis of Determinate Numbers (3 h.)
37. General and Special Geology (6 h.)
38. Zootomy (4 h.)
39. Historical Exercises (1 h.)
40. Modern History of England and of her Parliament (4 h.)
41. History of Politics (1 h.)
42. The Syriac Language (1 h.)
43. Grammar of the Semitic Languages (1 h.)

44. Explanation of the Psalms (5 h.)
45. Principles of Arabic Grammar (3 h.)
46. Comparison of Persian with Sanscrit (1 h.)
47. Crystallography (1 h.)
48. Mineralogy (6 h.)
49. The sixth book of Aristotle's *Nicomach. Eth.* (2 h.)
50. Psychology (4 h.)
51. History of Philosophy (5 h.)
52. Theory of Analytical Functions (6 h.)
53. Algebraical Equations (6 h.)

Assistant Professors.

54. History of Modern Philosophy (2 h.)
55. Logic (4 h.)
56. General History of Philosophy in 17th century (4 h.)
57. Theory of Determinants (2 h.)
58. Algebra (4 h.)
59. Differential Calculus (4 h.)
60. Physical Geography, and History of the Mediterranean (3 h.)
61. Simple Drugs examined with the Microscope (1 h.)
62. Botany of Medical Plants (6 h.)
63. Pharmacognosy (4 h.)
64. Certain Arabic Authors explained (1 h.)
65. Arabic Grammar (3 h.)
66. The book of Genesis (5 h.)
67. Theory of Geographical Phenomena (3 h.)
68. Analytical Mechanics (1 h.)
69. History of Astronomy (2 h.)
70. Theory of the Motion of Planets and Comets (4 h.)
71. Exercises in Archæology (1 h.)
72. History of Greek Sculpture (3 h.)
73. National Economy (4 h.)
74. The *Epidicus* of Plautus (2 h.)
75. Roman Antiquities (4 h.)
76. History of Greek Philosophy (2 h.)
77. Æsthetics (2 h.)
78. Select Epistles of Cicero (1 h.)
79. Philological Exercises (1 h.)
80. Greek Mythology (3 h.)
81. Exercises in Palæography (1 h)
82. Latin Palæography (1 h.)
83. National History of Glumaceous Plants (1 h.)
84. Systems of Medical Plants (6 h.)
85. Exercises in Anatomy and Physiology (4 h.)
86. Ancient Geography (3 h.)
87. Botany, Diseases of Plants (4 h.)

88. Agronomical Science (1 h.)
89. Historical Exercises (1 h.)
90. History of Germany (4 h.)
91. Art of Singing, especially Church Singing (2 h.)
92. Musical Composition (4 h.)
93. Pædagogy (2 h.)
94. The *Nibelungen* (6 h.)
95. Exercises in deciphering Manuscripts (1 h.)
96. Logic; Encyclopædia of Philosophical Sciences (4 h.)
97. History of Philosophy (4 h.)
98. History of the New World (2 h.)
99. Geography and Ethnography of Europe (4 h.)
100. The Chaldee Language (1 h.)
101. History of the Armenians (3 h.)
102. General History of Physics since Galileo (2 h.)
103. Theory of Electricity (1 h.)
104. Physics applied to Mathematics, Acoustics (4 h.)
105. Chemical Metallurgy (3 h.)
106. Principles of Qualitative and Quantitative Analysis (1 h.)
107. Experimental Chemistry (6 h.)
108. Pharmacy (3 h.)
109. Chemical Experiments (8 h. *daily*.)
110. The Turkish Language (3 h.)
111. Principles of National Psychology (1 h.)
112. Philosophy of Language; General Grammar (4 h.)
113. Character of the Indo-Germanic Languages (4 h.)
114. Universal History of the Arts (5 h.)
115. The *Sacontala* of Calidása (2 h.)
116. Sanscrit Grammar (3 h.)
117. Zend or Páli Grammar (2 h.)
118. The Rigveda or the Atharvaveda explained (1 h.)
119. Course of Sanscrit, Zend, or Páli (1 h.)
120. The Dramatic Art (1 h.)
121. Psychology and Anthropology (3 h.)

Privatdocenten.

122. Experimental Organic Chemistry (4 h.)
123. Experiments in Organic Chemistry (6 h.)
124. Schleiermacher (1 h.)
125. Logic, and Encyclopædia of the Philosophical Sciences (4 h.)
126. The Limits between Poetry and Philosophy (1 h.)

127. The American Political Economist, Henry Carey
128. Logic and Metaphysics
129. Political Economy
130. History of Modern Civilisation
131. Agronomical Zoology (3 h.)*
132. Entomology (3 h.)
133. The Koran (2 h.)
134. The Semitic Dialects (1 h.)
135. Differential Calculus (4 h.)
136. Analytical Geometry (4 h.)
137. The Bhagvatgita (1 h.)
138. Panini's Sanscrit Grammar (3 h.)
139. Hindustani or Páli Grammar (2 h.)
140. Indian Philosophy (1 h.)
141. The Satires of Juvenal (2 h.)
142. Syntax of the Latin Language (4 h.)
143. Lucretius, *De Rerum Natura* (1 h.)
144. Rhetoric and Rhetorical Exercises (2 h.)
145. Aristotle, and the Natural Philosophy of the Ancients (4 h.)
146. History of the German Universities (1 h.)
147. Systems of Modern Philosophy since Kant (4 h.)
148. Experimental Chemistry (6 h.)
149. The Olynthiac Orations of Demosthenes (1 h.)
150. The Epistles of Horace (4 h.)
151. Physics applied to Mathematics, Acoustics, Optics, &c. (3 h.)
152. General Geology
153. Natural History of *Entozoa* (1 h.)
154. General Zoology
155. The Climate of Italy (1 h.)
156. Medical Climatology (2 h.)
157. Conversational Lecture on Chemistry (1 h.)
158. History of Chemistry (1 h.)
159. Qualitative and Quantitative part of Analytical Chemistry (3 h.)
160. Medico-Legal Chemistry (3 h.)
161. Chemical Experiments (8 h. *daily*)
162. Theory of Irrigation and Drainage (1 h.)
163. Principles of Agriculture (3 h.)
164. Management of Cattle (3 h.)
165. Book-keeping (1 h.)

Readers (for Modern Languages).

166. Lectures in Italian on Italian Literature (2 h.)
167. Italian Grammar (2 h.)
168. Lectures on the Italian and French Languages (2 h.)
169. German Shorthand (2 h.)

* This course treats of the animals which do harm to agriculture.

170. German, English, French, and Italian Shorthand (2 h.)
171. Lectures in Polish on Persian Grammar and the Zend Language (2 h.)
172. The Turkish Language; *Kirk Vezir* read (3 h.)

173. Practical Lectures on the Persian and Turkish Languages (2 h.)
174. Lectures in English on English Literature down to the 16th century (1 h.)
175. Lectures on the English Language (2 h.)

11. TABLE showing the NUMBER, POPULATION, SCHOOL ABSENCES, and SCHOOL FUNDS of the POPULAR SCHOOLS of all kinds (*Volksschulen*) of CANTON ZURICH, for the Year 1863-1864.

Kinds of Schools.	Number of Schools.	Number of Teachers.	Number of Scholars.	School Absences.			Average per Scholar.	School Funds.
				Ex-plained.	Punish-able.	Total.		
Common Day Schools (*Allgemeine Volks-schulen, Alltagsschulen*)	365	515	25,797	318,496	30,151	348,647	13·12	fr. c. 5,320,647 93
Finishing and Singing Schools (*Ergänzungs-und Singschulen*)	—	—	{ 10,441 11,428 }	46,354	33,176	79,530	3.13	—
Küsnacht Practising School (attached to Normal School)	1	1	155	1,031	63	1,094	7·06	—
Secondary Schools (*Höhere Volksschulen, Secundarschulen*)	57	74	2,398	31,190	1,363	32,553	13·13	469,653 45
Needlework Schools (*Arbeitschulen*)	320	322	7,827	13,624	7,336	20,960	2·53	—
	743	912	48,046	410,695	72,089	482,784	8·18	5,790,301 38

12. Table showing the estimated Income and Expenditure of the Town of Zurich for its Popular Schools of all kinds, for the Year 1864; and drawn up by the *Schulpflege* of the Commune of Zurich in September of the preceding Year.

Income.	fr.	Expenditure.	fr.
Interest on School Funds .	26,000	Teachers' Salaries :	
Rent of Property . . .	1,105	1. Primary Schools.	
School Fees :		*a.* Day School :	
1. Primary Schools.		15 Masters at from 2,000	
a. Day School : fr.		fr. to 2,600 fr. in Boys'	
Boys: 630 at 6 fr. 3,780		School . . .	34,400
Girls: 730 at 6 fr. 4,380		5 Mistresses at from	
———	8,160	1,500 fr. to 2,000 fr.,	
b. Finishing School :		and 12 Masters at	
Boys: 25 at 3 fr. . 75		from 2,000 fr. to 2,400	
Girls: 80 at 3 fr. . 240		fr. in Girls' School .	35,200
———	315	Instructresses in needle-	
c. Singing School :		work . . .	8,750
Boys: 120 at 1 fr. 120		*b.* Finishing School :	
Girls: 120 at 1 fr. 120		Masters . . .	2,900
———	240	Mistresses and instruc-	
2. Secondary Schools.		tion in needlework .	840
Boys . . . 3,680		*c.* Singing School :	500
Girls . . . 5,600		2. Secondary Schools :	
———	9,280	Masters at from 2,400 fr.	
3. Fees from Scholars in		to 2,800 fr., and assist-	
Private Schools . .	100	ants, in Boys' School .	20,000
School fines	8,000	Masters at 2,800 fr., as-	
Settlement dues . . .	12,000	sistants, and instruction	
State grant	4,000	in needlework, in Girls'	
	———	School	19,920
	69,200	3. Instruction in gymnastics	1,000
		Retiring pensions . .	18,895
		Apparatus and maps . .	1,800
		Writing materials and books .	500
		Cleaning and warming . .	6,000
		Building and repairs . .	6,000
		Ground rents . . .	2,400
		Administration . . .	4,400
		Sundries (office expenses, print-	
		ing, &c.)	5,000
			———
			168,505

Balanced Account.

		fr.
Expenditure for 1864		168,505
Income for 1864		69,200
		———
Excess of expenditure over income .		99,305
Deduct surplus from preceding year .		12,000
		———
Actual deficit for 1864 * . .		87,305

* This estimated deficit is made up by a municipal rate of from 76 centimes to 1 franc on every 1,000 francs of assessed property of each inhabitant of the town of Zurich.

LONDON
PRINTED BY SPOTTISWOODE AND CO.
NEW-STREET SQUARE

December, 1867.

16, BEDFORD STREET, COVENT GARDEN, LONDON.

MACMILLAN AND CO.'S

List of Publications.

A Book of Thoughts.
By H. A. 18mo. cloth extra, gilt. 3*s.* 6*d.*

A Son of the Soil.
Crown 8vo. 6*s.*

ACLAND.—*The Harveian Oration,* 1865.
By HENRY W. ACLAND, M.D. Crown 8vo. 2*s.* 6*d.*

Æschyli Eumenides.
The Greek Text with English Notes, and an Introduction. By
BERNARD DRAKE, M.A. 8vo. 7*s.* 6*d.*

Agnes Hopetoun.
16mo. cloth. *See* OLIPHANT.

**AIRY.—*Works by* G. B. AIRY, M.A. LL.D. D.C.L. *Astronomer
Royal, &c.***

*Treatise on the Algebraical and Numerical Theory of
Errors of Observations and the Combination of Obser-
vations.*
Crown 8vo. 6*s.* 6*d.*

Popular Astronomy.
A Series of Lectures delivered at Ipswich. 18mo. cloth, 4*s.* 6*d.*
With Illustrations. Uniform with MACMILLAN'S SCHOOL CLASS
BOOKS.

*An Elementary Treatise on Partial Differential
Equations.*
With Stereoscopic Cards of Diagrams. Crown 8vo. **5*s.* 6*d.***

On the Undulatory Theory of Optics.
Designed for the use of Students in the University. Crown
8vo. 6*s.* 6*d.*

A

A.
2000.12.67.

Algebraical Exercises.
> Progressively arranged by Rev. C. A. JONES, M.A. and C. H. CHEYNE, M.A. Mathematical Masters in Westminster School. Pott 8vo. cloth. 2*s.* 6*d.*

Alice's Adventures in Wonderland.
> By LEWIS CARROLL. With Forty-two Illustrations by TENNIEL. Crown 8vo. cloth. 6*s.*

ALLINGHAM.—*Laurence Bloomfield in Ireland.*
> A Modern Poem. By WILLIAM ALLINGHAM. Fcap. 8vo. 7*s.*

ANSTED.—*The Great Stone Book of Nature.*
> By DAVID THOMAS ANSTED, M.A. F.R.S. F.G.S. Fcap. 8vo. 5*s.*

ANSTIE.—*Stimulants and Narcotics, their Mutual Relations,*
> With Special Researches on the Action of Alcohol, Æther, and Chloroform on the Vital Organism. By FRANCIS E. ANSTIE, M.D. M.R.C.P. 8vo. 14*s.*

Aristotle on Fallacies ; or, the Sophistici Elenchi.
> With a Translation and Notes by EDWARD POSTE, M.A. 8vo. 8*s.* 6*d.*

ARNOLD.   *Works by* MATTHEW ARNOLD.

New Poems.
> Extra fcap. 8vo. cloth. 6*s.* 6*d.*

A French Eton ; or, Middle-Class Education and the State.
> Fcap. 8vo. 2*s.* 6*d.*

Essays in Criticism.
> Extra fcap. 8vo. cloth. 6*s.*

Artist and Craftsman.
> A Novel. Crown 8vo. 6*s.*

BAKER.—*Works by* SIR SAMUEL W. BAKER, M.A. F.R.G.S.

The Nile Tributaries of Abyssinia, and the Sword Hunters of the Hamran Arabs.
> 8vo. 21*s.*

The Albert N'yanza Great Basin of the Nile, and Exploration of the Nile Sources.
> Two Vols. Crown 8vo. 16*s.*

BARWELL —*Guide in the Sick Room.*
> By RICHARD BARWELL, F.R.C.S. Extra fcap. 8vo. 3*s.* 6*d.*

BAYMA.—*Elements of Molecular Mechanics.*
> By JOSEPH BAYMA, S. J. 8vo. cloth. 10*s.* 6*d.*

BEASLEY.—*An Elementary Treatise on Plane Trigonometry*
With a Numerous Collection of Examples.   By R. D. BEASLEY
M.A.   *Second Edition.*   Crown 8vo.   3*s.* 6*d.*

BELL.—*Romances and Minor Poems.*
By HENRY GLASSFORD BELL.   Fcap. 8vo.   6*s.*

BERNARD.—*The Progress of Doctrine in the New Testament.*
In Eight Lectures preached before the University of Oxford.
By THOMAS DEHANY BERNARD, M.A.   *Second Edition.*   8vo.
8*s.* 6*d.*

BIRKS.   *Works by* THOMAS RAWSON BIRKS, M.A.

*The Difficulties of Belief in connexion with the Creation
and the Fall.*
Crown 8vo.   4*s.* 6*d.*

*On Matter and Ether ; or, the Secret Laws of Physical
Change.*
Crown 8vo.   5*s.* 6*d.*

BLAKE.—*The Life of William Blake, the Artist.*
By ALEXANDER GILCHRIST.   With numerous Illustrations from
Blake's Designs and Fac-similes of his Studies of the "Book of
Job."   Two Vols.   Medium 8vo.   32*s.*

BLAKE.—*A Visit to some American Schools and Colleges.*
By SOPHIA JEX BLAKE.   Crown 8vo   6*s.*

Blanche Lisle, and other Poems.
By CECIL HOME.   Fcap. 8vo.   4*s.* 6*d.*

BOOLE.—*Works by the late* GEORGE BOOLE, F.R.S.   *Professor
of Mathematics in the Queen's University, Ireland, &c.*

A Treatise on Differential Equations.
New Edition.   Edited by I. TODHUNTER, M.A. F.R.S.   8vo.
cloth.   14*s.*

Treatise on Differential Equations.
Supplementary Volume.   Crown 8vo.   8*s.* 6*d.*

A Treatise on the Calculus of Finite Differences.
Crown 8vo.   10*s.* 6*d.*

BRADSHAW.—*An Attempt to ascertain the state of Chaucer's Works, as they were Left at his Death,*
With some Notices of their Subsequent History. By HENRY BRADSHAW, of King's College, and the University Library, Cambridge.   [In the Press.

BRIMLEY.—*Essays by the late* GEORGE BRIMLEY, M.A.
Edited by W. G. CLARK, M.A. With Portrait. *Cheaper Edition.* Fcap. 8vo. 3s. 6d.

BROOK SMITH.—*Arithmetic in Theory and Practice.*
For Advanced Pupils. Part First. By J. BROOK SMITH, M.A. Crown 8vo. 3s. 6d.

BRYCE.—*The Holy Roman Empire.*
By JAMES BRYCE, B.C.L. Fellow of Oriel College, Oxford. *A New Edition, revised and enlarged.* Crown 8vo. 9s.

BULLOCK.   *Works by* W. H. BULLOCK.

Polish Experiences during the Insurrection of 1863-4.
Crown 8vo. With Map. 8s. 6d.

Across Mexico in 1864-5.
With Coloured Map and Illustrations. Crown 8vo. 10s. 6d.

BURGON.—*A Treatise on the Pastoral Office.*
Addressed chiefly to Candidates for Holy Orders, or to those who have recently undertaken the cure of souls. By the Rev. JOHN W. BURGON, M.A. 8vo. 12s.

BUTLER (ARCHER).—*Works by the Rev.* WILLIAM ARCHER BUTLER, M.A. *late Professor of Moral Philosophy in the University of Dublin.*

Sermons, Doctrinal and Practical.
Edited with a Memoir of the Author's Life, by THOMAS WOODWARD, M.A. With Portrait. *Seventh Edition.* 8vo. 8s.

A Second Series of Sermons.
Edited by J. A. JEREMIE, D.D. *Fifth Edition.* 8vo. 7s.

History of Ancient Philosophy.
Edited by WM. H. THOMPSON, M.A. Master of Trinity College, Cambridge. Two Vols. 8vo. 1l. 5s.

Letters on Romanism, in reply to Dr. Newman's Essay on Development.
Edited by the Very Rev. T. WOODWARD. *Second Edition,* revised by Archdeacon HARDWICK. 8vo. 10s. 6d.

BUTLER (MONTAGU).—*Sermons preached in the Chapel of Harrow School.*
By H. MONTAGU BUTLER, Head Master. Crown 8vo. 7*s.* 6*d.*

BUTLER (GEORGE). *Works by the Rev.* GEORGE BUTLER.

Family Prayers. ˗
Crown 8vo. 5*s.*

Sermons preached in Cheltenham College Chapel.
Crown 8vo. 7*s.* 6*d.*

CAIRNES.—*The Slave Power; its Character, Career, and Probable Designs.*
Being an Attempt to Explain the Real Issues Involved in the American Contest. By J. E. CAIRNES, M.A. *Second Edition.* 8vo. 10*s.* 6*d.*

CALDERWOOD.—*Philosophy of the Infinite.*
A Treatise on Man's Knowledge of the Infinite Being, in answer to Sir W. Hamilton and Dr. Mansel. By the Rev. HENRY CALDERWOOD, M.A. *Second Edition.* 8vo. 14*s.*

Cambridge Senate-House Problems and Riders, with Solutions.

1848—1851.—*Problems.*
By FERRERS and JACKSON. 15*s.* 6*d.*

1848—1851.—*Riders.*
By JAMESON. 7*s.* 6*d.*

1854.—*Problems and Riders.*
By WALTON and MACKENZIE, M.A. 10*s.* 6*d.*

1857.—*Problems and Riders.*
By CAMPION and WALTON. 8*s.* 6*d.*

1860.—*Problems and Riders.*
By WATSON and ROUTH. 7*s.* 6*d.*

1864.—*Problems and Riders.*
By WALTON and WILKINSON. 8vo. 10*s.* 6*d.*

Cambridge Lent Sermons.—
Sermons preached during Lent, 1864, in Great St. Mary's Church, Cambridge. By the BISHOP of OXFORD, Rev. H. P. LIDDON, T. L. CLAUGHTON, J. R. WOODFORD, Dr. GOULBURN, J. W. BURGON, T. T. CARTER, Dr. PUSEY, DEAN HOOK, W. J. BUTLER, DEAN GOODWIN. Crown 8vo. 7*s.* 6*d.*

Cambridge Course of Elementary Natural Philosophy, for the Degree of B.A.
> Originally compiled by J. C. SNOWBALL, M.A., late Fellow of St. John's College. *Fifth Edition,* revised and enlarged, and adapted for the Middle-Class Examinations by THOMAS LUND, B.D. Crown 8vo. 5*s.*

Cambridge and Dublin Mathematical Journal.
> The Complete Work, in Nine Vols. 8vo. Cloth. 7*l.* 4*s.* Only a few copies remain on hand.

Cambridge Characteristics in the Seventeenth Century.
> By JAMES BASS MULLINGER, B.A. Crown 8vo. 4*s.* 6*d.*

CAMPBELL.   *Works by* JOHN M'LEOD CAMPBELL.
Thoughts on Revelation, with Special Reference to the Present Time.
> Crown 8vo. 5*s.*

The Nature of the Atonement, and its Relation to Remission of Sins and Eternal Life.
> Second Edition revised. 8vo. 10*s.* 6*d.*

Catherines, The Two, or Which is the Heroine?
> A Novel. Two Vols. Crown 8vo. 21*s.*

Catulli Veronensis Liber Recognovit.
> R. ELLIS. 18mo. 3*s.* 6*d.*

CHALLIS.—*Creation in Plan and in Progress:*
> Being an Essay on the First Chapter of Genesis. By the Rev. JAMES CHALLIS, M.A. F.R.S. F.R.A.S. Crown 8vo. 3*s.* 6*d.*

CHATTERTON.—*Leonore; a Tale.*
> By GEORGIANA LADY CHATTERTON. *A New Edition.* Beautifully printed on thick toned paper. Crown 8vo. with Frontispiece and Vignette. Title engraved by JEENS. 7*s.* 6*d.*

CHEYNE.—*An Elementary Treatise on the Planetary Theory.*
> With a Collection of Problems. By C. H. H. CHEYNE, B.A. Crown 8vo. 6*s.* 6*d.*

CHRISTIE (J. R.)—*Elementary Test Questions in Pure and Mixed Mathematics.*
> Crown 8vo. 8*s.* 6*d.*

CICERO.—*The Second Philippic Oration.*
> With an Introduction and Notes, translated from KARL HALM. Edited, with Corrections and Additions, by JOHN E. B. MAYOR, M.A. *Second Edition.* Fcap. 8vo. 5*s.*

CLARK.—*Four Sermons preached in the Chapel of Trinity College, Cambridge.*
By W. G. CLARK, M.A. Fcap. 8vo. 2*s*. 6*d*.

CLAY.—*The Prison Chaplain.*
A Memoir of the Rev. JOHN CLAY, B.D. late Chaplain of the Preston Goal. With Selections from his Reports and Correspondence, and a Sketch of Prison Discipline in England. By his Son, the Rev. W. L. CLAY, M.A. 8vo. 15*s*.

The Power of the Keys.
Sermons preached in Coventry. By the Rev. W. L. CLAY, M.A. Fcap. 8vo. 3*s*. 6*d*.

Clemency Franklyn.
By the Author of "Janet's Home. Crown 8vo. 6*s*.

Clergyman's Self-Examination concerning the Apostles' Creed.
Extra fcap. 8vo. 1*s*. 6*d*.

Clever Woman of the Family.
By the Author of "The Heir of Redclyffe." Crown 8vo. cloth. 6*s*.

CLOUGH.—*The Poems of Arthur Hugh Clough,*
sometime Fellow of Oriel College, Oxford. With a Memoir by by F. T. PALGRAVE. *Second Edition.* Fcap. 8vo. 6*s*.

COLENSO.—*Works by the Right Rev.* J. W. COLENSO, D.D. *Bishop of Natal.*

The Colony of Natal.
A Journal of Visitation. With a Map and Illustrations. Fcap. 8vo. 5*s*.

Village Sermons.
Second Edition. Fcap. 8vo. 2*s*. 6*d*.

Four Sermons on Ordination and on Missions.
18mo. 1*s*.

Companion to the Holy Communion,
Containing the Service and Select Readings from the writings of Mr. MAURICE. *Fine Edition,* morocco, antique style, 6*s*. ; or in cloth, 2*s*. 6*d*. *Common paper,* 1*s*.

St. Paul's Epistle to the Romans.
Newly Translated and Explained from a Missionary point of View. Crown 8vo. 7*s*. 6*d*.

COLENSO.—*Letter to His Grace the Archbishop of Canterbury,*
Upon the Question of Polygamy, as found already existing in
Converts from Heathenism. *Second Edition.* Crown 8vo. 1*s.* 6*d.*

Cookery for English Households.
By a FRENCH LADY. Extra fcap. 8vo. 5*s.*

COOPER.—*Athenae Cantabrigienses.*
By CHARLES HENRY COOPER, F.S.A. and THOMPSON COOPER,
F.S.A. Vol. I. 8vo. 1500—85, 18*s.* Vol. II. 1586—1609, 18*s.*

COPE.—*An Introduction to Aristotle's Rhetoric.*
With Analysis, Notes, and Appendices. By E. M. COPE,
Senior Fellow and Tutor of Trinity College, Cambridge.
8vo. 14*s.*

COTTON.—*Works by the late* GEORGE EDWARD LYNCH
COTTON, D.D. *Bishop of Calcutta.*

*Sermons and Addresses delivered in Marlborough College
during Six Years.*
Crown 8vo. 10*s.* 6*d.*

*A Charge to the Clergy of the Diocese and Province of
Calcutta at the Second Diocesan and First Metropolitan
Visitation.*
8vo. 3*s.* 6*d.*

Sermons, chiefly connected with Public Events of 1854.
Fcap. 8vo. 3*s.*

Sermons preached to English Congregations in India.
Fcap. 8vo. 7*s.* 6*d.*

*Expository Sermons on the Epistles for the Sundays of
the Christian Year.*
Two Vols. Crown 8vo. 15*s.*

CRAIK.—*My First Journal.*
A Book for the Young. By GEORGIANA M. CRAIK, Author of
"Riverston," "Lost and Won," &c. Royal 16mo. Cloth, gilt
leaves, 3*s.* 6*d.*

DALTON.—*Arithmetical Examples progressively arranged;
together with Miscellaneous Exercises and Examination
Papers.*
By the Rev. T. DALTON, M.A. Assistant Master at Eton
College. 18mo. 2*s.* 6*d.*

Dante.—*Dante's Comedy, The Hell.*
Translated by W. M. Rosetti. Fcap. 8vo. cloth. **5s.**

Davies.—*Works by the Rev. J. Llewelyn Davies, M.A. Rector of Christ Church, St. Marylebone, &c.*

Sermons on the Manifestation of the Son of God.
With a Preface addressed to Laymen on the present position of the Clergy of the Church of England : and an Appendix, on the Testimony of Scripture and the Church as to the Possibility of Pardon in the Future State. Fcap. 8vo. **6s. 6d.**

The Work of Christ ; or, the World Reconciled to God.
With a Preface on the Atonement Controversy. Fcap. 8vo. **6s.**

Baptism, Confirmation and the Lord's Supper.
As interpreted by their outward signs. Three Expository Addresses for Parochial Use. Limp cloth. **1s. 6d.**

Morality according to the Sacrament of the Lord's Supper.
Crown 8vo. **3s. 6d.**

The Epistles of St. Paul to the Ephesians, the Colossians, and Philemon.
With Introductions and Notes, and an Essay on the Traces of Foreign Elements in the Theology of these Epistles. 8vo. **7s. 6d.**

Days of Old ; Stories from Old English History.
By the Author of "Ruth and her Friends." *New Edition*, 18mo. cloth, gilt leaves. **3s. 6d.**

Demosthenes, De Corona.
The Greek Text with English Notes. By B. Drake, M.A. *Third Edition*, to which is prefixed Æschines against Ctesiphon, with English Notes. Fcap 8vo. **5s.**

De Teissier. *Works by G. F. De Teissier, B.D.*

Village Sermons.
Crown 8vo. **9s.**

Second Series.
Crown 8vo. cloth, **8s. 6d.**

The House of Prayer ; or, a Practical Exposition of the Order for Morning and Evening Prayer in the Church of England.
18mo. extra cloth. **4s. 6d.**

DE VERE.—*The Infant Bridal, and other Poems.*
By AUBREY DE VERE. Fcap. 8vo. 7s. 6d.

DICEY.—*A Month in Russia during the Marriage of the Czarevitch.*
By EDWARD DICEY. 8vo. 10s. 6d.

DONALDSON.—*A Critical History of Christian Literature and Doctrine, from the Death of the Apostles to the Nicene Council.*
By JAMES DONALDSON, LL.D. Three Vols. 8vo. cloth. 31s.

DOYLE.—*The Return of the Guards, and other Poems.*
By Sir FRANCIS HASTINGS DOYLE, Professor of Poetry in the University of Oxford. Fcap. 8vo. 7s.

DREW. *Works by* W. H. DREW, M.A.

A Geometrical Treatise on Conic Sections.
Third Edition. Crown 8vo. 4s. 6d.

Solutions to Problems contained in Mr. Drew's Treatise on Conic Sections.
Crown 8vo. 4s. 6d.

Early Egyptian History for the Young.
With Descriptions of the Tombs and Monuments. *New Edition,* with Frontispiece. Fcap. 8vo. 5s.

East India Association Journal.
2s. 6d.

EASTWOOD.—*The Bible Word Book.*
A Glossary of Old English Bible Words. By J. EASTWOOD, M.A. of St. John's College, and W. ALDIS WRIGHT, M.A. Trinity College, Cambridge. 18mo. 5s. 6d. Uniform with Macmillan's School Class Books.

Ecce Homo.
A Survey of the Life and Work of Jesus Christ. Crown 8vo. 6s.

Echoes of Many Voices from Many Lands.
By A. F. 18mo. cloth, extra gilt. 3s. 6d.

ELLICE.—*English Idylls.*
By JANE ELLICE. Fcap. 8vo. cloth. 6s.

Essays on a Liberal Education.
By Various Writers. Edited by the Rev. F. W. FARRAR, M.A. F.R.S. &c. [In the Press.

EVANS.—*Brother Fabian's Manuscript, and other Poems.*
By SEBASTIAN EVANS. Fcap. 8vo. cloth. 6s.

FAWCETT.　　　*Works by* HENRY FAWCETT. M.P.
The Economic Position of the British Labourer.
Extra fcap. 8vo. cloth. 5s.

Manual of Political Economy.
Second Edition. Crown 8vo. 12s.

FERRERS.—*A Treatise on Trilinear Co-ordinates, the Method of Reciprocal Polars, and the Theory of Projections.*
By the Rev. N. M. FERRERS, M.A. *Second Edition.* Crown 8vo. 6s. 6d.

FLETCHER.—*Thoughts from a Girl's Life.*
By LUCY FLETCHER. *Second Edition.* Fcap. 8vo. 4s. 6d.

FORBES.—*Life of Edward Forbes, F.R.S.*
By GEORGE WILSON, M.D. F.R.S.E., and ARCHIBALD GEIKIE, F.R.S. 8vo. with Portrait. 14s.

FORBES.—*The Voice of God in the Psalms.*
By GRANVILLE FORBES, Rector of Broughton. Crown 8vo. 6s. 6d.

FOX.—*On the Diagnosis and Treatment of the Varieties of Dyspepsia, considered in Relation to the Pathological Origin of the different Forms of Indigestion.*
By WILSON FOX, M.D. Lond. F.R.C.P. Professor of Pathological Anatomy at University College, London, and Physician to University College Hospital. Demy 8vo. cloth. 7s. 6d.

FREELAND.—*The Fountain of Youth.*
Translated from the Danish of Frederick Paludan Müller. By HUMPHREY WILLIAM FREELAND, late M.P. for Chichester. With Illustrations designed by Walter Allen. Crown 8vo. 6s.

FREEMAN.—*History of Federal Government from the Foundation of the Achaian League to the Disruption of the United States.*
By EDWARD A. FREEMAN, M.A. Vol. I. General Introduction. —History of the Greek Federations. 8vo. 21s.

FROST.—*The First Three Sections of Newton's Principia.*
With Notes and Problems in Illustration of the Subject. By PERCIVAL FROST, M.A. *Second Edition.* 8vo. 10s. 6d.

FROST AND WOLSTENHOLME.—*A Treatise on Solid Geometry.*
By the Rev. PERCIVAL FROST, M.A. and the Rev. J. WOLSTENHOLME, M.A. 8vo. 18s.

FURNIVALL.—*Le Morte Arthur.*
> Edited fiom the Harleian M.S. 2252, in the British Museum. By F. J. FURNIVALL, M.A. With Essay by the late HERBERT COLERIDGE. Fcap. 8vo. cloth. 7s. 6d.

GALTON.—*Meteorographica, or Methods of Mapping the Weather.*
> Illustrated by upwards of 600 Printed Lithographed Diagrams. By FRANCIS GALTON, F.R.S. 4to. 9s.

GEIKIE.—*Works by* ARCHIBALD GEIKIE, F.R.S. *Director of the Geological Survey of Scotland.*

Story of a Boulder; or, Gleanings by a Field Geologist.
> Illustrated with Woodcuts. Crown 8vo. 5s.

Scenery of Scotland, viewed in connexion with its Physical Geology.
> With Illustrations and a New Geological Map. Crown 8vo. cloth, 10s. 6d.

Elementary Lessons in Physical Geology.
> [Preparing.

GIFFORD.—*The Glory of God in Man.*
> By E. H. GIFFORD, D.D. Fcap. 8vo. cloth. 3s. 6d.

Globe Editions :

The Complete Works of William Shakespeare.
> Edited by W. G. CLARK and W. ALDIS WRIGHT. Eighty-first Thousand. Royal fcap. 3s. 6d. ; paper covers, 2s. 6d.

The Poetical Works of Sir Walter Scott.
> With Biographical and Critical Memoir by FRANCIS TURNER PALGRAVE, and New Introductions to the larger Poems. Royal fcap. 3s. 6d.

The Poetical Works of John Milton.
> Edited, with Introduction and Notes, by Professor MASSON.
> [In the Press.

The Poetical Works and Letters of Robert Burns.
> Edited, with Life, by ALEXANDER SMITH.   [In the Press.

The Adventures of Robinson Crusoe.
> Edited, with Introduction, by HENRY KINGSLEY.
> [In the Press.

Globe Atlas of Europe.
> Uniform in Size with MACMILLAN'S GLOBE SERIES. Containing Forty-Eight Coloured Maps, Plans of London and Paris, and a Copious Index. Strongly bound in half morocco, with flexible back, 9s.

GODFRAY.—*An Elementary Treatise on the Lunar Theory.*
With a brief Sketch of the Problem up to he time of Newton.
By HUGH GODFRAY, M.A. *Second Edition revised.* Crown 8vo.
5*s.* 6*d.*

*A Treatise on Astronomy, for the Use of Colleges and
Schools.*
By HUGH GODFRAY, M.A. 8vo. 12*s.* 6*d.*

Golden Treasury Series :
Uniformly printed in 18mo. with Vignette Titles by Sir NOEL
PATON, T. WOOLNER, W. HOLMAN HUNT J. E. MILLAIS, &c.
Engraved on Steel by JEENS. Bound in extra cloth, 4*s.* 6*d.* ;
morocco plain, 7*s.* 6*d.* ; morocco extra, 10*s.* 6*d.* each volume.

*The Golden Treasury of the Best Songs and Lyrical
Poems in the English Language.*
Selected and arranged, with Notes, by FRANCIS TURNER PAL-
GRAVE.

The Children's Garland from the Best Poets.
Selected and arranged by COVENTRY PATMORE.

The Book of Praise.
From the Best English Hymn Writers. Selected and arranged
by Sir ROUNDELL PALMER. *A New and Enlarged Edition.*

The Fairy Book: the Best Popular Fairy Stories.
Selected and rendered anew by the Author of "John Halifax,
Gentleman."

The Ballad Book.
A Selection of the choicest British Ballads. Edited by WILLIAM
ALLINGHAM.

The Jest Book.
The choicest Anecdotes and Sayings. Selected and arranged by
MARK LEMON.

Bacon's Essays and Colours of Good and Evil.
With Notes and Glossarial Index, by W. ALDIS WRIGHT, M.A.
Large paper copies, crown 8vo. 7*s.* 6*d.* ; or bound in half
morocco, 10*s.* 6*d.*

The Pilgrim's Progress
From this World to that which is to Come. By JOHN BUNYAN.
* * Large p per copies, crown 8vo. cloth, 7*s.* 6*d.*; or bound in
half morocco, 10*s.* 6*d.*

The Sunday Book of Poetry for the Young.
Selected and arranged by C. F. ALEXANDER.

Golden Treasury Series—continued.

A Book of Golden Deeds of all Times and all Countries.
Gathered and Narrated anew by the Author of "The Heir of Redclyffe."

The Poetical Works of Robert Burns.
Edited, with Biographical Memoir, by ALEXANDER SMITH. Two Vols.

The Adventures of Robinson Crusoe.
Edited from the Original Editions by J. W. CLARK, M.A.

The Republic of Plato.
Translated into English with Notes by J. LL. DAVIES, M.A. and D. J. VAUGHAN, M.A. New Edition, with Vignette Portraits of Plato and Socrates engraved by JEENS from an Antique Gem.

The Song Book.
Words and Tunes from the best Poets and Musicians, selected and arranged by JOHN HULLAH. With Vignette by CAROLINE E. HULLAH, engraved by JEENS.

La Lyre Francaise.
Selected and arranged, with Notes, by GUSTAVE MASSON. With Vignette of BERANGER, engraved by JEENS.

Milton.
Edited by DAVID MASSON.　　　　　　　　　[In the Press.

Cowper.　　　　　　　　　　　　　　　　　[In the Press.

Book of Worthies.
By the Author of "The Heir of Redclyffe."　　[In the Press.

Religio Medici.
By SIR T. BROWNE.　　　　　　　　　　　[In the Press.

GORDON.—*Letters from Egypt, 1863—5.*
By LADY DUFF GORDON. *Third Edition.* Crown 8vo. cloth. 8s. 6d.

GORST.—*The Maori King;*
Or, the Story of our Quarrel with the Natives of New Zealand. By J. E. GORST, M.A. With a Portrait of William Thompson, and a Map of the Seat of War. Crown 8vo. 10s. 6d.

GREEN.—*Spiritual Philosophy.*
Founded on the Teaching of the late SAMUEL TAYLOR COLERIDGE. By the late JOSEPH HENRY GREEN, F.R.S. D.C.L. Edited, with a Memoir of the Author's Life, by JOHN SIMON, F.R.S. Two Vols. 8vo. cloth. 25s.

Guesses at Truth.
>By Two BROTHERS. With Vignette Title and Frontispiece. *New Edition.* Fcap. 6s.

GUIZOT, M.—*Memoir of M. de Barante.*
>Translated by the Author of "John Halifax, Gentleman." Crown 8vo. 6s. 6d.

Guide to the Unprotected
>In Every Day Matters relating to Property and Income. By a BANKER'S DAUGHTER. *Second Edition.* Extra fcap. 8vo. 3s. 6d.

HAMERTON.—*A Painter's Camp in the Highlands;*
>And Thoughts about Art. By P. G. HAMERTON. Two Vols. Crown 8vo. 21s. *New and Cheaper Edition,* one vol. 6s.

HAMILTON.—*On Truth and Error.*
>Thoughts on the Principles of Truth, and the Causes and Effect of Error. By JOHN HAMILTON. Crown 8vo. 5s.

HARDWICK.—*Works by the Ven.* ARCHDEACON HARDWICK.

Christ and other Masters.
>A Historical Inquiry into some of the Chief Parallelisms and Contrasts between Christianity and the Religious Systems of the Ancient World. *New Edition,* revised, and a Prefatory Memoir by the Rev. FRANCIS PROCTER. Two Vols. crown 8vo. 15s.

A History of the Christian Church.
>Middle Age. From Gregory the Great to the Excommunication of Luther. Edited by FRANCIS PROCTER, M.A. With Four Maps constructed for this work by A. KEITH JOHNSTON. *Second Edition.* Crown 8vo. 10s. 6d.

A History of the Christian Church during the Reformation.
>Revised by FRANCIS PROCTER, M.A. *Second Edition.* Crown 8vo. 10s. 6d.

Twenty Sermons for Town Congregations.
>Crown 8vo. 6s. 6d.

HEARN.—*Plutology ;*
>Or, the Theory of the Efforts to Satisfy Human Wants. By W. E. HEARN, LL.D. 8vo. 14s.

HEMMING.—*An Elementary Treatise on the Differential and Integral Calculus.*
>By G. W. HEMMING, M.A. *Second Edition.* 8vo. 9s.

HERSCHEL.—*The Iliad of Homer.*
>Translated into English Hexameters. By Sir JOHN HERSCHEL, Bart. 8vo. 18s.

HERVEY.—*The Genealogies of our Lord and Saviour Jesus Christ,*
As contained in the Gospels of St. Matthew and St. Luke, reconciled with each other, and shown to be in harmony with the true Chronology of the Times. By Lord ARTHUR HERVEY, M.A. 8vo. 10*s.* 6*d.*

HERVEY (ROSAMOND). *Works by* ROSAMOND HERVEY.

The Aarbergs.
Two Vols. crown 8vo. cloth. 21*s.*

Duke Ernest,
A Tragedy ; and other Poems. Fcap. 8vo. 6*s.*

HISTORICUS.—*Letters on some Questions of International Law.*
Reprinted from the *Times,* with considerable Additions. 8vo. 7*s.* 6*d.* Also, ADDITIONAL LETTERS. 8vo. 2*s.* 6*d.*

HODGSON.—*Mythology for Latin Versification.*
A Brief Sketch of the Fables of the Ancients. prepared to be rendered into Latin Verse for Schools. By F. HODGSON, B.D. late Provost of Eton. *New Edition,* revised by F. C. HODGSON, M.A. 18mo. 3*s.*

HOLE.—*Works by* CHARLES HOLE, M.A. *Trinity College, Cambridge.*

A Brief Biographical Dictionary.
Compiled and arranged by CHARLES HOLE, M.A. Trinity College, Cambridge. In Pott 8vo. (same size as the "Golden Treasury Series,") neatly and strongly bound in cloth. *Second Edition.* 4*s.* 6*d.*

Genealogical Stemma of the Kings of England and France.
In One Sheet.

HORNER.—*The Tuscan Poet Guiseppe Giusti and his Times.*
By SUSAN HORNER. Crown 8vo. 7*s.* 6*d.*

HOWARD.—*The Pentateuch ;*
Or, the Five Books of Moses. Translated into English from the Version of the LXX. With Notes on its Omissions and Insertions, and also on the Passages in which it differs from the Authorized Version. By the Hon. HENRY HOWARD, D.D. Crown 8vo. GENESIS, One Volume, 8*s.* 6*d.* ; EXODUS AND LEVITICUS, One Volume, 10*s.* 6*d.* ; NUMBERS AND DEUTERONOMY, One Volume, 10*s.* 6*d.*

HOZIER.—*The Seven Weeks' War ;*
Its Antecedents, and its Incidents. By H. M. HOZIER. With Maps and Plans. Two Vols. 8vo. 28*s.*

HUMPHRY.—*Works by* GEORGE MURRAY HUMPHRY, M.D.
F.R.S.

The Human Skeleton (including the Joints).
With Two Hundred and Sixty Illustrations drawn from Nature.
Medium 8vo. 1*l.* 8*s.*

The Human Hand and the Human Foot.
With numerous Illustrations. Fcap. 8vo. 4*s.* 6*d.*

HUXLEY.—*Lessons in Elementary Physiology.*
With numerous Illustrations. By T. H. HUXLEY, F.R.S. Pro-
fessor of Natural History in the Government School of Mines.
Uniform with Macmillans' School Class Books. 18mo. **4*s.* 6*d.***

Hymni Ecclesiæ.
Fcap. 8vo. cloth. 7*s.* 6*d.*

JAMESON. *Works by the Rev.* F. J. JAMESON, M.A.

Life's Work, in Preparation and in Retrospect.
Sermons preached before the University of Cambridge. Fcap.
8vo. 1*s.* 6*d.*

Brotherly Counsels to Students.
Sermons preached in the Chapel of St. Catharine's College,
Cambridge. Fcap. 8vo. 1*s.* 6*d.*

Janet's Home.
A Novel. *New Edition.* Crown 8vo. 6*s.*

JEVONS.—*The Coal Question.*
By W. STANLEY JEVONS, M.A. Fellow of University College,
London. *Second Edition, revised.* 8vo. 10*s.* 6*d.*

JONES.—*The Church of England and Common Sense.*
By HARRY JONES, M.A. Fcap. 8vo. cloth. 3*s.* 6*d.*

Journal of Anatomy and Physiology.
Conducted by Professors HUMPHRY and NEWTON, and Mr.
CLARK of Cambridge ; Professor TURNER, of Edinburgh ; and
Dr. WRIGHT, of Dublin. Published twice a year. Price to
subscribers, 14*s.* per annum. Price 7*s.* 6*d.* each Part. Vol. 1.
containing Parts I. and II. Royal 8vo. 16*s.*

JUVENAL.—*Juvenal, for Schools.*
With English Notes. By J. E. B. MAYOR, M.A. *New and
Cheaper Edition.* Crown 8vo. [In the Press.

KEARY.—*The Little Wanderlin,*
> And other Fairy Tales. By A. and E. KEARY. 18mo. cloth.
> 3s. 6d.

KENNEDY.—*Legendary Fictions of the Irish Celts.*
> Collected and Narrated by PATRICK KENNEDY. Crown 8vo.
> 7s. 6d.

KINGSLEY.—*Works by the Rev.* CHARLES KINGSLEY, *M.A. Rector of Eversley, and Professor of Modern History in the University of Cambridge.*

The Roman and the Teuton.
> A Series of Lectures delivered before the University of Cambridge. 8vo. 12s.

Two Years Ago.
> *Fourth Edition.* Crown 8vo. 6s.

" Westward Ho ! "
> *Fifth Edition.* Crown 8vo. 6s.

Alton Locke.
> *New Edition.* With a New Preface. Crown 8vo. 4s. 6d.

Hypatia.
> *Fourth Edition.* Crown 8vo. 6s.

Yeast.
> *Fourth Edition.* Fcap. 8vo. 5s.

Hereward the Wake—Last of the English.
> Crown 8vo. 6s.

Miscellanies.
> *Second Edition.* Two Vols. crown 8vo. 12s.

The Saint's Tragedy.
> *Third Edition.* Fcap. 8vo. 5s.

Andromeda,
> And other Poems. *Third Edition.* Fcap. 8vo. 5s.

The Water Babies.
> A Fairy Tale for a Land Baby. With Two Illustrations by Sir NOEL PATON, R.S.A. *Third Edition.* Crown 8vo. 6s.

Glaucus :
> Or, the Wonders of the Shore. *New and Illustrated Edition,* containing beautifully Coloured Illustrations. 5s.

KINGSLEY (*Rev.* CHARLES).—*The Heroes;*
Or, Greek Fairy Tales for my Children. With Eight Illustrations. *New Edition.* 18mo. 3*s.* 6*d.*

Three Lectures delivered at the Royal Institution on the Ancien Regime.
Crown 8vo. 6*s.*

The Water of Life,
And other Sermons. Fcap. 8vo. 6*s.*

Village Sermons.
Seventh Edition. Fcap. 8vo. 2*s.* 6*d.*

The Gospel of the Pentateuch.
Second Edition. Fcap. 8vo. 4*s.* 6*d.*

Good News of God.
Fourth Edition. Fcap. 8vo. 4*s.* 6*d.*

Sermons for the Times.
Third Edition. Fcap. 8vo. 3*s.* 6*d.*

Town and Country Sermons.
Fcap. 8vo. 6*s.*

Sermons on National Subjects.
First Series. *Second Edition.* Fcap. 8vo. 5*s.*

Sermons on National Subjects.
Second Series. *Second Edition.* Fcap. 8vo. 5*s.*

Discipline
And other Sermons. Fcap. 8vo. 6*s.*   [In the Press.

Alexandria and her Schools.
With a Preface. Crown 8vo. 5*s.*

The Limits of Exact Science as applied to History.
An Inaugural Lecture delivered before the University of Cambridge. Crown 8vo. 2*s.*

Phaethon; or, Loose Thoughts for Loose Thinkers.
Third Edition. Crown 8vo. 2*s.*

David.
Four Sermons: David's Weakness—David's Strength—David's Anger—David's Deserts. Fcap. 8vo. cloth. 2*s.* 6*d.*

KINGSLEY.   *Works by* HENRY KINGSLEY.

Silcote of Silcotes.
Three Vols. Crown 8vo. 31s. 6d.

Austin Elliot.
New Edition. Crown 8vo. 6s.

The Recollections of Geoffrey Hamlyn.
Second Edition. Crown 8vo. 6s.

The Hillyars and the Burtons: A Story of Two Families.
Crown 8vo. 6s.

Ravenshoe.
New Edition. Crown 8vo. 6s.

Leighton Court.
New Edition. Crown 8vo. 6s.

KIRCHHOFF.—*Researches on the Solar Spectrum and the Spectra of the Chemical Elements.*
By G. KIRCHHOFF, of Heidelberg. Translated by HENRY E. ROSCOE, B.A. Second Part. 4to. 5s. with 2 Plates.

LANCASTER.—*Works by* WILLIAM LANCASTER.
Præterita.
Poems. Extra fcap. 8vo. 4s. 6d.

Studies in Verse.
Extra fcap. 8vo. cloth, 4s. 6d.

Eclogues and Mono-dramas; or, a Collection of Verses.
Extra fcap. 8vo. 4s. 6d.

LATHAM.—*The Construction of Wrought-iron Bridges.*
Embracing the Practical Application of the Principles of Mechanics to Wrought-Iron Girder Work. By J. H. LATHAM, ESQ. Civil Engineer. 8vo. With numerous detail Plates. *Second Edition.*   [Preparing.

LAW.—*The Alps of Hannibal.*
By WILLIAM JOHN LAW, M.A. Two Vols. 8vo. 21s.

Lectures to Ladies on Practical Subjects.
Third Edition, revised. Crown 8vo. 7s. 6d.

LEMON.—*Legends of Number Nip.*
By MARK LEMON. With Six Illustrations by CHARLES KEENE. Extra fcap. 8vo. 5s.

LIGHTFOOT. *Works by* J. B. LIGHTFOOT, D.D.
St. Paul's Epistle to the Galatians.
A Revised Text, with Notes and Dissertations. *Second Edition, revised.* 8vo. cloth. 10*s.* 6*d.*

St. Paul's Epistle to the Philippians.
A Revised Text, with Notes and Dissertations. [In the Press.

Little Estella.
And other Fairy Tales for the Young. Royal 16mo. 3*s.* 6*d.*

LOCKYER.—*Class-Book of Astronomy.*
By J. NORMAN LOCKYER. [In the Press.

LOWELL.—*Fireside Travels.*
By JAMES RUSSELL LOWELL, Author of "The Biglow Papers." Fcap. 8vo. 4*s.* 6*d.*

LUDLOW.—*Popular Epics of the Middle Ages, of the Norse-German and Carlovingian Cycles.*
By JOHN MALCOLM LUDLOW. Two Volumes. Fcap. 8vo. cloth. 14*s.*

LUDLOW and HUGHES.—*A Sketch of the History of the United States from Independence to Secession.*
By J. M. LUDLOW, Author of "British India, its Races and its History," "The Policy of the Crown towards India," &c.
To which is added, "The Struggle for Kansas." By THOMAS HUGHES, Author of "Tom Brown's School Days," "Tom Brown at Oxford," &c. Crown 8vo. 8*s.* 6*d.*

LUSHINGTON.—*The Italian War,* 1848-9, *and the Last Italian Poet.*
By the late HENRY LUSHINGTON. With a Biographical Preface by G. S. VENABLES. Crown 8vo. 6*s.* 6*d.*

LYTTELTON.—*The Comus of Milton rendered into Greek Verse.*
By LORD LYTTELTON. Extra fcap. 8vo. *Second Edition.* 5*s.*

MACKENZIE.—*The Christian Clergy of the First Ten Centuries, and their Influence on European Civilization.*
By HENRY MACKENZIE, B.A. Scholar of Trinity College, Cambridge. Crown 8vo. 6*s.* 6*d.*

MACLAREN.—*Sermons preached at Manchester.*
By ALEXANDER MACLAREN. *Second Edition.* Fcap. 8vo.
4s. 6d. A Second Series in the Press.

MACLAREN.—*On Training.*
By A. MACLAREN, Oxford. With Frontispiece, and other Illustrations. 8vo. Handsomely bound in cloth. 7s. 6d.

MACLEAR.—*Works by* G. F. MACLEAR, B.D. *Head Master of King's College School, and Preacher at the Temple Church :*—

A History of Christian Missions during the Middle Ages.
Crown 8vo. 10s. 6d.

The Witness of the Eucharist ; or, The Institution and Early Celebration of the Lord's Supper, considered as an Evidence of the Historical Truth of the Gospel Narrative and of the Atonement.
Crown 8vo. 4s. 6d.

A Class-Book of Old Testament History.
With Four Maps. *Third Edition.* 18mo. cloth. 4s. 6d.

A Class-Book of New Testament History.
Including the connexion of the Old and New Testament. 18mo. cloth. 5s. 6d.

A Shilling Book of Old Testament History.
18mo. cloth. 1s.

A Shilling Book of New Testament History.
18mo. cloth. 1s.

Church Catechism.   [In the Press.

MACMILLAN.—*Works by the Rev.* HUGH MACMILLAN.
Bible Teachings in Nature.
Crown 8vo. 6s!

Foot-notes from the Page of Nature.
With numerous Illustrations. Fcap. 8vo. 5s.

Macmillan's Magazine.
Published Monthly, price One Shilling. Volumes I.—XVI. are now ready, 7s. 6d. each.

McCosh.—*Works by* JAMES McCosh, LL.D. *Professor of Logic and Metaphysics, Queen's College, Belfast, &c.*

The Method of the Divine Government, Physical and Moral.
Eighth Edition. 8vo. 10s. 6d.

The Supernatural in Relation to the Natural.
Crown 8vo. 7s. 6d.

The Intuitions of the Mind.
A New Edition. 8vo. cloth. 10s. 6d.

An Examination of Mr. J. S. Mill's Philosophy.
Being a Defence of Fundamental Truth. Crown 8vo. 7s. 6d.

Mansfield. *Works by* CHARLES BLANCHFORD MANSFIELD, M.A.

Paraguay, Brazil, and the Plate.
With a Map, and numerous Woodcuts. With a Sketch of his Life, by the Rev. CHARLES KINGSLEY. Crown 8vo. 12s. 6d.

A Theory of Salts.
A Treatise on the Constitution of Bipolar (two membered) Chemical Compounds. Crown 8vo. cloth. 14s.

Marriner.—*Sermons preached at Lyme Regis.*
By E. T. MARRINER, Curate. Fcap. 8vo. 4s. 6d.

Marshall.—*A Table of Irregular Greek Verbs.*
8vo. 1s.

Marston.—*A Lady in her Own Right.*
By WESTLAND MARSTON. Crown 8vo. 6s.

Martin. *Works by* FREDERICK MARTIN.

The Statesman's Year Book for 1867. (*Fourth Annual Publication.*)
A Statistical, Genealogical, and Historical Account of the Civilized World for the Year 1867. Crown 8vo. 10s. 6d.

Stories of Banks and Bankers.
Fcap. 8vo. cloth. 3s. 6d.

Masson.—*Works by* DAVID MASSON, M.A. *Professor of Rhetoric and English Literature in the University of Edinburgh.*

Essays, Biographical and Critical.
Chiefly on the English Poets. 8vo. 12s. 6d.

MASSON.—*British Novelists and their Styles.*
Being a Critical Sketch of the History of British Prose Fiction.
Crown 8vo. 7s. 6d.

Life of John Milton.
Narrated in connexion with the Political, Ecclesiastical, and
Literary History of his Time. Vol. I. with Portraits. 8vo. 18s.

Recent British Philosophy.
A Review, with Criticisms, including some Comments on Mr.
Mill's Answer to Sir William Hamilton. *New and Cheaper
Edition.* Crown 8vo. 6s.

MAUDSLEY.—*The Physiology and Pathology of the Mind.*
By HENRY MAUDSLEY, M.D. 8vo. 16s.

MAURICE.—*Works by the Rev.* FREDERICK DENISON
MAURICE, M.A. *Professor of Moral Philosophy in the
University of Cambridge.*

The Claims of the Bible and of Science.
A Correspondence on some questions respecting the Pentateuch.
Crown 8vo. 4s. 6d.

Dialogues on Family Worship.
Crown 8vo. 6s.

The Patriarchs and Lawgivers of the Old Testament.
Third Edition. Crown 8vo. 5s.
This volume contains Discourses on the Pentateuch, Joshua,
Judges, and the beginning of the First Book of Samuel.

The Prophets and Kings of the Old Testament.
Second Edition. Crown 8vo. 10s. 6d.
This volume contains Discourses on Samuel I. and II.; Kings I.
and II.; Amos, Joel, Hosea, Isaiah, Micah, Nahum, Habakkuk,
Jeremiah, and Ezekiel.

The Gospel of the Kingdom of Heaven.
A Series of Lectures on the Gospel of St. Luke. Crown 8vo. 9s.

The Gospel of St. John.
A Series of Discourses. *Third Edition.* Crown 8vo. 6s.

The Epistles of St. John.
A Series of Lectures on Christian Ethics. *Second Edition.*
Crown 8vo. 6s.

MAURICE.—*The Commandments considered as Instruments of National Reformation.*
Crown 8vo. 4s. 6d.

Expository Sermons on the Prayer-book.

The Prayer-book considered especially in reference to the Romish System.
Second Edition. Fcap. 8vo. 5s. 6d.

Lectures on the Apocalypse,
Or Book of the Revelation of St. John the Divine. Crown 8vo. 10s. 6d.

What is Revelation?
A Series of Sermons on the Epiphany; to which are added Letters to a Theological Student on the Bampton Lectures of Mr. MANSEL. Crown 8vo. 10s. 6d.

Sequel to the Inquiry, " What is Revelation? "
Letters in Reply to Mr. Mansel's Examination of "Strictures on the Bampton Lectures." Crown 8vo. 6s.

Lectures on Ecclesiastical History.
8vo. 10s. 6d.

Theological Essays.
Second Edition. Crown 8vo. 10s. 6d.

The Doctrine of Sacrifice deduced from the Scriptures.
Crown 8vo. 7s. 6d.

The Religions of the World,
And their Relations to Christianity. *Fourth Edition.* Fcap. 8vo. 5s.

On the Lord's Prayer.
Fourth Edition. Fcap. 8vo. 2s. 6d.

On the Sabbath Day;
The Character of the Warrior; and on the Interpretation of History. Fcap. 8vo. 2s. 6d.

Learning and Working.
Six Lectures on the Foundation of Colleges for Working Men. Crown 8vo. 5s.

MAURICE.—*Law's Remarks on the Fable of the Bees.*
With an Introduction by F. D. MAURICE, M.A. Fcap. 8vo.
4*s*. 6*d*.

MAYOR.—*Autobiography of Matthew Robinson.*
By JOHN E. B. MAYOR, M.A. Fcap. 8vo. 5*s*. 6*d*.

MERIVALE.—*Sallust for Schools.*
By C. MERIVALE, B.D. *Second Edition.* Fcap. 8vo. 4*s*. 6*d*.

    *** The Jugurtha and the Catalina may be had separately, price
2*s*. 6*d*. each.

    Keats' Hyperion rendered into Latin Verse.
By C. MERIVALE, B.D. *Second Edition.* Extra fcap. 8vo.
3*s*. 6*d*.

Moor Cottage.
A Tale of Home Life. By the Author of "Little Estella."
Crown 8vo. 6*s*.

MOORHOUSE.—*Some Modern Difficulties respecting the Facts
of Nature and Revelation.*
By JAMES MOORHOUSE, M.A. Fcap. 8vo. 2*s*. 6*d*.

MORGAN.—*A Collection of Mathematical Problems and
Examples.*
By H. A. MORGAN, M.A. Crown 8vo. 6*s*. 6*d*.

MORLEY, JOHN.—*Edmund Burke—a Historical Sketch.*
[In the Press.

MORSE.—*Working for God,*
And other Practical Sermons. By FRANCIS MORSE, M.A.
Second Edition. Fcap. 8vo. 5*s*.

NAVILLE.—*The Heavenly Father.*
By ERNEST NAVILLE. Translated by HENRY DOWNTON, M.A.
Extra fcap. 8vo. 7*s*. 6*d*.

NOEL.—*Behind the Veil,*
And other Poems. By the Hon. RODEN NOEL. Fcap. 8vo. 7*s*.

Northern Circuit.
Brief Notes of Travel in Sweden, Finland, and Russia. With a
Frontispiece. Crown 8vo. 5*s*.

NORTON.—*The Lady of La Garaye.*
By the Hon. Mrs. NORTON. With Vignette and Frontispiece.
New Edition. 4*s*. 6*d*.

O'BRIEN.—*Works by* JAMES THOMAS O'BRIEN, D.D. *Bishop of Ossory.*

An Attempt to Explain and Establish the Doctrine of Justification by Faith only.
Third Edition. 8vo. 12s.

Charge delivered at the Visitation in 1863.
Second Edition. 8vo. 2s.

OLIPHANT.—*Agnes Hopetoun's Schools and Holidays.*
By Mrs. OLIPHANT. Royal 16mo. cloth, gilt leaves. 3s. 6d.

OLIVER.—*Lessons in Elementary Botany.*
With nearly 200 Illustrations. By DANIEL OLIVER, F.R.S. F.L.S. 18mo. 4s. 6d.

OPPEN.—*French Reader,*
For the Use of Colleges and Schools. By EDWARD A. OPPEN. Fcap. 8vo. cloth. 4s. 6d.

ORWELL.—*The Bishop's Walk and the Bishop's Times.*
Poems on the Days of Archbishop Leighton and the Scottish Covenant. By ORWELL. Fcap. 8vo. 5s.

Our Year.
A Child's Book, in Prose and Verse. By the Author of "John Halifax, Gentleman." Illustrated by CLARENCE DOBELL. Royal 16mo. cloth. 3s. 6d.

PALGRAVE.—*History of Normandy and of England.*
By Sir FRANCIS PALGRAVE. Completing the History to the Death of William Rufus. Vols. I. to IV. 8vo. each 21s.

PALGRAVE.—*A Narrative of a Year's Journey through Central and Eastern Arabia, 1862-3.*
By WILLIAM GIFFORD PALGRAVE (late of the Eighth Regiment Bombay N.I.). *Third Edition.* Two Vols. 8vo. cloth. 28s.

PALGRAVE.—*Works by* FRANCIS TURNER PALGRAVE, M.A. *late Fellow of Exeter College, Oxford.*

Essays on Art.
Mulready—Dyce—Holman Hunt—Herbert—Poetry, Prose, and Sensationalism in Art—Sculpture in England—The Albert Cross, &c. Extra fcap. 8vo. 6s. (Uniform with "Arnold's Essays.")

PALGRAVE (F.T.).—*Sonnets and Songs.*
By WILLIAM SHAKESPEARE. GEM EDITION. With Vignette Title by JEENS. 3s. 6d.

Original Hymns.
1s.

PALMER.—*The Book of Praise:*
From the Best English Hymn Writers. Selected and arranged by ROUNDELL PALMER. With Vignette by WOOLNER. Pott 8vo. 4s. 6d. *Large Type Edition*, demy 8vo. 10s. 6d. ; morocco. 21s.

A Hymnal.
Chiefly from the BOOK OF PRAISE. In various sizes.
[In the Press.
Ditto, with Music by J. HULLAH.

PARKINSON.   *Works by* S. PARKINSON, B.D.

A Treatise on Elementary Mechanics.
For the Use of the Junior Classes at the University and the Higher Classes in Schools. With a Collection of Examples. *Third Edition, revised.* Crown 8vo. 9s. 6d.

A Treatise on Optics.
Second Edition, revised. Crown 8vo. 10s. 6d.

PATMORE.   *Works by* COVENTRY PATMORE.

The Angel in the House.
Book I. The Betrothal.—Book II. The Espousals.—Book III. Faithful for Ever. With Tamerton Church Tower. Two Vols. fcap. 8vo. 12s.
. A New and Cheap Edition, in One Vol. 18mo. beautifully printed on toned paper, price 2s. 6d.

The Victories of Love.
Fcap. 8vo. 4s. 6d.

PAULI.—*Pictures of Old England.*
By Dr. REINHOLD PAULI. Translated by E. C. OTTE. Crown 8vo. 8s. 6d.

PHEAR.—*Elementary Hydrostatics.*
By J. B. PHEAR, M.A. *Third Edition.* Crown 8vo. 5s. 6d.

PHILLIMORE.—*Private Law among the Romans.*
From the Pandects. By JOHN GEORGE PHILLIMORE, Q.C. 8vo. 16s.

Philology.
The Journal of Sacred and Classical Philology. Four Vols. 8vo. 12s. 6d. each.

PLATO.—*The Republic of Plato.*
Translated into English, with Notes. By Two Fellows of Trinity College, Cambridge (J. Ll. Davies, M.A. and D. J. Vaughan, M.A.). With Vignette Portraits of Plato and Socrates engraved by JEENS from an Antique Gem. (Golden Treasury Series) *New Edition,* 18mo. 4s. 6d.

Platonic Dialogues, The.
For English Readers. By the late W. WHEWELL, D.D. F.R.S. Master of Trinity College, Cambridge. Vol. I. *Second Edition,* containing *The Socratic Dialogues,* fcap. 8vo. 7s. 6d.; Vol. II. containing *The Anti-Sophist Dialogues,* 6s. 6d.; Vol. III. containing *The Republic,* 7s. 6d.

Plea for a New English Version of the Scriptures.
By a Licentiate of the Church of Scotland. 8vo. 6s.

POTTER.—*A Voice from the Church in Australia :*
Sermons preached in Melbourne. By the Rev. ROBERT POTTER, M.A. Extra fcap. 8vo. 4s. 6d.

PRATT.—*Treatise on Attractions, La Place's Functions, and the Figure of the Earth.*
By J. H. PRATT, M.A. *Second Edition.* Crown 8vo. 6s. 6d.

PROCTER. *Works by* FRANCIS PROCTER, M.A.

A History of the Book of Common Prayer :
With a Rationale of its Offices. *Sixth Edition, revised and enlarged.* Crown 8vo. 10s. 6d.

An Elementary History of the Book of Common Prayer.
18mo. 2s. 6d.

Psalms of David chronologically arranged.
Crown 8vo. 10s. 6d.

PUCKLE.—*An Elementary Treatise on Conic Sections and Algebraic Geometry,*
Especially designed for the Use of Schools and Beginners. By G. HALE PUCKLE, M.A. *Second Edition.* Crown 8vo. 7s. 6d.

RALEGH, SIR WALTER.—*Life.*
By E. EDWARDS. [In the Press.

RAMSAY.—*The Catechiser's Manual ;*
Or, the Church Catechism Illustrated and Explained, for the Use of Clergymen, Schoolmasters, and Teachers. By ARTHUR RAMSAY, M.A. *Second Edition.* 18mo. 1s. 6d.

RAWLINSON.—*Elementary Statics.*
> By G. RAWLINSON, M.A.   Edited by EDWARD STURGES, M.A.
> Crown 8vo. 4s. 6d.

Rays of Sunlight for Dark Days.
> A Book of Selections for the Suffering.   With a Preface by C.
> J. VAUGHAN, D.D.   18mo. *New Edition.* 3s. 6d. Morocco,
> old style, 9s.

Reform.—Essays on Reform.
> By the Hon. G. C. BRODRICK, R. H. HUTTON, LORD HOUGHTON,
> A. V. DICEY, LESLIE STEPHEN, J. B. KINNEAR, B. CRACROFT,
> C. H. PEARSON, GOLDWIN SMITH, JAMES BRYCE, A. L. RUTSON,
> and Sir GEO. YOUNG.   8vo. cloth.   10s. 6d.

Reform.—Questions for a Reformed Parliament.
> By F. H. HILL, GODFREY LUSHINGTON, MEREDITH TOWNSEND,
> W. L. NEWMAN, C. S. PARKER, J. B. KINNEAR, G. HOOPER,
> F. HARRISON, Rev. J. E. T. ROGERS, J. M. LUDLOW, and LLOYD
> JONES.   8vo. cloth.   10s. 6d.

REYNOLDS.—*A System of Medicine.*
> Edited by J. RUSSELL REYNOLDS, M.D. F.R.C.P. London. The
> First Volume contains :—PART I. GENERAL DISEASES, or
> Affections of the Whole System.   § I.—Those determined by
> agents operating from without, such as the exanthemata, malarial
> diseases, and their allies.   § II.—Those determined by conditions
> existing within the body, such as Gout, Rheumatism, Rickets,
> &c.   PART II. LOCAL DISEASES, or Affections of particular
> Systems.   § I.—Diseases of the Skin.   Vol. I. 8vo. cloth.   25s.

A System of Medicine.
> Vol. II. containing Diseases of the Nervous System, the Res-
> piratory System, and the Circulatory System.   [In the Press.

REYNOLDS.—*Notes of the Christian Life.*
> A Selection of Sermons by HENRY ROBERT REYNOLDS, B.A.
> President of Cheshunt College, and Fellow of University College,
> London.   Crown 8vo. cloth.   7s. 6d.

ROBERTS.—*Discussions on the Gospels.*
> By the Rev. ALEXANDER ROBERTS, D.D. *Second Edition,
> revised and enlarged.* 8vo. cloth.   16s.

ROBERTSON.—*Pastoral Counsels.*
> By the late JOHN ROBERTSON, D.D. of Glasgow Cathedral.
> With Biographical Sketch by the Author of "Recreations of
> a Country Parson." Extra Fcap. 8vo.   [In the Press.

ROBINSON CRABB.—*Life and Reminiscences.*
>   [In the Press.

ROBY.—*An Elementary Latin Grammar.*
> By H. J. ROBY, M.A. 18mo. *New Edition.*   [In the Press.

ROBY.—*Story of a Household, and other Poems.*
By MARY K. ROBY. Fcap. 8vo. *5s.*

ROMANIS.—*Sermons preached at St. Mary's, Reading.*
By WILLIAM ROMANIS, M.A. *First Series.* Fcap. 8vo. *6s.*
Also, *Second Series. 6s.*

ROSCOE.—*Lessons in Elementary Chemistry, Inorganic and Organic.*
By H. E. ROSCOE, F.R.S. 18mo. *4s. 6d.*

ROSSETTI.   *Works by* CHRISTINA ROSSETTI.

Goblin Market, and other Poems.
With Two Designs by D. G. ROSSETTI. *Second Edition.* Fcap. 8vo. *5s.*

The Prince's Progress, and other Poems.
With Two Designs by D. G. ROSSETTI. Fcap. 8vo. *6s.*

ROSETTI.   *Works by* WILLIAM MICHAEL ROSSETTI.

Dante's Comedy, The Hell.
Translated into Literal Blank Verse. Fcap. 8vo. cloth. *5s.*

Fine Art, chiefly Contemporary.
Crown 8vo. cloth. *10s. 6d.*

ROUTH.—*Treatise on Dynamics of Rigid Bodies.*
With Numerous Examples. By E. J. ROUTH, M.A. Crown 8vo. *10s. 6d.*

ROWSELL.   *Works by* T. J. ROWSELL, M.A.

The English Universities and the English Poor.
Sermons preached before the University of Cambridge. Fcap. 8vo. *2s.*

Man's Labour and God's Harvest.
Sermons preached before the University of Cambridge in Lent. 1861. Fcap. 8vo. *3s.*

RUFFINI.—*Vincenzo ; or, Sunken Rocks.*
By JOHN RUFFINI. Three Vols. crown 8vo. *31s. 6d.*

Ruth and her Friends.
A Story for Girls. With a Frontispiece. *Fourth Edition.* Royal 16mo. *3s. 6d.*

SARPI.—*The Life of Fra Paolo Sarpi.*
Theologian and Councillor of State to the Most Serene Republic of Venice, and Author of "The History of the Council of Trent." From Original MSS. By A. G. CAMPBELL. [*Preparing.*

Scouring of the White Horse.
Or, the Long Vacation Ramble of a London Clerk. By the Author of "Tom Brown's School Days." Illustrated by DOYLE. *Eighth Thousand.* Imp. 16mo. **6s. 6d.**

SELKIRK.—*A Handbook on Cricket.*
By G. H. SELKIRK. Extra Fcap. 8vo.   [In the Press.

SELWYN.—*The Work of Christ in the World.* ·
By G. A. SELWYN, D.D. *Third Edition.* Crown 8vo. **2s.**

SHAKESPEARE.—*The Works of Willia ɴ Shakespeare.*
Edited by WM. GEORGE CLARK, M.A. and W. ALDIS WRIGHT, M.A. Nine Vols. 8vo. cloth. **4l. 14s. 6d.**

Shakespeare's Tempest.
With Glossarial and Explanatory Notes. By the Rev. J. M. JEPHSON. 18mo. **1s. 6d.**

SHAIRP.—*Kilmahoe, and other Poems.*
By J. CAMPBELL SHAIRP. Fcap. 18mo. **5s.**

SHIRLEY.—*Elijah ; Four University Sermons.*
I. Samaria. II. Carmel. III. Kishon. IV. Horeb. By W. W. SHIRLEY, D.D. Fcap. 8vo. **2s. 6d.**

SIMEON.—*Stray Notes on Fishing and on Natural History.*
By CORNWALL SIMEON. Crown 8vo. **7s. 6d.**

SIMPSON.—*An Epitome of the History of the Christian Church.*
By WILLIAM SIMPSON, M.A. *Fourth Edition.* Fcap. 8vo. **3s. 6d.**

SMITH.   *Works by* ALEXANDER SMITH.

A Life Drama, and other Poems.
Fcap. 8vo. **2s. 6d.**

City Poems.
Fcap. 8vo. **5s.**

Edwin of Deira.
Second Edition. Fcap. 8vo. **5s.**

SMITH.   *Works by* GOLDWIN SMITH.

A Letter to a Whig Member of the Southern Independence Association.
Extra fcap. 8vo. **2s.**

Three English Statesmen ; Pym, Cromwell, and Pitt.
A Course of Lectures on the Political History of England. By Crown 8vo. Cloth extra. **6s. 6d.**

SMITH.—*Works by* BARNARD SMITH, *M.A. Rector of Glaston, Rutland, &c.*

Arithmetic and Algebra.
Ninth Edition. Crown 8vo. cloth. 10s. 6d.

Arithmetic for the Use of Schools.
New Edition. Crown 8vo. cloth. 4s. 6d.

A Key to the Arithmetic for Schools.
Fifth Edition. Crown 8vo. cloth. 8s. 6d.

Exercises in Arithmetic.
With Answers. Cr. 8vo. limp cloth, 2s. 6d. Or sold separately
as follows:—Part I. 1s. Part II. 1s. Answers, 6d.

School Class Book of Arithmetic.
18mo. cloth, 3s. Or sold separately, Parts I. and II. 10d. each.
Part III. 1s.

Keys to School Class Book of Arithmetic.
Complete in One Volume, 18mo. 6s. 6d.; or Parts I. II. and III.
2s. 6d. each.

Shilling Book of Arithmetic for National and Elementary Schools.
18mo. cloth. Or separately, Part I. 2d.; II. 3d.; III. 7d.

Answers to the Shilling Book of Arithmetic.
18mo. cloth. 6d.

Key to the Shilling Book of Arithmetic.
Fcap. 8vo. cloth. 4s. 6d.

Examination Papers in Arithmetic.
In Four Parts. 18mo. 1s. 6d.

Key to Examination Papers in Arithmetic.
18mo. 4s. 6d.

SMITH.—*Hymns of Christ and the Christian Life.*
By the Rev. WALTER C. SMITH, M.A. Fcap. 8vo. 6s.

SNOWBALL.—*The Elements of Plane and Spherical Trigonometry.*
By J. C. SNOWBALL, M.A. Tenth Edition. Crown 8vo. 7s. 6d.

Social Duties considered with Reference to the Organization of Effort in Works of Benevolence and Public Utility.
By a MAN OF BUSINESS. Fcap. 8vo. 4s. 6d.

SPENCER.—*Elements of Qualitative Chemical Analysis.*
By W. H. SPENCER, B.A.   4to.   10s. 6d.

Spring Songs.
By a WEST HIGHLANDER. With a Vignette Illustration by
GOURLAY STEELE. Fcap. 8vo. 1s. 6d.

STEPHEN.—*General View of the Criminal Law of England.*
By J. FITZ-JAMES STEPHEN. 8vo. 18s.

STORY.—*Memoir of the Rev. Robert Story.*
By R. H. STORY. Crown 8vo. 7s. 6d.

STRATFORD DE REDCLIFFE.—*Shadows of the Past, in Verse.*
By VISCOUNT STRATFORD DE REDCLIFFE. Crown 8vo. 10s. 6d.

STRICKLAND.—*On Cottage Construction and Design.*
By C. W. STRICKLAND. With Specifications and Plans.   8vo.
7s. 6d.

SWAINSON.   *Works by* C. A. SWAINSON, D.D.

A Handbook to Butler's Analogy.
Crown 8vo. 1s. 6d.

*The Creeds of the Church in their Relations to Holy
Scripture and the Conscience of the Christian.*
8vo. cloth. 9s.

The Authority of the New Testament,
And other Lectures, delivered before the University of Cambridge. 8vo. cloth. 12s.

TACITUS.—*The History of Tacitus translated into English.*
By A. J. CHURCH, M.A. and W. J. BRODRIBB, M.A.   With a
Map and Notes. 8vo. 10s. 6d.

TAIT AND STEELE.—*A Treatise on Dynamics.*
With numerous Examples. By P. G. TAIT and W. J. STEELE.
Second Edition. Crown 8vo. 10s. 6d.

TAYLOR.   *Works by the Rev.* ISAAC TAYLOR.

Words and Places ;
Or, Etymological Illustrations of History, Ethnology, and
Geography. By the Rev. ISAAC TAYLOR. *Second Edition.*
Crown 8vo. 12s. 6d.

TAYLOR.—*The Restoration of Belief.*
New and Revised Edition. By ISAAC TAYLOR, Esq. Crown
8vo. 8s. 6d.

TAYLOR.—*Ballads and Songs of Brittany.*
By TOM TAYLOR. With Illustrations by TISSOT, MILLAIS,
TENNIEL, KEENE, and H. K. BROWNE. Small 4to. cloth gilt.
12s.

TAYLOR.—*Geometrical Conics.*
By C. TAYLOR, B.A. Crown 8vo. 7s. 6d.

TEMPLE.—*Sermons preached in the Chapel of Rugby School.*
By F. TEMPLE, D.D. *New and Cheaper Edition.* Crown 8vo.
7s. 6d.

THORPE.—*Diplomatarium Anglicum Ævi Saxonici.*
A Collection of English Charters, from the Reign of King
Æthelberht of Kent, A.D. DC.V. to that of William the Con-
queror. With a Translation of the Anglo-Saxon. By BEN-
JAMIN THORPE, Member of the Royal Academy of Sciences.
Munich. 8vo. cloth. 21s.

THRING.—*Works by* EDWARD THRING, M.A. *Head Master of Uppingham.*

A Construing Book.
Fcap. 8vo. 2s. 6d.

A Latin Gradual.
A First Latin Construing Book for Beginners. Fcap. 8vo. 2s. 6d.

The Elements of Grammar taught in English.
Fourth Edition. 18mo. 2s.

The Child's Grammar.
A New Edition. 18mo. 1s.

Sermons delivered at Uppingham School.
Crown 8vo. 5s.

School Songs.
With the Music arranged for Four Voices. Edited by the Rev.
EDWARD THRING, M.A. and H. RICCIUS. Small folio. 7s. 6d.

Education and School.
Crown 8vo. 6s. 6d.

A Manual of Mood Constructions.
Extra Fcap. 8vo. 1s. 6d.

THRUPP.   *Works by the Rev.* J. F. THRUPP.

The Song of Songs.
A New Translation, with a Commentary and an Introduction. Crown 8vo. *7s. 6d.*

Introduction to the Study and Use of the Psalms.
Two Vols. 21*s.*

Antient Jerusalem.
A New Investigation into the History, Topography, and Plan of the City, Environs, and Temple. With Map and Plans. 8vo. 15*s.*

Psalms and Hymns for Public Worship.
Selected and Edited by the Rev. J. F. THRUPP, M.A. 18mo. 2*s.* Common paper, 1*s.* 4*d.*

THUCYDIDES.—*The Sicilian Expedition :*
Being Books VI. and VII. of Thucydides, with Notes. By the Rev. PERCIVAL FROST, M.A. Fcap. 8vo. *5s.*

TOCQUEVILLE.—*Memoir, Letters, and Remains of Alexis de Tocqueville.*
Translated from the French by the Translator of "Napoleon's Correspondence with King Joseph." With numerous Additions. Two Vols. Crown 8vo. 21*s.*

TODD.—*The Books of the Vaudois.*
The Waldensian Manuscripts preserved in the Library of Trinity College, Dublin, with an Appendix by JAMES HENTHORN TODD, D.D. Crown 8vo. cloth. *6s.*

TODHUNTER.   *Works by* ISAAC TODHUNTER, M.A. F.R.S.

Euclid for Colleges and Schools.
New Edition. 18mo. 3*s.* 6*d.*

Algebra for Beginners.
With numerous Examples. *New Edition.* 18mo. 2*s.* 6*d.*

Mechanics for Beginners.
With numerous Examples. 18mo. 4*s.* 6*d.*

A Treatise on the Differential Calculus.
With numerous Examples. *Fourth Edition.* Crown 8vo. 10*s.* 6*d.*

A Treatise on the Integral Calculus.
Second Edition. With numerous Examples. Crown 8vo. 10*s.* 6*d.*

TODHUNTER.—*A Treatise on Analytical Statics.*
Third Edition. Crown 8vo. 10s. 6d.

A Treatise on Conic Sections.
Fourth Edition. Crown 8vo. 7s. 6d.

Algebra for the Use of Colleges and Schools.
Fourth Edition. Crown 8vo. 7s. 6d.

Plane Trigonometry for Colleges and Schools.
Third Edition. Crown 8vo. 5s.

A Treatise on Spherical Trigonometry for the Use of Colleges and Schools.
Second Edition. Crown 8vo. 4s. 6d.

Trigonometry for Beginners.
With numerous Examples. 18mo. 2s. 6d.

Critical History of the Progress of the Calculus of Variations during the Nineteenth Century.
8vo. 12s.

Examples of Analytical Geometry of Three Dimensions.
Second Edition. Crown 8vo. 4s.

A Treatise on the Theory of Equations.
Second Edition. Crown 8vo. cloth. 7s. 6d.

Mathematical Theory of Probability.
8vo. cloth. 18s.

Tom Brown's School Days.
By an OLD BOY. 31st *Thousand.* Fcap. 8vo. 5s.
(PEOPLE'S EDITION, 2s.)

Tom Brown at Oxford.
By the Author of "Tom Brown's School Days." *New Edition.*
Crown 8vo. 6s.

Tracts for Priests and People. (By various Writers.)
THE FIRST SERIES, Crown 8vo. 8s.
THE SECOND SERIES, Crown 8vo. 8s.
The whole Series of Fifteen Tracts may be had separately, price One Shilling each.

TRENCH.—*Works by* R. CHENEVIX TRENCH, D.D. *Archbishop of Dublin.*

Notes on the Parables of Our Lord.
Tenth Edition. 8vo. 12s.

Notes on the Miracles of Our Lord.
Eighth Edition. 8vo. 12s.

Synonyms of the New Testament.
New Edition. One Vol. 8vo. cloth. 10s. 6d.

On the Study of Words.
Twelfth Edition. Fcap. 8vo. 4s.

English Past and Present.
Fifth Edition. Fcap. 8vo. 4s.

Proverbs and their Lessons.
Fifth Edition. Fcap. 8vo. 3s.

Select Glossary of English Words used formerly in senses different from the present.
Fourth Edition. 4s.

On some Deficiencies in our English Dictionaries.
Second Edition. 8vo. 3s.

Sermons preached in Westminster Abbey.
Second Edition. 8vo. 10s. 6d.

The Fitness of Holy Scripture for Unfolding the Spiritual Life of Man :
Christ the Desire of all Nations; or, the Unconscious Prophecies of Heathendom. Hulsean Lectures. Fcap. 8vo. *Fourth Edition.* 5s.

On the Authorized Version of the New Testament.
Second Edition. 7s.

Justin Martyr, and other Poems.
Fifth Edition. Fcap. 8vo. 6s.

Gustavus Adolphus.—Social Aspects of the Thirty Years' War.
Fcap. 8vo. cloth. 2s. 6d.

Poems.
Collected and arranged anew. Fcap. 8vo. 7s. 6d.

TRENCH (R. CHENEVIX)—*Poems from Eastern sources, Geno-veva, and other Poems.*
> Second Edition. Fcap. 8vo. 5s. 6d.

Elegiac Poems.
> Third Edition. Fcap. 8vo. 2s. 6d.

Calderon's Life's a Dream :
> The Great Theatre of the World. With an Essay on his Life and Genius. Fcap. 8vo. 4s. 6d.

Remains of the late Mrs. Richard Trench.
> Being Selections from her Journals, Letters, and other Papers. *Second Edition.* With Portrait. 8vo. 15s.

Commentary on the Epistles to the Seven Churches in Asia.
> Third Edition, revised. 8s. 6d.

Sacred Latin Poetry.
> Chiefly Lyrical. Selected and arranged for Use. *Second Edition.* Corrected and Improved. Fcap. 8vo. 7s.

Studies in the Gospels.
> 8vo. 10s. 6d.

Shipwrecks of Faith :
> Three Sermons preached before the University of Cambridge in May, 1867. Fcap. 8vo. 2s. 6d.

TRENCH. *Works by the Rev.* FRANCIS TRENCH, M.A.

Brief Notes on the Greek of the New Testament (for English Readers).
> Crown 8vo. cloth. 6s.

Four Assize Sermons,
> Preached at York and Leeds. Crown 8vo. cloth. 2s. 6d.

TREVELYAN. *Works by* G. O. TREVELYAN, M.P.

The Competition Wallah.
> New Edition. Crown 8vo. 6s.

Cawnpore,
> Illustrated with Plan. *Second Edition.* Crown 8vo. 6s.

TUDOR.—*The Decalogue viewed as the Christian's Law.*
With Special Reference to the Questions and Wants of the Times.
By the Rev. RICH. TUDOR, B.A. Crown 8vo. 10s. 6d.

TULLOCH.—*The Christ of the Gospels and the Christ of Modern Criticism.*
Lectures on M. RENAN's "Vie de Jésus." By JOHN TULLOCH,
D.D. Principal of the College of St. Mary, in the University of
St. Andrew. Extra fcap. 8vo. 4s. 6d.

TURNER.—*Sonnets.*
By the Rev. CHARLES TENNYSON TURNER. Dedicated to his
Brother, the Poet Laureate. Fcap. 8vo. 4s. 6d.

TYRWHITT.—*The Schooling of Life.*
By R. St. JOHN TYRWHITT, M.A. Vicar of St. Mary Magdalen,
Oxford. Fcap. 8vo. 3s. 6d.

Vacation Tourists ;
And Notes of Travel in 1861. Edited by F. GALTON, F.R.S.
With Ten Maps illustrating the Routes. 8vo. 14s.

Vacation Tourists ;
And Notes of Travel in 1862 and 1863. Edited by FRANCIS
GALTON, F.R.S. 8vo. 16s.

VAUGHAN.—*Works by* CHARLES J. VAUGHAN, D.D. *Vicar of Doncaster.*

Notes for Lectures on Confirmation.
With suitable Prayers. *Sixth Edition.* 1s. 6d.

Lectures on the Epistle to the Philippians.
Second Edition. 7s. 6d.

Lectures on the Revelation of St. John.
Second Edition. Two Vols. crown 8vo. 15s.

Epiphany, Lent, and Easter.
A Selection of Expository Sermons. *Second Edition.* Crown 8vo.
10s. 6d.

The Book and the Life,
And other Sermons, preached before the University of Cambridge. *New Edition.* Fcap. 8vo. 4s. 6d.

Memorials of Harrow Sundays.
A Selection of Sermons preached in Harrow School Chapel.
With a View of the Chapel. *Fourth Edition.* Crown 8vo.
10s. 6d.

VAUGHAN (CHARLES J.).—*St. Paul's Epistle to the Romans.*
The Greek Text with English Notes. *Second Edition.* Crown 8vo. red leaves. 5*s.*

Revision of the Liturgy.
Twelve Discourses on Liturgical Subjects.   [In the Press.

Lessons of Life and Godliness.
A Selection of Sermons preached in the Parish Church of Doncaster. *Third Edition.* Fcap. 8vo. 4*s.* 6*d.*

Words from the Gospels.
A Second Selection of Sermons preached in the Parish Church of Doncaster. *Second Edition.* Fcap. 8vo. 4*s.* 6*d.*

The Epistles of St. Paul.
For English Readers. Part I. containing the First Epistle to the Thessalonians. *Second Edition.* 8vo. 1*s.* 6*d.* Each Epistle will be published separately.

The Church of the First Days.
Series I. The Church of Jerusalem. *Second Edition.*
   ,, II. The Church of the Gentiles. *Second Edition.*
   ,, III. The Church of the World. *Second Edition.*
Fcap. 8vo. cloth. 4*s.* 6*d.* each.

Life's Work and God's Discipline.
Three Sermons. Fcap. 8vo. cloth. 2*s.* 6*d.*

The Wholesome Words of Jesus Christ.
Four Sermons preached before the University of Cambridge in November, 1866. Fcap. 8vo. cloth. 3*s.* 6*d.*

VAUGHAN.—*Works by* DAVID J. VAUGHAN, M.A. *Vicar of St. Martin's, Leicester.*

Sermons preached in St. John's Church, Leicester,
During the Years 1855 and 1856. Crown 8vo. 5*s.* 6*d.*

Sermons on the Resurrection.
With a Preface. Fcap. 8vo. 3*s.*

· *Three Sermons on the Atonement.*
1*s.* 6*d.*

Sermons on Sacrifice and Propitiation.
2*s.* 6*d.*

Christian Evidences and the Bible.
New Edition. Revised and enlarged. Fcap. 8vo. cloth. 5*s.* 6*d.*

VAUGHAN.—*Memoir of Robert A. Vaughan,*
Author of "Hours with the Mystics." By ROBERT VAUGHAN, D.D. *Second Edition.* Revised and enlarged. Extra fcap. 8vo. 5s.

VENN.—*The Logic of Chance.*
An Essay on the Foundations and Province of the Theory of Probability, with special reference to its application to Moral and Social Science. By the Rev. J. VENN, M.A. Fcap. 8vo. 7s. 6d.

Village Sermons.
By a NORTHAMPTONSHIRE RECTOR. With a Preface on the Inspiration of Holy Scripture. Crown 8vo. 6s.

Vittoria Colonna.—Life.
Crown 8vo. [In the Press.

Volunteer's Scrap Book.
By the Author of "The Cambridge Scrap Book." Crown 4to. 7s. 6d.

WAGNER.—*Memoir of the Rev. George Wagner,*
late of St. Stephen's, Brighton. By J. N. SIMPKINSON, M.A. *Third and Cheaper Edition.* 5s.

WARREN.—*An Essay on Greek Federal Coinage.*
By the Hon. J. LEICESTER WARREN, M.A. 8vo. 2s. 6d.

WEBSTER.—*Dramatic Studies.*
By AUGUSTA WEBSTER. Extra fcap. 8vo. 5s.

A Woman Sold,
And other Poems. By AUGUSTA WEBSTER. Crown 8vo. 7s. 6d.

Prometheus Bound, of Æschylus,
Literally Translated into English Verse. Extra fcap. 8vo. 3s. 6d.

WESTCOTT. *Works by* BROOKE FOSS WESTCOTT. B.D.

A General Survey of the History of the Canon of the New Testament during the First Four Centuries.
Crown 8vo. *Second Edition, revised.* 10s. 6d.

Characteristics of the Gospel Miracles.
Sermons preached before the University of Cambridge. *With Notes.* Crown 8vo. 4s. 6d.

Introduction to the Study of the Four Gospels.
Third Edition. Crown 8vo. 10s. 6d.

WESTCOTT (BROOKE FOSS).—*The Gospel of the Resurrection.*
Thoughts on its Relation to Reason and History. *New Edition.*
Fcap. 8vo. , 4s. 6d.

The Bible in the Church.
A Popular Account of the Collection and Reception of the Holy
Scriptures in the Christian Churches. *Second Edition.* 18mo.
4s. 6d.

Westminster Plays.
Lusus Alteri Westmonasteriense, Sive Prologi et Epilogi ad
Fabulas in Sti Petri Collegio : actas qui Exstabant collecti et
justa quoad licuit annorum serie ordinati, quibus accedit Decla-
mationum quæ vocantur et Epigrammatum Delectus   Curan-
tibus J. MURE, A.M., H. BULL, A.M., C. B. SCOTT, B.D.
8vo. 12s. 6d.
IDEM.—Pars Secunda, 1820—1865. Quibus accedit Epigrammatum Delectus. 8vo. 12s. 6d.

WILSON.   *Works by* GEORGE WILSON, M.D.

Counsels of an Invalid.
Letters on Religious Subjects. With Vignette Portrait. Fcap.
8vo. 4s. 6d.

Religio Chemici.
With a Vignette beautifully engraved after a Design by Sir
NOEL PATON. Crown 8vo. 8s. 6d.

The Five Gateways of Knowledge.
New Edition. Fcap. 8vo. 2s. 6d. Or in Paper Covers, 1s.

The Progress of the Telegraph.
Fcap. 8vo. 1s.

WILSON.—*Memoir of George Wilson*, M.D. F.R.S.E.
Regius Professor of Technology in the University of Edinburgh.
BY HIS SISTER. *New Edition.* Crown 8vo. 6s.

WILSON.   *Works by* DANIEL WILSON, D.D.

Prehistoric Annals of Scotland.
Two Vols. demy 8vo. *New Edition.* With numerous Illustrations. 36s.

Prehistoric Man.
New Edition. Revised and partly re-written, with numerous
Illustrations. One Vol. 8vo. 21s.

WILSON.—*A Treatise on Dynamics.*
By W. P. WILSON, M.A. 8vo. 9s. 6d.

WOLSTANHOLME.—*A Book of Mathematical Problems.*
Crown 8vo. 8*s*. 6*d*.

WOODFORD.—*Christian Sanctity.*
By JAMES RUSSELL WOODFORD, M.A. Fcap. 8vo. cloth. 3*s*.

WOODWARD.—*Works by the Rev.* HENRY WOODWARD, *edited by his Son,* THOMAS WOODWARD, M.A. *Dean of Down.*

Essays, Thoughts and Reflections, and Letters.
Fifth Edition. 8vo. cloth. 10*s*. 6*d*.

The Shunammite.
Second Edition. Crown 8vo. cloth. 10*s*. 6*d*.

Sermons.
Fifth Edition. Crown 8vo. cloth. 10*s*. 6*d*.

WOOLLEY.—*Lectures delivered in Australia.*
By the late JOHN WOOLLEY, D.C.L. Crown 8vo. 8*s*. 6*d*.

WOOLNER.—*My Beautiful Lady.*
By THOMAS WOOLNER. With a Vignette by ARTHUR HUGHES.
Third Edition. Fcap. 8vo. 5*s*.

Words from the Poets.
Selected by the Editor of " Rays of Sunlight." With a Vignette
and Frontispiece. 18mo. Extra cloth gilt. 2*s*. 6*d*. *Cheaper
Edition,* 18mo. limp. 1*s*.

Worship (The) of God and Fellowship among Men.
Sermons on Public Worship. By MAURICE, and Others. Fcap.
8vo. cloth. 3*s*. 6*d*.

WORSLEY.—*Christian Drift of Cambridge Work.*
Eight Lectures. By T. WORSLEY, D.D. Crown 8vo. cloth. 6*s*.

WRIGHT.   *Works by* J. WRIGHT, M.A.

Hellenica;
Or, a History of Greece in Greek, as related by Diodorus
and Thucydides, being a First Greek : Reading Book, with
Explanatory Notes Critical and Historical. *Second Edition,*
WITH A VOCABULARY. 12mo. 3*s*. 6*d*.

A Vocabulary and Exercises on the " Seven Kings of Rome."
Fcap. 8vo. 2*s*. 6*d*.
⁎ The Vocabulary and Exercises may also be had bound up
with "The Seven Kings of Rome."

WRIGHT (J., M.A.).—*A Help to Latin Grammar;*
Or, the Form and Use of Words in Latin, with Progressive
Exercises. Crown 8vo. 4s. 6d.

The Seven Kings of Rome.
An Easy Narrative, abridged from the First Book of Livy by the
omission of difficult passages, being a First Latin Reading Book,
with Grammatical Notes. Fçap. 8vo. 3s.

David, King of Israel.
Readings for the Young. With Six Illustrations. Royal 16mo.
cloth, gilt. 3s. 6d.

YOUMANS.—*Modern Culture,*
Its True Aims and Requirements. A Series of Addresses and
Arguments on the Claims of Scientific Education. Edited by
EDWARD L. YOUMANS, M.D. Crown 8vo. 8s. 6d.

𝔚orks by the 𝔄uthor of

"THE HEIR OF REDCLYFFE."

The Prince and the Page. A Book for the Young. 18mo. 3s. 6d.

A Book of Golden Deeds. 18mo. 4s. 6d.

History of Christian Names. Two. Vols. Crown 8vo. 1l. 1s.

The Heir of Redclyffe. Fifteenth Edition. Crown 8vo. 6s.

Dynevor Terrace. Third Edition. Crown 8vo. 6s.

The Daisy Chain. Eighth Edition. Crown 8vo. 6s.

The Trial: More Links of the Daisy Chain. Third Edition. Crown
8vo. 6s.

Heartsease. Ninth Edition. Crown 8vo. 6s.

Hopes and Fears. Third Edition. Crown 8vo. 6s.

The Young Stepmother. Second Edition. Crown 8vo. 6s.

The Lances of Lynwood. 18mo. cloth. 3s. 6d.

The Little Duke. New Edition. 18mo. cloth. 3s. 6d.

Clever Woman of the Family. Crown. 8vo. 6s.

Danvers Papers; an Invention. Crown 8vo. 4s. 6d.

ELEMENTARY SCHOOL CLASS BOOKS.

The Volumes of this Series of ELEMENTARY SCHOOL CLASS BOOKS *are handsomely printed in a form that, it is hoped, will assist the young Student as much as clearness of type and distinctness of arrangement can effect. They are published at a moderate price, to insure an extensive sale in the Schools of the United Kingdom and the Colonies.*

1. *Euclid for Colleges and Schools.*
   By I. TODHUNTER, M.A. F.R.S. 18mo. 3s. 6d.

2. *Algebra for Beginners.*
   By I. TODHUNTER, M.A. F.R.S. 18mo. 2s. 6d.
   A KEY to this work will shortly be published.

3. *The School Class Book of Arithmetic.*
   By BARNARD SMITH, M.A. Parts I. and II. 18mo. limp cloth, price 10d. each. Part III. 1s. ; or Three Parts in one Volume, price 3s.
   KEY TO CLASS BOOK OF ARITHMETIC.
   Complete, 18mo. cloth, price 6s. 6d. Or separately, Parts I. II. & III. 2s. 6d. each.

4. *Mythology for Latin Versification.*
   A Brief Sketch of the Fables of the Antients, prepared to be rendered into Latin Verse for Schools. By F. HODGSON, B.D. *New Edition.* Revised by F. C. HODGSON, M.A. Fellow of King's College, Cambridge. 18mo. 3s.

5. *A Latin Gradual for Beginners.*
   A First Latin Construing Book. By EDWARD THRING, M.A. 18mo. 2s. 6d.

6. *Shakespeare's Tempest.*
   The Text taken from "The Cambridge Shakespeare." With Glossarial and Explanatory Notes. By the Rev. J. M. JEPHSON. 18mo. cloth. 1s. 6d.

7. *Lessons in Elementary Botany.*
   The Part on Systematic Botany based upon Material left in Manuscript by the late Professor HENSLOW. With nearly Two Hundred Illustrations. By DANIEL OLIVER, F.R.S. F.L.S. 18mo. cloth. 4s. 6d.

8. *Lessons in Elementary Physiology.*
   With numerous Illustrations. By T. H. HUXLEY, F.R.S. Professor of Natural History in the Government School of Mines. 18mo. 4s. 6d.

9. *Popular Astronomy.*
   A Series of Lectures delivered at Ipswich. By GEORGE BIDDELL AIRY, Astronomer Royal. 18mo. cloth. 4s. 6d.

10. *Lessons in Elementary Chemistry.*
    By HENRY ROSCOE, F.R.S. Professor of Chemistry in Owens College, Manchester. With numerous Illustrations. 18mo. cloth. 4s. 6d.

11. *An Elementary History of the Book of Common Prayer.*
    By FRANCIS PROCTER, M.A. 18mo. 2s. 6d.

12. *Algebraical Exercises.*
    Progressively arranged by Rev. C. A. JONES, M.A. and C. H. CHEYNE, M.A. Mathematical Masters in Westminster School. Pott 8vo. cloth. 2s. 6d.

13. *The Bible in the Church.*
    A Popular Account of the Collection and Reception of the Holy Scriptures in the Christian Churches. By BROOKE FOSS WESTCOTT, B.D. 18mo. 4s. 6d.

14. *The Bible Word Book.*
    A Glossary of Old English Bible Words. By J. EASTWOOD, M.A. and W. ALDIS WRIGHT, M.A. 18mo. 5s. 6d.

MACMILLAN AND CO. LONDON.